Chocolate Soufflé

Trish Ahjel

©Copyright 2015 Chocolate Soufflé by Trish Ahjel

First Edition: January 2016

Printed in the United States of America

Cover design by:
Lenox Avenue Publishing & Publicity

Photo credit:
Trish Ahjel

ISBN-13:
978-1522906735

ISBN-10:
1522906738

This book is dedicated
to my mother,
Dorothy,
who loved this story
and never stopped encouraging me
to publish it.

And to my sister,
Chrissy,
who kept pushing me
when my mother left this earth
and no longer could.

Chocolate Soufflé:

(noun) A dessert painstakingly crafted and extremely delicious

Urbandictionary.com

Aura, Ocean & Sophia Spring 1995

Aura rushed into the lobby of the hotel frantically; her pale yellow business suit and white blouse complemented her dark skin and long black hair nicely, like a slice of lemon meringue pie cooling on a mahogany table. Her bone pumps clicked loudly on the marble floors, as if playing an instrument in the cacophony of other clicking heels, padding shoe bottoms and conversation. It was lunchtime in midtown Manhattan, and it seemed every worker who spilled out of a high-rise building was walking through the hotel's lobby. She had been told that Ocean was eating here with one of his business associates, a woman named Sophia, so Aura asked the restaurant's maitre d' if he'd seen a dreadlocked black man with a very light-skinned black woman. (Ocean and Sophia wouldn't be hard to find.) The short Italian man quickly smiled and nodded. Yes, he had seen them but they finished their meal about an hour ago.

Aura thanked the man and turned to leave. She was surprised when she ran into one of her own co-workers on the way out—a tall, bearded, light-skinned brother named Marc. The two chatted near the hotel elevators for a few minutes before heading toward the glass revolving doors which led to the noisy street. Aura was shocked when she saw Ocean exiting one of the elevators with Sophia's arm slid possessively around his waist.

A dizzying wave of hurt and anger overwhelmed Aura

as she watched them exit the hotel, unaware of her presence. *Did this mean what she thought it meant? Was he screwing around?* She knew she hadn't been totally honest with him, and she was partially to blame, but she had made a promise to herself that she would never tolerate a man who cheated.

Marc quickly grabbed Aura's hand. "I'm so sorry this had to happen..." he began, recognizing her shock and hoping this would give him an opportunity to get closer to her. But, he had a strange feeling he knew this other man. He hadn't seen his full face, but his walk seemed oddly familiar.

***

Ocean leaned against Sophia as they exited the hotel. His denim shirt and jeans covered phat brown work boots. He felt much better now. With just enough martinis in him to drown out his pain, he figured he could handle the rest of the day. Or maybe he'd take the rest of the day off. After all, Sophia was the boss. *She wouldn't throw him off the account if he decided to take the afternoon off, would she?* She could be harsh with others, but she clearly had a soft spot for him. It was beginning to seem as if she treated him better than his own woman. That thought brought back his feelings of betrayal and disillusionment. *How could Aura do this to them?*

Through the pleasant euphoria manifested by his earlier cocktails, Ocean rested a hand casually on Sophia's burgundy-draped thigh.

***

Sophia wore a head-wrap which matched her long-sleeved blouse and burgundy palazzo pants. It was of her own design, as was most of her wardrobe. The light-weight rayon brushed lightly against her voluptuous figure as she hailed a cab in the spring breeze. Sophia was genuinely thrilled when she and Ocean left the hotel together. He was an amazing man, and she had wanted him for a long time. It was fascinating to her that he was still so interested in Aura. Aura *was* beautiful, but so were a lot of women. She supposed Ocean had not yet learned what she already knew: love just doesn't last. It cannot. If it did the divorce courts of the world wouldn't be brimming with brides-were and grooms-had-been. It wasn't that she wanted to split them up, but as far as she could tell, they were never really together anyway.

As she sat beside Ocean in the yellow cab, she let thoughts of her previous relationships wash over her easily. There had been good ones and bad ones, but they all had one thing in common: they ended, just as Ocean's would. When she felt his hand on her thigh, it deepened her feeling of prophecy.

Aura Olivier
Spring 1987

"I don't think this is such a good idea..." Aura mumbled under Tony's kiss. "Are, you sure no one can see us?"

"Come on, baby, how many times do I have to tell you? I checked out everything. Your moms and pops are sleeping. Mostly everybody else is gone now anyway... Just relax..." He slid his right hand under the soft purple leather of the mini-skirt, fully exploring the smooth black skin that lay beneath. "Damn, baby, you drive me crazy."

"And you're sure Mom and Dad went to bed?"

"Yeah." The skirt slid down to her ankles and she stepped out of it, revealing white stretch lace panties barely held together with looping strings at her hips. She pulled away at the backs of her sandals with her toes, freeing her carefully pedicured feet to the soft grass below.

"Turn around, girl." She spun around to face him after giving him a full view of her rounded behind. He eyed her from head to toe. Aura was beautiful. She was probably the most beautiful of all the black girls at Syracuse University. She was tall, only a few inches shorter than him, and he was six feet. Her skin was deep ebony all over, with wide hips, a round full butt, small, perfectly rounded breasts and a tiny waist. He was rock-hard as he was most of the time he was with her. They sometimes thought they only did one thing, but they were twenty-one, and maybe that's all you're supposed to do.

Aura slid closer in Tony's arms, running her hands down the back of his loose T-shirt. She could feel the tight muscles in his back contract under her touch. She loved the feel of his body, the smell of his skin. He *always* smelled like a shower. Even at the end of a long, hectic day, this brother always smelled like a fresh shower. Smiling, she pulled the shirt over his head. Nothing could be better than laying her eyes on Tony when he took his shirt off. His upper body was precisely cut, as if a sculptor had painstakingly chiseled each perfect muscle. At 6', 180 lbs., he was tall, muscular and lean. This brother wasn't carrying a layer of fat over his stuff for that teddy bear effect. This brother had stuff that go *ping*! His chest was honey-brown with thick strands of curly black dispersed sparingly around his dark brown nipples. Aura leaned into him, stroking his nipple lightly with her tongue, then biting gently. He let out a shallow moan as he lifted her onto the picnic table in the backyard. Although Aura's guests were still inside the house, they had the cover of a sprawling oak tree and the late spring night. He leaned his head back, opening his eyes occasionally to glance the evening stars as Aura nibbled at him as she did so well. When he had his fill of her teasing, he pulled her out of the white spandex crop-top she was wearing, braless as usual. He took his time gently teasing her as he stroked his bare hard-on against her thigh, his hand nestled in her thick, black hair. It was at times like this that he knew there was a God.

"Aura!?" a voice called from the back porch.

"Oh, shit!" Aura mumbled sliding quickly to the grass with Tony in one noiseless motion.

"Aura!" the voice called out again as Aura glimpsed the moon with soft grass against her back and a hungry tongue between her legs. Tony licked her determinedly; he loved her taste. This girl was so beautiful he couldn't resist the urge to lick her everywhere, especially there where her passion rose, and she filled up with milk for him. Aura only slept with him and, most of the time, he only slept with Aura.

"Put it in..." she mumbled. Tony had no idea what she was saying until she grabbed his ass hard, cutting her nails into his cheeks. "Put it in!" she rumbled.

Aura could get scary when she got really horny. If Tony got up and tried to leave right then, he wouldn't be surprised if she'd stab him in the neck! He smiled—she was beautiful, smart and horny...could this be love? He moved his mouth back up to hers and kissed her deeply as he pressed his erection into her. She moaned loudly, jolting him for a second. Whoever came out before had left, but if she started making too much noise somebody might come out again. As if she read his mind, she quieted into slow, rhythmic gasps, barely audible unless your ear was pressed against her mouth, like Tony's was.

***

"So what were you and Tony doing in the backyard all that time?" Dana joked. "I sent Robin out to call for you, make sure you're not getting in any trouble out there."

"Shut up, Dana," Aura laughed. "Tony and I were just checking out the moonlight. We decided the moon looks good tonight, *okay*? Besides, you seemed to be missing in action with Bobby for a while tonight yourself."

"Well I'm sure we weren't checking the moonlight like you and Tony checked it." Dana slid her hand to her hips over the slim dress she wore. Her playful smile showed off her endearing prettiness, smooth caramel skin and bright white teeth.

"Let me tell you something, Tony is one helluva good moonlight checker." She looked over at an amused Tony.

"Hey, don't look at me, I don't know what you fool women are talking about...I'm hungry."

"Mike and the rest of the guys are in the basement. They're probably down there eating, anyway. Go find them," Aura suggested.

"Oh sure, just *use* me and then send me off." He mimicked her voice with a high whine, "Go *find* them!"

"Come on, baby, it's late anyway, let me chill with my girls for awhile. I'm about ready to kick everyone outta here pretty soon, anyway."

"Yeah? What time?"

"Probably around five; it's almost four right now anyway. My DJ stops at four, so we can hang out for awhile after, but that's about it."

"Maybe more moonlight later?" Tony slid his hand over his stomach and let his eyes rest directly on Aura's breasts.

"Tony, move it baby, you *know* I'll catch you later." With a wave of the hand and a subtle exchange, Aura and Tony parted.

Dana stretched her bare feet out on the textured burgundy sofa. "Girl, I don't know what you're doing to that boy, got him acting like that. Maybe you need to teach the rest of us some of your tricks." She leaned back, admiring the high ceilings and bay windows of the Brooklyn brownstone. She wished she had been so fortunate to grow up in a house like this. The apartment she shared with her parents was only a few blocks away, but since she and Aura were children, she'd been playing in Aura's backyard. College was the first time they were really separated, when Aura decided to go upstate New York and Dana stayed in the city.

"Dana, you could have any man you want if you didn't have to have your own way all the time. Look at Brian...," Aura began.

"I didn't like Brian. He was stupid."

"Brian was nice. What about Dexter?"

"All Dexter ever talked about was that stupid car of his."

"You should have been happy to have a guy with a ride. What about John?"

"All John wanted to do was fuck!"

"Dana, all anyone wants to do is fuck!"

"No, Aura, all you and Tony want to do is fuck. Normal people like Robin and me like to do other things too." Dana looked in Robin's direction for agreement.

"Don't look over here, honey. You're on your own." Robin sat cross-legged on the hard wood floor of Aura's living room.

"So, what's the deal with you and Bobby anyway? You sure were hanging by the door with him for a long time before he left. Is this the guy or what?" asked Aura.

"I don't know. I think he's starting to bore me. I mean, he's nice and all, but I think his deepest thought is deciding if wearing a Yankees baseball cap with a Knicks T-shirt will cause some sort of intergalactic chaos. I tell you, though, that man has a dick to make a nun go to hell! Uhmm…" Dana leaned her head back, enjoying the thought.

"You better keep a condom on that intergalactic dick, before I have to come visit your ass in the hospital," Aura countered.

"Yes, oh mighty Aura, we know all about AIDS. We all took Health 101 and all that shit, and God knows this shit is scary. Honestly, though, I can't imagine anyone our age having it. It still seems like it's mostly gays and junkies."

"Dana, just use the condoms so I can sleep at night. You know how the shit goes, first they'll say it's gays then they'll say it's your cousin. You just never know. It's only been around a few years now, and so many people have died. It's really scary. And you're my oldest and best friend. I'm not ready to lose you."

"With all the talking you do, you'd think you actually use the things yourself," Robin interjected. "Aura, you're full of shit, 'cause I know you don't use condoms with Tony."

"I don't fuck anybody but Tony!"

"That's not gonna help you if Tony's not fucking only you!" Robin countered.

"You think Tony's sleeping with someone else?" Aura sounded hurt.

"No, Aura, I don't think that, but, I'm just saying... you never know..."

"So what's going on with you Robin? It's been awhile since I've seen you. Got that degree going on now, I know you must be feeling good." Dana was scrambling to change the subject.

"Yeah, it does feel good...really good. School was fun, but I'm glad it's over with. It's time to get on with the rest of my life. I'm just not really sure what to do next." Robin pulled her knees into her chest as she sat pensively on the floor, her braided extensions dangled as she nestled her nose into her knees. She had majored in communications like Aura and did a few gigs as a radio DJ on campus, but she hadn't really decided what her next step would be. Aura already had a job lined up with one of the major ad agencies in Manhattan. It didn't pay much, but she was happy about the work. Robin didn't want to work for "free" the way Aura would. She was waiting for something better to come along. The problem was, along from where?

"Well, we've all got to figure out where to go from here. I'm thinking about getting my MBA now and just getting it over with. I know I'm gonna want one eventually. I just can't figure out where to get the money from. I'm already up to my ears in student loans..." Dana started.

"Please, don't even say that word..." Robin whined.

"I know what you mean. I'm scared to even figure out how much I owe," Dana agreed. She paused briefly, "Is that 'Moments in Love' playing downstairs? Now you *know* that's my jam! Let me go get a little busy now! Makin' me wanna go to the Garage!" she said referring to an area dance club. She let out a yelp and shook her hips rhythmically before taking off down the steps to the basement. Robin was right behind her waving her hands in the air and yelling, "Where's the party at?!" as she boogied down the stairs.

Although many of Aura's guests had left, there were still about twenty people in the basement eating and dancing. A few clearly had a bit too much to drink.

"Robin, baby you're looking D-E-licious tonight," a very drunk man mumbled.

"Peter, shut up. You should be ashamed of yourself smelling like that. You're liable to catch fire with all the beer you've put away."

"Bitch," Peter responded and headed to a corner.

Robin laughed. "Peter's gonna hate himself in the morning. Hey, Tony..." She noticed Tony talking to a couple of guys in a corner. "Wanna dance? Aura's upstairs and I'm all alone." She batted her eyelashes dramatically.

Tony laughed and excused himself from his friends. They danced to three songs in a row with Dana and another partially sober friend dancing alongside them screaming "Say Ho!" and "Party over here!" Aura joined them for one song, a remix of Michael Jackson's "Billy Jean," before heading back upstairs.

Aura headed to the bathroom for some painkillers. She

hated the pains which sometimes shot through her back and legs, but there was nothing she could do about it. She had been diagnosed with sickle-cell anemia when she was seven years old. Neither of her parents had the disease, but they both carried the trait. Her older brother and sister inherited the trait, but it was only Aura who endured the burden of the disease itself. Mostly she just had pain caused by the inability of her little sickle-shaped blood cells to move freely in her veins. Sometimes the pain got so severe she had to be hospitalized, but that hadn't happened in years.

"Hey sis, what's up?" Angela asked passing the open bathroom door. "Feeling bad, huh?" Her sister's voice was filled with concern.

"I'm okay. You know the deal." Aura mumbled before swallowing the Tylenol® & Codeine tablets. "Where've you been anyway? I thought you were in bed."

"I was for awhile, but with all the thumping going on down here, I figured I'd come see how things are going. I can hear your friends screaming in the basement from upstairs." Angela was an older version of Aura, tall and dark with a beautiful body and full lips. She put a hand on Aura's shoulder. "So who's spending the night?"

"Puh-leeze, the way they're drinking down there, we'll probably wake up with twenty people knocked out on the basement floor." Aura laughed.

"That's all right, just as long as they don't want breakfast! Where's Ace?" Angela asked, referring to their brother, Aaron.

"I think he's downstairs acting the fool with everybody else. If I see him, I'll let him know you're looking for him."

"It's no big deal. I just wanted to run some things past him."

"The usual guy stuff?" Aura guessed. They both went

straight to Aaron when they had problems with men. It was stupid, really, as if he was some sort of authority on male-female relationships. He always did seem to bring a useful male perspective into play when they were totally at a loss.

"Yeah." Angela's smile was a bit on the giddy side. It didn't occur to Aura at that moment to ask why.

***

Angela and Aura started cleaning the upstairs rooms while the sounds of "Moody" by ESG pulsated through the floor. "Feelin' Mooody, yeah, yeah, yeah... Like this!" Aura sang along with her sister. She loved that damn song!

"Thanks for helping out, Angie."

"How can I not help out when my baby sister's graduating from college... And with a B+ average? I don't say a whole lot of mushy stuff to you often, but, you know, I'm proud of you." She flashed her sister a warm smile. "So how are things going with you and Tony? You guys seemed pretty cozy tonight."

Aura smiled in recollection. "Things are really good. He's sweet and attentive. I really can't complain about anything."

"That's good to hear. It's nice to be in a good relationship with a man. I can only hope that you and I will be able to have long lasting marriages like Mom and Dad. Sometimes, I swear I don't know how they've kept from killing each other over all these years. It's gonna be what... thirty-five years this October? We should throw them a party or something."

"We could throw them a party, or maybe put them up in a hotel for a weekend."

"Yeah, well we've got months to figure that one out.

When do you start your new job?"

"Not until next month. July tenth. I wanted to start even later, but I really need the money."

"Well, little sister, welcome to the real world. Remember what Dad always says: get a job doing something you enjoy and are good at and the money will follow."

"Yeah, I just hope Dad knows what he's talking about. I really hope I'm good at the things I think I'm good at. Oh, let me not even start..." Aura sighed. All this talk about working full-time and real responsibility wasn't thrilling her. She and Tony had been together for over a year, and he hadn't mentioned marriage even in passing. Although she wasn't ready to start having children, she was ready to starting planning a life with someone. When Tony talked about the future, he made sure to use very vague terms so Aura couldn't figure out if she was going to be a part of it or not.

Without even realizing it, Aura was shaking a little groove with her hips and shoulders as she loaded the dishwasher and wiped down the sink and counter.

* * *

"The party was great Aura. Congratulations, again." Peter held her hand earnestly before waiting on the front stoop for his cab to arrive. He was the last of the guests to leave, except for Robin, Dana and Tony who would spend the night.

"All right, you guys, that's the last person. I'm tired. Dana, you and Robin can sleep on the couch in the living room. Tony and I will stay downstairs." Basically, her family had a "don't ask/don't tell" attitude when it came to her boyfriends. She didn't flaunt any overnight guests and her parents pretended she never had any. It had been that way since her eighteenth birthday, and although her other friends were sometimes shocked and even feigned disgust, she realized they were largely motivated by jealousy. Thankfully, she didn't have to sneak around guys' houses or pay for cheap motels. Her friends had sex in cars, on rooftops, behind buildings, in classrooms... not because they were looking for a new experience, but because they had no place else to go. All those precariously planned encounters led to a number of unexpected pregnancies and the requisite abortions. She didn't know any girls who continued with their pregnancies. Like dropping a course from their schedule, they would terminate the life of their little tadpoles methodically, automatically, selfishly. Luckily, Aura had not found herself in that position—forced to choose her own future over the future of an unborn life. Among her friends, with only days before her twenty-second birthday, she was a minority.

"Why don't you guys hang out with us for awhile?" Robin called out as Aura and Tony approached the stairs to the basement.

The two exchanged brief glances before turning around. "Dana are you gonna stay up too?"

"It's almost five o'clock. Aren't you people tired?" Dana responded playfully.

"Let's play a game of spades!" Robin beamed. "We can watch the sun come up and then go to the park or something!"

"Aura, what have you been feeding that girl? I think she's out of her mind!" Dana proclaimed. She had known Aura for what felt like forever. Robin was Aura's best friend from Syracuse University, and although she liked her well enough, sometimes Robin got on Dana's last nerve. She hated to admit it, but sometimes she was jealous of Aura's relationship with Robin. She couldn't compare notes on Syracuse guys the way they could. And, although she enjoyed NYU, she never got to have the experience of going away to school.

"It doesn't matter to me," Tony added, clearly leaning towards staying up. "Let's play Truth or Dare!"

Aura gave him a suspicious look. "Why do you need to play Truth or Dare with my girlfriends?"

"Baby, come on, now... I didn't say strip poker or anything." He winked at Robin.

"Well, whatever... Let's do something before I fall asleep," Dana said.

Aura located a marble incense holder and lit a stick of Cocomango. She placed the fragrant ensemble carefully on the dining room table as her guests followed her into the room. The area was sparsely furnished with mahogany china cabinet, piano and serving station. She took a seat at the head of the glossy table, covered decoratively with a hand-crocheted cloth. "So what's it gonna be, guys?" she asked.

"Truth or dare, Tony?" Robin queried, eyeing Tony carefully.

A bit startled, Tony responded, "Truth."

"Are you in love with Aura?"

"What kind of question is that?" Tony asked.

"Thanks a lot," Aura remarked sarcastically, glaring at Tony.

He rested a hand on Aura's bare thigh. "Honestly, I care a lot about Aura. I have very deep feelings for her, but I don't know if this is what people call love." Tony gave Aura a sincerely apologetic gaze. She put her hand over his. Although she was sure she was in love with him, his response was nothing new to her. "So Robin, truth or dare?" Tony asked.

"Truth."

"When's the last time you got laid?" Tony asked with

a smirk.

"I guess about a week ago."

"With who?"

"Now, that's another question." Robin smiled, enjoying the attention. "Dana, when's the last time you got laid?"

"You sure are some nosey people. But that's all right. Let's see Bobby gave me some lovin' before we came over here. Okay?!" Dana tried to get comfortable in the straight-backed chair. "Look, if we're not playing cards, there's no point in sitting at this table. Don't you people want to go in the living room or something? My butt's starting to hurt."

"Sounds good to me." Aura got up and headed back into the living room. She and Tony stretched out on the burgundy sofa, Dana curled up on the love seat and Robin sat on the floor beside the sofa.

The questions went back and forth. Who slept with who, who sucked and fucked who, who had homosexual fantasies. They finally managed to tire of prying into each other's personal lives in an attempt to confirm the validity of their own thoughts. The game was one they had each played many times before with many other groups of people. Partly, it satisfied their voyeuristic desires to watch the dares carried out: "lick the wall" or "kiss the neck of the person next to you." In many ways, it was a team-building game: anything goes during the game, everything goes unspoken after the game. Mainly, it was just a way of killing time when you're twenty-two with plenty of time to kill and not many worries. Bills are paid; food simply exists. It's only the looming, foggy forest of a future that swirls and confuses, convincing you that you have nothing and everything at the same time. Every opportunity is available, the world might just be your oyster, but nothing is yet accomplished, except maybe a degree in some sort of abstraction.

"Look, people, the sun's coming up," Dana announced blearily. "It's time for this sister to go to sleep. And no, Robin I don't want to have sex with Michael Jackson. You folks are obsessed!" Dana sat up on the loveseat she had been sprawled over for the past two hours. She looked at Aura and Tony cozily wrapped in each other's arms on the sofa. "Go away, you guys! I'm *pooped*!"

Aura and Tony rose slowly and went to the basement. Robin flopped onto the opened sofa-bed next to Dana. "That Tony sure is a cutie, isn't he?" she offered smiling.

Dana's eyebrow rose as she peered down at Robin. *Was she serious?* "Yeah, I like Tony. He seems nice."

"Aura sure is lucky to have him…"

"Yeah, whatever. Go to sleep before I smack you," Dana mumbled before falling off to sleep in her T-shirt and jeans.

***

"So how did the party turn out last night? You kids were sure making a lot of noise," Mrs. Olivier commented to a well-fatigued Aura. It was past noon already, but Aura felt as if it were 8:00am. Although she had cleared six hours of sleep, she felt as if someone had beaten her up. She sat at the kitchen table with her hands wrapped around a cup of instant coffee. What she really needed was a shower.

"Oh, it went really well," Aura smiled dazedly. "Everyone seemed to have a good time. I know I'm gonna have my hands full cleaning up. Who's up?"

"Who do you think?" Sylvia Olivier frowned at her daughter. "You know everyone manages to wake up before you do." She patted Aura on the shoulder. "Even Robin crawled out of bed awhile ago."

"I think you people are all crazy. I slept barely six hours! It's not normal for people to sleep less time than that. Dana and Robin are only awake because they're not in their house."

"You weren't in your bed"

"Mom, give me a break!" Aura's look was pleading.

Seeing that her daughter was not up to any playful sparring, Sylvia left her alone. She felt she had a good relationship with all of her three children, and she was sure that moving her family to the States had been the right thing to do, although there were times when they all missed the small Caribbean island of St. Lucia where they were all born. Her kids made her proud every day. Or, almost every day. Aura was the youngest, and now even she was an adult. She tried to let her children make their own decisions about who they wanted to spend time with, but for some reason she just didn't like Tony. He and Aura had been going out for about a year she guessed, but to her it seemed an eternity. It wasn't that he wasn't nice enough. He was certainly good-looking. He seemed bright enough, and he seemed to treat her well. Aura seemed so happy with him too. It was nearly inexplicable, maybe a mother's sixth sense. Just something about the way the way he looked at her as if he knew he "had" her. Maybe it was as if Aura was a prize or a showpiece. After all, Aura was a very attractive woman and many men would love to have her on their arm and in their bed. She couldn't really put a finger on it, but something definitely bothered her about their relationship. She would never mention anything to her daughter without first being asked, though. She hated the stereotype of the overbearing, interfering, know-it-all mother, and she tried her best to avoid that type of behavior. She wondered if maybe in trying to be a good mother, she missed the point sometimes.

***

"You look like you've been slaving over a dirty basement all day," Angela laughed at her sister who was knee-deep in after-party clean up. It was nearly 4:00pm and Aura was feeling about as bright-eyed as she expected to for the day. Dana and Robin had left hours ago. "What are you doing later? Leave the rest of the work for tomorrow and catch a movie with me. I want to see 'Hollywood Shuffle.' It's got a black director and it's supposed to be good."

Angela got Aura's attention. "Hmmm, I heard about it. I do want to see that. Tony and I are supposed to be getting together later tonight, but even if we see a movie, we can see something different." She placed her hands on her hips with the exhaustion of cleaning all day. It seemed she hadn't stopped moving for hours, picking up paper cups and plates, throwing out food, sweeping up chips and pretzels, cleaning spills, stacking records. It was amazing how much mess remained after a simple party. She knew she didn't have more than a hundred people, but a hundred people could sure eat a lot!

"It's playing at Forty-Fifth Street at five-thirty. How quickly can you get dressed?"

"If it means getting out of this basement, try twenty minutes." Aura relaxed with the idea of getting out of the house. She and Angie hadn't been out together in awhile. It seemed they barely spent any time together at all since the graduation. She had been so busy with finals, then the ceremony and preparing to be separated from her college buddies, and finally her party. Taking in a movie with her sis sounded like a pleasant reprieve. Sometimes it's the people you care about most who are so easily taken for granted.

Aura ran upstairs and jumped in the shower for the second time that day, taking care not to wet her carefully curled hair. The warm water left soapy trails along her smooth, black skin. She almost forgot she was rushing as she allowed herself to enjoy the scented soap and shower steam. It was at times like this that she appreciated her mother's bold, geometrically designed shower clock. Ten minutes had passed. She exited the shower with a jolt, slathered herself in lotion and tip-toed to her bedroom. She quickly located a pair of well-worn, body-hugging jeans and a cut-off T-shirt. She knew she had a body well-worth flaunting, and she enjoyed showing it off. Angie wore cut-off denim shorts and a white Tee when she met up with her in the living room. "Are you ready?" Aura asked.

"Let's do this," Angie replied as she grabbed her shoulder bag.

The weather was beautiful, and the short walk to the subway allowed the opportunity to comment on their respective situations. Or, it would have, if the men on the street would allow the two young women to have a conversation.

"I think I've died and gone to heaven!" one old man blathered through a haze of Wild Irish Rose.

"Can I speak to you ladies for a moment?" a forty-something minister-looking brother wondered.

"Are you twins?" another man suggested, his hand tucked wearily in his waistband.

Basically, they spent their walk smiling "no's" and "no thank you's." It was an annoyance to which they had grown accustomed, like when their mother reminded them to put on a scarf in the winter. It was annoying, but if it stopped it would be sorely missed. They could only wonder what it would be like to walk down the street and have no one speak to them. Even covered from head to toe in the winter, they got a full range of comments, compliments and suggestions, from "Can I help you with your bags?" to "What can I do to get wit'chu?" Men...who could figure?

The subway ride was better. The cars were lightly filled with passengers, and Angie and Aura had their pick of available seats. Angie gave Aura an update on Pascal, her newest boyfriend. Although there were four years between them, it often seemed like much less. Aura, being the youngest was always so anxious to grow up, it seemed she had the maturity of a much older woman. Angie spoke to her as a peer. "I think Pascal and I might be getting serious!" Angie beamed as if twenty-six was the respectable limit on being unmarried.

"Gosh, Angie, couldn't you find a guy with a better name than *Pascal*? I knew a guy named Pascal in junior high school and he was so retarded! What's his last name?" Aura cringed at the idea of having to call someone Pascal for the rest of her life, even if it was only her brother-in-law. "I hope he doesn't look like the Pascal I know."

"Shut up, Aura!" Angie laughed. "Let me tell you. My Pascal looks *good*! His last name is Rogers."

"Hmmm…Angela Rogers...I guess that's acceptable. Oh my god!" Aura nearly fell out of her seat, "You're marrying *Mr. Rogers*!"

"Shut up, Aura!" Angela feigned embarrassment. "You *are* stupid!" She couldn't help but laugh in spite of herself. She was actually going out with a guy named Pascal Rogers. "You know Aura, a lot of people think your name is pretty stupid too."

"That's true, but they're just stupid people, and you're just jealous because Mom and Dad put some thought into my name," Aura teased. She enjoyed her unusual name, despite the fact that most of her professors still called her

Laura or Aurora, both of which pissed her off.

When they arrived at the theater, it was nearly show time and they hurried in to get their seats. Aura carried in a couple of sodas that they bought. Angie had a big popcorn. It was as she nestled a piece of the buttery stuff in her mouth that she caught a glimpse of Robin in one of the rear rows. "Hey, Robin, what's up?" Angie asked, getting Aura's attention.

"Hey, girl, what's up? Why are you sitting so far back here? You should have told me you were coming to the movie, we could have come together!" Aura's enthusiasm over seeing her friend was so complete and her words so rapid, that she did not see the horror in Robin's eyes as they shifted fearfully to the doorway. "Robin?" Aura's voice could not hide her concern as she allowed her eyes to fall gently over Robin's uneasy gaze. "Are you okay?" she asked.

"Oh, shit," Robin mumbled, lowering her expensively braided head. Tony walked in the theater and nearly bumped into Angie as he absently headed towards the seat next to Robin.

"Tell me this isn't happening," Aura said, her voice thin and shallow. She smiled pensively and finally laughed. "You know something, you two are both *assholes*!" She stormed off to a seat nearer to the screen just as the lights began to dim. Angie followed closely behind her.

Tony remained standing in the middle of the aisle, dumbfounded. Should he follow her? It seemed so rude to just sit with Robin, but what could he do? Aura would never take him back and Robin sucked a mean dick...then, again Aura sucked a mean dick too...shit, how did he always end up thinking about sex during important shit? The movie started, people started screaming for him to sit down and he sat next to Robin.

Aura stared at the movie screen blankly. She was determined not to let Tony see how much he had hurt her, so she forced herself to sit through the movie. She rested her head on Angie's shoulder and folded her arms across her chest as she fought and eventually lost the battle against her tears.

Eddie Ryder
Spring 1987

"I need two gin and tonics, a kamikaze and one sex on the beach," Brenda demanded. Her aging flesh fought with the constraints of her short black skirt, while her full, talcum-powdered bosom peered out of the restrictive push-up bra she wore below a V-neck sweater. She pushed out a hip and gave Eddie a halfhearted smile. They both hated their jobs and hated even more the requirement that they see each other six days a week. Eddie had an attitude she just couldn't stand, like he was God's gift to women or something. He looked at her with disregard and sometimes even disgust because she wasn't one of his twenty-year-old floozies. What could she do? But, then again, Eddie sure was easy on the eyes. She remembered when men thought she was pretty easy on the eyes herself. Shit, that was a long time ago, though.

"Sure Bren," Eddie replied in a deep baritone. His long-sleeved T-shirt rested carefully over his well-defined body as he expertly prepared the drinks. No one at "Caribbean Corner" would have ever guessed he was only twenty! He was 6'2" with a full mustache, deep cocoa-brown skin, thick eyebrows and long black lashes. Although he had been in the States for four years, his skin held a slight reddish undertone as if he were unwilling to part with his Bahamian tan. Eddie was a dangerous brother: fine and smart *and* he knew it. He made small talk with the unsightly Brenda as he arranged the concoctions on her tray. It didn't bother him so much that Brenda was not a particularly good-looking woman, or that she was overweight and over fifty. It was her grooming and her loud mouth that disgusted him. She insisted on squeezing into clothes that didn't fit, exposing her powdery boobs, smoking and allowing her oily skin to seep through her makeup. She was the kind of woman Eddie had no interest in ever touching, although at times he wondered if she had always been that way. Maybe she had just gotten lazy with herself over the years. It didn't matter, because Brenda wasn't going anywhere. She'd been working at Caribbean Corner since its inception in 1980, and Louie wasn't going to fire her now. He sometimes got the feeling she and Louie slept together, although he couldn't fathom what Louie could possibly see in her, especially when he already had a beautiful young wife.

"Thanks," Brenda mumbled as she walked off with the serving tray. Eddie was giving her that stupid look again, like he was better than her or something. She swore if he wasn't so damn good-looking she'd give him a quality piece of her mind.

Eddie watched Brenda's crooked little tip-toe of a walk on her ridiculously high-heeled pumps as she headed towards one of the rear tables. The restaurant was filled with folks from all over the city and the scent of jerk chicken, conch chowder, curried goat and other favorites filled the air. He always felt at home when he came to work. That was one positive aspect of it, and Brenda was one of many waitresses working with him, he was thankful for that. Of course, like nearly every other bartender in New York City, he was really a model/actor waiting for his big break. Here he couldn't complain, though. The restaurant's ambience was very appealing— hard wood floors, African art, black and white photos of the greats: Bob Marley, Jimi Hendrix, Malcolm X, Louis Armstrong, Dr. King. So much intermingled culture of the African diaspora in various forms that it created an earthy homeland feeling, but most importantly the food was varied and good in large portions at reasonable prices. These were the things that made Caribbean Corner a huge success and its owner, Louie Robbins, a reasonably well-to-do man.

It was approaching 6:00pm and the wave of people filing into the restaurant increased as the after-work, pre-theater, pre-movie and eventually pre-party dinner crowd rolled in. The soft amber lighting at the bar made Eddie's strong square jaw and full lips even more appealing to the women as they entered the establishment in everything from business suits to jeans to tiny spandex dresses.

"Hey Eddie, what's going on with you lately?" a petite, long-haired, light-skinned sister asked pouting full peach lips. Eddie allowed his eyes to rest gently on her eyes then her lips before carefully taking in every inch of her, the bright apricot business suit, long peach nails, high taupe pumps and matching bag.

Smiling he began to respond, "Everything's good, Sherri... I haven't seen you in here in awhile. How've you been keeping?"

The woman squeezed between bodies at the cramped bar to get closer. "Oh, I've been real good, Eddie... You're looking great!" She smiled assuredly. She had known Eddie for nearly a year and had known his bed a number of times. It was Friday night, and although she hadn't seen him in months, she was certain she could end up in his bed tonight.

As Eddie turned to prepare drinks for the now very busy crowd, Sherri secured a stool at the bar. She relaxed a bit as Eddie approached her with a glass of Chardonnay. "Your favorite," he smiled, leaning in to her. Sherri was very pretty with an awesome body and at thirty-five she had a great job, a huge apartment and money to burn. Eddie might have taken her seriously when they dated in the past if not for her three screaming brats. It wasn't that he didn't plan to have his own kids one day, just not somebody else's kids today. As his eyes rested on the hint of cleavage below Sherri's clearly overpriced suit, he wondered if one night with the kids securely locked up in their bedrooms would hurt.

"*Eddie!*" a familiar voice called out from the manager's office, beyond the bar area. It was Mona Robbins, Louie's wife, Brenda's arch enemy and Caribbean Corner's amiable co-owner. Eddie's smile quickly faded. He threw Sherri an apologetic wink, before heading back to the manager's office.

"Hey, Mona, I didn't see you come in," Eddie commented as he entered the room. It looked more like a lounge than an office, with dimly lit antique floor lamps, a small mahogany desk, shaggy beige carpeting and tawny calfskin sofa and recliner. Carved and shellacked tree trunks served as coffee tables and a few large rubber plants were scattered throughout.

Mona leaned casually against the desk "I know you didn't see me come in, Eddie, you were too busy ogling that little girl," she remarked knowingly. "I bet you didn't see Louie go out either." Her full blackberry lips curled provocatively as she tilted her head back slightly. Mona was tall and beautiful, with skin the color of a Hershey bar and long hair dyed burgundy-black. She wore no makeup, except the lipstick and thick false lashes. In a body-hugging, plum-colored crushed velvet dress and sequined black pumps, Mona had a look all her own.

"Actually, I didn't." Eddie laughed at his predicament. He actually felt like he owed Mona some sort of explanation for talking to Sherri. How ridiculous!

Realizing impending opportunity, Eddie stepped closer to Mona, "Where is Louie, anyway?"

Mona flashed a devilish grin, "He's gone for the evening... I'm in charge."

"Oh, you are, are you?" As if on cue, Eddie quickly flipped the lock on the office door. "Do you think we can work through some recipes together?" he asked playfully as he reached his hand into the thick forest of Mona's hair, pulling her head to his mouth he pressed his lips against hers, gently kissing her lower lip, then her upper. Finally he thrust his tongue into her mouth gently, probingly. He kissed the lids of her eyes and her cheeks, working his way over to her ear lobes and carefully down her neck. He lingered there, breathing the scent of her hair, enjoying the feel of her dress.

Mona grabbed Eddie's hair which had become quite an unruly 'fro lately. It was coarse and curly, and she loved it. She could feel his full erection moving against her body as he ran his tongue and teeth along her neck. She reached under the back of his shirt and scratched along the valleys of his muscular back with her long, berry-colored nails. Before she knew what had happened, Eddie had her on the desk with her dress hitched under her breasts and her silk panty discarded on the soft shag carpet.

He held a sequined shoe in his hand as he ran his tongue along the outline of her slim calf, pausing to bite the back of her knee before continuing the journey along her inner thigh. He relished in the soft tautness of her flesh under his mouth as he approached her warm wetness.

Mona leaned back into the desk, propped up on her elbows as Eddie teased her with his tongue. She loosened a breast from the confines of her dress and bra, gently sucking her own nipple as she watched Eddie enjoying her body.

Once Eddie tired of teasing Mona, he finally lifted his mouth to the joining of her thighs, gently running his tongue along her love button. He pushed his tongue inside her as far as he could; tasting her thoroughly before pushing his forefinger inside of her and moving his mouth back to her fully engorged clitoris. As he gently suckled, he penetrated her vagina repeatedly with his fingers steadily, confidently, until he felt her body quake. She let out a little yelp as she came, and Eddie kissed the sweat off her thighs as he lifted her body to the floor and mounted her quickly, nearly tearing her dress as he pulled it over her head. She had been sucking her own breast and the sight of it made him almost unbearably excited, her puffy berry lips against the large round blacks of her nipples... He quickly removed his pants and threw them in the pile with her dress before pinning her face below his hips and thrusting his penis into her mouth. She suckled him greedily at first before relaxing and allowing him to control the strokes, enjoying the feel of his smooth flesh against her lips. She looked at his square jaw, finely chiseled body and wild hair as he moved his hips rhythmically. She would have smiled, had her mouth not been so completely occupied. She felt Eddie's aching and just as she thought he might let her taste him, he pulled out of her mouth, kissed her forehead and smiled. Reaching behind her head, he pulled a condom out of his pants pocket and slid it over his swollen penis, pausing to regain his composure so as not to displease his lover.

Mona's body was raw with desire as she watched Eddie slide the sheath over his erection. He looked into her eyes for guidance, quickly recognizing her longing; he grabbed her thighs and forced himself into her in one sharp stroke. She released a throaty moan and Eddie covered her mouth quickly with his as he slid in and out of her with sharp motions. As he approached his own orgasm he could no longer control her moans with his mouth, and simply bit her lower lip abstractly before blindly releasing himself in ecstasy. As waves of delight rippled through him, he could not help but think heaven really was between a woman's legs.

***

"Eddie, is that you?" Tasha mumbled groggily. It was nearly 5:00am.

"Yeah, baby, it's me," Eddie whispered as he turned the dimmer switch on their bedroom light, slightly illuminating a half-awake Tasha tucked under white sheets and a pale blue blanket. "Go back to sleep."

"What time is it?" Tasha asked.

"It's late, honey. I've been working all night. I'm just gonna jump in the shower and hit the sack."

"All right, baby. That Louie sure works you like a slave," Tasha mumbled halfheartedly. Eddie couldn't help but smile.

***

"So how'd you like my breakfast?" Eddie asked the neatly business-suited Tasha as she rushed out the door of the apartment they shared.

"It was wonderful, as usual, Eddie," she responded enthusiastically, before quickly running back into the kitchen to kiss him goodbye.

Eddie watched Tasha's long brown legs sprinting to the elevator. She was always "running late" to her job as a legal secretary for one of Manhattan's premier law firms. He couldn't blame her because, although he functioned on little sleep and habitually got up at the same time as her to make breakfast, he rarely went out before 10:00am. Waking up was one thing, braving the subway and hordes of people, another thing entirely. Eddie settled down with his cup of coffee and the *New York Times*. It was after 9:00am when the phone rang.

"Hello?"

"Yes, I'm calling for Mr. Eddie Ryder" a male voice stated.

"This is Eddie."

"Yes, Eddie. I'm calling on behalf of Reeva Johnson at Esquire Models. It looks like Ms. Johnson was impressed with your photos. She'd like you to come in ASAP. I suppose she has something in mind for you." The voice sounded very bored and very nasal.

Eddie was ecstatic, but he tried to sound cool. "I can come in today if that's convenient for Ms. Johnson," he offered.

"Let's say three o'clock, then. And, don't be late. Ms. Johnson is a very busy woman." The man hung up.

Eddie sat at the kitchen table stunned. This was it! Finally a major modeling agency was interested in him! What he wouldn't do to kiss Brenda goodbye for good. His mind wandered...he would be surrounded by beautiful models instead of the fat Brenda. Although he would definitely Miss Mona...shit, he could always visit her.

He had barely recovered from the phone call before the phone rang again. He swallowed before saying, "Hello?"

"Hey, man, what's up?" a deep, husky voice wondered. It was his best friend, Marc Bryant.

"Ay, Marc, man, how you doin'? Shit, I haven't heard your voice in awhile!" Eddie bellowed.

"I know you haven't! I've just been so busy with all this job shit. All this shit's finally starting to pay off, though."

"That's good to hear, man," Eddie responded,

thoughtfully nodding his head. "Listen, I've got good news. I was just hoping you could *partake* in the *merriment*," Marc played with his words. "Anyway, a bunch of us are getting together tonight to celebrate my promotion to Local Sales Manager at the radio station. You're my man, Eddie you've got to join us."

"I'd love to, man. I don't think I can, though. I've got a big appointment this afternoon and I'm working damn near all night." Eddie paused, quickly thinking. "Or, you know what you *could* do...Why don't you bring your friends over to Caribbean Corner? I can set you up with a nice table, private, if you'd like. Were you planning on dinner or just drinks?"

"I was thinking about drinks, but I suppose we really *should* eat. With the kind of money I'm gonna be pulling in, why don't you set it up for dinner for ten. I'll call the restaurant if there's any change."

"What time?" Eddie asked.

"Do it for eight...When will you get off?"

"I'll be off at midnight. I can catch up with you after dinner. Who knows maybe leave a little early?"

"Cool. I'll see you tonight then."

"Yeah, man, cool." Eddie hung up the phone smiling. Maybe he'd have something to celebrate tonight too! He wrote a note to Tasha on a piece of the Friday *Times*, "Sony, Tash. Have to meet Marc after work. Will be home late again. I'll call. Ed." He secured the note to the refrigerator with one of Tasha's butterfly magnets.

***

Eddie left the Fifth Avenue office with a huge grin. This really was it! Esquire wanted to represent him, and appointments were already set up for next week. He couldn't wait to tell his dad and Tasha. He had been living with Tasha for just about six months now. She had always taken care of him when he was short with the rent or just money in general. Bartending at Louie's made him pretty good money in tips, but between his portfolio, acting lessons and Tasha's high-priced Park Slope apartment, it always seemed he was broke.

He stopped off at a nearby park to enjoy the beautiful weather while he wrapped his mind around the meaning of this new opportunity. Although Esquire specialized in male models, they didn't represent very many blacks. He had never heard of an Esquire model that didn't rack in the bucks. And if an Esquire account needed a black model, he would be one of only a few. No matter how it worked out, he was bound to get the type of exposure that would send him over the top.

He pulled off the bold black and violet-patterned tie he wore and stuffed it in his pants pocket. At moments like this he really wished his mother lived in the States. He loved his dad, but he couldn't really talk to him about anything important—just women and dominoes. Neville Ryder lived in Fort Greene, Brooklyn with his girlfriend for years, but slept around like a college kid. It was his dad, but Eddie had a hard time taking him seriously. He never thought he'd feel this way. He had great news but no one he cared much about in particular to share it with. He found the realization annoying and dismissed it. He had more important things to think about, like what he might want to use as his professional name. Ms. Johnson suggested he come up with a more appealing name, something "racy" was her word. He liked the idea of choosing a second identity. It was like a new beginning or something.

***

"Hey, I see you made it!" Eddie called out to Marc as he entered the restaurant with a group of business-suited men and women. Eddie had made sure not to reserve one of Brenda's tables for Marc. He was his friend, after all. Mona greeted the party and directed them to one of the rear dining tables waitressed by Jackie, quite possibly the prettiest waitress at Caribbean Corner and one Eddie hadn't already slept with. After all, Marc *was* his friend.

"Hi, Eddie," Jackie said cheerfully as she leaned into the bar. "Your friends need a couple pitchers of margaritas to start." She lowered her voice and winked before adding, "You can put some in a cup for me on the side."

As Eddie took Jackie in, he wondered why he hadn't slept with her. He quickly remembered Mona, Tasha, Sherri and the others. The fact was he just didn't have the time. He blended the drinks quickly, poured a paper-cup-full for Jackie and put the pitchers on her tray. He smiled as he watched Jackie ambling towards the rear area, her thick calves and thighs fully displayed in her short black skirt. All the waitresses wore black skirts and white blouses; some just wore them better than others.

"Eddie, you really are a womanizer aren't you?" Suddenly Mona was sitting at the bar right in front of him.

Eddie had allowed his mind to wander. "Huh?" he responded dumbfounded. "What did you say, Mona?" he asked, his eyes still on Jackie.

Mona laughed. "You know, Eddie, I think you need to have your testosterone levels checked; you're horny all the time."

Eddie turned to look at Mona in her cranberry jumpsuit and bolero jacket. As always, she looked great. He couldn't help laughing at himself. It did seem he was always watching women, but how could he help it?

"Mona, you know I only have eyes for you," he joked.

"Yeah, sure." Mona rolled her eyes playfully.

"So where's your husband, Mrs. Robbins?" Eddie asked, his voice barely audible.

Mona swallowed. Louie wasn't in, but she knew he'd be back shortly. Maybe if they were fast… Just as Mona seriously toyed with the thought of taking Eddie into the office, Louie walked in the front door. She sighed. That could have been a really bad scene. She shouldn't let Eddie tempt her so...

Eddie stood up straight when Louie approached the bar. "What's up boss?" he asked.

"Gimme a scotch straight up," Louie responded bleakly.

"What's the matter, baby?" Mona asked her husband.

"Nothing, babe. I just need a drink, that's all."

Mona gave Eddie a perplexed look. Eddie just shrugged his shoulders. "Look, Louie, I hate to be a pain, but I need to leave a little early tonight. Mona or Brenda can handle the bar."

"How early?" Louie asked.

"Around ten."

"No problem." Louie turned towards Mona, "Are you sure you don't want to leave early with Eddie?" he asked before throwing the liquor to the back of his throat. He tapped his glass on the table indicating his need for a refill. Eddie obliged expressionless.

"What are you talking about, Louie? Why would I want to leave with Eddie?" Mona was giving an Oscar-caliber performance.

"I have no idea," Louie mumbled. "You know what, Eddie, since your friends are here, why don't you go ahead and join them for dessert? I know you don't really want to work tonight, and I can handle the bar." Louie's voice was surprisingly friendly.

"Thanks, Louie, you're a prince." Eddie smiled. He really had nothing against the guy, despite the fact that he was screwing his wife. He actually liked Louie a lot, but he wasn't much of a looker and Eddie could see why Mona went elsewhere for her physical pleasures. Besides, from what Mona told him, Louie wasn't particularly skilled or inventive in bed. He knew how a bad lover bored the hell out of him.

Mona purposefully ignored Eddie as he left the bar and headed over to Marc's table.

***

"Looks like I'm available a little earlier than anticipated," Eddie remarked as he approached Marc's table. Jackie was flirting unabashedly, nearly sitting in Marc's lap. Eddie frowned, she must have been hitting those margaritas a bit more heavily than he'd realized.

Marc and Eddie were both good-looking, but like night and day to any observer. While Eddie was tall, dark and lean, clean-shaven except for his mustache with wild hair and beautiful big eyes, Marc was a light-skinned brother, still pretty tall at 5'11", but stocky and bearded. The two of them together made an interesting combination. Marc in his tailored suits with his closely cropped beard and carefully chosen jewelry, and Eddie all jeans, button-down T-shirts and work boots come rain or shine. Women went nuts when the two of them were together; they seemed such an unlikely pair. No one would have guessed the ten year difference in their ages, not even Marc, who thought Eddie, was in his mid-twenties. Eddie's welcome was apparent on the faces of the women in Marc's group. He knew it as they began adjusting their clothes and hair nervously. Eddie didn't smile at all as Marc introduced him to the various men and women. It was stupid, but sometimes he liked to put on an aloof demeanor when he met people, particularly women but men too. He thought it made for more interesting introductions.

Eddie settled into one of the available chairs at the table as the group ordered a variety of confections and liquored coffees. He suggested his favorites: the rum pecan pie and Louie's special Bahamian coffee, a blended mixture of coconut, overproof and dark rums, hazelnut liqueur, condensed milk and espresso. Anyone could have guessed Eddie was a bit partial to rum in general, coconut rum in particular. Marc and most of his guests followed Eddie's lead. A few with aversions to pecans or rum chose other items.

"So, Eddie, I see you've joined Mr. Bryant's table," Jackie commented as she took the individual dessert orders. He could hear the alcohol in her voice. She wasn't drunk, but he could see the subtle difference in her mannerisms: the way she let the dessert menus flop, the way she allowed her skirt to slide up, her tendency to fan herself. He'd seen her drink many times, but he'd never really seen it affect her. As much as he hated to admit it, seeing Jackie ever so slightly out of control turned him on, and he had to wonder why he gave Marc a table in her section.

"Marc and I go way back," Eddie commented, exaggerating their two-year friendship. They met in '85 when they attended a weekend acting class together. Eddie sought to enhance his acting skills while Marc sought to enhance his selling skills. They hit it off immediately and kept in touch ever since. While their relationship certainly wasn't deep, they had become best friends to each other.

"Really?" Jackie commented noticing Eddie's displeasure. She had been flirting with Eddie for as long as she'd been working at Caribbean Corner, and he never seemed to pay her much mind. He was friendly and he *looked*, but that was it. He never asked her out or came on to her. It had been driving her crazy. She found him wildly attractive, but she just wasn't the forward type. So now that she was flirting with his outrageously handsome friend, now he wanted to play the jealous boyfriend? At twenty-five, she gave up on figuring out men a long time ago. It seemed silly, but she knew she'd never understand them from age eighteen. She never understood her father or her brothers or her early boyfriends, why start now? But, she could have fun with it.

"So, how late are you working tonight?" Marc asked Jackie, gently running his index finger along her thigh.

"I'll be trapped here all night, Marc." She leaned in close to him, lightly resting her lips against his ear before adding in a whisper, "Maybe another time."

Eddie watched Jackie's display with annoyance. The more she bent over the more he really wished he could suck her thighs, but he had already passed her up and it would be rude to cut in on Marc's action now, so he resigned himself to tolerating their behavior until Jackie was gone. Thankfully, Jackie didn't offer to leave work early to jump into Marc's bed, and Eddie knew the group wouldn't linger too long after dessert. After all, he worked at Caribbean Corner, they couldn't possibly want to subject him to spending all his free time there as well.

Jackie sauntered off to put in the dessert orders and check on her other tables. Eddie's eyes followed her until she was well out earshot before suggesting a reggae lounge in the area for their after-dinner entertainment. The group seemed in agreement for the most part especially one dark-skinned beauty named Erikka who'd been eyeing Eddie all night.

***

The lounge was dimly lit by red light bulbs dangling loosely from the high pipe-covered ceiling. Bob Marley's "Buffalo Soldier" played in the background as the group of dashikied, business-suited, spandexed and baggy-pantsed men and women gyrated, rocked, swayed and rotated their bodies to the music. Eddie, Marc and two of the women from dinner entered the place together.

"Hey, it's good to see you!" the bartender shouted to Eddie and Marc over the sound of the music.

"Hey, what's up man?!" the two nearly chimed in response, slapping palms with the brother behind the bar. They had no idea what his name was, despite the fact that they'd both been in the "Redlite" Lounge many times.

"I see you brought some beautiful ladies with you," the bartender commented, smiling at the women.

"Yeah, *you* don't have to worry about these ladies," Eddie said feigning jealousy and playfully tugging on Erikka's arm as if steering her clear of the lascivious bartender. They laughed together and ordered beers and a pitcher of water for their table.

Smooth black lacquer tables were set into faux-leather booths along the walls of the club. Groups of fresh carnations where bundled into small white bud vases on each table. They served only drinks and limited appetizers. Redlite was an after-dinner watering hole where people came primarily to drink, party and smoke the occasional joint. The sticky scent of cannabis could be detected creeping from the passageway to the rest rooms or the rear lounge area at random intervals.

Eddie and Erikka were getting comfortable in their side of the booth, while Marc cozied up to a temp from his office named Roxi. The women were young, pretty and looking for a good time. They drank their beers haphazardly, told each other raunchy jokes and laughed about the office. Eddie finally had the opportunity to tell Marc about his deal with Esquire, much to Erikka's pleasure. After all, who wanted to date a poor bartender? They danced to reggae, calypso, ska and soca with occasional house and R&B mixed in. Eddie held Erikka close to him as they moved their hips rhythmically, whining to the Caribbean beats. He could feel her perspiration, hot and sticky through her navy blue spandex dress; and was determined to find out whether or not she wore panties. He would have bet money that she didn't. The looking was killing him though, and he had to mentally control an impending hard-on a number of times.

Eddie couldn't think of a time when he felt so free. Being around Marc was always fun, partly because Marc was just a really a cool guy and also because he usually picked up the tab. He looked forward to the time when he'd be able to reciprocate. But tonight was just about good news...good news for both of them. He and Erikka sat together while Marc and Roxi went at it on the dance floor. "Don't hurt'em now!" Erikka screamed out to Roxi and she rocked her body low to the ground, suggesting excellent muscle control.

"Stop screaming at those people," Eddie said as he placed a hand on Erikka's bare thigh and kissed her. He could taste the beer and the salt from her sweat, and he loved it. He leaned into her a bit more, lingering on the taste and feel of her lips. Erikka was a beautiful shade of ebony, with a short braided bob and a gorgeous smile. He ran his tongue over the tops of her teeth.

"Hey, what's going on over here?" Roxi asked spiritedly as she sat across from them. Marc was right behind her.

"You know, Eddie, I can't take you anywhere!" Marc laughed.

"Hey, mind your business," Eddie retorted. "I'm getting exhausted. What time is it anyway?" The four of them began squinting ridiculously at their respective watches. Between the alcohol in their bodies and the dim lighting, they couldn't see to save their lives!

"Why don't we head back to my place? We can get away from all this noise," Marc offered throwing Eddie a knowing glance. "I'll call a car." Marc asked and answered his own offer without any objections.

**

Sunlight flooded the guest bedroom at Marc's Upper West Side apartment uncontrollably. Eddie covered his head with a pillow in a pitiful attempt to protect himself, but the sun shot past the venetian blinds, under the pillow and straight to his hangover.

"Mmmm" the woman next to him mumbled.

God, it was worse than he thought. He wasn't even alone. Eddie looked around quickly for a clock. It was nearly 2:00pm. *Holy shit!* He scrambled for his pants. Tasha would definitely kill him; there was no question about it. He was a dead man.

Marc was in the living room watching TV and eating when Eddie entered the room.

"Ugh!" Eddie grumbled.

Marc laughed. "So you made it! I thought you were dead. I was about to dial nine-one-one!"

"Help," Eddie mumbled holding his head. "Please tell me you have aspirin," he said very softly.

Marc bellowed, "SURE I DO!"

Eddie looked at him harshly. "That was entirely unnecessary, Marc. Don't torture me."

Marc smiled sympathetically. "Sorry man. There's aspirin in the john."

"Thanks. I'm going take about twelve, and then I'm gonna take a shower. Remind me never to hang out with you again."

"Nobody told you to drink vodka shots, Eddie."

"Vodka?..." Eddie paused trying to remember the vodka. As he ran through the prior evening in his mind, he realized the last thing he remembered was coming back to Marc's place and dancing in the living room with Erikka. He couldn't remember precisely what happened after that. It was *very* fuzzy. Shit, he definitely didn't remember getting naked with Erikka...he at least wanted to know if it was good or not.

He popped two aspirins in his mouth and drank a large glass of orange juice before getting into the shower. The warm water massaged his scalp and cascaded along the ripples of his tense muscles. With his head under the crashing noise of the shower, he couldn't hear Erikka enter the steamy bathroom. Before he knew what happened, he felt her next to him, her head nuzzled in his chest. He immediately felt a hard-on coming.

"Good morning," she uttered softly.

"Mmmm… Good morning to you," he responded grabbing her butt and pulling her body closer to his. As his erection became complete, he could no longer feel the pounding in his head. He looked down on her soft brown face as rivers of water dripped off her chin and her tiny braids. She had the look of a sleepy baby, her skin a little oily, her makeup all but gone, but such pretty clear skin it really didn't matter. Eddie ran his fingers along her closed eyelids before allowing his eyes to drop to her bare breasts. Her nipples were hard and rivulets of water made careful arcs around them. He grabbed both of her nipples quickly with each hand, pinching firmly. Her gentle moan blended harmonically with the sound of the water crashing against their bodies.

"You're beautiful," he said.

She smiled and opened her eyes to look at him. Eddie looked better wet than dry. His deep complexion glistened as water traveled along his broad shoulders and chest. She noticed his nipples were hard and began nibbling them gently as she held his trim waist in her arms. She grabbed a bar of soap and began washing his chest, then his back. She slid the soap between his legs and washed him there, running her hands along the soft rounded flesh of his testicles, before massaging the length of his penis. Eddie let out a moan and she smiled, dropping to her knees. Not only was this brother fine and skilled in bed, he had the kind of dick like a lollipop; she couldn't help but want to suck it.

Erikka took him in her mouth then, gently licking the head of his penis before increasing the pressure and picking up the pace. She enjoyed the feel of his smooth skin in her mouth and on her lips as the water ran through her braids and down her bare body. She couldn't resist touching her own clitoris as she felt Eddie rocking in her mouth, but it was becoming unbearable for her, she had to have him. She stood up to kiss him and pressed her body against his trying desperately to slip his erection into her. Eddie moved away from her. She couldn't stand it, her desire was too urgent.

Eddie held her by the shoulders and stepped away from her slightly. Erikka was hot, but he wasn't about to skinny-dip. "One second," he said. He jumped out of the shower and pulled a condom out of his jeans pocket. He dried himself quickly from the waist doom and turned the shower head down, so the water wouldn't hit them directly, "Put your hands up," he said as he motioned for Erikka to put her hands against the shower wall so her body would be bent slightly with her butt sticking out.

She did as she was told.

Eddie enjoyed the view of her cutely rounded behind stuck out waiting for him to give it to her. He slapped her butt with his hand, then bit her gently. Finally, he took hold of her hips and slid himself inside of her, she nearly screamed.

"Are you OK?" he had to ask.

"Uhmm hmmm..." she trailed off, rocking her body against him as she alternated between moans, yelps and near screams.

Eddie didn't really care how much noise she made; he knew Marc couldn't hear much over the sound of the water, and who really cared if he could? He stroked her expertly as he played with her body. She was getting out of control, so he toyed with her more...slapping her butt and firmly telling her to calm down when he knew she couldn't. He bit her earlobe and rubbed her breasts and belly. His hands were all over her when he felt her body shudder with one of many climaxes. When her moans softened, he relaxed into her, stroking her gently then faster, grabbing her breasts firmly he was shocked by the power of his own orgasm as he exploded in her. At that point, Eddie knew he had just discovered the cure for a hangover.

***

When Eddie arrived home it was nearly 6:00pm that Saturday. He knew Tasha would be furious no matter what time he showed up, so he went for a burger and a few antidotal beers with Marc before heading back to Brooklyn. He hadn't called, although he knew he should have. He knew he was being selfish, but he just didn't want to deal with being screamed at twice. He really screwed up big time. There was no way he could expect her to be happy about the modeling thing now. *Maybe if he cooked her dinner and made her a nice bubble bath...*

Eddie noticed something was different from before his key even went into the apartment door lock. He couldn't believe his eyes, when he opened the door. The place was practically empty! The TV, VCR and sofa were missing from the living room. For a moment he thought they had been robbed. He walked into the bedroom; the entire bedroom set was gone! He opened the closets, her clothes were gone! As he frantically roamed the apartment, he realized they had not been robbed, Tasha had left! His head was reeling and he went to open the fridge to grab a beer. There was a note on it, "You're so busy sticking people all night, now you're stuck in a two-year lease, you ASSHOLE!"

"Shit," Eddie grumbled, sitting on the kitchen floor with his brew. "Shit, shit, shit."

***

By 9:00pm Eddie had grown comfortable with the idea of living alone. If things worked out with Esquire he'd have the money, and he knew his six month relationship with Tasha was lost. Although he had sometimes wished they were closer; theirs had been a relationship of convenience. He never loved her. He had known and enjoyed the company of many women in his twenty years, back in the Bahamas and in Brooklyn. Maybe now was the time to start his life anew. His mind wandered back to Abaco, the land of his birth. He remembered the beauty of the water, the tranquility of the sea. Just as he pondered memories of home, the thought struck him with a certainty that astonished him. His professional name would be Ocean Ryder; there was no question about it!

"Ocean," he said, feeling the name move across his lips. He smiled, feeling a renewed vitality. Maybe he'd give Erikka a call after all.

Sophia Boyd
Summer 1987

Sophia taped the closures on her son's diapers carefully, making sure each little leg was securely wrapped. Timothy was only a year old, but he seemed to make enough mess for a child five times his age. At twenty-five, Sophia had felt she was ready for children. With another year and a son under her belt, she wondered how things might have been had she waited. It seemed there would never be a "right" time to have children, so when she found out she was pregnant a year ago, she decided it was as good a time as any. Ron said he loved her and the decision was hers, so she brought a new life into the world with barely a thought except to fulfill her natural longing to procreate.

"Heeey, baby... Heecy, baby," she cooed at her boy nuzzling a stuffed animal against his tiny face. Thankfully, he had his father's complexion, a light shade of caramel. Sophia's natural complexion was ivory, so light in fact that she was slightly embarrassed by it. She wouldn't leave the house without her bronzer and lipstick to give her "some color." While she was busy trying to get color, other women were busy trying to bleach themselves or wear yellow contacts to get the effect of Sophia's pale skin and light brown eyes.

She fed Timothy his bottle in front of the television. The nightly news was on, and a series of young black boys in handcuffs were paraded across the screen. As she held her son in her arms she was moved to tears. How would he turn out? Luckily, her job with a fashion company allowed her to live in prestigious Brooklyn Heights, but she knew she couldn't shelter him from the world around him. New York City was huge with just about every type of scourge and every type of beauty wildly intermingled. She loved the city and remembered her own college years filled with sex and drugs. She had managed to come away with what she felt was a clearer understanding of the world: she could address a sidewalk hustler in one second and a senior executive in the next, obtaining equal respect from each. But she knew she was one of the lucky ones. Many of her friends from back home in Mississippi had not been so fortunate, falling to the wayside with addiction, lack of education, crime, you name it…she had pretty much seen it. She held her son in her arms as the thoughts flooded her. How could she possibly ensure her son's future? He would grow to be bigger and stronger than she ever would, and probably as obstinate as she was as a young woman. At twenty-six, Sophia was confronted with one of the great dilemmas of motherhood: how do you protect your children from learning from their own mistakes? If only you could just tell them how to live, and they would listen. If only you could convince yourself that you even knew what to tell them.

She brushed a tear from her cheek realizing just how far her thoughts had run away from her. Just then, the phone rang. She answered quickly so as not to awaken her son, who had quietly dozed off.

"Hello?"

The voice on the other end cracked with anguish and pain. "Sophia? I'm so glad you're home. I need to talk to you. Can I come over?" The woman's voice was pleading.

"Sandy? Of course you can!" Sophia assured her, raising her voice in recognition of her friend's distress.

"I'm across the street," Sandy said before hanging up.

Sophia glared at the phone with disbelief. Sandy was her best friend, but it was totally unlike her to call freaked out from across the street. Was it her family? Her lover? She put Timothy in his bed and waited for her apartment buzzer to ring.

Sophia turned the television off and popped a Miriam Makeba cassette into her new stereo system. Her ankle bracelets and wrist bangles jingled softly as she walked barefoot across the parquet wood floor of her living room. The kente-style wrap-around skirt and head wrap she wore fluttered softly in the breeze of her ceiling fan as she adjusted the various African sculptures in her wall unit. *Maybe she should make some tea.*

When her buzzer rang, she let Sandy in the downstairs door quickly. Before she knew it, Sandy was knocking on her apartment door.

"Hey, girl..." she said comfortingly as she opened the door. "What's going on with you?"

"Oh, Sophia, it's just fucking unbelievable. You'll never believe what I've been through in the past few days. I hope you have time. I really need to talk!" Sandy was clearly exasperated. The rims around her eyes were red as if she'd been crying. Her hands fiddled nervously with the pockets of her jeans and her short natural 'do.

"It's not your family is it?"

"My family?" Sandy paused for a moment, confused. "No, no, it's Lana. I left her tonight... You'll never believe..."

"Hey, relax." Sophia gave her friend a hug. "I'm gonna make some tea. Why don't you sit down and get comfortable. Tell me the whole story." Sophia and Sandy graduated from Fashion Institute of Technology six years earlier. Sophia had majored in Fashion Design while Sandy majored in Marketing. It was nearly ten years since they had become friends, sharing just about every conceivable crisis together. Some of her other friends thought it was strange to be so close to a gay woman, but Sophia had always been with men so Sandy's sexuality had never been much of an issue. She had relationships just like anyone else.

Sandy sat on Sophia's large beige sofa, resting her small brown face in her hands. Sandy was an attractive woman with interesting features: full pouty lips, big dimples, wide eyes and a sharp nose with a tiny mole. Unlike the stereotypical lesbian, she was not at all boyish. She was 5'5" with a voluptuous figure and feminine good-looks which complemented her short "fade" haircut.

"She was cheating on me," Sandy began.

Sophia raised an eyebrow. "Did you know the woman?" she asked.

"It was a man!" Sandy exclaimed. "I saw the two of them leave our place yesterday afternoon."

"A *man*?!" Sophia couldn't believe her ears. She thought Lana was the gayest woman she had ever met! She never gave the slightest inclination of an interest in men. Sophia paused to fully absorb the idea of Lana with a man before asking quite off-handedly, "What were you doing at the apartment in the afternoon anyway?"

"I had to pick up a disk for a project I was working on. I saw them coming out of the building... Lana and this man I didn't know... She had her hand on his arm and she was smiling." Sandy's voice cracked. She pulled a tissue from a dispenser on an antique wooden end table and blew her nose before continuing. "I knew immediately. I could tell right away, you know?" She looked at Sophia, her eyes pleading.

"Yeah, I know," Sophia responded sympathetically.

She patted her friend on the back of her heavy black T-shirt. "Sometimes these things happen..." Her voice trailed off soothingly.

"But what makes it so much worse, I can't even begin to tell you..." Sandy continued, adjusting her body on the sofa. She lowered her voice to almost a whisper, "You wouldn't believe how perfect our lovemaking was the night before. I mean, it was just unbelievable."

Sophia's interest was definitely piqued. She leaned in closer to absorb the more titillating information. It wasn't that she wasn't concerned about her friend's pain, but throwing some juicy detail certainly helped her maintain her attention.

Sandy continued, "Then after this awesome love...nothing, zero, zilch..." Her voice trailed off.

"You're not making any sense," Sophia commented. "What happened?"

"Sorry. Anyway, I saw them, but I didn't confront them... I just went upstairs to do what I had to do... I found the condoms..." Her voice broke again and she paused to steal another tissue away from its holder.

"Shhh... go on, honey," Sophia coaxed.

"I just went back to work and tried to forget about it. I had a busy day... But, when I got home and I saw her. I told her what I saw...what I found..."

"What did she have to say?!" Sophia asked excitedly.

"She just admitted it like it was no big deal." Sandy sniffled and rolled her eyes. "She said it was different with a man. She said it wasn't like she was really cheating because it wasn't a woman." Sandy's sentences took on a staccato rhythm, then she added, "She invited me into their bed!" That was it. Sandy started shaking horribly as the tears rolled down her cheeks. She tried to continue talking but the power of her tears wouldn't allow it.

"Shhh..." Sophia consoled, wrapping her arms around

her friend. She rocked her gently in her arms as Sandy rested her head on her shoulders. "Shhh… It's okay…"

When Sandy regained her composure she continued, "I can't believe she asked me to join them? I mean, what kind of person would do that? Sex is something special between two people... Wasn't it bad enough that what I thought was special between us wasn't? Couldn't she just leave it at that? Why did she have to cheapen it? God, and when I think how moved I was when we were together... When I think that all along she was doing the same shit with someone else. I feel like such a sucker..." Her voice went from anger to despair to disgust to longing as the words trailed from her lips. Sandy was obviously feeling the deep burn of a love gone bad.

"Well, so what are you going to do now?" Sophia asked gently.

"I'm not exactly sure. I mean, I moved all my stuff out with my brother today. It wasn't that much. Maybe I'll stay with him for a little while until I can get it together."

"I'd love to have you here if you'd like," Sophia offered.

"You know I'd love to, but wouldn't that cause problems with Ron?"

"Ron doesn't live here, you know. You're my best friend. You're more than welcome to stay."

"Are you sure?" Sandy asked meekly.

"Of course," Sophia responded, nodding her head happily. She was sure she'd enjoy having someone to talk to for a few months. She enjoyed her relationship with Ron, but sometimes he really annoyed her, and she thought it would be nice to have someone to let off some steam with.

"That's great!" Sandy gushed, curling her socked feet under her body. She hadn't seriously considered living with Sophia figuring that between Ron and little Timothy, she'd just be in the way. Thankfully, Sophia didn't seem to feel that way.

"Waahhh," Timothy cried out from the bedroom. The women exchanged smiles. Sophia patted Sandy's denim-covered thigh quickly in acknowledgement of their agreement before rushing to check on her baby.

***

Sophia enjoyed Sandy's company for the next few months. They took Timothy to the park together, went to movies, cooked dinner and shared household chores. Sandy was an early riser and meticulously neat, so her presence on the living room sofa-bed was barely detectable. Lana called nearly every day at first, then once a week, finally tapering off to once every three weeks or so.

This Saturday was one of the last days of Indian summer and Sophia busied herself with straightening out the house to the sound of Anita Baker's "Rapture" album while waiting for Ron to arrive. They had made plans to spend the day at the park with Timothy, and she was looking forward to enjoying the pleasant weather with her two favorite guys. She smiled thinking about all the good times and good news they had shared together as she dusted the Venetian blinds in her bedroom. She realized it was getting a bit late so she adjusted the stereo volume to make sure she wouldn't miss Ron's arrival. Just as she lowered the stereo she heard the apartment buzzer and let him in.

"I've been ringing the door bell for half an hour," an annoyed Ron grumbled when she opened her apartment door. He didn't kiss her hello the way he normally would. "Isn't it working?" Ron stood in Sophia's living room with his hands in his jeans pockets, the bow of his legs tapered out as he locked his knees. His denim jacket hung half open at his waist and revealed a Keith Haring "Free South Africa" T-shirt.

"Sorry, Ron, I didn't hear it. I was in the back with the baby and the stereo was on loud."

"But you knew I was coming to get you," Ron continued annoyed.

"Look, Ron, I'm sorry. I didn't realize I wouldn't hear the bell."

"Where's Miss Sandy, is she deaf too?" Ron's voice was raised.

"Ron, you're being obnoxious. Sandy's in the shower." Sophia's pale brown eyes glared at the tall black man before her with agitation. While she was attracted to Ron partly because he was a big man (he was about 6'3", 200 lbs.), when they argued his size sometimes made him seem more menacing.

"Were you in the shower too?" Ron asked suggestively. He hated homosexuals in general and Sandy in particular. It really wasn't a personal thing. He just hated the fact that some lesbian was living with his woman—a cute one, at that. Maybe he was just jealous that his woman was closer to her gay friend than she was to him. He had asked Sophia on many occasions to live with him, especially since she had the baby, but she refused claiming she needed her independence whether or not she had his child.

"Ron, you're really being an *asshole*!" Sophia screamed before turning to the back room to get Timothy.

"What did you say?!" Ron roared as he charged after her watching the way her thin brown wrap-around jumper moved over her curves.

Sophia turned quickly when she heard Ron's footsteps. When she faced him she saw blankness in his eyes, like he barely knew her. He grabbed her by the arm and pulled her back towards the living room. "Who the hell do you think you're talking to?" he rumbled.

In an attempt to cool things down, Sophia responded gently, "My lover?"

Ron pushed her shoulder so hard she had to take a few steps back to regain her balance. "Your lover?!" he screamed. "Now, she's even got you talking like one of them! I AM NOT YOUR LOVER, SOPHIE, I'M YOUR FUCKING MAN!"

Sophia looked at Ron in disbelief, was this man she loved? He had never raised a hand to her before, and now he was practically throwing her on the floor! "Ron, get out." She spoke calmly, turning her body away from him At 5'6", 145 lbs. she was no physical match for him. The most she could do was get him away from her so he could calm down. If she provoked him now, who knew what he might do.

"Look, Sophie," Ron began, his voice suddenly softening.

"Just leave."

"What about our date?"

"I'll talk to you later," Sophia dismissed him with her words. Her actions confirmed her resolve as she walked over to the front door and held it open for him. She stared at the floor.

"Look, Sophie, I'm sorry. I'll call you. I don't know what came over me. It's just that damn girl..." He gestured towards the bathroom where Sandy was getting dressed.

"Fine, Ron. We'll talk another time. I need some time alone now." Sophia's eyes did not shift from the square she examined in the parquet pattern of her floor.

***

Sophia and Sandy hadn't talked much about relationships since that day in June when Sandy showed up in Sophia's doorway teary-eyed, so Sandy was surprised when Sophia told her she needed advice about Ron.

"I thought the two of you were going out today," Sandy commented.

"I thought so too..." Sophia's voice trailed off.

"What's going on?" Sandy asked, resting her elbows on Sophia's glass-topped kitchen table.

"First promise you won't tell anyone else what I'm about to tell you," Sophia implored.

Sandy nodded quickly.

Sophia sat at the kitchen table in her brown jumper and sandals, holding her head in her hands. She stroked the soft brown strands of her bob as they peaked out the sides of her carefully arranged head wrap. "Shit," she mumbled. When she raised her head to look at Sandy, her eyes had welled with tears. "I don't know what to do." A lone tear traced a winding pattern along her cheek before being brushed away by the back of her hand.

"Hey," Sandy's voice was consoling as she recognized the severity of the situation. She touched her friend's hand across the table. She hadn't thought anything was going wrong with Sophia. She knew her career wasn't on track as much as she had hoped and her relationship with Ron was a little rocky, but none of that was out of the ordinary for women their age, or anybody really.

"Sorry," Sophia whispered, apologizing more for her loss of control than for her tears.

"Did you and Ron have a fight?" Sandy asked. She had a feeling something happened while she was dressing, but she really couldn't hear much. All she knew was that instead of leaving, Sophia had stayed.

"Yeah."

"What happened?" Sandy asked again, pressing her hand into her friends. Sophia exhaled loudly releasing the words, "He pushed me."

"WHAT?!" Sandy couldn't believe her ears. She never thought for a moment that Ron could be violent. He was a police officer, after all. If he had stress to release he could take it out on his suspects. And, he always talked about the extent of his love for Sophia. He seemed so enamored with her; it was hard to believe he would raise a finger to her. And, they had been going out for years. Surely, something like this would have come up sooner. She looked at Sophia in disbelief.

Sophia responded to Sandy's facial expression. "How do you think I feel? Ron and I have had a lot of arguments, but I never thought he would hit me. He nearly knocked me down!" She bit her lip before continuing, "I haven't even told him, or anybody... I'm pregnant again."

Sandy was stunned again. She looked at her friend in disbelief. "Weren't you using anything?"

"I was getting lazy with the diaphragm, it's my fault. I should have known better. I want this baby, though. I want to give Timothy a little brother or sister, and who knows..." Sophia held her chin in her hands as she stared up at the ceiling light fixture. "I was beginning to think Ron was the person for me."

"I'm beginning to think you should leave that moron, and find a man who doesn't need to strut around with a badge and a gun for a living. What about his safety? Could you even deal with planning a life with a cop? And as for this pushing stuff, it just sounds like something that's bound to escalate." Sandy folded her arms across her chest with resolution.

Sophia paused in an attempt to select her words carefully. "Ron has a real problem with you living here."

Sandy's expression changed from anger to annoyance. "Ron doesn't live here," she stated matter-of-factly. As she reached the end of her statement she immediately realized that maybe she wouldn't be living there for much longer.

Sophia's expression was emotionless. What could she do? She loved Sandy, but she didn't want Sandy to come between her and Ron. "You're right, Ron doesn't live here. Look, do you mind staying with Timothy for a little while? I need to take a walk or something. I've got to think about what I'm going to do."

"Sure." Sandy was careful not to create anymore unnecessary friction. She didn't want to move out just yet and she knew Sophia would need a lot of support to end her relationship with Ron. Even if Ron never hit her again, dealing with their arguments and another unplanned pregnancy would be difficult.

"Thanks," Sophia muttered dazedly. She grabbed her leather carry-all and headed for the street.

***

The day seemed to pass quickly once Sophia left the apartment. She took the subway to SoHo, in lower Manhattan, and visited a few art galleries. She gathered her thoughts in Washington Square Park and stopped to catch a movie. By the time she returned home it was nearly 6:00pm. Sandy stared at her blankly when she entered the apartment. She had been gone for over five hours.

"Hi," Sophia stated quietly when she entered the room. Sandy was curled up on the sofa with Timothy.

"Hi," Sandy replied.

Sophia threw her bag onto the kitchen table. "How did Timothy behave?"

"He was no problem at all," Sandy responded. "So how are you feeling?"

Sophia sat on the sofa next to Sandy and Timothy. "I'm still in love with Ron; I'm not ready to end our relationship, and I'm having this baby. I'm sure we can work through this." Sophia looked at Sandy for approval before continuing, "Ron's been under a lot of stress lately. I know he wants us to be together. I kept telling him I needed to live alone, so he can't understand your being here. Maybe it's time for Ron and me to live together."

Sandy's face was covered with a combination of horror and amazement. "You mean you're going to *reward* Ron for pushing you by offering to move in with him?!" She could barely believe her ears!

Sophia rolled her eyes. "No, I'm not going to *reward* him," she explained sarcastically, "It's just that, to an extent, I can understand his frustration."

Sandy was fascinated by Sophia's attitude. "You're scaring me, Sophie; you sound like one of those battered women on 'Oprah.'"

"Sandy, you're acting like he punched me or something. He didn't even slap me! He got upset and he *pushed* me. I'm sure he didn't realize how much force he used." Her eyes begged her friend to understand her predicament. How could she throw away a three-year relationship over one incident?

"What's the difference if it was a slap a punch or a push, Sophie?! It's all the same to me! I know you want to have the baby, but *living* with Ron? It just doesn't make any sense. Please, just think about it more before you make him any offers. Can you do that?" Sandy's eyes had softened with the feeling that maybe, just maybe, she was getting through to her friend.

"Okay, okay, I'll think about it for awhile before I call

him. If I do decide to live with him, I'll tell him face-to-face anyway, and I don't want to see him for at least a couple of days." She smiled apologetically at Sandy. "I promise I'll wait." She took her son from Sandy's arms and carried him to his bed.

***

That night Ron didn't even call.

Sophia and Sandy rented a few videos and ordered Chinese take-out. Sophia fell asleep on the sofa during the second movie. Sandy paused the VCR to throw a crocheted Afghan across her friend's legs. As she leaned over to cover Sophia, she noticed her sleeping face in a way she hadn't before. She noticed the silkiness of her hair, the pale prettiness of her skin, the softness of her lips... Suddenly she was overwhelmed with the desire to kiss Sophia.

Her heart pounded loudly in her chest and she felt her face flush as she lowered her head to quickly kiss her friend's lips. When she kissed her briefly, Sophia began to respond slightly, encouraging her to kiss her further. Sandy parted her lips slightly, probing her friend's mouth with her tongue.

Sophia jerked away from her quickly, "What the hell are you DOING?!!" she screamed, looking sleepy-eyed at Sandy with horror and disbelief. She wiped her mouth with the back of her hand. "Shit, Sandy! Fuck!" Sophia jumped off the sofa, stormed into her bedroom and closed the door.

***

"I do love you, Ron," Sophia murmured softly in her new husband's ear. They had married the day before at

City Hall and were waking up together for the first time as husband and wife. Timothy was with her aunt, as they decided to spend a long weekend together at a couples-only resort in the Pocono Mountains of Pennsylvania.

"I love you too, Sophie," Ron mumbled, wrapping his arm possessively around Sophia's slightly rounded belly.

It had been nearly two months since the kissing incident with Sandy. She had felt so violated at the time she was unable to speak to Sandy for days after. When Sandy first started to kiss her, in her sleep she thought it was Ron and kissed back until she realized what was happening. It confirmed what Ron had been seemingly trying to warn her about all along. She felt that Sandy couldn't be trusted after that. The one scary part about it was that in a way it did feel good. She ignored that part, hoping it would vanish from her memory. She didn't want a woman; she wanted a man, and Ron was her man. She still loved Sandy, but she loved Ron the way a woman loves a man: affectionately and sexually.

Almost immediately after the kissing incident she had asked Sandy if she wanted to take over her lease. Sandy loved the apartment but couldn't afford it alone, so Lana was quickly allowed back into her life. So Sandy and Lana lived in her old place, and she moved her belongings to Ron's house in Queens.

When Ron first proposed marriage it was the last thing on her mind, but after giving some thought to Timothy and her unborn child, she decided it would probably be in their best interest. She loved Ron, and he apologized endlessly for the shoving incident. He bought her a beautiful diamond solitaire and gold band which she knew he couldn't afford.

They hadn't argued at all once Sandy was out of the picture.

As Sophia Boyd Henderson rested her head on the

white satin sheets of the resort suite, she finally felt a resounding happiness and fulfillment. Maybe she too would know the joy of a long-lasting relationship like Mr. and Mrs. Boyd were so lucky to share. She had been meaning to visit her family in Mississippi for months. She supposed a new husband and a baby on the way would make a good reason for a call. She had no idea how bad her timing would be.

Aura Olivier
Winter 1989

"I need your help on the WNTL buy," John Wiexler explained to an attentive Aura. "I hope you don't mind working late."

"Not at all, John. I do have plans for lunch, though," Aura responded smoothing her knit dress over her knees. It was late February and there had been a wave of particularly cold days. On this Tuesday the temperature had dropped below zero.

"Of course." John turned on his heels in his tailored business suit and returned to his office, leaving Aura alone at her desk.

John Wiexler was Aura's boss at the ad agency she'd been working at for over two years. Although she liked her job as a media buying assistant, she worked hard for low pay while the more senior buyers, like her boss, cleaned up in bonuses. Even the radio and TV salespeople she arranged buys from made more money than she did. It was very frustrating at times, but she knew that since this was her first full-time job out of college she was expected to "pay her dues" for the next few years before she could begin to reap the rewards of her education and her efforts. She just hoped that she wasn't chasing a rainbow with a booby prize at the end.

Aura busied herself with her work, assisting her boss in his media buys, but also doing clerical work: answering phones, typing and making copies. It was just minutes past noon when her phone rang.

"WBG Advertising, Aura Olivier speaking."

"Hey Aura, are you ready?" It was Dana.

"Yeah, girl, but it's cold out there. Are you sure you want to do this?" Aura asked.

"Aura, you know cold weather don't bother me. I've got my fly wool cap, my crazy Russian ice age boots and a scarf to die for! I've got two inch tights and a wool suit! Girl, when I go outside I can't feel a thing! As a matter of fact, this office has me sweating!" Dana laughed. "So do you want me to meet you or what?"

"Hey if you can brave the cold, then so can I!" Aura said knowing full well she should be careful in such severe weather. Sometimes the cold weather aggravated her sickle-cell condition, but it had been nearly six months since she suffered a pain crisis so she didn't give too much thought to the weather. "I'm good as long as it's someplace cheap. How about the Empire Coffee Shop?"

"Sounds good to me. Meet you at one, okay?"

"Okay," Aura responded before hanging up. By the time she wrapped up a few loose ends at the office it was nearly one. She grabbed her coat and headed down a few partially snow-covered blocks to the coffee shop to meet Dana. When she arrived Dana was seated, waving at her.

"Hi!" Dana greeted, showing off dimples as she smiled. Her deep caramel skin was slightly pink at the cheeks and nose in response to the bitter weather, and her loose shoulder-length hair was a bit fuzzy from removing her wool cap.

"What's up?" Aura responded as she took a seat across from Dana in the red leather booth. I've been so busy at work. I have to work late again; I swear John's trying to kill me. I don't think I'll be able to get away for lunch again for awhile."

"You know you love it. If you weren't busy all the

time you'd be miserable. Brace yourself though; I've been dying to tell you who I bumped into yesterday. I didn't want to tell you on the phone 'cause I just had to see your expression."

Aura's cheery face grew stony. "Is this gonna piss me off?" she asked her friend.

"Stop being so goddamn serious all the time, Aura. No it's not going to piss you off... Okay, maybe it'll piss you off just a little... I saw Tony."

"That little shit. What was he up to?" Her mind ran quickly over the scene that ended her year-long relationship with Tony. His stupid face in that movie theater with Robin! She and Robin had been friends for so long it was hard to believe she was sneaking around behind her back like that, but when she saw the two of them together it had been perfectly clear. Suddenly little innuendos made sense and their presence together could not have been explained.

"He was with Robin," Dana blurted out, partially proud to have dirt to dish on Robin after all these years. She had never trusted that girl.

"Where did you see them?"

Dana cringed before revealing, "AT THE MOVIES!" She couldn't help but laugh as she said it—the coincidence was so ridiculous. And, although she knew Aura was still a bit bruised by that particular heartache, after all, it wasn't just her boyfriend it was one of her best friends too, she also knew Aura was in a new relationship for the past six months and seemed relatively happy.

"Oh," Aura looked at Dana in partial disbelief before laughing. "I hate them both."

"That's not all," Dana continued relishing in her mammoth-sized wallop of gossip.

"Gosh, Dana. You mean there's more? What else? They're married? Robin had his three sons and named them all Tony? What?" If Aura were a few shades lighter, Dana might have been able to tell she was blushing with a combination of embarrassment and anger.

"Robin was wearing a little diamond ring. She said they're *engaged*!"

"That's all right. Better her than me. That Tony is a dog and Robin is pathetic. They deserve each other."

The conversation paused while they gave their orders to a blonde-haired waitress in a peach smock.

"So what have you been doing besides scouting out the latest gossip on my ex-boyfriends?" Aura asked wearily.

"Same shit. *You* know." Dana feigned a yawn to dramatize her boredom. It's been two years since I started working at the publishing company and I'm still basically a secretary slash executive gofer. At least they're paying me well."

Aura smiled in acknowledgement. "Yeah, I hope that means you're buying lunch."

"No, I'm not, but maybe you and I should move out and get a place together. We're almost equally poor."

"I wish I were equally poor, Dana, I'd be doing a lot better than I am now. Nah, there's no way I can afford to move out now. Maybe in another year."

The waitress returned with their sandwiches. Dana had hot pastrami and cheese and Aura ate a turkey and cheddar melt.

"So what's with you and Robert?" Dana asked between bites of her sandwich.

"Same ole thing, I guess," Aura responded nonchalantly.

"You act like you're an old married couple or something. I thought this was the hot new man on the scene?"

Dana paused awaiting a response. Aura gave her none. "Well???" she prodded.

"Dana, there's really nothing to tell. Things with Robert are fine. He's kind; he's attentive; he's generous. I have nothing to complain about."

"Sounds like you don't have much to brag about either." Dana smiled knowingly.

"Shut up, Dana."

Dana laughed. "Well, I'm so glad you asked about me and Peter. We've been fucking like rabbits every other night, but we still can't seem to take each other too seriously after the dirty deed is done. Ohhh, but honey when the deed's being done, I'M HIS."

Aura laughed at her best friend. "You know, Dana, you really are a slut!" she joked.

"Yes. Aura, but I'm a satisfied slut, and that's important!" Dana dabbed at her lips with her napkin as she finished her meal.

"Who said I'm not satisfied?" Aura questioned.

"Who said I'm not satisfied?" Dana mimicked in a sing-song voice.

"You know, Dana you are absolutely intolerable. What are you doing this weekend? We haven't hung out in a long time. We should really do something."

"Aura, do you realize how often we say that and we never go anywhere? Men... If it weren't for men, we'd hang out all the time but when they say 'let's go' we run to them like a couple of school girls!" Dana covered her forehead with the back of her hand dramatically, like Scarlet from "Gone with the Wind."

"That's just 'cause they usually pay. When you and I go out we're both broke after!" Aura explained.

Dana frowned. "You're probably right."

The waitress slipped their check onto the table.

"Anyway, I need to start heading back. I'll give you a call before the week's out, maybe we can hook up?"

"Sounds good," Dana responded, taking the money

Aura handed her for the bill.

Aura rushed out of the restaurant and along Madison Avenue back to her office.

***

"Hi. I'm meeting someone here. The name is Olivier," Aura explained to the restaurant host. Her eyes scanned the room as she spoke, quickly noticing Ace at a corner table. "Oh, I see him," she said as she headed towards her brother's table.

"Hi!" she said, kissing his cheek. "You look good!" Aura beamed.

"So do you!" Ace replied in a gravelly bass. At 25, he was wedged perfectly between Angela and Aura in age: Angie was 27 and Aura 23. Like his sisters, he was tall with a clear deep chocolate complexion. Women loved to chase him around, but Ace had always been a one-woman man. And, although his relationships never seemed to last long, they were always one woman at a time.

"I see you ordered wine," Aura commented, quite impressed. "Is this where you bring your newest woman?" she asked playfully. It was a nice Italian restaurant with large floor-to-ceiling windows which allowed for a dramatic view of the city.

"Yeah, I've been here with Toffee."

"Toffee? That's an interesting name. I like it." Aura lied. *What kind of name was that? It sounded like a porn star's!* "So tell me about her."

"Let's see. She's medium-height, brown-skinned, pretty, long hair."

Aura laughed. "I know your type by now Ace!"

"I guess you would, huh. Anyway, she's an attorney...very smart, organized, nice family. So far it's going pretty well. I can't complain."

"Gosh, you sound like me with Robert. I went to lunch with Dana on Tuesday and I think I said the same thing, 'I can't complain.' You know Dana, she's my girl but she's a pain in the neck. I guess she's probably right, though."

"Right about what?" Aaron broke in between bites of buttered bread.

"Oh, I guess, that things aren't really working with me and Robert. It's not that he's doing anything wrong; it's just that he's not really doing anything. You know what I mean?"

Ace looked in his sister's eyes like he knew all too well. "Like everything's okay, but you're not feeling anything special in particular?" he asked.

"Yeah! I mean I figure I should just wait and see what happens. I suppose I'll feel something eventually. After all, Robert and I have been seeing each other for quite some time now."

Ace frowned. "From my experience, if you're not feeling it now, you definitely won't be feeling it later..." He paused realizing he would do well to listen to his own advice with Toffee. She was beautiful and smart and totally into him, but he sometimes felt she was more into what he represented—an educated, employed, good-looking, available black man—than what he was. It was like she wanted to own him, not to get to know him. They'd only been dating three months; maybe he was jumping the gun a little. Maybe he'd ask Aura what she suggested.

"So you think I should get rid of him?" Aura asked, interrupting Aaron's drifting thoughts.

"I can't say all that. Just set a limit. Maybe give it a month or something."

Aura's brows furrowed as she thought about her brother's words. Finally, she said, "I know what I'll do." She paused smiling. Looking up at her handsome brother she continued, "So what's the deal with this Toffee person?"

"Who knows? I'm beginning to wonder if I shouldn't take my own advice, 'cause whatever it is with Toffee, I'm just not feeling it."

"I think we have opposite problems," Aura observed. "I give things too much time and you don't give them enough. Don't throw the sister away yet, for chrissake's! Give the girl a chance...talk to her...let her know what you want... *Then* get rid of her if you have to!" Aura laughed. She loved her brother. He had grown to become one of her best friends, and it was his turn to pay for dinner.

***

Aura let herself into Robert Levy's West Village apartment with two brown bags of groceries in her arms. It was 8:00pm on Friday and Robert had promised to be home no later than 10:00pm. As an associate at one of the larger corporate law firms in the city, he was often required to work late into the night.

Aura tossed her charcoal gray swing coat onto the black leather sofa in Robert's sparsely decorated living room. She pulled a stick of opium incense from one of the bags and arranged it so the ashes fell in one of Robert's marble ashtrays. She popped a Luther Vandross cassette in the stereo and began preparing Robert's favorite dish: lasagna. If she could get it in the over by 9:00pm, it would be ready by 9:45pm or so, giving her plenty of time to relax and freshen up before Robert got home. She poured herself a glass of red wine and allowed the worries of the day to leave her as she went about draining the noodles and mixing the sauce.

Aura hummed along with the music as she arranged the layers of pasta, cheese and sauce in a roasting pan and put it in the oven. With that done, she went about getting herself ready for Robert's arrival. She showered and changed into the emerald green silk camisole and lounge pants Robert had given her as a gift along with little glass slippers with green fur. Robert called them "fuck me" slippers. Aura called them uncomfortable, but she knew he liked to see her in them, so she paraded around in them often and in a variety of colors: the green fur could be detached and replaced with black, red, blue or yellow. She released her long black hair from the tie which had held it all day, fluffing it into a desirable mane and spritzed herself with opium perfume.

By the time she was finished, the lasagna was cooked, so she put an apron on to quickly throw together a salad and garlic bread. She finished just in time to see Robert enter the apartment. She could not have planned better timing, except for the fact that Robert looked exhausted and run-down.

Aura kissed him at the door.

"Uhmm," he responded. "You look absolutely beautiful," he said holding her rounded behind in his hands as he breathed in the scent of her soap and fragrance intermingled. She smelled wonderful. The room smelled wonderful; the freshly cooked food and incense all intermingled for a delightful aroma. "I'm exhausted, but you sure are a sight for sore eyes." He ran his hands up and down the back of Aura's thin camisole, kissing her bare shoulders gently.

Aura smiled. She had hoped tonight would be a good night to get Robert to loosen up a little. "Well, dinner's ready. Maybe you'd like a glass of wine first?" she offered.

"That would be wonderful," he said walking towards the kitchen area.

"Sit down, Robert. I'll bring it to you."

Robert smiled and threw himself on the sofa. He pulled the red and blue paisley tie from around his neck and threw it on his mahogany coffee table. Kicking off his shoes, he grabbed the television remote and began channel surfing.

Aura brought him a glass of Bordeaux. "I thought we could skip the TV tonight, honey," she suggested.

"Aura you're absolutely adorable," he responded taking the wine glass from her and placing it carefully on the table. He grabbed her waist and threw her off balance so she fell into his lap. He kissed her on the forehead as he peeped at The Wall St. Journal Report on the TV screen behind her. "Please don't be a nag, honey. You know TV helps me unwind when I'm absolutely neurotic from work."

"I know," Aura admitted, nestling her face into Robert's neck.

The two sat quietly in front of the television for a few minutes. Robert carefully digested a rebroadcast of financial news while Aura just enjoyed being in his slim, sinewy arms. Robert was tall, fine and educated with a salary in the upper 80's. He was the classic BUPPIE personified: clean-cut with a solid middle-class upbringing, well-spoken save the occasional curse word, and, for the most part, mild-mannered. He was caring, considerate and easy to get along with. He was also boring her to tears.

"Are you ready to eat?" Aura asked, gently stroking the green silk covering her thigh.

Robert moved slowly as if he could not understand the background noise which interfered with his TV reception. In a sudden jolt, he turned to her and responded in his most interested voice, "That sounds great!" He turned back to the television as if listening to another few words would help him gain some last bit of essential knowledge, before he forced himself to turn the set off. He rose and followed Aura to the kitchen area which looked out onto his dining area. The table had already been set with candles.

"What can I help you with?" he asked.

"You can put the lasagna on the table. It's pretty heavy. I'll bring out the rest." Aura went about arranging the salad and bread on the table with the lasagna.

"Let me make a toast," Robert said as they sat to eat.

"Okay," Aura smiled. She had never actually prepared a candlelight dinner for two before. The reality of it was making her feel giddy, especially, with Robert getting all romantic and mushy.

"Here's to us! Solid careers and warm winters!" Robert winked. His black skin looked stunning in the soft glow of the candlelight.

"To us!" Aura chimed in, clinking her crystal flute with his.

The dinner conversation quickly went in the direction of Robert's latest work triumph/tragedy. It seemed all Robert's triumphs had some sort of sinister dark side, and all his tragedies won him the respect of his peers, or somebody. He dominated the conversation, but Aura didn't mind. She was more concerned with what was to follow dinner: actions, not conversation. She had been dating Robert on and off for over a year, but it was only in the past six months that they had decided to become exclusive. With exclusivity she had hoped he would "open up" a little more sexually, but it had not yet happened. She was convinced that a sensual evening at home would be just the thing to get him going.

After they finished their meals, Aura's voice softened considerably. "Robert, why don't you take a shower and let me give you a nice massage?" She rubbed the back of his starched white shirt.

"Sounds like a good idea. I know I must need one," he stated only half-joking. It was nearly midnight and he hadn't been in water since 7:00am.

While Robert showered, Aura cleared away the dishes and loaded the dishwasher. She removed the light bulbs in Robert's living room and bedroom lamps and replaced them with soft amber lights, lit fresh incense and flipped the Luther cassette. Removing her pants, she revealed emerald green high-cut panties, and covered an area of Robert's brown down comforter with a large white bath sheet. When Robert entered the bedroom she was waiting for him with a new bottle of peppermint massage oil.

"Feel better?" she asked.

"Much," he responded adjusting a small towel around his waist.

Aura was surprised by the frown on his face. "What's wrong?" she asked.

Robert spoke slowly as if embarrassed by his own words. "It's just... I've asked you before not to lie on the comforter. It will ruin it."

Aura got up from the bed quickly and folded the comforter back. She laid the bath sheet atop his velour blanket. "Is that better?" she asked.

"Thanks," Robert said as he lay his body out on the bath sheet.

Aura began kneading the muscles in his back scrupulously with the oils, taking care to give each protruding muscle a thorough massage. "How's that feel?" she asked.

"Uhrrgh," Robert groaned.

"How's this?" she asked pounding his lower back rhythmically with her fists.

"Hmmm," he sighed.

Aura took her time, carefully watching his smooth black skin absorb the oil as it dripped from her reddening palms. She took painstaking care with each muscle in an attempt to relax him completely. Unfortunately, her plan succeeded, and by the time all the rubbing and kneading of his skin had made her uncontrollably horny, she discovered Robert had fallen asleep.

***

It was nearly 4:00am when Aura felt the hands groping her legs and breasts. She was barely awake, but her initial reaction was pleasant surprise. As she ran her hand along her side, she was surprised to discover that her underwear had been removed. As she slowly opened her eyes, she felt Robert entering her sharply. She blinked a few times to take in the form above her. She could barely see him, with only street lights illuminating the dark room. She jerked away from him slightly, but he grabbed her hips quickly. "Relax, baby," he mumbled softly.

Aura breathed in, allowing her body to relax as Robert moved his body inside of her. She felt surprisingly numb and barely awake. A few moments passed before Robert groaned with release and rolled over onto his side. Another few moments and the rhythmic sounds of his snores could be heard.

***

"Dana called you," Sylvia Olivier mentioned as Aura flipped through Friday and Saturday's mail.

"Thanks, Ma. Hi, Dad. Did anyone else call?" she asked, walking over to kiss her mother and father 'hello' as they sat curled up on the sofa with half of the Sunday *Times*. It was late Saturday morning, and she had not been home since she left for work the previous day.

"That's the only call I know of," her mother

responded. Her father just shrugged his shoulders.

"Thanks, guys." Aura ascended the stairs to her bedroom, grabbed the phone at her bedside and dialed Dana's number.

"Hello?" Dana answered.

"Hey, what's up?" Aura responded.

"Hi, Aura! Did you make plans for tonight?"

"I had plans with Robert, but I think I need to cancel."

"Oh, really?" Dana commented, suddenly interested. "Don't get me started... So do you want to go out?"

"Why don't we go for dinner. I'm starving and my mom's cooking pig's feet tonight. I can't stand those little piggy toes!"

"That's 'cause your mom doesn't know how to cook those little piggy toes!"

"Aura, I can't believe you really eat that shit," Dana commented in exasperation and disgust.

"Anyway, Dana Dane, where do you want to eat?"

"I could go for some BBQ's," she said referring to a popular barbecue spot in Manhattan.

"All right. How fast can you get here?"

"Give me about half an hour."

"See you then."

"Later."

***

"Damn, Aura, you can't just leave the guy 'cause he fell asleep!" Dana leaned back in the restaurant's black wooden chair laughing.

"It's not just that, Dana. It's everything."

"What's everything?"

Aura frowned. "He's got a little bit of a habit too."

"Please Aura, don't tell me any kinky sexual stuff... You know I'll love it too much, and then you'll never get rid of me!" Dana grinned from ear to ear before leaning across the basket of onion rings between them and half-whispering, "So what is it?"

"Dana, you're absolutely *depraved!*" Aura laughed at her friend. "No, it's nothing like that. Not sexual, just like a habit, you know... He's got a little recreational drug thing going on."

"Oh..." Dana paused trying to figure out what Aura would consider a little recreational drug thing. Lots of people they knew smoked an occasional joint, so it couldn't be that bothering her so much. "Is he a real pot-head or something? I know he's not smoking crack!" Dana stared into Aura's face, expecting her expression to give an answer before her mouth could.

"Yeah, he does smoke weed sort of too much, but I know that sometimes he puts cocaine in it. It's not like I've seen him acting strange or anything, but I just don't like it."

"Yeah, that's not too cool. Plus Robert's older, he should have grown out of that shit by now," Dana added wisely.

"So, I guess between his weed thing, and the sex thing, and the working all the time thing, I'm just kind of through, you know?" Aura looked defeated "He's a really nice guy, though. He doesn't look at other women. He doesn't hang out with other men. He's got a great job, a great place, a great body, a great car. He treats me really well."

"Are you trying to convince me of something? Gimme a break, cut him loose, you're just doing time with that man. Aura you're too smart and pretty and squeaky clean to have to deal with some goofy druggie. So what he has a nice place? Is he giving it to you? And you and that body stuff. I want you to find a nice guy with a nice round beer belly."

"Dana, shut up! You know I hate men with big bellies!" Aura laughed. She had always been a stickler for a nice male physique. She didn't mind if a guy was a little skinny, but she couldn't take it if they were a little fat. Even at twenty-three, it seemed the older she got the fewer washboard-stomached men she could find. It wasn't so bad at eighteen, twenty or twenty-two, but now that the average guy she dated was between twenty-five and thirty, the slim waists were getting to be few and far between.

"I don't know what the big deal is. Those bellies make a nice cushion sometimes." Dana winked suggestively.

"Dana, you really are disgusting!" Aura exclaimed.

"At least I don't eat those piggy toes, like you do!" Dana countered.

"Will you lay off the pigs feet, already? Listen maybe we should do something after dinner since I'm a single woman again."

Dana laughed. "Oh, you're single now, huh? Just don't forget to tell Robert. With your luck, you'll probably bump into him while you're rubbing up on some other man."

"It's a big city, Dana. What are the odds of that?" Aura popped an onion ring between her blackberry lips.

***

Aura and Dana fit right in at the trendy night club they selected. In body-hugging jeans and short leather jackets, the bouncers at the club let them in immediately while others shivered in the late February cold hoping to be allowed inside. The club was huge, with music blaring from nearly every room.

"Ooh, this is fun, girl," Dana commented looking at the large sampling of men and women. "There are some fine brothers here tonight, too," she said emphatically as she sipped a sea breeze. "Some of these guys make poor Peter look seriously tired."

"What?" Aura asked.

Dana repeated herself directly into Aura's ear.

Aura turned to Dana's ear. "Dana, I hate to bust your bubble, but Peter always was seriously tired!" She laughed. Realizing they wouldn't be able to talk much with the deafening music, they finished their drinks quietly before heading out to the dance floor. Fragrant smoke was released from vents in the ceiling, video screens dotted the walls with kaleidoscopic displays, laser lights danced along the walls, and the music played relentlessly. Aura found an attractive Puerto Rican to dance with, and Dana shook her body dramatically with a tall cocoa-colored guy. When they tired of the two, they found more: a short Dominican, a husky Panamanian, a couple of Jamaicans, three guys from Southern California. Before they knew what had happened they had passed hours in the company of many strangers.

***

"So how many numbers did you get?" Dana asked.

"Three." Aura responded between bites of her pancakes. It was 5:00am when they left the club, so they decided breakfast was in order. She pulled pieces of paper out of her jeans' pocket. "Tony, Byron and Leo. Byron was pretty cute, maybe I'll call him. So, how many did you get? Twelve? Thirteen?"

"Ha, ha," Dana replied in mock sarcasm. "No, but I did lose count. Let's see..." She began pulling wads of tissues, napkins, matchbooks and slips of paper from her jeans, purse and jacket. She threw them on the table and laughed, "I have no idea who these people are!"

"I thought there was someone you liked," Aura suggested.

"Yeah, maybe," Dana began pondering. "Nah, not really," she concluded, popping a strip of bacon in her mouth.

***

"Aura, what's going on with us?" Robert asked, his face full of fear.

Aura sat in his leather recliner staring at the ceiling. "I don't know, Robert."

"You must know something. You cancelled our date last Saturday at the last minute. You haven't returned my calls all week, and I find you in my apartment when I come home on Friday."

"Robert, *you* gave me the key!" Aura shouted.

"I'll talk to you another time," the woman next to Robert muttered as she quickly exited the apartment.

"I didn't think you would just show up whenever you wanted!" Robert countered.

Aura glared at him before asking, "Robert, why did you give me a key if you didn't think I'd use it to let myself in on a Friday night?"

Robert was at a loss for words.

Aura was unable to quell her anger. "Look, I know I should have called you back, but you make it sound like you called me ten times or something. You called me *one fucking time*, Robert!" She lowered her voice before continuing, "I had been giving a lot of thought to our relationship, you know?" She looked at him softly for a moment.

"Rita is just a friend from the office," he began.

Anger overcame Aura. "I DON'T CARE WHO RITA IS. You really don't get it do you? It's after midnight! It doesn't matter who she is!"

"We've never slept together..." Robert started.

"Lucky her. " Aura mumbled.

"What?"

"Nothing."

"Look, Aura, if you have something to say, we might as well clear the air."

"Really, Robert, I don't have anything to say. I just want to end this thing. Maybe you'll make Rita a happy woman or something."

"Aura, don't do this," Robert begged.

Aura stood up. "Honestly, Robert, I don't know which one of us is more stupid: me for staying around you, or you for giving me the key to your apartment and not expecting me to be here on a Friday. What were you thinking? Even if I wasn't here tonight, I could have pranced in with the paper at 8:00am while Rita was doing her encore belly-dance or something."

"Aura, don't be ridiculous."

"Robert, this isn't even worth discussing." She reached into the pocket of her velveteen slacks and produced a house key. "Here. Enjoy." She grabbed her scarf and short leather jacket and calmly left his apartment.

***

"Hey, what's up?"

"Aura?" Dana mumbled half-sleeping.

"Yeah. What are you doing?"

"Aura, what time is it?"

"I know it's late. I thought you'd be up. What happened to Peter?"

"Peter? I didn't see him tonight. Where are you?"

"I just got home. I broke up with Robert. He's a real asshole! I've got the car if you want to hang out!"

"Aura, go to sleep!"

"Come on, Dana, stop acting so old. You'll hate yourself in the morning!"

"Urgghh...give me a half hour. I'll meet you outside." Dana hung up.

***

"Why do I ever listen to you?" Dana mumbled. It was 7:00am and she was just being dropped back at her house.

"You know you loved it!" Aura shouted out of the car window as Dana turned the key for her apartment building.

She drove the few blocks to her house and parked. When she got to her bedroom, she nearly fell asleep before her head hit the pillow. Suddenly her body felt achingly exhausted and a sharp throbbing pain began its course up the backs of her thighs and through her lower back. It seemed she overdid it, and now her sickle-cell was rearing its ugly head. She sighed and attempted to fall asleep despite the pain. After dozing on and off uncomfortably for a few hours, she stumbled to the bathroom for a couple of Tylenol® and Codeine tablets. She focused her mind on the previous evening in an attempt to distract her from her pain. She really was single again, but with three new phone numbers... Not too bad. As the drugs took their effect, she drifted off to sleep.

Eddie "Ocean" Ryder
Winter 1989

"Tilt your head back a bit more," the photographer urged an already weary Eddie. He had spent the previous night bar-hopping with his good friend and occasional bedmate, Mona, and was not in the best shape.

"Good. Now, just relax."

Eddie's mind wandered as the photographer shot a few rolls of film. He absently followed the directions as they were given. It had been over two years since he first started modeling for Esquire, and the jobs had been rolling in quite nicely. He had become accustomed to doing print shoots and had worked with this particular photographer from a male fashion magazine a few times in the past.

Many wardrobe changes and hours passed before his work day was finally over. It was 7:00pm before he grabbed his duffle bag and brown hooded leather jacket and headed back to the same Park Slope apartment he once shared with Tasha. It was a nice place, so he had renewed the lease for another two years. He was sure Tasha was somewhere annoyed as hell, but he couldn't do anything for her now. If she had tolerated his infidelities, he would have at least been able to let her reap the benefits of his success, but the timing had been off for both of them.

As he entered his apartment he heard his answering machine taking a call. "Hey, you know what I want, so do it at the beep..." his throaty baritone demanded. Eddie cracked a smile upon hearing his own voice but did not rush to answer the phone. Instead, he grabbed a beer from the fridge and listened to the message being left for him: "Hi, Ocean, it's Crystal. I'm just calling to make sure you don't miss my party tonight. Call me when you get this message."

Eddie smiled. Crystal was an outrageous-looking, ebony-skinned, platinum blonde model. They both worked for Esquire. She was wild and funny and amazing between the sheets. Even with all that, he really wasn't sure he wanted to go to another party tonight, although he knew his presence was important to her.

He rewound the tape and played back his other messages:

"Hey, Eddie, it's Marc. Sorry I've been so hard to catch up with. I'm heading out of town again and I've been kind of settled down with my new lady. I'll try to catch up with you when I get back. Later." Eddie sucked his teeth. It seemed he and Marc had been playing phone tag on and off for about a year. *Fuck'm.*

"Hey, baby, it's Mona. Hope you weren't too tired at the shoot today. I've got a big surprise for you, and I mean big. Louie's going out of town for a few days this weekend. Let's get together and I'll tell you what it is. Believe me, it's to die for. I'll talk to you soon, babe." Eddie smiled. Mona was really a prize. It had reached the point where she was probably his best friend.

"Hey, babe, just calling to see what your plans are for the weekend. I want to see you. Call me." It was Erikka, still sexy as hell, but he didn't know if he wanted to see her this weekend. It had been nearly a month since he saw her last, but sometimes the weeks just flew by. *Oh well.*

"Hi, sexy, gimme a call when you get the chance. Miss you. Six-two-nine-four-eight-seven-six." It was Jackie.

They started dating on and off nearly immediately after the big dinner Marc had at Caribbean Corner over two years ago. She always left a number for him so he had no excuse not to call.

"Eddie, it's your father. Listen, I've got a couple of ideas I want to run by you. Call me when you get in." His father's thick Bahamian accent demanded attention, so Eddie dialed his father's number after running through the last couple of messages: information from the office on a new gig and a second call from Mona.

"Hello?" a female voice answered. It was Karen, his father's girlfriend of the past four years.

"Hi, Karen, it's Eddie. Is my dad available?"

"Oh, sure Eddie!" Karen responded enthusiastically. Eddie could hear the fuss in the background as she called his father for the phone.

"Hey, boy, what's good with you? You don't call your old man anymore?" Neville Ryder asked.

"Everything's real cool dad, what's up?"

"Listen, I've got a friend who's interested in modeling, right?" Mr. Ryder began.

Eddie's mind was already wandering. Before the money started rolling in, his dad was entirely uninterested in his modeling and not particularly interested in him period. But since he started doing pretty well, the requests began. First, he needed loans, which Eddie didn't mind. Then he wanted Karen to model, which he really couldn't help him with. Then, he periodically wanted his help in getting modeling jobs for his array of girlfriends. No matter how much he tried explaining, he just couldn't convince his father that it just didn't work that way. First, the women were usually a bit too old to start modeling— late twenties and early thirties; and second, they didn't realize a lot of hard work and investment was involved. You needed photos and you had to pound the pavement to get work. There was no free lunch to be had. Finally, although Esquire dealt with female models, they specialized in males and they wouldn't even consider someone with no experience. Competition for modeling jobs in New York City was downright fierce.

Eddie's mind continued to wander as his father explained about his new "friend" who was interested in modeling. It was obvious that Karen was somewhere within earshot, as he explained this was a friend from work, blah, blah... in an attempt to make his relationship with his so-called "friend" sound clean. It was really a silly exercise out of some shade of respect for Karen, because everyone in his household knew he fooled around, even Karen's kids from a previous relationship. Only little David, Karen's ten-month-old son for his father, could have been fooled.

"So what do you think you can do?" Neville Ryder finally asked.

"I'll talk to some of my contacts and work on it for you," Eddie lied. There was no other way to end the conversation.

"Thanks. So when am I going to see you around here? Karen and the kids have been asking for you. I know you're busy nowadays, but you should be able to make some time to have dinner with your family."

"Sure, Dad. I'd love to come over for dinner. When would be good?"

"How about next Saturday?"

"I don't think Saturday will be good for me," Eddie mumbled rifling through the pages of his planner.

"What about the following Saturday?" his father asked.

"Saturdays are going to be really bad for me for awhile. Maybe during the week?" he offered.

"You know how late I work at the airport during the

week. I'm not here at a reasonable dinner hour."

"Sorry, Dad. I'll call you and we'll set something up a little later."

"Fine," Mr. Ryder stated softly. His disappointment was apparent. He never thought there would be a time when Eddie wouldn't make time for him. Out of the six kids he fathered with Eddie's mother, Eddie had been the most like himself. At sixteen, Eddie had been anxious to head for the States with him, following in his footsteps with everything he did from his love for beers to women. He missed the time they used to spend together playing basketball or dominoes. Really he just missed seeing one of his creations every now and then. All his other grown kids were still in the Bahamas.

"Bye, Dad."

"Bye."

Eddie hung up quickly. He wanted to go for dinner, but a part of him just didn't want to deal with it. He already had more brothers and sisters in the Bahamas than he could possibly count. As far as he knew little David was his only brother in the States, but it was getting to be pretty ridiculous. He had tons of family, but still no real family. Maybe he saw too many "Brady Bunch" reruns since moving to the U.S., but he was beginning to wish he had a traditional intact nuclear family. His thoughts wandered to his mother in Abaco, Bahamas. How nice it might have been if his parents had remained together... As he enjoyed the fantasy of it, the reality struck him—If his parents had remained together, would he have left the Bahamas for such a pleasant life in the U.S.? If he had to choose one over the other which would he have selected? As the questions abounded in his mind, he realized there was no answer. If he had to choose, he wouldn't and he would never have to choose.

***

"Ocean, meet Dawn!" Mona exclaimed excitedly as she introduced Eddie to one of her good friends. She had met Dawn on a vacation to Trinidad a few years back.

"It's very nice to meet you," Eddie said as he let the two women into his apartment. He helped them off with their coats and hung them quickly on the large hand-carved Kenyan sculpture which sometimes doubled as a coat rack. Eddie smiled as he surveyed Dawn. She was tall, slim and caramel-colored with short natural hair that curled into tight ringlets atop a perfectly shaped head. She wore a short black and mustard plaid wool skirt with thigh-high black patent leather boots and a heavy mustard turtleneck sweater. The colors complemented her skin tone dramatically. As usual Mona was stunning in a forest green pants suit, her long black hair cascading over her shoulders.

This was Mona's big surprise. After much discussion over the past year, she finally found a girlfriend of hers who was interested in being part of a threesome. Mona had admitted to being curious about lesbian sex, and Eddie had always wondered what it would be like to be with two women, but up until this point the reality of it had never been so imminent. Conveniently enough, Dawn lived in Trinidad, so they didn't have to worry about bumping into her in case things didn't turn out as expected.

"What would you ladies like to drink?" Eddie asked.

Dawn smiled suggestively. "Whatever you have is fine with me," she responded.

Mona just shrugged her shoulders; she was busying herself with Eddie's VCR.

Eddie mixed a few rum & cokes and placed them on a tray while Dawn got comfortable on the navy velour sofa.

"This is a nice place, Ocean. How long have you been living here?" she asked. Her eyes took in the navy, black and white Oriental rug which came between the smoked glass coffee table and the hardwood floor. She noticed how dust-free the black mini-blinds were and the exquisite 27" TV encased in a black lacquer wall unit. The kitchen was spotless as well.

"Oh, about two years," he responded as he placed the drinks on the coffee table. "Do you get high?" he asked as he pulled a small bag of weed and rolling paper from a side drawer.

Dawn smiled. "I've been known to indulge."

"Is it working?" Eddie asked Mona, referring to the VCR.

"Yeah, I think so... Let's see..." Mona pushed the play button on the remote. "Great!" she said as the tape began playing. "I heard this is a really good one," she commented about the porno tape she put in the VCR. "You know how hard it is to find good black porno."

Dawn took a pull on the joint Eddie rolled before offering it to Mona. "Mona, you're absolutely unbelievable," she stated without exhaling as she held the potent smoke in her lungs.

Mona looked at Dawn curiously in response to her comment.

"I mean, you never told me Ocean was so goddamn gorgeous! People think models are always good-looking. I've known some models that were downright ugly. They must have been modeling their feet!" She laughed and looked at Eddie for his reaction. He was smiling.

"Oops! I almost forgot!" Mona jumped off the couch and pulled a small package from her coat pocket. "My friend, Frank hooked me up with some nice blow. I told him it was a special occasion, you know. Of course, I didn't tell him what the occasion was." She winked at

Eddie, and Eddie winked back. "Anyway, Ta-Da!" she showed her package to the two proudly. "Eddie, where's your mirror?"

Eddie walked to the kitchen area and produced a small mirrored tray backed with marble which he bought specifically for this purpose. He handed the tray to Mona, and she went about breaking the rocks of cocaine with a razor and arranging lines on the mirror. She found a straw and cut it down to a usable size. After sniffing a line, she passed the mirror to Eddie. For the next half hour they did a few lines, smoked a few joints, watched the porno flick and got comfortable with each other and their surroundings.

"Do you mind if I touch your hair?" Dawn asked Eddie. He had shiny black shoulder-length dreadlocks which had been driving her crazy since she first arrived.

"I'd love it," Eddie replied, moving closer to her on the sofa.

"I'm hot," she mumbled removing the heavy wool sweater she wore and revealing a sheer black bra which did nothing to hide her nipples. She rested the back of Eddie's head in her breasts so they were both comfortably facing the TV. With Dawn and Eddie so close together on the sofa, Mona got up from the chaise she had been lounging in and sat on the sofa at Eddie's feet.

Dawn began massaging Eddie's scalp and twisting his locks around her fingers while Mona removed his shoes and socks and began massaging his feet.

Eddie was in heaven. He relaxed under the women's touch, watching as Mona removed her blouse to reveal a white lace bra which barely covered her full chocolate-colored breasts. By now his erection was in full effect. To his surprise he felt a little nervous. He had been with many women and with Mona many times, and although he never ran into trouble satisfying one woman, two women might be a challenge.

As his anxiety rose, Dawn quickly calmed him down with a kiss. She had slid off the soft velour sofa, her boot-covered knees atop Eddie's Oriental rug. She kissed him timidly at first, sampling the newness of his full mouth as she played in his thick black hair. She felt his breathing shift from shallow breaths to full, relaxed exhalations.

He kissed the smooth caramel of her skin: her cheeks, nose, and neck as he ran his hand along the back of her head, enjoying the sensation of the tight waves of her hair under his now sensitive palms. He could see her beginning to flush with arousal, and he relaxed. She liked him.

Mona's hands were hot with the scented oil she rubbed aggressively along the soles of Eddie's feet. She forced her fingers between his toes and tugged gently, knowing the sensation created would be a combination of pleasure and pain like any good massage. She made fists and kneaded his arches while watching him and Dawn go at it. They looked beautiful together. She looked at Eddie's feet as she worked on them. Eddie really was fine, even his feet were smooth, deep brown and perfectly manicured. She bit his large toe playfully before popping it into her mouth.

Eddie had to look when he felt Mona sucking his toe. She had never done that to him before, actually nobody had. He was surprised by how good it felt, and when he looked at her and saw her full blackberry lips around his protrusion, her eyes set dead on his, he was jolted by his own excitement.

Dawn looked to see what had gotten Eddie's attention, and saw Mona greedily sucking a toe. She smiled and crawled a few motions to Mona. She grabbed Mona by the back of her hair and kissed her mouth quickly, their lips barely touching, then brushing repeatedly until they kissed more deeply, her tongue stroking Mona's gently.

Eddie had never seen two real women kiss before! He smiled and watched closely, enjoying the gentle torture of wanting to interrupt, and then again not. He sat up on the sofa and removed his black turtleneck revealing a hard, aesthetically chiseled body and smooth cocoa brown skin. His hair rested gently on his shoulders, and for a moment he didn't know what to do, so he watched quietly as the women tugged at each other's bras.

"Hey, let's go in the bedroom and get comfortable," he suggested.

"Uhhmm," Mona said rising. Her mouth had been occupied with Dawn's small sprightly breasts. She laughed. "This is kind of fun, Eddie."

The three entered Eddie's dimly lit bedroom, shedding their clothes quickly, they fell onto the soft cotton cover of the bed.

Mona quickly nestled her head between the honey softness of Dawn's long legs.

Eddie sucked greedily at Dawn's breasts. Dawn's hands confidently stroked Eddie's erection, until he moved into a position to enter her mouth. She took his penis gently and with some distraction while Mona licked and sucked her clitoris, finally bringing her to orgasm.

When Mona felt Dawn's orgasm, she moved her mouth away from her and began kissing Eddie greedily along his body, first the hard ripples of his stomach then his neck and finally his mouth. She knew him well and scratched his back in a way she knew he liked. She bit his neck and earlobes gently before returning her mouth to his. At that moment, she wished they were alone, but there was really nothing she could do, so she resigned herself to enjoy the situation. She pushed Eddie onto his back, forcing his penis free from Dawn's mouth, and straddled him. She was flush with excitement as she slid a condom over Eddie's hard shiny extremity. Raising her hips high above Eddie's body, she began to take him slowly inside of her aching vagina.

Eddie sighed as Mona worked her full black hips rhythmically, her breasts bouncing busily in his face while Dawn nibbled at his nipples. The visual combined with the reality of his fantasy come true erupted in a sweet, though somewhat early climax. Mona continued to ride his half-erect penis with slow controlled movements until he regained a full erection. Her moans grew throatier, her hip movements more unpredictable, until finally she came with a shiver and collapsed. After resting briefly, she moved her body so that she could lie on her side and spoon with Eddie, her face nestled in the back of his thick black hair.

Dawn sandwiched Eddie, pressing her firm round behind against his stomach, barely touching his penis and then moving away. She teased him until he could no longer bear it.

Eddie quietly reached for another condom to slide over his swollen penis. Once done, he began massaging Dawn's butt roughly.

Dawn moaned in appreciation.

Eddie bit the back of her neck and slid his penis into her sharply. Once he was secure inside of her, he stroked slowly, teasing her body with his hands. He felt her movements change from slow deliberation to frenetic as he picked up the pace. As their pleasure mounted, her frenzy set him off and they came together, rocking wildly.

***

Eddie was the first to rise in the morning. Mona and Dawn looked beautiful, sleeping in each other's arms. They were beautiful, but he felt weird. He really liked

Mona, and Dawn seemed nice, but something about the evening's activities just didn't sit well with him. He must have been crazy; there were men who would pay big bucks for the experience he just had. He should have considered himself lucky.

Eddie got busy preparing breakfast: eggs, sausage, pancakes, coffee. As the aroma drifted to the bedroom, he heard Mona and Dawn rustling out of bed and into the bathroom. By the time the two of them got out of the shower, the breakfast was cold and Eddie was annoyed.

Mona was beaming. "We thought you might have joined us," she explained apologetically to Eddie's disturbed countenance.

"Don't worry about it. You can microwave your food." Eddie smiled, but his smile was a lie. He really just wanted them both out of his apartment. *Was that so bad?*

"Eddie, you're a sweetheart!" Mona exclaimed.

"I thought your name was Ocean," Dawn said baffled.

Eddie looked at her stupidly. "My professional name is Ocean, but I was born Eddie. My new friends call me Ocean." His smile was polite.

"Oh," Dawn said uncomfortably. She felt the negative vibes from Ocean and understood why; it was as if they were living a cliché: she didn't even know his name. She and Mona ate their breakfasts without much exchange and left quickly afterward. Eddie sighed when they were both gone. *What had he done?*

***

Eddie spent the morning cleaning up the mess he and his guests had made the night before. He washed the breakfast dishes, changed the bed sheets, swept and vacuumed. When he finished he lit a stick of sandalwood incense and relaxed with the newspaper. He still had a solid hour before he was to meet his "little brother" Darryl, the fatherless eleven-year-old he volunteered to spend time with. He had agreed to take him to a movie if Darryl would also visit a museum. It took some talking to convince Darryl that cool guys occasionally went to museums. Sometimes Darryl broke his heart: He was a good kid like most, gangling like Eddie was as a child, but at eleven he was already so disillusioned. He rarely left the neighborhood of the housing projects he lived in, so he hadn't experienced much of the low cost and free events the city had to offer. Eddie was trying to change that, to be a positive influence in his life. He was worried that with the onset of adolescence, things could start getting really rough. It wasn't that Darryl's mother didn't try, but with three young boys and a job as a cafeteria worker, she was barely making ends meet, let alone finding time to act as a social worker to her three sons. In the heart of the ghetto, that's what kids really needed: therapy. Eddie laughed at the outlandishness of his own thoughts. Although he spent a few years in a not-so-hot section of Fort Greene, Brooklyn, he never experienced the type of jailhouse living projects lent themselves to. There were just too many damn people in one place, piled on top of each other like so much cattle, with guns and drugs sprinkled on top and poverty fencing them in.

He looked at his watch; it was nearly noon so he grabbed his jacket, put his feet in his Timbs and headed for the subway where he was to meet Darryl. When he got to the station, Darryl had not yet arrived, so he waited. First it was noon, then quarter past, half past, quarter to. He waited a full hour before returning to his apartment. When he returned he had one message:

"Ocean, you're a shit. Where were you Friday? Call me." It was Crystal, he had totally forgotten about her party after Mona made her offer. Now he wondered if maybe he should have gone to Crystal's party after all. He pictured Dawn and Mona kissing in his living room. Nah, he decided; he made the right choice.

He dialed Crystal's number. Maybe he'd meet her for lunch since it looked like Darryl was a no-show. He got her machine and left a message. *Oh, well.*

He dialed Darryl's house. His mother answered, but Darryl wasn't home. He left a message.

When he hung up, the phone rang.

"Hello?" Eddie asked.

"Eddie?" a young male voice queried.

"Yeah?"

"Yo, man. What's up? Yo, man, check this out. I'm coming down with some shit...like a flu or something, man. I can't do that movie with you today, man...maybe next week we can do it, okay?"

"Darryl, don't lie to me like I'm some sort of ASSHOLE!" His voice deepened with authority. It wasn't so much that he was angry, but he figured it was important to let Darryl know that he cared, that it wasn't okay to cancel at the last minute and lie like that. The funny thing with kids like Darryl was that they missed having parents to yell at them. In Darryl's case, his dad wasn't around at all and his mother was too tired of yelling already. "Look, I know you're not sick. If you don't want to go out, we don't have to, but don't lie to me like I'm one of your playmates." He softened his voice as he finished his reprimand, hoping that his message was understood.

Darryl paused for a few moments. "Hey, how do you know I'm not home?" he asked sheepishly.

Eddie sighed. "Look, Darryl, if you're gonna tell a lie like that, at least call sooner. I already spoke to your mother."

Darryl exhaled. "Oh."

"So are you going to tell me what the problem is?"

"I just wanted to hang out with some of my boys. That's all..."

"Good, so I'll see you tomorrow, same place at noon, and if you let me wait on you for an hour like you did today, I'll lay into that ass like we really *are* related. Do you understand me?" Eddie's threat was polite, yet serious, and Darryl didn't argue with it. When Eddie got off the phone with Darryl he felt kind of proud of himself.

***

Eddie met up with Erikka at a movie theater in Manhattan's West Village. By the time they went for dinner and arrived back at Eddie's apartment it was 8:00pm. Eddie made a couple of cocktails and threw himself onto the sofa.

"Ugh, what a life," he moaned melodramatically.

Erikka laughed. It was nearly a month since she had last seen Eddie and he seemed a bit distant. "What's your beef?" she asked.

Eddie released his hair from the black band which held it in a pony tail. His dark locks cascaded to his shoulders. His biceps flexed under the deep green sweater he wore as he held his chin in his hands. He shifted anxiously, finally finding a comfortable position reclining on the sofa. He turned his deep brown eyes in Erikka's direction. "Erikka, you've known me for, what, two year's now? How do you feel about me?"

Erikka was shocked by the question. Something must really be bothering Eddie. "I think you're adorable," she said moving closer to him and kissing him on the lips. Eddie moved away quickly. "Erikka, that's not what I'm asking you!"

Erikka gave him a dumbfounded stare. "Look, Eddie, I

don't know what's wrong with you today. Maybe you need some time to yourself." She stood up quickly.

Eddie looked at her in disbelief. Partially he couldn't believe her, and partially he couldn't believe himself. She wanted to leave because he wouldn't let her kiss him at that particular moment, and *he wouldn't let her kiss him at that particular moment!* "You know what, Erikka, you're probably right. I'm just feeling a little out of sorts. Why don't I give you a call another time?"

Clearly, Erikka didn't expect Eddie to agree with her, but her pride wouldn't allow her to stay after being so clearly dismissed. "Sure, Eddie. I'll call you," She grabbed her coat and promptly walked toward the door.

***

When Erikka left, Eddie called his mother. It had been quite a few weeks since he last spoke to her. When he heard her voice he felt the stinging sensation of a tear in his eye. *Maybe he was just homesick.*

He asked her to come and visit him, but she said she had too much to do there and she would miss the island far too much.

She asked him to come visit her. After all it was overdue for him to come back home. Bring a girlfriend, she said.

He said he would.

They caught up on a few little things.

He felt a bit better.

Or, at least he thought he felt a bit better until he realized that there wasn't a single woman he felt close to...and there wasn't a single woman he would feel comfortable introducing to his family.

When Eddie hung up with his mother he felt that damn stinging sensation again. He dismissed it, grabbed a beer out of the fridge and watched Video Soul until he couldn't take anymore, then he picked up the crossword he had been toying with earlier. He didn't have time to feel sorry for himself he had a hot date with Darryl the following afternoon. Maybe an evening at home alone was exactly what he needed.

Sophia Boyd Henderson
Winter 1989

Sophia couldn't believe it was happening again. She locked herself in the bedroom with the children and dialed 911. The phone rang more than ten times. She hung up and tried again, still no answer.

"YOU BETTER OPEN THE FUCKING DOOR, BITCH!" Ron screamed. The scent of alcohol was so heavy it permeated the light wood door of her bedroom. "I'M NOT GONNA FUCKING TOUCH YOU, I JUST WANT TO GET MY SHIT AND I'LL LEAVE. WHAT DON'T YOU FUCKING UNDERSTAND?!"

Sophia shook with fear as she struggled to dial the three digits again. She still couldn't get through... The phone plummeted to the floor. *Shit!* She was dressed in only a cotton night shirt with Marcus sleeping in the crib and Timothy in the bed. She tried to calm herself down. Maybe this was a sign that she shouldn't call the police. It would probably only make Ron angrier anyway. Besides, it seemed the police weren't even home... The rude irony of that thought ripped through what remained of her fragile sense of equilibrium. She paced the soft brown carpet of the bedroom she and Ron shared. *What to do?*

"Sophia," Ron's tone had quieted. "Look, I know you're scared. I'm not gonna hit you, I swear. Just open the door; I need to get my jacket."

Timothy shifted in his sleep. It was nearly 2:00am.

Sophia slipped into a pair of jeans and sneakers. Her

eyes scanned the room for Ron's jacket, finally recognizing it strewn on the lazy chair. She picked up the jacket, her heart beating loudly, her hands trembling. She walked slowly to the door.

"Ron, I'm gonna give you the jacket," she said, her voice weak with fear.

Ron didn't respond.

She unlocked the bedroom door quietly, and cracked it just enough to push the jacket through.

Ron quickly grabbed her hand and yanked her out of the bedroom.

Sophia sobbed hysterically with her fear. She squinted her eyes, as if in doing so it would minimize the effect of any potential blow.

Ron closed the bedroom door behind her. "What do you think you're doing?" he demanded. "Are you trying to wake up my kids?" he asked. He raised his hand as if he would slap her, but he didn't.

It didn't matter, because Sophia was paralyzed with fear. Ron was a huge man with 9" and nearly 100 lbs. on her; she knew there was no way to beat him, unless she killed him. And if she killed him, what would happen to her kids? The Bureau of Child Welfare could take them away if they even knew this kind of activity was going on in the house. But it hadn't always been this way. The first year of their marriage was wonderful—it wasn't until Ron was shot in the line of duty by another officer that he began drinking heavily and having these violent episodes. He had always been given to rash behavior, but it had never been like this before.

"ANSWER ME, BITCH!" Ron demanded as he shoved her body away from the bedroom, leaving his jacket crumpled on the cool, tile floor.

Sophia stumbled backwards.

"ANSWER ME!" he yelled, pushing Sophia into the

living room wall.

Sophia stared in her husband's eyes for a glint of the man who used to be there. All she saw was bitter vengeance and hate; she didn't know this man at all, and apparently he didn't recognize her either. She tried to appease the man before her, whoever he was. "I'm sorry. I don't want to wake up the kids," she mumbled.

"WHAT?!" he bellowed.

"I said, I'm sorry, I don't want to wake up the kids..."

Ron raised his hand far from her head, and slapped her so hard she fell to the floor. A hint of blood began trickling from her ear. He looked at her with venom, "You disgust me," he stated almost matter-of-factly.

Sophia looked at him with the wide-eyed expression of the proverbial deer in the headlights. She did not move as she heard the sound of Ron picking his jacket up from the floor and leaving, closing the door gently behind him.

***

"Oh, Sophia," Tyra Halsey said empathetically. It was nearly 4:00am on a Tuesday morning, barely twenty degrees outside, and here was her niece on her doorstep with red eyes, a baseball night shirt and two sleeping children wrapped in blankets. Tyra had wondered why Sophia had begun leaving so much of the kids' clothes at her house in the Bronx. Although she babysat a few times a month, they lived so far apart (over an hour's drive) that she figured it had to be inconvenient for Sophia. She had no idea Ron was hitting her. It wasn't like on TV; she never saw any bruises.

Sophia put the kids in Aunt Tyra's second bedroom, carefully building a wall around the bed with chairs and pillows so they couldn't fall out. Timothy was now two and a half, but little Marcus was only eight months old.

She turned the night light on in the room and cracked the door slightly before returning to where Aunt Tyra was in the kitchen.

Aunt Tyra lived in half of a small two-story house; she and her husband, Mac, rented the top floor out to a young married couple and lived on the two lower floors. She placed a cup of hot chocolate before Sophia. "I never knew things with Ron were so bad. He actually hit you?" she asked knowing full well he had. Sophia had told her on the phone before catching the cab over, but now, with Sophia before her with nothing more visible than a pair of red-rimmed eyes, it was almost difficult to believe. *Maybe she could still work things out...*

"Yeah...my ear's bleeding," Sophia said in a near-whisper, turning her head to reveal a barely noticeable cut inside her ear from the force with which Ron's palm had hit her head. She grabbed a napkin from the holder on the table, as if she had just remembered her ear. Thankfully, there wasn't much blood as she dabbed the site.

"Did you tell your mom about this?" Aunt Tyra asked.

"No, Aunt Tyra. You know what Mom's been going through with the divorce. I just didn't want to trouble her. I've actually been having a really bad time with Mom and Dad's separation. They were married for almost thirty years..." her voice trailed off and she paused to dab the corner of her eye with a napkin.

"I know, Honey," her aunt soothed.

"I never thought anything like that could happen..." Sophia's voice cracked and her tears fell rapidly before she could stop them. "Shit," she mumbled. "Oh, I'm so sorry Aunt Tyra!" she said, apologizing both for her tears and for the curse word.

"It's okay, honey." Tyra Halsey had been shocked too, when her sister Beverly told her she was switching back to her maiden name, Brown, and divorcing Leon Boyd after 29 years of marriage. Tyra knew the marriage was off to a bad start when Beverly got pregnant for Leon soon after meeting him when she was only 18. He was good-looking, college-educated and politically active. With Leon's upbringing and the norm in 1960 Mississippi, he had to either marry her or leave town, so he married her and they seemed to live a reasonably happy life. Leon went on to get elected to the state legislature. They had two more children: Denise and Marion, but apparently Leon always held some hostility towards his wife, and at the age of 50 he decided, after years of fooling around with other women, that he wanted to be entirely free. After all, he had been a reasonably respectable husband for nearly thirty years. He didn't owe Beverly any more than that, did he?

Tyra pitied them both. She pitied her sister for being so desperate to purposely trap a man, and she really pitied poor Leon for letting his pants guide him into a marriage which never seemed to fulfill him. Of course, to others a thirty-year marriage looked like a success. Tyra knew better though: it didn't matter how long you stayed, what mattered was how much love you owned. She thanked God every day for her Mac. She still loved him the same as the day they married, twenty years ago, and he still treated her like a princess. She looked over at poor Sophia, initially her mother's pawn to catch a man, and now some man's form of enraged therapy. She loved her niece, but she enjoyed being alone with her husband now that her kids were away in college. She didn't want Sophia staying with them.

"Is it okay if I stay here for a little while?" Sophia asked. Her eyes dissected the patterned linoleum floor in her aunt's kitchen: brown box, white box, brown box, white box...

"Of course!" Tyra responded, realizing she had

absolutely no choice.

Sophia looked up and smiled. Fresh tears slid down her cheeks. "Thank you so much, Aunt Tyra! It'll only be for a little while, I swear. I just need a little time to get back on my feet." She hugged her aunt tightly and poured the half-empty cup of now lukewarm chocolate in the sink.

***

As the weeks passed, Sophia had a hard time controlling the anger which grew in the pit of her belly, every time Ron called, every time he apologized, every time he threatened to come get her, every time he threatened to take away the kids. She had a legal order of protection, so if Ron came anywhere near her home or office, she could have him arrested. She knew in reality, though, that by the time she saw Ron it would probably be too late, so she carried a twenty-two caliber revolver illegally. After all if she never had to use it, it wouldn't matter if it was legal or not, and she didn't have time to apply for a legal weapon. Besides, she knew there was no way the City of New York would give her a carry permit to protect herself from her husband. So, basically Leon and Beverly's daughter was packing in the big city... 'Cause if it had to be her or Ron, it sure as shit wasn't going to be her.

Sophia sat at the drafting table in her office. It was already after 5:00pm, but she enjoyed the quiet of working there, and Aunt Tyra didn't mind getting the kids from the sitter in the afternoons as long as she wasn't left watching them for too long. Sophia's hand boldly color sketched the designs for a new line of sportswear. Ideas flooded her mind and cascaded onto the paper as a salve to her despair. The job was beginning to take off, and if these designs were well received by her superiors, she could well be on her way to starting her own signature collection. She'd been working at the same clothing design firm for the past eight years learning the ropes and giving it her best, and now she was ready. She looked at the completed pages and smiled. Her work was looking really good, and she felt confident about it. It was strange, as if her anger had been transformed into beauty and purpose. She put the drawings away, grabbed her purse, felt quickly for her weapon, and left the office. It was now 6:00pm.

***

When Sophia entered her Aunt Tyra's house, Tyra was on the phone looking frustrated. "Hold on," she said to the caller before looking at Sophia and mouthing, "It's Ron" in a questioning manner.

Sophia nodded her head and took the phone. She only spoke to Ron to keep him from getting angry and scaring her aunt. "Hi, Ron," she stated blandly.

"Oh, Sophie," Ron began. "I've been doing a lot of thinking I've figured out what it is that makes me act that way..."

Sophia's eyebrow rose. This she *had* to hear. She removed her coat and stood in the kitchen with her hand on her hip.

"I think when I got shot a year and a half ago... I think it changed me..."

Sophia rolled her eyes. Well, shit, even *she* knew that. She already told him that!

"Another cop shot me! I mean it still hurts me. I think I'm still angry. I mean, you know I always had a bad temper...but I used to be able to control myself."

Sophia just listened quietly. A part of her still loved

Ron, but she knew there was no way she could go back to him.

Ron's voice cracked as he spoke, "Sophie, you've got to give me another chance... I miss you and the kids... I'll do anything... I'll go for therapy... Anything..." He paused. "Shit, Sophie, I'll even quit my job for you... I'll get a job as a janitor or something..." He laughed. "Sophie... Say something..."

Sophia didn't respond. A tear welled in her eye.

"Sophie?"

"Ron, you know you're breaking my heart," she sniffled. "I can't do it, though. If you can straighten your life out, I'm happy for you, but I can't be a part of it." Her voice trailed off.

"Are you positive Sophie?" Ron asked.

"Yes," she responded.

"Then I guess there's nothing else for me to do. I needed you..." Ron said softly. Then, the loud resonant explosion of a gunshot could be heard.

The telephone receiver crashed to the hard tile of Aunt Tyra's kitchen floor as Sophia screamed and fell to her knees, "Oh, dear God!" Her face contorted in fear, shock and disbelief and she breathed quick, shallow breaths. "Oh, dear God..." her voice trailed off into a whisper and she rocked her body wildly, sitting on the cold floor. "Oh, dear God..." Her voice was a high staccato, as she released the three words repeatedly, rocking her body against the wall. "Oh, dear God..."

***

"Hey, how *are* you?" Sandy asked, hugging her friend.

"I'm keeping it together," Sophia responded, rising from the bench she had been relaxing on waiting for Sandy to meet her in the museum. As they walked through the wide halls and large open rooms, they talked softly between intervals of absorbing the modern paintings before them. It had been nearly a year since they had last seen each other.

"Why don't you come back to the apartment with me?" Sandy offered as they exited the museum. "You haven't been by since you moved out way back when."

"Yeah, I know," Sophia smiled ashamedly. "I totally overreacted back then. I'm sorry. Not to say what you did was right, but my response was a little off the deep end. I mean if I had a cute guy friend sleeping on my couch, I can see the potential to get the urge, you know?"

"Sophie, stop apologizing! It was my fault! I was so embarrassed... Anyway, forget about it. You're my best friend; it was stupid of me. Listen, Lana's away this weekend, so why don't you let me cook dinner for you?"

"I can't stay late, though, Aunt Tyra will kill me, and the trek back to the Bronx is over an hour."

"I know. Let's just have dinner and send you home."

"Thanks."

When Sophia arrived at the apartment she once lived in, she was surprised to see how different it was. Sandy had painted dramatic designs on the walls, making the place look like some sort of adult romper-room. Large, black stick figures appeared against red, yellow and white brush strokes; large flowers, giant suns, playschool houses. It was really very interesting.

"Wow!" Sophia said.

"So what do you think?"

"I think you're becoming eccentric!" Sophia responded playfully, walking through the candy-colored rooms. "I love it! You could probably make money doing this!"

"I'm glad you said that. I'm thinking about starting a business for home murals. You know, children's rooms or whatever... I mean I love doing this, and people get paid to put plain ole boring paint on walls. I can charge more for this. And I'm sick of my day job, you know."

"Why, what's been going on?" Sophia asked.

"Well, you know, I'm still hiding in the closet. I work for a financial company, for godsake, they're just not ready to find out their marketing manager is gay. I mean, I just know everyone would freak out if they knew. I've been there for five years now. I'm getting tired of playing hetero every day, you know?" She sighed and looked around, her hands stuffed into her jeans pockets. Suddenly, with a burst of energy, she added, "This way I can be free from all the society shit. Look, I paint clothing too..." She pulled a large chest away from the wall and opened it, pulling out painted denim jackets, T-shirts and jeans. All had bold primary colors and childlike brush strokes. "What do you think?" she asked.

"I love it!" Sophia responded, her mind racing. This could really be a hit. Maybe she could get Sandy involved with her designs. She wandered through the rooms of the apartment. They had all been transformed into veritable works of art. "What are you going to do when you move?" she asked Sandy, who was busy preparing dinner in the kitchen.

"Well, if I'm rich and famous, I can make the owner pay me for my work. If I'm not, I guess I'll just paint over it. I like it here, though. I'll probably stay for a while." She paused before asking Sophia what she really wanted to know, "So how are the kids doing?"

Sophia smiled. "Oh, they're fine. Timothy understands what happened a little, and Marcus has no idea what's going on. I took them both to the funeral, of course..."

"I'm sorry I wasn't there."

"Sandy, you didn't even know about it, how can you be sorry?"

"I would have known if I read newspapers like everyone else," Sandy offered.

"Be glad you don't read newspapers like everyone else. They're awful." Sophia tilted her ivory chin toward the ceiling, in an attempt to prevent any potential tears from falling. She breathed deeply.

"So how are you handling it?" Sandy asked with concern.

"It's hard. I mean, you know I loved Ron. I still feel sort of responsible...I just...I keep telling myself it wasn't my responsibility to save Ron from Ron. Only he could have saved himself from himself. I mean, I *know* that. You know, it's like my head knows that, but my heart keeps saying maybe I could have saved him or something. Then I feel even more guilty because there's a part of me that I hate to admit exists... The part that's happy...The part that says 'ding-dong Ron's dead' just because having him alive had gotten to be so scary." She looked into Sandy's eyes for understanding.

Sandy smiled. "You're doing just fine. It sounds to me like you're dealing with it. Facing it and giving it time. That's all you need."

The two enjoyed a quick dinner together before Sophia caught the subway back to Aunt Tyra's house in the Bronx.

***

Sophia tapped her fingers on the painted metal desk in her office. Her managers had spent the morning reviewing her designs and those of other firm designers. They were deciding who would be awarded their own signature collection. Sophia had been doing designs for the firm for a long time, but it didn't mean as much when you didn't get real credit for it. A signature line would be her coup de grace: a final sign that her contribution to the company was valued.

Her mocha colored nails made a rattling noise against the desk as she stared blindly at her children's photos. Finally, her line rang.

"Sophia Boyd speaking," she answered.

"Sophia, it's Joe, could you come into my office?" her boss asked.

"Sure," she said, hanging up. She wiped her now-moist palms on the brown tweed slacks she wore as she walked the steps to Joe's office, trying to maintain her cool. When she entered, Joe was alone behind his desk. He smiled and she smiled back, following his lead.

"Sophia, congratulations!"

Sophia felt a tear forming in her eye. This was what she had spent the past eight years dreaming of! "You mean..." she started.

"Our signature collection will be your own line... 'Sophia'... I think the first name alone suffices, don't you?"

"Oh, yeah. That's fine! I mean that's great!" She jumped up and down wildly for a couple of seconds, before regaining her composure, still grinning widely.

"No, Sophia, you've been great." Joe lowered his voice, "I know you've been going through some tough personal problems. Everyone here is impressed by how well you've handled yourself. And honestly, the work you've done over the past few months is the best work I've seen from you yet!"

Sophia blushed a pale pink. "Thanks, Joe. It means a lot to me to hear you say that."

"You more than deserve it. Keep up the good work."

Sophia left her boss's office beaming. The extra money this could bring in would allow her to move into a nice two-bedroom place and get out of Aunt Tyra's house before she overstayed her welcome. For a moment her thoughts drifted to Ron and she felt dizzy... She didn't know how long it would be before she'd be ready to enter a new relationship with a man. Thankfully, she'd be able to focus all her energy on her job and her kids. It took her twenty-eight years, but it seemed things were finally starting to fall into place.

Aura Olivier
Spring 1991

"Congratulations, Aura!" the heavy, brunette woman stated. She leaned on Aura's desk, her bright pink lips curving into a sincere smile.

"Thanks, Mary," Aura responded, smiling in kind. Her boss, John Wiexler, had called her into his office to offer her a promotion to Media Negotiator at the ad agency. She was thrilled by the opportunity and accepted the offer without hesitation. Finally she'd clear $40,000 in base salary alone. The news immediately spread like wildfire throughout the Media Department and many of her co-workers made a point of stopping by her desk to congratulate her. She would move into her own office at the end of the week. She could hardly believe it! Her own office!

She would have been ecstatic had it not been for the distracting pains she'd been feeling in her chest for the past two days. It seemed they were only intensifying, instead of going away as she had hoped.

A tall, blonde man approached her cubicle. "Aura, I heard the news. That's just fabulous! So what are you doing after work? The folks in the office want to take you out to celebrate!"

"Oh, I don't know..." Aura began.

"Don't say you don't know... Say yes! You absolutely have to come have a drink with us!" He gestured to a group of co-workers near the pantry. Aura looked at the smiling white faces. Oh great, she thought. It wasn't that she had anything in particular against white people, except maybe slavery and four hundred years of oppression, Jim Crow, delayed right to vote, desegregation, re-segregation, black exploitation and affirmative action backlash. Okay, maybe she did have a slight chip on her shoulder. But, she did realize that she didn't choose to be black so she couldn't blame white people for being born white... Right? She could blame them for not saving her race from self-destruction, but on most days she could barely save herself from self-destruction, and even if she blamed it on the "white man" she knew it would only be self-defeating—they weren't even thinking about her and her race's problems because they were too busy thinking about themselves. Just like everybody else...trying to stay afloat in a chaotic world.

She never forgot her father's old adage: "Everybody hates everybody." He said it for as long as she could remember, using the word "hate" loosely. When she was young she really didn't understand what he meant. It wasn't until they had conversations when she got older that she realized that he was talking about fear of the unknown. Everybody feared the unknown. Her dad summed it up one Halloween, after Aura had been pelted with rotten eggs by a group of kids from a rival high school by saying, "Whites hate Blacks. Blacks hate Jews. Jews hate Muslims. Muslims hate Protestants. Protestants hate Catholics. Catholics hate Gays. And kids at that school hate kids at your school. Everyone wants to have someone to hate so they can feel superior. Don't let anyone convince you that because you're a young woman or because you're black that you can't hate just as much as anyone else. We all hate because our hate is part of our fear, and we fear what we don't know, and in this world there's so much we'll never know, why not just hate it?

Then we never have to deal with our own ignorance." Her father took the rotten egg incident far more seriously than she had. She was guilty of tossing a full dozen herself, so when she got caught in the backlash, she shrugged it off. Of course, she "forgot" to tell her parents she was a participant, knowing at sixteen that the sympathy points earned could prove valuable come the weekend.

Her parents owned and operated a travel agency, which had grown over the years to include many offices. It still fascinated her that her father, a St. Lucian immigrant who worked twelve hour days for as long as she could remember, had such wisdom to share. His theory went against a lot of her longings over the years. She often wanted to blame whites so badly it hurt. But she knew that "everybody hated everybody," something most people just didn't realize, because ironically they were too busy hating their particular target or minding their own particular business to care.

In any event, Aura had chosen a field which was at least 95% white, and she knew that as she reached higher levels, the black population would decrease even further. She also knew that she was needed in her field to open it up for other black people that she hoped would follow.

Aura grinned at the blonde-haired man. "Sure, I suppose I could *drag* myself to the bar and let you folks buy me drinks if you must!" she answered playfully. She figured it would be best to go out and celebrate. She was sure her boss would be there, and socializing was a critical aspect of her job, especially now, since with the promotion she'd be required to entertain clients.

"That's the spirit, darling!" The man beamed. Todd was a really pleasant guy, but his mannerisms were so flamboyant at times, everyone in the office pretty much assumed he was gay. He walked over to the group of people who had been watching; Aura's promotion was the hot gossip topic for the day, and after the announcement, more people than usual seemed to be hanging around her area.

Aura smiled. When she first started at WBG Advertising she really did feel the "hate" her father described. Despite her college days at a predominantly white institution, Aura was essentially a product of her racially segregated Brooklyn neighborhood. And, even in college, the black and white students lived as if on two separate campuses. So, when she first came to WBG she was unaccustomed to interacting with white people, and the newness was disturbing. But she adjusted, and what was unfamiliar became more familiar until finally she realized they weren't so different after all. Lots of them were from immigrant families too, from Italy, Ireland, and Poland...and their cultures were as different as the Caribbean immigrants she was accustomed to dealing with in her community, from Jamaica, Haiti, Trinidad. And while she was still getting used to spending her work days primarily with whites, she found them no more "different" than some segments of the black community.

She hated to admit it at times, but she felt very far removed from some of the poorer blacks in her neighborhood. She spent many years joking about sisters in the projects going grocery shopping with curlers in their hair, or brothers with the afro picks on call in the back of their 'fros. Now that she was older, she still thought the jokes were funny; most of that stuff was rampant in the late seventies, with a lot of other frightening fashion trends. But now she tried for a more thorough understanding of the cultural attitudes that made going outside partially dressed acceptable or even "cool." She felt a world apart on the socioeconomic spectrum. She'd *die* before she left the house with curlers in her hair on any day. She smiled; actually Dana would *kill* her if she left the house with curlers in her hair. Aura's mind wandered on the possibility. Her *whole family* would *beat* her if they saw her on the street with *curlers* in her hair! She couldn't help breaking a grin with the thought, but as she did a sharp pain struck the right side of her lung and half her chest, causing her to double over at her desk. Her smile quickly slid away.

***

Tears poured down Aura's cheeks as she lay in the nurse's office. "I need to get out of here; my painkillers aren't working!" Her voice pleaded with the nurse; her body racked with pain. Aura normally carried a few strong painkillers in case the sickle-cell acted up during the day, but this day was unlike any she had experienced in years.

The moments passed like hours as she huddled in the fetal position on the soft black vinyl of the examining table. Her jaws were clenched shut as she ground her teeth repeatedly, creating a scraping noise. Her hair was beginning to matte against her face and neck from perspiration. She had already removed her suit jacket and opened her blouse. She felt as if she were on fire.

The nurse looked at her nervously. "You said you have what kind of anemia? I've got lots of iron pills."

Aura's face was sore from the instinctive need to clench her mouth. Her body felt tight from the tension of stiffening up in response to the pain. It was more than she could possibly endure. She wanted to jump out of her own skin! She wiped her tears and sweat with the back of her hand and watched her black mascara smear against her clammy skin. The veins in her hand seemed to be straining against the confines of her skin. She shook her head around on her neck in an attempt to get the pain to leave her body, but it wouldn't. She wiggled her arms. She moved her legs. She tried to control her breathing, hoping to keep it together; she didn't want her boss to regret his decision to promote her. No matter how she turned her body, the pain wouldn't move, not an inch.

She jumped off the examining table with exasperation. "Just call me an ambulance, please," Aura begged the red-haired woman in the white uniform. "Call my doctor, just get me out of here...urggh..." The energy required to speak, to stand, was suddenly too much for her. She threw her body back onto the soft examining table and immediately curled up in a ball. She lay very still for a few minutes, rocking herself with abstraction as her teeth continued the quiet scraping sound of the grinding, like chalk on a blackboard.

The woman leaned over a desk, her white nurse's uniform crumpled casually. It seemed the over-the-counter medication she had given this girl wasn't helping, but she couldn't dispense anything stronger. What the hell was this "sickle-cell" thing, anyway? Maybe, if she called her supervisor they could tell her what to do. She dialed the number quickly and got the head physician on the phone. "Thank goodness you're there, Dr. Steinberg!" she began.

But Aura couldn't take it anymore. With a last bit of energy, she grabbed the phone and screamed, "Call an ambulance! I think I'm dying!" With that done, she threw her body back onto the examining table and rocked herself until an ambulance arrived. The paramedics quickly set her up with an IV and rushed her to the nearest hospital. It had been hours since the pains had become severe, and by the time she was given intravenous injections of morphine, she was exhausted from fighting the excruciating aching that racked her chest, arms, back and legs. The drug quickly put her into a deep sleep.

***

When Aura opened her eyes the next morning, her parents were at her bedside with flowers and candies. She smiled and they kissed her, but she couldn't stay awake. The drugs which poured into her system kept putting her back to sleep, which was fine with her...anything to avoid the pain.

***

That evening, a nurse came into her room with dinner: a sirloin steak with onions, green beans, mashed potatoes and tapioca pudding. Aura ate and fell back asleep while her parents explained to her physician that they could not approve a blood transfusion without Aura's approval.

***

Three days had passed since Aura's sickle-cell "crisis" as the doctors liked to refer to it. The pains had, for the most part, subsided, replaced only by Aura's depression. She felt as if she had failed. She let the disease get the best of her. She knew that she was being unfair to herself, but she just didn't know how to handle her predicament. She was angry, very angry...with herself for having the disease, with her parents for giving her the disease, with her siblings for not having the disease, with white people because it was primarily a black disease, with God for choosing her to give the disease to, and with all the disease-free people in the world for not appreciating their own good health. The list went on and on in her mind as she struggled with how to live her life when it seemed so out of control. One moment she felt fine, and the next, she was screaming bloody murder in the nurse's office of her company! She allowed her mind to briefly relive the pain, and the memory alone made her cringe! How would she go on? It had been over five years since she had last been hospitalized with a pain crisis, and she had been convinced she was getting better. She had become somewhat accustomed to the weekly and sometimes daily pains she experienced and controlled with strong pain killers. But, it seemed right when she thought things were getting better, they only got worse. She had never experienced pain this severe before, and now she felt as if her life were suddenly out of control.

The phone at her bedside rang in the late morning; it was Henry, one of her current boyfriends. He had apparently heard about her illness through her job. She sighed. Mike had already sent her flowers and promised to visit. With her luck, they'd show up at the same time. She tried to convince Henry that it really wasn't necessary, but he wouldn't listen, promising to stop by either that night or the following day. But exactly what day? she asked. Unfortunately, he wouldn't get specific, saying it depended on his workload. Henry knew they were not exclusive, but he wanted to be, so she figured this was some plot on his part. *Yeah, whatever...*

She sat up quickly when she saw Dana entering her room.

"Hey, girl, what's up?" Dana asked in her usual bubbly manner "Here, I brought these for you," she said handing her a bouquet of condom lollipops in various colors, "in case you get lucky with a doctor." She laughed.

Aura examined the gift: they were real condoms attached to lollipop sticks. She smiled. "Are these any good?" she asked.

"Girl, these puppies are nonoxynol-9 *down*. You *know*

I don't play!" Dana slapped her knee, laughing at her own good sense. It was early April and she still wore a coat to counter the effects of the post-winter chill.

"Why aren't you working today?" Aura asked. Dana had recently landed her dream job at Mahogany Enterprises, a black publishing company.

"Why do you think, Aura? I came to see you." She paused, lowering her voice slightly before continuing, "How are you anyway?"

Aura could see the fear in her friend's eyes, and it scared her. She felt the burning sensation of tears trying to form, but she fought them. "I'm okay," she said simply.

Dana's eyes questioned her further.

"*I said I'm okay.* I'll be out of here soon. They just want to make sure I'm full of fluids and the pain is over before they let me go." Her words made a futile attempt to reassure Dana and herself. Seeing Dana was unconvinced, she added firmly, "I don't want to talk about it."

She looked over at the door and saw her brother entering her room. She was surprised to see him; he should have been working as well. "Ace!" she cried out, raising her arms for a hug.

"Hey, little sis!" He hugged his sister tightly. "I wanted to come sooner, but Mom and Dad said I should wait."

Aura nodded, "Yeah, I was pretty out of it for awhile."

"Don't worry about a thing, the next dinner's on me, even though you owe me one." He smiled. Even though Aaron had moved to Connecticut in the past year, they still went out for dinner about once a month. Sometimes Angie joined them.

"Ace, you remember my friend Dana..." Aura began. It had been years since the two of them saw each other.

"Daanaa," Aaron said her name slowly, looking at her as if they had never met before. She was beautiful with smooth deep caramel skin, pretty eyes and a fierce haircut. She wore her hair in a sharp, black blunt cut, tapered carefully at her ears.

Dana curved her lightly glossed lips into a quick smile and stood up. She wore a pale pink angora sweater with a pair of fitted black jeans over low heeled boots. "Hi, Ace," she greeted. "Last time I saw you was at Aura's college graduation party... That's a long time ago..." she began. She didn't remember Ace looking this good four years ago. Actually, she barely remembered him at all from the party. She just knew he was there. The brother before her now was not only handsome, but he had a certain smoothness about him. She was embarrassed when the word "debonair" popped into her mind. She allowed her eyes to take him in slowly... nice hands, nice shoes, nice earring, nice close-cropped beard, nice mustache...

"All right, you guys, you're grossing me out!" Aura exclaimed, seeing what was happening.

"What?" Dana asked feigning innocence.

Aura looked at the two of them and had a new fear. Suppose they started dating or something? Ace wouldn't want to talk about women problems to her if the woman was Dana. And Aura couldn't stand it if Dana started bitching to her about her own brother! She watched the two of them watching each other and hoped for the best. Aaron had brought fried chicken, so the three sat watching TV and eating. Dana and Aaron flirted unabashedly, and Aura was sad when they left at about 3:00pm; they had definitely taken her mind off her problems for awhile.

***

"Hi Mike!" she said as gracefully as she could muster to the tall, light-skinned brother entering her room. It was just minutes past 7:00pm, the start of the evening visiting hours.

"Hey, baby, how are you feeling?" he asked, his tone concerned. He kissed Aura's forehead. Her long, black hair was pulled back into a pony tail.

"Oh, I'm doing okay."

"I brought you cheesecake."

"You're a god!" Aura joked nervously. She really hoped Henry wouldn't show up while Mike was in her room.

"So, how's the job? Did you ever find out about the promotion?" he asked.

"Oh, yeah! I didn't talk to you, huh? I guess I ended up here..." She turned her face away for a moment, controlling her urge to cry.

"Hey, what's the big deal?" Mike asked, sensing her despair. "You're okay aren't you?" His question was out of concern for both Aura and himself. He really liked Aura, but he wasn't sure he could deal with a chronically ill girlfriend.

How could she tell him 'no' she wasn't okay. She had some dumb-ass disease to live with for her whole life. "I'm fine," Aura lied. Then, it occurred to her she didn't have to deal with anyone's shit when she was the one who was sick. "Look, Mike, I hate to be a bitch, but I'm having a hard time with this, and I'd rather just spend some time alone. I hope you don't mind. Call you in the morning, okay?"

"Aura, are you sure?" Mike frowned looking dejected.

"Yeah, I'm sure. I'm sorry, really. I'll call you."

"Well, you're the boss. Take it easy." He kissed her forehead and left. When he boarded the elevator to the lobby, a dark-skinned man carrying a box of roses passed him on his way to Aura's room.

***

"Henry, you're too good to me!" Aura smiled nervously, hoping Mike didn't have to come back for anything.

She really enjoyed dating two men. When one was busy, the other one was available. When one pissed her off, she could always call the other. One was dark; one was light. One was skinny; one was husky. Of course, they both had the requisite flat stomachs...she had to maintain her standards, after all... And, they were both exquisitely horny.

Aura opened the box Henry handed her, a dozen long-stemmed white roses. He kissed her quickly, then a bit more longingly. He sighed. He loved Aura, but he hadn't told her yet.

"Hey, what's going on in here?" a voice called out from the doorway.

Henry moved away from her quickly.

"Hey, Angie!" Aura said, spotting her sister.

"How are you feeling?" Angie kissed her sister on the cheek. "Mom and Dad wanted to come, but they got tied up with work. They send their love."

"Thanks. I feel much better. I think they're letting me out tomorrow. I'm supposed to find out later tonight."

"That's great..." Angie glanced toward Henry.

"Oh, I'm sorry! Angie this is my friend Henry. Henry this is my sister Angie."

"So, you're Angie! Aura speaks very highly of you."

"Oh, she does, does she?" Angie smiled at her sister. "Look, I brought you cheesecake!"

"Gosh, you folks are trying to fill me up with

cheesecake!"

"Really? Who brought you cheesecake?" Angie asked.

"Mi...My friend, Dana..." Aura fumbled, nearly spilling Mike's name, but proud of her quick thinking.

Angie gave her a curious grin, knowing something was up. She paused briefly, before realizing Aura nearly said Mike. "Oh... Dana's *my* friend too..." she said teasing. Henry looked at Aura curiously.

"Dana and I went to school together, but Angie knows her too. Sometimes, I forget who I'm speaking to and I just say 'my friend,' you know?" Aura was doing a messy clean-up job. She wouldn't have had to if Angie didn't decide to screw around, but that's what sisters are for, she supposed.

"Anyway," Angie said, deciding to save her sister from gracelessly continuing with the topic. "I hear you got the big promotion!"

"How'd you know?"

"You told Mom and Dad."

"I did?"

"Yeah, you did. I think you were pretty groggy at the time, though."

"Ugh, it sucks to be drugged. I can't remember the first couple of days after I got here."

"Yeah, don't worry about it. You'll get out of here and everything will be fine."

"Sure it will," Aura said sarcastically. She was still annoyed about having to be in the hospital anyway.

Angie and Henry exchanged worried glances before talking Aura into a game of spades.

***

Aura spent four days in the hospital before being released. Her parents came to pick her up the following morning. They drove through Manhattan and back into Brooklyn mostly in silence. The air was crisp with the newness of spring, and puffy white clouds soared against a blue canvas of sky. Aura breathed deeply of the air as if she had forgotten what a new day smelled like. She watched people through the car window—beggars, invalids, executives, runners, mothers, lovers, school children... As her father steered through the cool paved streets, she looked quietly at the car window come movie screen. *Was life just a show that she couldn't be part of?*

"I don't like the way you look," her father stated, glancing Aura's face in the rear view mirror.

"Leave her alone, Don," her mother warned.

Her father glanced wearily at his wife before continuing. "Aura, I just hope you're not back there feeling sorry for yourself. It's too much."

"Why, Dad? What do you mean?" Aura pulled herself out of her distracted window gazing.

"You have too much to be thankful for," her father stated simply.

"I know."

"Do you really?" Donald Olivier probed.

"I know... I have a great family and great friends, what more could I want, right?" Aura's voice was monotone, and she rolled her eyes with exasperation.

Her father smiled. "You have no idea what you *really* have; do you?"

"What do you mean?"

"You know, sometimes people are so busy concentrating on their own problems, they don't have time to appreciate all the problems they could have but don't." Her father paused. "Your existence in this world is a miracle in and of itself, Aura. If my one particular sperm didn't catch your mom's one particular egg on one particular evening you would never have come to be."

"Don, what *are* you talking about?" Sylvia laughed.

"Yeah, Dad, what's the point?" Aura folded her arms across her chest with defiance.

"The point is that you could have been anyone anywhere, but you were lucky enough to be you here. You live in one of the richest countries in the world. That's good odds just to start. You come from a family of decent means. Let's just say the top 25% in this country. That's better odds still... It almost makes you seem lucky."

"I don't feel lucky."

"You don't feel lucky because you compare yourself to people who you think have more than you. You want to compare yourself to people who don't have sickle-cell and convince yourself that they're better off than you, but it's not true. What's true is some of them are and some of them aren't."

"Yeah, whatever."

"Don't 'yeah, whatever' me, Aura. Listen. I'm trying to tell you something that makes sense. You see, just because people don't have sickle-cell doesn't mean they don't have problems."

"Dad, my life expectancy is probably around forty."

"Aura, the average black man in the ghetto has a life expectancy of around forty. And, there are children all over the world dying every day. Who says you have the right to live to fifty or eighty or a hundred? No one. But, you see no one knows how much time they have. That's why you must spend your time wisely and cherish all your moments." Sylvia smiled under the cover of her loosely wrapped silk scarf; she did not want Aura to see her expression. Don was always good at talking a little sense into Aura when she needed it.

"Dad, why are you telling me this stuff? It's not going to make any difference."

"Oh, Aura, that's where you're *really* wrong! Anything you need or want in this world comes from within, from your mind. If you believe you can overcome this illness and you fight it, and if you believe you can live a worthwhile life in spite of it then you can..." Her father paused for a moment. Overwhelmed by his own emotions, he swallowed before continuing, "But Aura, if you let this thing kill your spirit... If you let it win, then all the medicine men and modern technology in the world won't be able to help you."

Aura paused for a moment, a bit taken aback by the intensity in her father's voice. "But, Dad, there are so many people who have their health and don't appreciate it."

"Just like *you* did, before this last crisis. Do you know how many people would love to live where you live, have a job like you have, look the way you look. People would line up to have the mind you have! And you have the nerve to be upset because you're not perfect when 99% of the world is suffering! People are starving and you and I walk to the grocery store and buy a chicken for three dollars!"

"When I watch TV, I don't see suffering, Dad. I see Bel Air, Hollywood, penthouse apartments."

"Stop watching soap operas, Aura. Watch the news! People overcome obstacles every day. Obstacles and change, Aura, those are the only things you can really count on."

Sylvia caught Aura's face in the rear view mirror. Don's words were definitely having an impact.

"I understand all that, Dad. It's just, in the back of my mind, I keep thinking why me? I know it's self-defeating, but I can't help it." Her eyes pleaded with her father for sympathy.

Donald Olivier gave his daughter something better

than sympathy, he gave her outrage. "WHY ME?" he bellowed, then laughed. "I didn't hear you say 'why me?' when you got good grades in school, when you graduated college, when you got this promotion. When men chase you around like you're some sort of princess, I don't hear you say 'why me?'" Now he mimicked her, "Oh, why am I so beautiful? Why am I so smart? Why are my parents together? Why does my dad drive a nice car?" He winked in the rear view mirror.

Aura smiled. The old fart did have a point. *Obstacles and change, huh?* "Dad, it sounds as if you're saying 'life sucks deal with it.' Is that supposed to make me feel better?" Aura knew she had him now.

Her father laughed heartily upon hearing her words. He mimicked her again, "Life sucks, deal with it," then paused before continuing. "Now, Aura, you may have spent four days in the hospital honey, and I know you were in a ton of pain, but you've had enough laughter and joy in your life to make up for it so many times it would be crazy to even discuss it. Life sucks? Give me a break, all you have to do is look at the beauty of a sunny day to know that life doesn't suck. And why do you have me using that stupid slang term, anyway? Life is full of pleasure Aura, you know that. If it didn't have a little pain too, you'd be too giddy to appreciate the pleasure. Maybe you'll have a little more pain than most, but maybe not. Keep your head up and you'll at least find out."

Aura sighed. "I love you Daddy."

"I love you too baby."

Sylvia finally exhaled. It wasn't only Aura who was worn out by the disease. After all it was Sylvia who gave Aura life, and it was Sylvia who supplied the sickle-cell gene which met with Donald's to give Aura a life replete with physical pain. And no matter how she might try to empathize with her daughter, she couldn't. She had no means of understanding the horror of chronic pain. She was just thankful that, so far, Aura was able to lead a normal life.

Maybe they could make it through this after all.

Ocean Ryder
Spring 1991

Ocean rolled over in his bed. The sun streamed into the smoky room and he rose with a cough. He stared stupidly at the pack of Newport cigarettes on the night stand. He didn't know what made him take up a new bad habit. He already had too many, and at the still-tender age of twenty-four his habits were beginning to catch up with him. He wasn't a drunk, a pothead, a coke addict or even a smoker. But he did indulge in an array of vices on occasion, and the occasions were increasing in frequency.

He stood up at the side of his bed, reaching his hands over his head to stretch his long naked body out. He rocked his head from side to side in an attempt to remove the kinks from his neck and spine. His long dreads swept across his broad shoulders. He released a gravelly groan laden with the sound of morning, and roamed into the living room.

When he saw a woman on his sofa, he jumped. Shit, he had to stop living like this! "Good morning, Diane," he muttered. Why couldn't they just *leave* in the morning? Why did they always want to hang out? Women...who could figure?

"Morning sexy!" the woman responded.

"What time is it?" Ocean asked abruptly.

"It's nine-thirty," she said looking at her watch.

"Oh, shit!" Ocean faked. "I have a meeting at ten-thirty. You've got to get out of here!" He grabbed her jacket and began heading toward the door.

Diane smiled at Ocean's nude body. "You'd better get dressed," she spoke suggestively, allowing her eyes to linger on his manhood.

"Ha, ha," Ocean stated with annoyance. "Thanks. I'll call you."

When Diane left the apartment, he leaned his back against the door and breathed deeply. This was getting ridiculous. Was he becoming one of those sex addicts you see on 'Oprah?' Nah, he was just a horny guy doing what horny guys do...right?

* * *

The small aircraft landed safely on the open area of the Great Abaco airport. Ocean exited the plane feeling relaxed. He hadn't been home since he left in 1983; it was hard for him to believe it had been eight years. He didn't know how he let so much time pass without seeing any of his five brothers and sisters, his mother or his aunts and uncles. In the beginning it was a lack of money, then a lack of time, and then he reached the point where it had been so long it didn't seem to matter when a few more months were tacked on. As he set foot on the earth of his homeland, he knew he should never have stayed away so long. The air was so different, even steps away from an airplane engine, he could feel its clarity and the purity of his people.

When he reached his mother's home, she was sitting on the front porch awaiting his arrival. She wore a starched white blouse and smooth peach skirt. When he laid his eyes on her he was shocked by the emotions which engulfed him... It had been far too long. Her complexion was smooth and light brown, the color of coffee with too much cream. She wore no makeup, save a swish of burnt sienna lipstick and brown mascara, as if she made a special effort just for this occasion. Her face was soft and full, her body pleasantly plump. She looked wholesome and beautiful the way a mother should.

Ocean walked up the stairs of the house he had lived in for so many years. "Mom!" he exclaimed, the words rolled off his full lips with a certain triumph.

His mother looked at him carefully from head to toe, unmoving from her sitting position. Her smile reached her cheeks slowly. "What's with the hair?" she finally asked.

"Oh!" Ocean breathed, placing his sole carry-on bag on the wood slats of the porch; he slowly fingered a loose lock of matted hair, then smiled fully. He hadn't mentioned his dreadlocks to his mother. Actually, he hadn't given it any thought at all. He walked the two steps to where she sat and kissed a soft brown cheek. It had been so long, he had to control the urge to pull her out of the chair and give her a full bear hug! "It's just the style in the States. It doesn't mean anything religious, you know." He looked at her for approval in a way she found familiar.

She examined the long pretty locks of her son's hair carefully. There was no mud or sun-bleaching like the dreadlocks she had heard about and occasionally saw. Eddie didn't profess to have joined a new religion, not that that would be worse than no religion at all. She hoped he wasn't smoking that marijuana all day. She looked into his clear eyes—he looked healthy as an ox! Her mouth curved into a full grin. His hair was jet black, clean and smoothly held into place by a covered rubber tie. The ends were all cut to the same length dangling near his shoulders. She hated to admit it, but if not for the fact that the length struck her as slightly feminine, it was beautiful. "It's good to have you home," she muttered with much thought. "So, what's the big delay?" she demanded, her smile soft yet stern. "Give your mother a hug!" Dorothy Ryder stood up and raised her arms.

Ocean was more than happy to nestle himself in her warmth. He held her tightly and experienced a somewhat trite yet startling revelation... A mother's love is like no other. He could feel emotion leave her body and enter his in a way he could barely comprehend, let alone attempt to express.

"I love you, Mom." The words crossed his lips with astounding ease. His mother *was* beautiful in a way so different from other woman he knew.

"Come inside," she offered.

Ocean picked up the bag that had settled comfortably on the deck of their patio and followed his mother into the house. There, before him, were the faces he remembered, almost... Each had changed slightly with the passage of time and knowledge.

"Eddie!" a young woman's voice cried out. It was his sister, Shana. She ran up to him from the worn brown couch which had beaten an impression on her long white skirt, and hugged him, lingering in his arms for a few moments longer than necessary. She buried her head into his chest, smiling a glowing face which he could not see. Shana was the only one who continued to write him over the years. When he left she was merely a baby girl of fourteen. Now she was twenty-two and wholly a woman.

He stepped away from her to take in the lacy starched white dress. She was beautiful and voluptuous. For a moment he wondered what man laid claim to her, but quickly realized it didn't matter... She was a woman now. And it had been too long; he could not play the role of the over-protective big brother.

"How are you?" he asked.

"I'm just fine, Eddie... just fine!" Eddie was not the oldest of her brothers, but to her and the rest of the family, he was the adventurous one. She was sure he had many tales of life in the big city to share with them all.

Eddie's joy spilled onto his sister in a way that brought him "Brady Bunch" memories. It always seemed that show crept into a lot of his corny fantasies of ideal family life. He then moved through the room to greet his other siblings. Marvin, George and Michael were all younger than he and looked somewhat distracted. His older brother Barry was not around. They hugged, and he smelled the warm moist scent of conch chowder simmering on the stove. It was his favorite, and he could sense a lot of care had been taken to prepare for his arrival. The living room was spotless, without a hint of dust on a drape or chair. There was no love that compared to family... He was busy exchanging 'hellos' when a shortish, older man walked towards him.

"Hello," the man said, as if such a simple word had been chosen with some thought.

"Hello," Ocean responded, his cadence tapered into something of a question.

His mother quickly walked over to the two men as they shook hands. "This is Andrew Miller," she stated without explanation.

"Eddie!" a voice called out. It was his Aunt Mary, his mother's sister, quickly descending the steps from the upper rooms with excitement. "Oh, you look so *good!*" She hugged him tightly.

Ocean held her closely; Aunt Mary's hugs were the next best thing to his mother's.

The laughter began as Ocean told tales of parties and people he had met in the States. His natural charisma came across smoothly as he described the day he got the phone call from Esquire, being careful to leave out the exquisite details of his evening with Marc and Erikka, and Tasha's unexpected reaction.

As if on cue, and somewhat inappropriately, the man

named Andrew Miller said, "So tell us about the woman in your life!"

Ocean looked at the man suspiciously. *Who was he any way?* His mind raced for a brief moment before he explained, "I'm still looking for the right woman, you know? I *am* only twenty-four after all!" He thought his response was excellent, but the room grew somewhat quiet as if that was not what his family wanted to hear, so he added, "Well there is this one woman, but I'm not sure if she's the right one."

His mother flashed his aunt a knowing glance. "What's her name?" she asked, leaning forward in her chair.

"Mona," Ocean blathered. He couldn't think of what else to say. Mona was still a friend of his, although not a particularly close one. He was satisfied with his response, though. He had known her the longest of all his female friends, and his mother didn't know she was married.

"Mona... So when will I get to meet her?"

Was she really serious? "I don't know, Ma," he managed to explain. His mother had to be kidding. It was bad enough he said Mona's name. Need he go on? He looked into his mother's eyes and suddenly felt a pang of embarrassment. She was absolutely beaming, and here he was lying to her, like a school boy. Was that why he came back home...to lie to his mother? After all, he *was* an adult now. He didn't have to lie to "get away" with things anymore. She couldn't punish him. He was single by choice. *So what?* He hated to do it, but he immediately needed to come clean. "Ma, forget what I said. Mona and I are not that close."

"Oh?" Dorothy Ryder frowned.

Ocean looked around the room at his family "I wish I could please you by saying I'm seeing someone special, but I'm not. Right now, I'm concentrating on other things...you know, my career. And you folks should stop trying to marry me off so quickly, anyway!"

Shana spoke first, her voice clear as a flute. "Nobody said anything about getting married, Eddie. We just want you to have someone in your life that cares about you. I mean, you're all alone out there in New York City. You shouldn't be alone."

Ocean smiled, at his sister. "Thanks, Shana, but I hardly spend any time alone at all."

The Andrew Miller person frowned.

Ocean's brothers began laughing and mumbling to each other. Clearly, big brother had become a ladies' man.

His mother and aunt exchanged perplexed glances. They couldn't imagine why anyone would want to spend his days the way it seemed Eddie did. "Well," Mrs. Ryder finally said, "It's just about dinner time, so let's stop hounding Eddie about his personal life. She and her sister stood up and began preparing for dinner.

When Ocean rose the following morning on a single bed in his brothers' room, he felt more relaxed than he had in a long time. He had been surprised by his family's reaction the previous night to his dating situation. His mother always asked about his newest girlfriend when they talked on the phone, but he never thought she cared to any great extent. He wasn't going to let it bother him, though. It was a typical mother's reaction, he supposed. Just as his typical reaction was to wonder who the hell Andrew Miller was, but his mother seemed so careful not to discuss it, that he decided not to bother her about it for now. After all, he had two weeks to spend with his family in Abaco.

He quietly wrestled his long brown legs into the charcoal grey nylon of his running pants, and slipped into a loose white T-shirt. He was careful not to awaken Marvin who had finally gotten a room to himself since Barry moved out a little less than a year earlier. It was 7:00am and he had promised himself he would run the beaches while he was out there. Abaco has some of the most beautiful sandy beaches and ports in the world. The sun was still low in the sky as he began his jog through the partially paved streets to the shoreline, and then over the rocks and sand. The air was cool with early morning and the salt from the sea gave him a certain clearness of mind. After running for a little over half an hour, he pulled the elastic bands of his pants legs high on his calves and removed his running shoes, freeing his feet to the soft sand below. The sun was daring its ascent higher as it approached 8:00am, and his stomach was beginning to grumble.

He stopped to rest and enjoy the early morning sun near a large group of rocks. The sky was a solid, bright blue and the breeze was slow and tranquil. He leaned back, turning his face toward the ceiling of sky and allowed his hair to fall back on his shoulders. The outline of his profile against the smooth blue backdrop made a pleasant portrait: the careful arch of his nose, the wide loose curve of his lips, and the deep cut angle of his chin.

A group of children appeared a few steps away from him. They were selling painted shells, but he didn't have money on him, so they walked on. He watched the outlines of their lean angular bodies making footprints in the sand as they walked away, and was sorry he left the house without even a bit of pocket change.

He jumped onto a huge boulder expertly, with the ease of the familiar. He sat, pulling his knees into his chest, and stared out onto the turquoise water and azure sky. The scent of the sea drifting on a blanket of breeze caressed his nostrils, gently freeing his thoughts. The pleasure of the experience was a bit astounding. He closed his eyes and relaxed as the passing minutes collected like rainwater into a puddle. Before he knew what happened, it was nearly 9:00am and he felt giddy with hunger and euphoria. He stretched out on top of the big rock, before jumping down and heading back to the house.

***

When Ocean got back home, the kitchen was quiet after a frenzy of early morning cooking. His siblings had gone off to their respective jobs: Shana was a bank teller, Marvin and George had jobs at one of the local hotels, and Michael worked on a fishing boat. Ocean sat at the table while his mother prepared a plate for him.

"You're looking good, Eddie, better than last night."

"I feel amazing, Ma. I don't know why I waited so long to come back."

Mrs. Ryder's eyes dropped slightly. "I wondered why too."

"There was no good reason, I guess. Just poor then busy, you know." He paused and added, "I had no idea how much I missed you guys. Shana looks beautiful, all woman like you now."

Dorothy Ryder's face got ruddy in response to her son's compliment.

Ocean continued, "Marvin, George and Michael all getting up early in the mornings to work. It's good to see they're keeping out of trouble. No pregnant girls, I take it?"

"Eddie!"

"Why are you so surprised Mom? You know the Ryder men are all good-looking."

"But they are *not* all like your father!" A quiet anger was apparent in Mrs. Ryder's voice.

"I'm sorry Mom. It's just nowadays, they have to be careful. You know AIDS is no joke. It's really spreading in the States. And with Marvin and George working at that hotel, you don't know what kind of women they may be meeting…"

"Marvin and George have girlfriends, nice girlfriends. You'll probably get a chance to meet them one day this week. And as for as that AIDS thing, if those Americans didn't subscribe to the kind of lewd behavior they do, that disease wouldn't be spreading so quickly."

"It's more than just about sex, Ma."

"It's *too* many *partners* Eddie." She glared at him with suggestive eyes, as her voice danced a sing-song, reminiscent of childhood exchanges.

Ocean looked at the ceiling in exasperation before directing his gaze again towards his mother. "I get the point, Ma." He forced himself to smile, then found he couldn't help but smile when he saw the plate of fried grouper, grits and Johnny cakes his mother placed before him—it had been a long time since he tasted food from home.

***

Ocean spent most of his first week running the shore, relaxing at his younger brother's boat gig and wandering among the bars at the few small hotels on the island. He spent his nights alone by choice. There was no shortage of beautiful and available women at his disposal. Although he didn't like what his mother suggested the first day he arrived, he couldn't ignore it. Maybe he *had* been with too many women over the past ten years. He had certainly been with more than he could name, count or remember. And not a single one had really moved him. There *had* been one girl when he was only eighteen and new to the States, but she wanted to spend all her time with him, and he just wasn't ready for that. He forced the relationship's destruction by indifference and lack of attention, and he was never faithful to her like she wanted.

Between the time he spent working in a bar for over a

year, then modeling for the past four, it seemed the women he met were flighty and fast, like him. But although he enjoyed their company, he always wished for a woman who would do the Sunday crossword with him at 8:00am, after spending the evening at home alone. *Maybe he had just been looking in the wrong places all along.* Ocean's mind wandered as he threw back a beer. His feet dangled off a local pier as his eyes canvassed the small boats docked and at shore. He knew he couldn't blame his predicament on the women he knew. Most of them, or at least half, would have been happy to spend a Sunday morning crossword session with him. The fact was, he had never asked any of them to. Maybe it was something he was scared to ask for. Sex was an easy request. Or dinner. Drinks. But, how do you tell a woman what you really want is a five letter word for tawny? Or unexplained silence? The sound of reading in unison? He knew there was a side of him that needed that, but not enough then...but more so now...?

Ocean stood on the pier and gazed out. The night was clear and black with a confetti sprinkling of lights in the sky. His mother had been aching to speak to him over the past few nights, but he avoided her attempts at intimate conversation. Partly, he was upset with the realization that Andrew Miller was her lover. Not that it wasn't obvious when he walked into their home a week ago, but when she stated it without apology one evening at dinner, it stirred something in him. Something he couldn't quite pinpoint. He knew his mother had a right to intimacy and affection like everyone else. His father certainly took care of his intimate requirements without restraint. But somehow the thought of his mother lying next to a man and doing the thing's Ocean loved to do with women who meant nothing to him, bothered him...a lot. And it didn't bother him because he didn't want his mother to have love. It bothered him because he wondered if Andrew Miller felt what Ocean felt when he fucked. Did Andrew Miller ever look at his mother and think what a tight pussy she had? Did he ever slap her ass and call her a sweet bitch? Did he laugh at how cute her legs looked when they stuck straight up in the air? Or how delightful her pussy smelled right after a shower? Or did Andrew Miller ever tell her how much he cared and then leave her and fuck another woman? Did Andrew Miller ever lie to his mother? Did Andrew Miller ever cheat on his mother? When he thought about his life, he knew he couldn't be his worst thoughts of Andrew Miller anymore. Because if every man was Ocean, then nobody had love.

***

Ocean's final farewell was ripe with melancholy. He hadn't seen much of his older brother, Barry, during his two weeks at home, but they embraced tightly at the airport. Everyone made time to see him off. Shana cried as she kissed his temple, promising to visit him in New York soon. He hugged and kissed his mother and his Aunt Mary for an extended time, before shaking Andrew Miller's hand and bear-hugging his three younger brothers.

When he boarded his plane his heart was heavy with love of home and yearning. But there was a certain satisfaction as he recalled a final dialogue with his mother. She had said, "At some point you have to face your emotions and yourself. So you've been with a lot of women; that doesn't mean you cannot find fulfillment from one woman. Maybe in your heart that's what you wanted all along, but with many women it was easier, you didn't have to get to know yourself and you didn't have to let these women know you. After all, no one who doesn't know you can ever have the ability to hurt you."

When his mother first spoke the words had bounced off him like so much Caribbean storm on a thatched roof. But while some words were initially deflected by the force of contact, some settled in making the interior moist, and sunk through to the ceiling and down the walls. Before hearing those words on that particular evening as he sat on their patio bench, it had never occurred to Ocean that there were benefits to having one woman instead of twenty. The numbers alone were illogical. It was simple: the more the merrier, the bigger the better. Maybe that was the problem; they were simply clichés which didn't address the void he'd been feeling for years. That night he admitted to his mother that he was lonely.

Ocean eyed the stewardess on flight, and for the first time began to wonder how people want to live. What's important? What do people seek to gain from their relationships with others? The stewardess was cute as hell... He wondered if she was in love with someone.

***

When Ocean got home, he cleared the usual messages on his answering machine: a few models he'd been screwing, Mona, Erikka, Jackie, Crystal, his father, Darryl... Shit!... He had almost forgotten Darryl was supposed to come over the following evening. Their relationship had developed over the past two years, and at the age of thirteen Darryl was coming along nicely—developing an appreciation for art and respect for hard work. Ocean had never imagined when he first took on his role as a "big brother," that it could be so satisfying. He had heard horror stories of "little brothers" who were unruly and beyond "repair," but even more about "big brothers" who didn't keep their commitment and dropped their protégées after a few months, because it wasn't exciting enough, or they found it too emotionally draining. They left behind young boys often abandoned by society, their parents, the educational system, and finally their "big brother." The damage was often irreparable.

Ocean called his father and agreed to dinner that week. His trip gave him a sense of the importance of family and he couldn't go on shutting his father out. Maybe it was time to tell his dad how he really felt.

***

"Hey, man, whassup?" Darryl asked slapping palms with Ocean as he entered his apartment the next night. "Yo, man. You got a phat crib!" Darryl's eyes widened as he took in the navy velour sofa, Oriental rug, wall unit and hard wood floors. Even more appealing to him were the large screen television, VCR and stereo system.

"Work hard and you can have nice things too. Hang out with little punk criminals and you'll end up in jail. A jail record is for life, you know. Then you can't have jack." Ocean eyed Darryl's face carefully. They had long talks in the past about the importance of keeping a clean slate. Young kids like Darryl often didn't realize building a rap sheet made it virtually impossible to get many of the city and state jobs that interested them later in life, or, to get any job for that matter.

"I know, I know. So what was it like going back home, man?" Darryl asked as he took a seat on the sofa. The laces in his high top sneakers were carefully unlaced, and cleaned with a toothbrush for hours the night before. He wore a navy warm-up suit and a white baseball cap turned backwards.

"Oh, it was great. It's real good to be with your family, you know?"

"Yeah," Darryl replied. He had never really experienced being away from his mother, so Ocean's words didn't mean much to him. His father didn't even cross his mind when Ocean said "family."

"You'd be surprised how much you miss family when they're not around."

"Yeah," Darryl hung his head slightly. His dad never was around. "Believe me, man, I know. It can be a real bitch sometimes. You know I never see my pops and shit."

Ocean eyed Darryl carefully. He put his hand on his shoulder. "Yeah, well, fuck'm. He doesn't know what he's missing. He's got a real cool kid."

Darryl smiled at Ocean. "Who you calling a kid, man?" He asked, playfully punching Ocean in the stomach. "Don't make me have to hurt you, boy!" He stood up and did a flighty bob and weave routine in the middle of the living room.

"Boooy!" Ocean stepped back. "Now I know you're not trying to step to this, you little scrub. I'll crush you like a grape." He let out a few playful jabs before quickly maneuvering Darryl into a sleeper hold.

"Uncle!" Darryl yelped, letting his body go limp.

Ocean let him go laughing. "You're all right, you know that, kid? You're getting kind of strong on me too. You keep messing around with those weights and you'll have girls chasing you for miles."

"You know I only see my girl, Maria."

Ocean rolled his eyes. *From the mouths of babes.* Was it him or was there a master conspiracy for him to settle down with one woman? The thing of it was, if it wasn't what he wanted he probably wouldn't even interpret Darryl's comment as some sort of sign. "Yeah, I know," Ocean mumbled. He grabbed a videocassette from the plastic bag they came in at the rental spot. "What do you want to see first: horror or action?"

"Action."

"Cool."

The two spent the evening watching videos until the early morning. Ocean hated it when evenings like this satisfied him more than slinging back beers and dancing with pretty women at a party. Something had to give.

***

"Eddie, you look wonderful!" Karen beamed. She wore a loose apricot dress with long sleeves that hid her still-round belly. She stepped back to allow Ocean to enter the dimly lit two-bedroom apartment. Ocean could smell the heavy scent of fried snapper and plantains as he slowly eyed the thickly carpeted living room. Karen's two boys, Nicholas and Ian, sat on the floor with a video game. Neville Ryder rose as his son entered the room.

"You're looking good Eddie. I'm glad you finally made it over." Neville patted his son on the back in a weak embrace.

"You look good too, Dad." Ocean smiled politely and shifted his weight to the other side of his body.

"Eddie, why don't you let me take that coat from you? Neville, get the boy a drink." Karen helped Ocean remove his warm-up jacket and hung it in the closet.

"What do you drink nowadays, Eddie?" his father asked.

"How about a rum and coke?" Ocean asked.

"Sounds right." Mr. Ryder headed toward the liquor caddy and fixed the drink for his son. While he was there, he refreshed his own drink. "Karen, how's your drink doing?"

"Oh, it's just fine," she responded winking at Ocean.

The three sat in the living room while Ocean relayed stories of his visit home. He made a point of mentioning Andrew Miller.

His father tried to contain his displeasure.

Ocean observed his father's reaction carefully. What was it that would make his father still want to think of his ex-wife as being alone? "Yeah, Mom seemed really happy with that man. And, the kids, they're all doing well. Tasha's beautiful. They're all in pretty steady relationships. They don't seem to be screwing around"

Neville Ryder laughed. "What it is and what it seems are very often two different things, my dear boy."

"You'd be surprised Dad, not everyone's a liar." Ocean's words fell coolly from his lips.

His father's eyebrows rose. "What are you trying to say, boy?"

"I'm just saying, not every man feels the need to cheat on his woman." Ocean raised his chin defiantly.

Karen turned flush. "I'm gonna go ahead and set the table for dinner." She rose quickly and left.

Mr. Ryder's eyes followed Karen out of the room, before quickly snapping his head around to confront Ocean. He lowered his voice to a near-whisper. "Look, Eddie, I don't know what the hell you think you're doing, but I didn't ask you to come over here to upset my woman. Do you understand that? I don't know what you're mother has you thinking, but there's no such thing as a faithful man. Men are dogs. Woof-woof!" He laughed. "Anything else is a compromise, and real men don't have to compromise for any goddamn body." He paused. "You see that woman in the kitchen working hard to cook up dinner for you and me. She's *my* woman and she does what *I* say. I care about her...she's my woman and she takes care of me. Shit, I might even say that I love her, but the thing in my pants is mine. It doesn't belong to her or anybody else. It belongs to me, and I can do what I goddamn well please with it." He paused. "Now, that doesn't mean that I want her to know about it, so *shut up already*. What are you trying to do, spoil a perfectly good meal?" Neville Ryder patted his son on the knee and laughed heartily. "Shit, you kids are something else."

Ocean threw back the drink he had, and then another, and then another. By the time he sat down to dinner he was feeling pleasant and comfortable. Karen's cooking was good and he enjoyed the meal. The conversation was kept to small talk about the goings on in the hospital where Karen worked as a nurse's aide and her kids' progress in school. Nicholas and Ian were getting big at thirteen and eleven and participated in the conversation with talk about sports and video games. Ocean talked about the potential of getting an exclusive contract with a major fragrance manufacturer and his relationship with Darryl. They had plans to go to a Knicks game together sometime that month.

After dinner, he got the opportunity to play with his three-year-old brother, David, before it became the child's bedtime. As he looked into his little brother's face, he was struck by the feeling that a great unfairness had been done to the boy. Didn't he have the right to a father who was committed to him and his family? Ocean didn't have that as a child, either, but at least his family was intact for a good deal of his youth. Oh, who was he kidding? It didn't matter. The baby had a mother and father who were together. They got along well enough. Karen's children were well-adjusted and seemed happy. Her ex-husband didn't take an interest in his sons, maybe because his new wife had a couple of sons for him too. So Karen's kids had additional siblings from a different mother. Just like Ocean had siblings from many different mothers in Abaco. Just like he had little David. It formed a big confusing circle. He supposed the complexities didn't matter. After all, a child was a child was a child. *What was the difference how a child's family was comprised?* Ocean immediately recognized the thought as a lie at the moment he conceived it. Maybe it didn't make a difference to anyone else, but he knew he wanted his children, *all his children* to live with him. And he wanted *all his children* to be fully related by the blood of both parents. He wanted *all his children* to be born of one woman's womb, to live under a single roof as a family— Ocean, his kids and his lover for life. God, he sounded like a woman. *Could he really be getting this corny at the age of twenty-four?* A part of him hated what he felt in his heart, it seemed to go against everything his father had ever taught him about relationships with women. But it seemed his father's choices were motivated more by machismo than real human need. Life is a journey, and Ocean didn't want to spend his travel trying to meet needs that didn't really exist. He didn't need a woman to boost his confidence or to make him feel male. He needed a woman to build a family.

***

The day after his dinner with his father, Ocean and Marc got together for drinks. It had been a long time since they touched base, and they met at one of Marc's regular hangouts. The place was full of beautiful caramel colored women, but there was one chocolate-colored sister with hair so short she was nearly bald, who kept eyeing him. Ocean made a mental note *not* to talk to her. He had too many women already. There was no point in complicating things, further.

"So, how's the job been treating you, man? I've been seeing your face around quite a bit." Marc looked pretty much the same as always, suited and bearded. He had recently taken a trip to the Caribbean so he looked darker than usual.

"The job's good. I can't complain. Money's fine. I've got a good savings going. I'll probably start looking into some investments."

"How's the ole love life?" Marc laughed, remembering the days of his and Eddie's jaunts through the city, looking for as many women as they could handle.

"Same stuff different day. You know. I still see Mona and Erikka." He was careful not to mention Jackie. Marc never knew they started screwing around right after the night Jackie started throwing herself at Marc. "So what's your story?" Ocean and Marc talked only a couple of times a year, and saw each other even less often. There were many things they didn't know about each other.

"Same girl. Shit, I've been seeing Melina for almost two years now. I think she might be the one, you know. She makes me want to give her my paycheck. Shit!"

Ocean looked at Marc stupidly. Love was one thing; passing over a paycheck was an entirely different experience. One he had no desire to have. "Well, I just hope she's worth it, if she's got you acting like that."

"Damn. I know she's worth it. I just love every goddamn thing about that woman." Marc smiled with the thought.

"Are you sure you didn't just let that girl whip that ass?" Ocean laughed. Marc was acting *real* strung out on the pussy. "What's she got, sparks flying out her shit?" Ocean asked jokingly. "Does the pussy come with a free ginsu knife set?" He couldn't help but laugh heartily at what he knew was an outrageously corny line of jokes.

Marc looked at him contemplatively. "Damn, Eddie, I guess the shit must have something hooking me, but fuck it. It feels good. You know, I wake up in the morning and she's there. I come home at night and she's there. It's nice. I never have to wonder who I'm gonna stick it in next!" Now Marc laughed heartily. He loved the girl, but

Eddie was his boy, and he had to laugh over being in love. If he didn't laugh he'd feel too out of control.

"So this love shit is really *all that?*" Ocean asked jealously.

"It's got its ups and downs like anything else. But for me for now it feels right." Marc popped a beer nut in his mouth.

After having a few drinks at the bar, Marc headed home. Ocean decided to hang around for awhile and watch the end of the game that was showing on the big screen TV. Before he knew what had happened the chocolate-colored girl was in his lap, then his bed.

***

When Ocean rolled over the next morning and saw Tamika sleeping beside him, he vowed never to have another one night stand.

Sophia Boyd
Spring 1991

Sophia laughed heartily with Sandy, and Timothy and Marcus giggled in unison as Sophia flipped the latch on the door of her downtown Manhattan apartment. Sandy was mimicking the antics of one of the circus clowns in such spectacular detail; the kids were going wild with laughter. It was after 5:00pm by the time they made it back to Sophia's Twelfth Street apartment—a small two-bedroom, but reasonably priced by Manhattan standards and very convenient.

Sophia and Sandy tossed their handbags on the sofa nearly simultaneously when they entered the small living room. "Ahhh, home, sweet home," Sophia sighed. She sat Marcus on her "new" antique sofa and removed his little blue sneakers. He and Timothy had been struggling to stay awake during the cab ride home, and she knew they'd probably both pass out once she got their clothes off. "So, you enjoyed your first circus, baby?" She cooed at her almost three-year-old son.

"Yup!" Marcus shuffled around restlessly, his eyes darting wildly around the room the way he sometimes did when he was fighting sleep. Sophia struggled to get his inattentive arms out of the bright green jacket he wore. He allowed his mother to distract him with the sight of his jacket being pulled off his arms, before continuing his conversation. "The clowns were the best... And the elephants... I liked them too!" By now Sophia was carrying him into the bedroom to get him into his pajamas. He still had a loose grip on the spinning souvenir penlight she had bought him earlier. By the time she got him out of his pants and sweatshirt, the penlight had fallen beside him on the Superman bed comforter, and he was fast asleep. She put him into his favorite pajamas, tucked him in and kissed him on the forehead.

Whenever one of her boys fell asleep, Sophia exhaled. She supposed it was the relief of making it through another day of mothering. She loved her boys, but it was this same love that took so much from her. They were stealing her heart every single day of their little lives, but they were too young to know it.

Sophia took the opportunity to gaze at her son's sleeping face. His hair was cut low and he looked adorable in his sleepwear. If only he looked this sweet and adorable all day long. Sometimes he drove her absolutely crazy! She brushed a forefinger along his temple. It was wonderful to see him on days like this when he was so excited and happy. Sometimes she was racked with guilt over Ron's death, as if it were her fault Ron killed himself. She often wondered if she hadn't been selfish when it came to him. She put her own needs before anyone else at the time, thinking about her own pride and well-being.

Sophia sat on the edge of her son's bed with her carefully scarved head in her hands. She felt that old feeling washing over her again, making her sick and dizzy. It had been over two years, but sometimes when she looked at her kids it hit her like yesterday. She had to keep reminding herself that it couldn't have been good for the children to see Ron hit her. She knew if she didn't leave him, it wouldn't have been the last time...and she knew if it wasn't the last time they would have divorced eventually...at least this way her kids had one *decent* parent...and all their dad's benefits. His life insurance policy had come in handy for all of them. That made her feel guilty too, but what could she do? She *did* have his kids, and she *was* his wife even if she *had* left him... Oh, who was she kidding? It *was* better this way. But how do your reconcile the guilt left by death? She could not argue with Ron anymore. She could not hate him or love him anymore. But as much as she could not interact with Ron, she couldn't just forget him either. Sophia rocked herself quietly, staring down at the way her winter white leggings tucked neatly inside her lace-up brown ankle boots. She felt the smart of her tears and tried to control her breathing. She knew she could get through this.

The kids would never have to know about the suicide... And, at least they wouldn't have to deal with *their* parents divorcing thirty years later.

She was telling herself what felt like a million different things. She knew she couldn't have helped Ron...but sometimes, it doesn't matter what you say to yourself when your pain is irrational, as pain often is.

***

"Where've you been?" Sandy asked nonchalantly when Sophia returned to the living room. "We thought you got lost back there!" she joked.

"Yeah, Ma!" Timothy chimed in. The two had been watching a Disney video while Sophia tucked Marcus in.

Sophia smiled halfheartedly. "Nothing, really, I was just putting the baby to bed."

"Marcus is not a baby!" Timothy offered haughtily.

"Oh, I'm *so* sorry," Sophia responded melodramatically. She raised her hand to her forehead as if saluting, and half-curtsied. Timothy was quickly satisfied and somewhat entertained by his mother's antics.

He smiled at her before returning his gaze to the movie he had been watching.

Sophia let out a quick sigh when her son turned away. Sometimes playing the happy mother role was tiresome, at best.

Sandy sensed her friend's displeasure. "How about finding a snack?" she suggested. Leaving Timothy alone on the tapestry sofa they had shared, she rose abruptly, straightened her crumpled blue jeans and walked around the corner toward the kitchen. "We've still got brie..." Sandy commented softly as she pulled the cheese from the refrigerator.

"Sandy, sometimes I think I'm going crazy," Sophia began; her voice was low and controlled. Her elbows rested wearily on the small, scuffed oak table in her modest eat-in kitchen. "I can't stop dreaming about Ron, and just now, I swear I got dizzy thinking about him. She felt the urge to lose control coming on, so she glanced quickly around the wall which separated the kitchen from the living room. Thankfully, Timothy was entirely engrossed in his movie. "I've been seriously considering going into therapy. I'm just at my wit's end, I guess. I feel guilty half the time, and the other half I can't get a decent night's sleep because I keep seeing Ron's face."

Sandy put a plate with brie and crackers in front of Sophia. "I think I'm gonna open the bottle of Chablis in the fridge. You want some?"

"Do I *ever!*"Sophia responded enthusiastically. A glass of wine was just what she needed! She picked up a cheese-smeared cracker and ate it heartily; she was already beginning to feel the dark cloud of her own self-pity beginning to clear. Sandy poured two glasses and handed one to Sophia. "So do you have any idea who you want to see?"

Sophia's eyes suddenly dropped, and she found herself

examining the little nicks and scratches in the rustic table. "I'm not even sure I want to go, let alone to whom. I mean, I'm *okay*. It's not like I can't handle this." She smiled and sipped her wine nervously.

Sandy gave her a reassuring smile. "You know, Sophie, there's nothing wrong with asking for help when you need it. It's the courageous thing to do. It's probably the harder thing to do. I mean, it's easy to sit back and say everything's fine while your life falls apart." She softened her voice before continuing, "If you're having nightmares, you really should talk to someone. It's nothing to be ashamed of."

"I don't know, Sandy. It's hard for me to justify spending money to talk to someone when I know I haven't done anything wrong. I don't *owe* Ron anything. It's almost like he's coming to get me from the grave..." Her voice cracked slightly when she said the word *grave*.

"Look, Sophie, you can lie to me all you want, but don't lie to yourself and try to convince me it's true. I know this thing has been bothering you for years, and you've been doing a great job handling it... I mean, I tip my hat to you Sophie. You've been through more than anyone should have to. With two young kids and an abusive husband, your parents' split, the suicide, our relationship... I know you've had a lot of things to work out." Sandy drained her wine glass. "Just don't sit there and try to tell me it's the money, when you and I both know that's not true. It's just pride."

Sophia gave Sandy an annoyed glance.

Sandy smiled. "Sophie, I love you to death, but you *know* I'm right." She smiled again, hoping to change Sophie's mood.

Sophia furrowed her brows and frowned. She adjusted the cotton scarf which was scrupulously wrapped around her head. "Could you pour me some more wine?" she asked. As Sandy poured the wine, Sophia adjusted the long beige V-neck sweater she wore over her leggings.

"Look, Sophie, why don't we start from the beginning. I asked if you had any idea what therapist you wanted to use."

"Just forget about it, Sandy. I know you only want to help, but I think I need to work through this on my own. I'm not ready to sit on a couch and tell some white man all my problems."

"Is that what's bothering you? You can get a black therapist. That's easy enough to do."

"It's not only that. I just can't see myself blabbing about my personal life to a complete stranger." She looked pleadingly at Sandy, "I guess I'm just not ready, that's all. It just scares me; sometimes I feel so out of control." Sophia leaned back in her chair, setting her eyes on the white painted ceiling.

"Look," Sandy said, gently resting a hand on Sophia's shoulder, "I love you, and you know there's nothing I wouldn't do for you...but, this thing with Ron is just something you have to figure out for yourself. I can't tell you what to do. You know this thing is bothering you more than you're saying, and you know the only thing between you and a good therapist is a little research and some old-fashioned feelings of pride. I just don't want you to wait until the burden is too much for you to bear."

Sophia looked into her pretty brown eyes, as Sandy bent over and kissed her on the lips. She closed her eyes and felt the moistness of her tears around their rims. She pushed her hands into the coarse curliness of Sandy's low-cut hair as their mouths joined, gently probing in a long kiss. "Uhmm…" Sophia moved from the table, "Let me check on Timothy." When she looked into the next room, she saw that Timothy had fallen asleep on the couch. "He's sleeping," she informed Sandy.

"Why don't you just sit down and relax," Sandy said as she refilled their wine glasses. "I'll go put him to bed." She flashed Sophie a knowing glance as she left the kitchen.

Sophia relaxed in the high-backed wood chair. She had purchased her entire kitchen set for two hundred dollars at a garage sale two years earlier, around the time she first moved into the apartment. The family she bought it from considered it old and ugly, but she loved the rough, beaten wood and old-fashioned styling of it. She had always liked old things, but her interest in them seemed to pique after Ron's death.

"Well, Timothy's all tucked in." Sandy beamed as she returned to the kitchen. "Why don't we sit out in the living room for awhile?" She picked up the plate which held a few remaining crackers and headed toward the living room. "Let's see what's on..." she began as she got comfortable on the sofa with the TV remote in hand, but Sophia sat next to her and quickly cradled her face into a kiss. "Hey," Sandy protested lightly.

Sophia smiled. "Who said I wanted to watch TV?" she asked provocatively. She took Sandy's hand in hers and led her into her bedroom. She switched the dimmer on the ceiling light, casting a soft white hue on the gray silk comforter which covered her bed. "Come here," she whispered as she pulled Sandy onto the bed with her, fully dressed. She ran her fingers along the smooth brown skin of Sandy's face and kissed her cheeks and lips longingly, while her hands massaged Sandy's body through her clothing.

Sandy moaned softly under her touch. She reached behind Sophia's head and pulled at the ties of her head wrap, releasing Sophia's soft, relaxed hair. She ran her fingers through the velvety, brown strands as she returned her kisses leisurely.

Sophia slowly unbuttoned Sandy's white cotton shirt and unhooked the front snap on her bra, releasing her full breasts. She massaged them thoroughly with her hands and bent her head to kiss them, lingering in the scent of Sandy's perfume. As she kissed Sandy's body, she felt Sandy tugging at the simple V-neck sweater she wore. Sophia sat up briefly on the soft cover of the bed while Sandy pulled the sweater over her head and removed her bra. Sophia removed her shoes and wiggled out of her leggings while Sandy slipped out of her jeans. She knelt on the bed allowing her eyes to absorb Sandy in nothing but a pink bikini panty against her chocolate brown skin. Sandy really was a cutie: smooth brown skin, a perky exquisitely moled nose, big dimples and an awesome smile. Sophia saw why women found her to be very sexy. Sometimes when Sophia looked at Sandy naked, she could hardly believe there was a time when they were strictly platonic friends, and Sophia had never 'been' with a woman.

Sandy moved toward Sophia on the bed, finally covering Sophia's nearly bare body with her own. She ran her hands through Sophia's shiny brown hair and then along her face, neck and breasts. Sophia's skin was a pearly ivory, and Sandy enjoyed watching the contrast of their complexions when they made love. She watched her own hands kneading Sophia's breasts, finally stroking her pale pink nipples before caressing them with her mouth and tongue.

Sophia rocked her body under Sandy's touch as she reached inside Sandy's pink panties to feel her slippery wetness.

Sandy moved her head from Sophia's swollen breasts to her face and began kissing her again. She pinned Sophia's body under her and pulled at the black panty she wore, which was now a dripping testament to Sophie's excitement. Finally, she removed Sophie's panty and nestled her head between the other woman's legs. She licked at her with the ease of the familiar, while Sophia moaned her approval.

Once Sandy knew Sophia 'came,' she moved her own body into position over Sophie's mouth, while she rested her head on Sophie's thigh. Sophia suckled her girlfriend enthusiastically as she penetrated Sandy with her fingers, until Sandy climaxed in a sweaty heap.

They held each other and rested before bringing each other to orgasm over and over again throughout the night.

***

The early April sun flickered softly through the sheer white curtains in Sophia's living room, giving her plants the energy they seemed to have been deprived of during the long, cold winter. It was nearly 11:00am on Sunday, and the kids had been up playing with miniature racing cars and building blocks for the past couple of hours. They had already had bowls of their favorite cold cereals for breakfast. Sophia and Sandy sat at the kitchen table, rifling through sections of the *Village Voice* and Sunday *Times.*

"So, what are you going to do today?" Sandy asked as she perused the *Times'* Arts and Leisure section.

"I don't know. I have some work I really want to catch up on, but it's such a beautiful day, I'm tempted to take the kids out for a little while."

"It's still too cold for the park, you know. It's barely sixty degrees out there. Now's a perfect time for them to get sick."

"I know. But, maybe just a walk or something I wouldn't keep them out for too long." Sophia took a sip from her coffee mug. "Are you going to come with us?"

she asked just as her telephone rang. "Hello?" she asked.

"Hi, baby, how are you?" her mother responded.

"Oh, hi mom!" Sophia replied enthusiastically. It was always good to hear from her mother, partly because she was so far away that she missed her most of the time, but also because she felt more needed since her parents' split. She hadn't spoken to her father in nearly two years, and it seemed that during that time her relationship with her mother deepened. She couldn't forgive her father and neither could her mother, so they had more in common than they used to. "So how's Denni and Marri," Sophia asked her mother referring to her two sisters.

"Oh, they're good. Both have some new men, you know." Her mother added disdainfully. "You're still not seeing anyone yourself, huh?" Her mother asked, knowing full well her daughter's answer and triumphing in the question alone.

"Nah, after Ron, I've decided to stay alone. I can't deal with being in another relationship with a man right now." She smiled at Sandy, who sat across from her at the kitchen table.

"That's good, dear, sometimes they're just more trouble than they're worth."

"I know," Sophia responded. "So have you spoken to my father lately?" she asked. As part of her schism from her father, she stopped calling him 'dad.'

"No. You know I'm not bothering with that man anymore."

"Good. It's not worth the trouble," Sophia agreed mindlessly.

"I know."

The conversation continued with tidbits of daily activities. Sophia told her mother how well her children's clothing line was going. Her company had purchased some of Sandy's artwork for Sophia's children's wear line and Sandy's home mural business was doing well with an upscale, mostly white clientele.

"Now let me speak to my grandbabies!" her mother asked affectionately but firmly, the way mothers often do.

Sophia put the boys on the phone one at a time to talk to Beverly Brown, the former Mrs. Boyd. Marcus couldn't remember his grandfather, but Timothy giddily asked for "grandpa." Sophia couldn't hear her mother's response, but she saw Timothy's expression quickly change from happiness to hurt. "Okay, now. You've talked to your grandma enough," she said, quickly grabbing the phone from her son. How dare her mother hurt his feelings! He was only a child! Sophia's voice was stern when she put the receiver back to her own ear. She made sure the kids were out of earshot before she spoke. "Mom, what did you say to Timothy?" She tried to quell her anger. She didn't care who was whose mother; she didn't stand for anybody upsetting her kids.

"I just told that child his grandfather doesn't exist anymore," Beverly Brown replied with disgust.

"Mom, you said *what?!*"

"You heard what I said. I don't want to deal with that man, and I don't want my grandsons dealing with him either. He's as good as dead to us!"

Sophia could not believe her ears! "Mom, what *are* you talking about?! I know you're not keeping much contact with my father, but how can you tell my son something that terrible?"

"What's so terrible about it? I didn't say the man fell off a roof or anything. I just said he doesn't exist anymore. The kids should forget about him."

Sophia stared at Sandy incredulously. *Was this shit real?* It *was* her mother, though. What could she do? She relaxed her tone of voice. "Well, Mom, I guess you're right," she stated knowing full well the next time her mother spoke to her kids would only be if they spoke in person.

When Sophia hung up she was overcome by a sense of disillusionment and loss, She had hoped that at least one positive thing could come from her parents' divorce. That thing was supposed to have been a newfound relationship between herself and her mother. Now, it seemed even that was impossible.

***

Sophia and Sandy took the kids to a matinee at a nearby theater. After the show, Sandy went home to her Brooklyn apartment and Sophia returned to her apartment to work on a couple of designs for work the following day. She was able to work steadily for a few hours before her telephone rang. She decided to screen the call.

"Hi, sweetie, it's your dad," the slightly southern-sounding voice on the answering machine declared. Sophia looked at the contraption on her bed stand with disbelief. She hadn't gotten a call from her father in months! She had an unlisted number to avoid his calls, but her sister Marion gave her father the number more than once. She screamed at Marion and changed her number every time, but it was getting ridiculous. The message continued, "I hope you're not still mad at me. I told you I'd keep calling whether you call me back or not, so here I am again... Well, if you're not going to answer or if you're not home, I'm going to leave my number for you. I'm in Florida now. You can reach me at three-oh-five-seven-three-nine-nine-five-five-oh. It's been a long time, Sophie, maybe it's time to forgive your Dad."

Sophie stared angrily at the answering machine for a moment before rewinding the tape and getting back to her work. She had a big presentation at work the following day, and she wanted to make sure everything went smoothly.

***

"Ohhh, baby" a young, dark-skinned man commented as Sophia walked the blocks to the subway. His eyes darted from her breasts to her legs, back to her breasts and finally to her face in one slow ogle.

Sophia gave him an annoyed glance.

"What's the matter baby?" the man asked as he walked in her pace. "Don't you like men?"

Sophia didn't respond, but picked up her pace as she headed for the subway stairs.

The man let her go on, but not without commenting, "Fucking dyke bitch!"

When Sophia reached the subway platform she was flush with anger and humiliation. How dare that asshole say that to her! It wasn't the first time a man had made an off-color remark to her on the street, but no one had ever called her a dyke before! Did this mean she looked like one now? She enjoyed her relationship with Sandy, and was happier than she had been in years, but she wasn't always sure she *wanted* to be a lesbian. She folded her arms across her chest as she waited for the train. No one but Sandy knew she was in a relationship with Sandy. When that stranger said what he said, she felt as if he was looking straight through her. *Were there signs?* Her mind raced... *Could people tell she made love to a woman?*

A good-looking man smiled at her. She turned away. She didn't want to have to deal with people right now. Shit, it was Monday morning and she had to start the week off this way! Well, she'd have to just focus on her presentation. She was developing a mass market extension to her children's clothing line which could really reach a lot of consumers if it was well-received by Joe and his superiors. She'd just have to keep her cool.

Her train pulled into the station and she boarded.

***

When she arrived at her office, she smiled the usual hellos to her co-workers as she walked through the halls to her office. Aubrey Clifford, an attractive young administrative assistant at the firm, stopped her in the corridor. "Good luck on your presentation today, Sophia!" The woman grabbed her hand and held it briefly. "I hope you get the new assignment!" she exclaimed, tossing her carefully weaved hairdo.

Sophia smiled back at her. "Thanks," she said. Aubrey and she had gone to lunch a few times in the past, but they were far from chums.

Aubrey held her hand for a few more moments. "That suit looks fabulous on you," she said, referring to the V-necked apricot peplum suit jacket and straight skirt Sophia wore.

"Thanks," Sophia replied. She was beginning to feel a little uncomfortable.

"We've *got* to get together soon. Maybe we can go for dinner after work one day." Aubrey smiled excitedly. "Look, talk to you later," she said quickly glancing around before kissing Sophia's cheek and returning to her desk.

Sophia was surprised and quite uncomfortable. Either it was her imagination or Aubrey lingered on her cheek longer than necessary. Not that she could vouch for the appropriateness of a kiss on the cheek between female co-workers, anyway. Suddenly, it hit her... Aubrey *knew*. Just like the man on the street *knew*. There must be something about her today that gave her away. She went into the ladies' room to check herself. Her hair looked straight. Her suit looked straight. What could it be? Was there some sort of subtle sign which let people know she was living as a lesbian? The crazy part about it was she didn't feel like a lesbian. She loved Sandy, and enjoyed their relationship, but she really didn't *feel* gay. But, then again, she didn't quite know what she thought gay was supposed to feel like. She stared into the bathroom mirror, but there seemed to be nothing different. Then, it occurred to her, maybe she didn't *look* different...maybe she just *was* different since she began the relationship with Sandy. The thought made her feel queasy. After all, what happened in her own home was her own business. She didn't want people to know.

***

Sophia finished her presentation before the dozen or so decision-makers in her company with a feeling of nervous anxiety. She wasn't sure it went very well. The responses she got to her ideas were hard to determine, and she knew after a hectic morning she wasn't up to her usual speed. Her boss simply thanked her for the presentation and told her he'd get back to her in the afternoon. It was now past three and she was becoming a basket case. It just seemed too many things had happened in the past few days: the stupid remark from her mother, her father's call, the conversation about therapy with Sandy, then that asshole this morning and Aubrey's creepy behavior. All that combined with her presentation and the fact that it was still only Monday, was more than she wanted to handle. She could barely get any work done. Finally she saw her boss heading toward her office.

"Sophia," Joe stated simply as he entered her office, closing the door behind him.

"So, how did it go, Joe?" Sophia asked.

Joe seemed surprised at her question. His voice was suddenly patronizing, "You were there, Sophia, you know there's no way we can use what you put together."

Sophia felt her face turn flush. "What do you mean?" she asked innocently.

Joe gave her a strange look "You practically lost it in there," he stated calmly as if trying to talk sense to a jumper on a window ledge. "Do you remember?" he asked.

Sophia chose her words carefully. "I know I wasn't up to speed today," she offered.

"Yes, that's true, but you snapped at our senior executives, Sophia. We just can't have that kind of behavior. You know I'm normally your staunchest supporter, but I wasn't happy with the designs you presented, either." He paused before asking, "Is everything okay with you?"

Sophia was beginning to feel the urge to cry. She had to keep it together at least until her boss left her office. Her face was hot and she felt her palms dampen with perspiration. "I think so," she mumbled ashamedly.

"Look, Sophia, why don't you take some time off? I checked with Human Resources, and it seems you have plenty of unused vacation time." He paused slowly, giving her time to absorb his words. "Take a week or two. Get away for awhile. It's obvious something's bothering you." Joe frowned at her partly with disappointment, and partly with concern.

"Really, it's not necessary..." Sophia began.

"Look, Sophia, just do it. I don't want to see you here for at least a week." Joe's words were conclusive, and he stood up from the chair in Sophia's office and quickly left.

***

"Well, look who finally made the time to visit her old mother!" Beverly Brown gushed when Sophia and the children arrived at the house with her two younger daughters, Denise and Marion.

"Hi, mom! It's good to see you!" After the disaster at work and her resultant feelings of inadequacy, Sophia *was* happy to be back at her mother's house in Jackson, Mississippi.

The last two times she had been home were hellish. Immediately after her marriage she visited with Ron and Timothy. Ron couldn't get along with anybody in her family, and her mother and father fought the whole time. It was the first time she realized her parent's marriage was heading down the tubes.

The next time was immediately after Ron's suicide. It had been a particularly difficult time for Sophia, partly because she never told her mother what happened with Ron. She let her think their marriage had been fine, and Ron died in the line of duty. It was easier than trying to explain the physical abuse and suicide at a time when her mother was mourning her own loss. Sophia had planned to grieve with family while helping to console her mother in her loss of a husband, but she just ended up feeling used. It seemed no one was available to console her in her loss of both a father *and* a husband, and she had vowed never to come back. But, that was over two years ago, and there was something about home that made you return even when you didn't want to. Something about roots and blood and family that served as a salve, even if the salve was sometimes delivered with a heavy hand. Sophia had felt the need to come home, so she asked Sandy to water her plants, and she left New York for a week. She loved her mother, but she wasn't stupid enough to plan a trip home for longer than that. She planned to take a second week off to stay in her apartment and relax for a change. Just sleep late and watch soap operas. Maybe she'd be able to return to work refreshed. She knew it would be a challenge to win back Joe's respect. The scary part was that she honestly couldn't remember what transpired in that damned meeting.

Her mother looked at her grandchildren. "So how did my babies like the trip on the big airplane?"

Timothy and Marcus expressed their delight with the plane ride. It had been a first for both of them. Because, although Timothy had travelled when he was a child, he couldn't remember it, and when Sophia came down after Ron's funeral, she had left the children with her Aunt Tyra.

Sophia quickly got settled into her mother's two-story home on their quiet block in Jackson. It seemed there were a lot of improvements on the house since the last time she had been there, and Sophia couldn't help but wonder if her father's divorce settlement paid for all the enhancements: new doorknobs and windows, a skylight over the patio, a new kitchen floor. She knew her father hadn't fought for much in the settlement. It seemed he just wanted out, no matter what the cost. His years in the state assembly, teaching at a local college and a host of business investments had garnered for the family a comfortable nest egg. Sophia couldn't argue with the fact that he had always been a good provider. And, as much as she hated to admit it, up until the separation, he had always been a good father.

***

Denise and Marion sat on the floral canopy bed in the guest room while Sophia packed the clothes she brought into the dresser drawers. She had never been close to her sisters growing up. Partly because they were so much younger than her: Denise was about five years younger at twenty-six and Marion was only twenty-four! With only months between her and her thirty-first birthday, Sophia felt a huge gap in their ages.

"So what are you gonna do tonight, Sophie?!" Marion asked excitedly with a slight southern lilt. "Do you mind if I smoke in your room?" Marion was as light-skinned as Sophia, with long honey-blonde hair, full lips and hazel eyes.

Sophia sighed. *"Please,* Marri. Don't smoke in my room. I've got to sleep here. You shouldn't be smoking anyway." Marion rolled her eyes at Denise while Sophia's back was turned. "You still didn't answer the question, you know. What are you doing tonight?"

"I don't know. I'm a guest. What do you want to do?"

"I was just thinking we could get the guys, go to a bar or something. Maybe we can find you a nice southern man!" Marion laughed, and Denise joined in. They both thought it odd that two years after Ron's death they hadn't heard any news of Sophia's love life. "Are you dating anyone in New York?" Marion asked.

"No, I'm not." Sophia grimaced. She had been home only a couple of hours, and she was already tired of hearing her sister's stupid accents.

"Why not?" Denise asked. She was quite a bit darker than. Sophia and Marion, with caramel skin and dark hair.

"I'm not ready."

"Shit, Sophie, you're saying you haven't had nookie in two years?!" Denise half-asked, half-stated. She and Marion exchanged glances and laughed.

Sophia was quickly beginning to wonder if she had made the wrong decision in visiting. She felt as if she had two strangers in her room. Or maybe, it was she who was the stranger. "Look, I didn't come down here to discuss *nookie* with you two." She frowned at her sisters. *Was she really related to these cold, mindless bimbos?*

"So-orry" Marion whined dramatically. "Come on, Denni, let's go call our *men.*" With that, the two left the room.

Sophia closed the door behind them and locked it. She threw her body on the bed trying to remember why she decided to come back home. It seemed she couldn't come up with anything. Then it finally occurred to her...the little brats were probably just *jealous!* After all, they were both still in Jackson working low-paying jobs. Denise was manager of one of the local convenience stores, and Marion worked as a receptionist at one of the cheaper hotels. From what her mother said, Denise was engaged to a carpenter from the outskirts of town with no wedding date in sight, and Marion just slept with whoever bought her dinner on any particular night. But no matter how she rationalized it, their behavior hurt her. She thought after not seeing her for years, and knowing all she's been through with the loss of her husband and raising two children, they would have some sympathy for her. She didn't realize that Denise and Marion would have sold their right arms for what she had: a job she loved that paid her well, her own apartment in Manhattan, two healthy children and a husband, even if he *was* dead.

***

Sophia leaned over the bed in the guest room, carefully packing the children's clothes for their flight the next day. The week passed slowly and painfully. Each day when she rose, she tried to remember what solace she thought she'd obtain by coming back home. And, each day she couldn't remember. The kids were enjoying the yard, but that was about all the pleasure she got out of the place. It was boring, and the people in the house were all miserable.

Her mother spent most of her time badmouthing Denise and Marion behind their backs and then smiling in their faces. It made Sophia wonder what she said about *her* when *she* left a room. And, of course a lot of time was spent badmouthing her father and men, in general. Denise and Marion just giggled mindlessly between romps with their boyfriends and excursions to the local bars. Sophia had no desire to discuss her problems with anyone in the house. It seemed they were all worse off than she was.

By the end of the week, Sophia was anxious to get back to *her* home. Maybe *that* was why she went back to Mississippi...to realize that this wasn't her home anymore and to rediscover how wonderful her life is in comparison! She enjoyed her job, her children and her relationship with Sandy. She enjoyed living in a city where she could pick which museum she felt like taking the kids to, visit the planetarium or the botanical gardens and see a Broadway play whenever she felt like kicking out the money. She liked having her choice of haute cuisine from around the world at her fingertips, and all deliverable! Sophia smiled as she packed for her flight the following morning. She couldn't wait to see Sandy.

***

When Sophia's plane landed at LaGuardia Airport in Queens, NY, the kids were exhausted, but she felt surprisingly renewed. The week with her mother was long and boring, but in a way it seemed to be what she needed to appreciate her own life.

Sandy drove her mother's car to pick up Sophia and the kids. "Hey, how are you doing?" she asked, giving her girlfriend a hug when she met up with her in the baggage claim area "Oh, look at my babies!" she exclaimed, taking a half-asleep Marcus from Sophia's arms, and kissing Timothy's cheek. "How'd did it go?" she asked a serene-looking Sophia.

Sophia smiled. "Not bad, after all… I'll tell you about it later."

***

When Sophia got back home, the kids seemed to get a new burst of energy and ran around the house playing for a couple of hours before calming down. Sophia unpacked, and Sandy made a pitcher of margaritas. It was wonderful to be back in her small, quirky apartment.

Sandy sat on the silk comforter which covered Sophia's four-poster bed, sipping her drink." Ohhh, this is *goood*. I haven't had a margarita in *ages.* Today is pretty special, though, huh?" Sandy placed her glass on Sophia's bed stand.

"Yeah it is." Sophia smiled as she tossed worn clothes into the wicker hamper in her bedroom.

"So, tell me about the trip."

"You know my mom. Same ole shit. She's a pain in the ass and so are my sisters. The week was long and boring."

Sandy looked shocked. "So then why do you seem so happy?" she asked.

"Because I don't live with them," Sophia replied matter-of-factly. She peered out her bedroom door briefly before moving towards Sandy for a kiss. She touched her hair and neck as she kissed her gently, and smiled before continuing, "Now I know what's important to me, and it's not in Jackson."

Sandy smiled. Maybe Sophia was really beginning to

come into herself with their relationship. "So how are you feeling about Ron and all that stuff? Did you have nightmares?"

Sophia's facial expression froze for a moment, before she could compose herself and respond. "Yeah, actually I did, but I've decided I'm going to find a therapist. What the hell?" She sighed. "I wish I could work through this thing on my own, but the dreaming thing's got to stop. That must mean my subconscious is really working overtime." She paused briefly to look directly into Sandy's eyes. "And, what you said was right all along. It was never a money issue...it was a pride issue. Besides, after what happened at work, I know something has to give. I think Joe will appreciate my decision also."

"Yeah," Sandy agreed, nodding her head.

"If I were to go back to work with nothing to offer...you know, with no change, I think Joe would just be waiting for me to have a nervous breakdown or something." Sophia smiled. "I really couldn't even blame him. I must have been really obnoxious for him to respond to me like that. I mean we've been working together for a long time now."

"Well, at least you know they can't let you go without releasing your line."

"Oh, they would never let me go over this one thing. I've been there too long. It would take more time than this. Plus, I do have a contract."

"Well, you can always do home murals with me."

"Yeah, sure!" Sophia laughed.

Sandy looked serious. "It's good that you feel so secure."

Sophia smiled and whispered in her ear, "It's good that I have you." She kissed Sandy on the forehead as Timothy looked on from the doorway.

Aura Olivier
Spring 1992

Aura tilted her head to the side, occasionally stealing glances out of her office window as her co-worker spoke. She was interested, disgusted and annoyed all at once. She didn't exactly know what to do with the combination of humiliation, outrage and sense of victimization the Rodney King verdict left her with. Yesterday she was doing all right. Today she was feeling oppressed. She hated it.

"I just can't *believe* the decision in LA.! I mean, I'm just so *totally* shocked! It *really* makes me understand more, you know?" The comments came from Todd, her tall, blonde, recently 'outed' co-worker. She always thought Todd was gay, and he finally began admitting it after WBG Advertising circulated a compliance memo to NYC's gay rights law.

Todd was *not* the person Aura wanted to vent with. "Yeah, Todd. It really disgusts me too. Listen, though... I've got work to do." Her tone was curt as she reached for papers on her desk.

Todd looked offended and somewhat hurt as he apologized for interrupting, backed out of her office and continued his journey down the hallway. Aura watched as he stopped at one of the black secretary's desks to express his outrage. The woman, Linda, appreciated his remarks and kept him in conversation for a good ten minutes. Aura could hear the occasional curse words as they were uttered. It was stressful and distracting, but she did not want to close her office door, partly because she hated the stuffiness when it was closed, and partly because she wanted to hear what was said.

When the telephone rang, she appreciated the interruption. "Aura Olivier speaking," she stated.

"Hey, baby, what's up? How you feelin'?" a man's voice greeted.

"Baby, how are *you* feeling?" Aura asked sincerely. If the Rodney King verdict hit her hard, she could only imagine how violated it made black men feel. "This thing's dragging my day way down. Did you hear about all the rumors of riots in New York?" Aura crossed her arms and legs and shifted in her chair in frustration.

"I just hope they stay rumors..." his voice trailed off pensively.

"Yeah." Aura paused to think about the potential for riots reaching all the way to New York.

"Why don't you let me pick you up from work today? Make sure you get home safe."

"Sure, Kenny, whose home?"

"Hey, your place or mine, baby?" Kenny laughed at his use of a tired old pick-up line.

"Ha, ha, ha," Aura replied drolly. Then she laughed for real, tossing her long curly hair. "Yeah, baby come get me. We can hang out at my place tonight. I don't want to go out." They had made dinner plans earlier in the week, but with all the talk of riots and Aura's feelings of disgust, anxiety and disillusionment, she figured they'd be better off indoors for the night and in the company of friends.

"You mean we have to hang out with Dana?" Kenny asked. He would have preferred to have Aura to himself for the evening.

"What's wrong with Dana?" Aura asked, quickly

jumping to her best friend's defense. They were roommates in a Brooklyn Heights apartment for the past six months. Aura continued her thought, "Besides, I don't even know if Dana will be home tonight. I'll give her a call."

"You know I'm only kidding, baby. I like Dana. Is she still seeing your brother?"

"I don't know what's going on with those two. They never mention each other, and whenever I ask Ace, he just changes the subject. It's probably better that way, anyway. No stress." Aura admired the picture collage on her desk; included were photos of her parents kissing on New Year's Eve, Angie and Ace's college graduations, and Dana and her on vacation together in Miami. She and Dana had known each other for practically their entire lives.

"Well, I'll come get you at about five-thirty. Is that cool?"

"Yeah, perfect." Aura smiled. "Listen, I'm behind in work like you wouldn't believe, but you did put a smile on my face... Thanks."

"I have better ways to put a smile on your face," Kenny added provocatively.

"I bet you do," Aura laughed. "Look, I'll talk to you later. I've got work to do; I've got a job, baby!" she referenced Vanessa Williams' hit record.

"All right, babe."

"Bye." Aura hung up. Kenny was a real gem, but sometimes she felt much more like a friend than a lover.

***

"Mahogany Publishing, Dana Carlton speaking." Dana pushed a pencil behind her ear and rolled her eyes as she answered the phone. It was nearly 4:00pm, and the day had been particularly hectic.

"What's uuup?!" Aura greeted.

"Hey, girrrl," Dana responded, then added, her voice lowered, "Your voice is like music to my ears, girl. You just don't *know* what kind of day I've been having... I meant to call you earlier. I hope you're not going out tonight 'cause I have a friend I want you to meet." Dana's words streamed out rapidly.

"Oh, really?" Aura's curiosity was definitely piqued. "What *kind* of friend?"

"A really good friend. You'll really like him. So what's the plan, anyway? Can we order in dinner or do you want to cook?"

"I know I'm not cooking tonight. If you want to cook, I'll supervise!" Aura laughed.

"Well, I guess we're calling in some Chinese then, huh? Or maybe Thai? Italian?"

"Whatever... you know I eat *everything*. It doesn't matter to me," Aura replied.

"Girl, don't run around tellin' people you eat *everything*. That's just *rude*" Dana chuckled.

"Hey, you know what I mean!"

"Yeah, I *do* know what you mean... That's the *problem!*"Dana laughed heartily. She knew Aura's appetite for all things oral was pretty serious. "But listen, on a real tip, I'll ask my friend what he'd prefer and we can just vote or something later."

"Sounds good to me. I can't wait to meet this guy. He must be pretty special."

"He's awesome."

"Great. So, I'll talk to you later. Peace."

"Cool." Dana hung up the phone and grinned at the half-carat solitaire on her left hand.

***

When Aura and Kenny arrived at the apartment, Dana was already home. The three exchanged their hellos as Aura and Kenny removed their jackets.

"So, is he *here?*" Aura asked looking around the mid-sized living room which the two of them kept decorated strictly in black and white. Dana was sprawled on their black gingham sofa wearing black jeans and a yellow T-shirt, with the TV remote in her hand. "How long have you been home?" Aura asked, wondering how Dana could look so comfortable when they traveled just about the same distance from midtown Manhattan.

"Oh, about half an hour, and *no* he's not here yet. He'll be here soon." Dana twisted the bottom of her T-shirt in her hands, toying with the idea of removing her ring, but finally deciding she was unwilling to do so.

"Okay, well, I'm gonna change." Aura walked with Kenny into one of the back bedrooms. They both found jeans and comfortable tops, and returned from the room feeling more relaxed. "Ugh," Aura moaned as she threw her body onto a black bean bag. Kenny sat in the white one next to her. A large rubber plant sprawled from a black and white painted ceramic pot behind them. "So what are we gonna eat?" Aura asked.

Dana smiled and twisted her body on the sofa; she was lying flat on her stomach. "My friend's bringing food," she said mysteriously.

Aura scrutinized Dana. From where she was sitting she could see only part of her face, so she stood up and walked over to the end of the couch where Dana's head was nestled into a pillow. She sat on the checkered black and white tile floor and eyed her friend suspiciously.

Dana quickly squeezed her eyes shut and released them when she met Aura's gaze. She smiled anxiously. *"Whaaat?"* she asked, pulling the throw pillow into her chest, her hands carefully hidden underneath.

"You're acting funny..." Aura began examining Dana from head to toe. She wore a loose-fitting pale yellow oversized T-shirt over black stretch jeans. It certainly wasn't her clothes that were weird. Her hair was the same micro-braided bob she'd been sporting for the past year. Aura frowned. "You're acting like you're hiding something. Come clean, girl!"

"What are you talking about Aura? There's nothing strange about me."

"So, sit up, then. Why are you lying down like that? It's only six."

"Okay, but promise you'll stop bugging me!" Dana whined melodramatically as she repositioned her body on the sofa, taking care to keep her hands tucked under her T-shirt.

"What's with the hands in the T-shirt?" Aura asked suspiciously, reaching for Dana's covered hands.

As Dana began to protest, the apartment buzzer rang, and she jumped to answer it, hastily allowing her visitor into the building.

Aura mumbled "saved by the bell" to a half-interested Kenny, who was now flipping wildly through available cable channels from his newly obtained position on the sofa.

A few minutes passed before there was a knocking at the door. Both women raced to answer it, but Aura managed to get to the peephole first. "Ace!" she cried out, quickly opening the door.

"Hey, sis, SURPRISE!" Ace roared in a throaty bass, quickly placing the shopping bags he brought on the living room floor.

"Aaace..." Aura let the word roll off her tongue while she tried to figure out why he was there. "What are *you* doing here?!..." Her mind was reeling. Was this the guy

Dana was talking about? That wouldn't make any sense... Why would Dana pretend Ace was someone else? "Daaana," she began her question slowly as she tried to anticipate the possible explanations for Ace's presence. "Why didn't you tell me Ace was coming over?" Aura put her hands on her hips and pouted like a little child who was not being let in on a joke.

Dana began giggling wildly and walked into Ace's arms. She wiggled her engagement ring in front of her chest for the two seconds it took Aura to notice.

Aura's bottom lip dropped, and for a moment she swore she couldn't speak a single word. "No you *didn't!*"she finally gasped. Ace and Dana nodded in unison, both with wide grins across their faces.

"How could you do this and not tell me?!" Aura looked from Dana's face to Ace's and then back to Dana's again. Her question was directed to *both* of them.

"You're the first one we're telling," Ace offered.

"You mean Angie doesn't know?" Aura was still dumbfounded. *Did this mean what she thought it meant?*

"She should be on her way over with Pascal," Ace explained.

Aura's mouth dropped again. "You mean, you guys were doing all this planning and concealing," a joyful tear formed in her eye. "I'm so happy for you... You're really getting *married?!!*"As the word crossed her lips she was overcome once again with disbelief. She felt Kenny walk up behind her and wrap his arms around her waist.

"Hey, boss," he greeted Ace with a nod. "Congratulations, man," he let go of Aura long enough to bump fists with her brother.

"But you *never* even *talk* about each other!" Aura continued in disbelief.

Dana pulled a bottle of champagne from one of Ace's bags and began removing glasses from the kitchen cabinets. "Oh, Aura, you know it was *killing* me! I was absolutely *dying* to tell you what was going on. But, you know Ace and I just didn't want to upset you if things didn't work out. You know, you're the one who said you wouldn't be able to handle us dating, so we just tried to spare you."

"But Ace is all the way in New Haven! How often did you guys even see each other?" Aura finally sat at the black-topped counter which separated their kitchen area from the rest of the living room.

"It only takes two hours to get to Connecticut. It was really no big deal. We saw each other all the time."

"But, I do have news!" Ace interjected.

"Good?" Aura asked misty-eyed. Dana and Ace were her absolute best friends in the world. The idea of them marrying was quite a bit to get used to.

"Of course it's good. I'm accepting a job at the Supreme Court in Brooklyn!"

"Oh, Ace, that's fabulous!" Aura hugged her brother again. She had always hated his living in another state. Plus, she felt he could better serve their community as a public defender in Brooklyn, not *Connecticut.*

Ace and Dana poured the champagne and passed around the glasses. "To my fiancé, I love you babe!" Dana toasted.

Ace grabbed her and kissed her neck "To *my* fiancée, when are we gonna start making some babies?!"

Dana smiled and rolled her eyes. "You say that now, but if I start sending you out for diapers at three AM, you'll be singing a whole different song"

Ace laughed. "Baby, you know I'd be more than happy to make a diaper run in about four years," he said, winking at Dana.

Aura looked from Ace's face to Dana's and back. She hadn't seen the two of them together since the previous year when she was in the hospital. It was clear they were in love; there was a level of familiarity, unspoken gestures, and a seemingly obvious fascination they had with each other. Her mind ran off with the idea... *Who would have thought?*

***

Angie and Pascal arrived just in time to finish off the second bottle of champagne with the newly engaged couple. Angie didn't seem quite as surprised by the news as Aura, but that was probably because Angie didn't actually *live* with Dana the way Aura did. Aura was not amazed by the fact that Ace fell in love with her best friend and vice versa, but she was shocked by the fact that all this happened right under her nose and she hadn't known a thing about it. During the lobster dinners which Ace brought in his shopping bags, the conversation drifted back to the unrelenting topic of the riots in Los Angeles. LA was miles away from NYC, but the realities of police brutality and inner city life were laid up in bed right next to each person in the room. The Oliviers, Dana, Kenny and Pascal were all raised in the concrete jungle of New York's inner cities. They each experienced different aspects of the ghettos from which they came, but the fact was, they each had their own story to tell when it came to being black and being raised in black neighborhoods in a predominantly white country.

"I can't believe we're just supposed to sit here and deal with this crap while white America sits around trying to figure out if racism still exists," Angie grumbled while Pascal sat quietly by her side.

"What do you suggest we do? Burn our businesses down over here? Rob and loot from each other, here in our own communities?" Ace countered pacing angrily.

The worst part of the LA situation for him was a feeling of helplessness. He had no faith in the legal system to begin with, and that was the primary reason he became a criminal attorney, figuring if he could stop one innocent brother from going to jail, he'd be satisfied. He already had, and to an extent he *was* satisfied. Then, this kind of crap came along and made it all seem worthless. He thought of the Martin Luther King quote: "Injustice anywhere is a threat to justice everywhere." What the hell difference did it make what he did in New York or Connecticut if Rodney King could be beaten mercilessly by a group of state-sanctioned thugs and get away with it? What difference could he make if twelve white folks could sit down and have the nerve to say, Rodney King brought it on himself?

Ace continued speaking: "You know I work with so-called 'criminals' every day. The fact of the matter is sometimes the cops pick up the right guy, sometimes they don't. No one cares who did it and who didn't; all they care about is whether or not they can convict someone." Ace paused for a few moments, "Shit, I don't even care who's innocent and who's not. All I can do is try to get my man off whatever...that's the job. Sometimes they did it and almost getting sent up scares them so much they keep out of trouble. Sometimes they didn't even do it, and if I wasn't around to give them a decent defense they'd be behind bars with hundreds of other guys who say they didn't do it either." Ace threw his hands up in the air. "Hell, who knows?" He turned towards Dana. "Baby, you want anything?"

"Nah," Dana responded.

Ace headed towards the kitchen area to refresh his now much-needed drink.

Dana turned to look at Angie before saying, "I *do* feel Ace's frustration with this whole thing. Obviously burning down your house or your neighbor's house, or anyone's house just isn't the move to make when you're angry, but what else is there to do? You know Martin Luther King said riots are the language of the unheard. I guess he had a point. I can't imagine not having a job, or food, or a place to live, or a good family. The level of frustration must be insane. And this system isn't designed to give you a hand up. It's designed for a beat down!" She tossed her braided bob, "I'll tell you one thing though," she lowered her voice lightly before adding with a forceful resonance. "Those muthafuckas will notice the black folks 'round that way now."

"Truth said, baby. Truth said." Ace nodded in solemn agreement as he returned with his glass.

Angie spoke next. "I'll tell you...one way to dig ourselves out of this shit is to be more active in our communities so we can address the problems that lead to the kind of social conditions that make our people ticking time bombs. We may not be able to stop racism in one day, but we can work to uplift our own goddamn race...'cause I'll tell you...if you're waiting for white folks to make and enforce a mandate saying 'be nice,' then you'll be waiting a long damn time!" Angie's argument was heartfelt. She had become very involved in the community over the years, first working at a couple of community outreach organizations and finally completing her Master's in Social Work and Public Policy.

Dana responded "Not everyone works in your field, Angie. I work long hours in the publishing industry. My work has virtually nothing to do with human rights or social activism. But I do try to donate money to important causes. I donate blood at company blood drives. I give to the United Way. I feel like I do as much as I can." Dana leaned back into Ace's arms with exhaustion from the whole conversation. She felt as if their words were making circles leading nowhere.

Angie responded. "It's easy to throw money at a problem when you have some to spare. And, that's truly great if you really don't have the time, but the fact of the matter is most of us *do* have the time, *we just don't make the effort.* Everybody's so busy running around trying to figure out what they can get, they forget to give... You know, it just balances things out." Angie held her chin in her hands as she leaned forward on the sofa.

"Gee, Angie, give the girl some credit for donating blood!" Aura laughed. "You know I've needed a couple of transfusions in my life." Aura felt a prickly sensation on the back of her neck as soon as the words left her mouth; she flinched.

Kenny quickly raised his eyebrows and nearly snapped his neck to look at Aura. *Did she say transfusions?*

"Yeah, I guess you're right. It's just that to me, donating blood is the least she should do as a healthy person, especially knowing our family for all these years. She knows about the need for blood in the black community," Angie added.

"Girl, I guess you *do* have a point," Dana began. "I never think a whole lot about investing my time. And, I always do think, okay, that's it, I've done enough. Sometimes, it's just so hard to know where to start." Her tone was pensive.

"Hey, every brick can build a bridge, baby," Ace smiled at Dana as he spoke. "Most of us really don't spend the time we should thinking about ways we can help those less fortunate than us. There are lots of folks out there who just need an outstretched hand." Ace's tone was hopeful.

Aura sighed. "Well, be glad for your health. Sometimes we take our own good health for granted. You know, not everyone is able to do the type of physical work you're talking about." Aura's remark was vague since she was in the habit of not telling the men she dated about her sickle-cell. She already screwed up with the transfusion comment. Since her last sickle-cell crisis a year ago, she had reduced her work hours, avoiding overtime as much as possible and concentrating on a healthy diet and regular sleep. She had been feeling pretty good for the past year, but still carried codeine in her purse at all times. It really pissed her off when people who were healthy were ambivalent, because there were so many things she felt she would do if she were physically able. Even her own sweet, healthy Kenny had a thousand excuses for not making a yearly blood donation. He had even more explanations for avoiding Aura's occasional jaunts to a local soup kitchen. He felt he deserved to be paid for his time, which Aura could understand, but must the payment always be *monetary?*

Sometimes, the rewards of doing a good deed are simple: personal satisfaction, a feeling of connection with the world around you and the right to wear your halo for a day. Aura remembered when she used to tutor students in college. Sometimes it annoyed her to have to fit it into her schedule, but she always felt so satisfied after. It was a strange feeling to be in the position to do something positive for another person; it created a dynamic of power. Suddenly Aura, a mere college student, was transformed into the seemingly omniscient tutor in the eyes of her student. The feeling was great even if it was rooted in some of the more base human emotions: the desire to control, the need for power. What's wrong with power in a symbiotic relationship? She was only human after all! And, both the means and the end were *positive.*

Angie smiled softly at the group, her eyes darted meaningfully from Aura, to Ace, to Dana and finally to Kenny, who didn't speak but seemed both enlightened and disturbed. Moments like this made her wish she could bottle up all the energy and hopefulness in the room and somehow make all the bad times go away. If only life were so simple.

***

After sharing in a few after-dinner drinks and conversation, Angie and Pascal left.

Aura watched until they were safely in the elevator before closing the apartment door. She turned to her brother and asked "What do you think about those two?"

"I don't know..." Ace looked a bit strained by his own response. "I think it's dead," he finally admitted.

"Yeah," Aura grimaced, "me too." They both referred to their sister's seemingly bleak relationship with her boyfriend of five years. At thirty, they both knew Angie would like to find the right guy to settle down with, but it was becoming increasingly apparent that Pascal was not the one. "When the two of them are in a room, they barely notice each other!" Aura exclaimed in frustration. "And, gosh, with all that shit we were talking about, Pascal has absolutely *no* opinion about anything!" She really wanted her sister to find a man she could be happy with, if only because she knew that was what *Angie* really wanted.

"Hey, sometimes you find love in the strangest places. There's hope for Angie yet," Dana said smiling in Ace's arms. He grabbed her hands in response.

"Yeah..." Aura mumbled. She didn't bother to look at Kenny.

***

It was late Monday morning when Aura arrived at the studio. WBG had a new account with a jeanswear company called "Jenson," and Aura was invited to visit the set of one of their commercial shoots to get a feel for the product line. Mainly, she was interested in checking out the models. After all, Kenny was nice, but she wasn't *in love* with him. Seeing Dana and Ace together on Friday night made her realize that more than ever. And, he'd been acting strange ever since she used the word 'transfusion.' He definitely wasn't ready for her reality.

She wore an elegant lavender pants suit which showed off her shapely figure with its sleek V-neck jacket and tapered legs. As she surveyed the area and watched the models, makeup artists and directors at work, she noticed a tall, extraordinarily handsome brother, with shoulder-length locks. He was with a young boy, who looked to be about thirteen or so, who she presumed was his son or some other family member. Actually, the boy seemed a bit too old to be his son, and they really didn't share any family resemblance. Aura's mind was working overtime as she peered in the direction of the man, trying to figure out who he was and what the boy was doing with him.

Aura was suddenly embarrassed by her own behavior. She was being paid to work, and here she was acting like a horny college girl! Besides, who was this guy? He was probably only twenty-eight with a thirteen year old son, clearly the signs of a maniac womanizer. *That* she could do without! At twenty-six, even Aura was tired of screwing around...the last thing she needed was to meet yet another man who wanted to be a mack daddy.

By the time she completed the thought, she had made herself disgusted with this man she hadn't even met, and stormed away, her heels clicking noisily on the tile floor. Ocean broke out of his conversation with one of the makeup artists and noticed the exquisite flurry of lavender and long black hair as Aura walked away.

***

"Hi. My name is Ocean Ryder. I'm one of the models on the Jenson account," Ocean extended his hand to Aura.

"I'm Aura Olivier," she offered in the perfunctory way, shaking his hand.

He motioned toward Darryl, "This is Darryl, my younger brother. I've been giving him a tour of the studio."

Darryl and Aura exchanged hellos and handshakes. This Ocean person had walked up to her totally unexpectedly. "Nice stage name," she commented before realizing she might have been putting her foot in her mouth. "It *is* your stage name, I'm guessing," she said with a sincerely apologetic smile.

"Oh, yeah," Ocean responded. "I'm Bahamian. I love the water, so it was natural, you know."

"Yeah." Aura smiled, but resisted the urge to continue the conversation. "Well, it's nice to meet you two," she stated simply. This guy was *too* good-looking *and* Caribbean with a mild, pleasant accent. It was making her nervous. "I hope you enjoyed your tour Darryl," she said conclusively.

"Oh, yeah. It was dope!" Darryl beamed.

"So what do you do here?" Ocean asked.

Suddenly, Aura was glad Ocean was drawing her into conversation. "Oh, I work for the ad agency in the media department. I buy air time for Jenson's spots."

"TV?"

"Yeah, TV, radio, print, whatever. I buy them all." Aura was getting a bit more interested. This Ocean person seemed really down-to-earth, not stuck-up like she initially expected.

"Hey, would it be too much of a bother to give Darryl a little office tour one of these days? I'm trying to give him ideas for career opportunities. Who knows? Maybe he'll want to work in advertising." He flashed Darryl a smile and then winked at her.

This was too much; this guy was *too* smooth. Maybe he was stupid or violent or crazy. There *had* to be *something* wrong with him. Finally it occurred to her, he was probably married. But what could she say? "Sure, Ocean, that wouldn't be a problem at all," she heard herself respond. She quickly reached into her handbag and handed him a business card, "Here, give me a call when you're ready to set something up."

Ocean took the card from her slowly, smiling. "Thank you. That's very generous of you," he said before leaving the studio to buy Darryl lunch.

.

***

"Girl, I met a new guy! And, this one is *fine* like you would not believe!" Aura shared with Dana at the end of the day.

"Yeah, I figured you needed someone to rescue you from Kenny. I mean Kenny's nice and all but, he's getting kind of *tired*... And I noticed his attitude the other night when you mentioned transfusions. Did he ever ask you anything about that?"

"No, and I'm not trying to bring it up either." Aura folded her arms.

"Anyway, forget it. Tell me about this new guy," Dana prodded.

"He seems real nice, but there's got to be something wrong with him," Aura admitted; she lost her smile as her voice trailed off. She hated when she got her hopes up over a man, only to find out it was all just a waste of time. Maybe he wouldn't even be interested in her. She knew most men found her to be very attractive, but she was sure this Ocean character had been around many beautiful women. What could make her any different?

"What's the matter with you?" Dana asked munching on a chocolate cookie. She immediately noticed the change in her friend's disposition.

Aura smiled briefly. "Oh, I'm just not too sure about this one."

"Tell me what happened? Do you have a date?" Dana queried between bites.

"Not really," Aura admitted.

"Well, what's the deal? How did you meet him?" Dana probed.

"I went down to the Jenson shoot today, and he was there with this kid. He says it's his younger brother, but they don't look at all alike. The kid looks more Hispanic. Anyway, he said he was giving the kid a tour of the studio..." Aura paused thinking how nice that was of him "Well," she grabbed one of Dana's cookies and continued, "we talked a little and he asked if I'd be willing to give his brother, Darryl, a tour of the agency."

Dana was glowing. A fine brother who takes his younger brother on company tours! Sounded like a man with some character. "Now, I *know* you said yes!" Dana responded.

"Of course!" Aura looked at the floor briefly. "I gave him my card, but..."

"But, what?!" Dana asked excitedly.

"But, I didn't get his number... Suppose he never calls? It was really stupid of me, huh?"

Dana frowned. They both knew never to give out their number without getting the digits too. "Yeah, girl...You broke the dating 101 rules...always get the digits...but, hey, I'm sure he'll call. If he doesn't, he's a dick. Don't worry about it."

"Yeah."

"Besides, you don't have to worry about if he loses the card or whatever. You have common job contacts. If he wants to find you, he easily can. No excuses. Just sit tight and screw Kenny while you're waiting." Dana laughed.

Aura shoved her friend in the shoulder playfully. "Yeah, that's *not* a bad idea. Where's the phone?" she asked, playfully motioning as if she were making a 'bootie call' to Kenny.

***

"Thanks for everything," Ocean said meaningfully to Aura as she ended the tour of WBG, nearly two weeks after they first met.

"I'm glad to be able to help out. We could use more young brothers in advertising, you know." Her remark was directed at Darryl.

"Who me?" he asked.

"Yeah you," Aura responded.

Darryl looked embarrassed and overwhelmed. He shifted in Aura's office chair, looking rather dashing in a white shirt and tie. I don't know," he smiled. "I guess I'll have to think about it."

"Yeah, it takes a lot of hard work to figure out what you want to do with the rest of your life. I hope you treat your big brother well; it's good of him to take you around like this." Aura grinned at Ocean.

"Yeah, he's all right," Darryl admitted with some embarrassed hesitation and a bit of restless shifting in the chair.

"Why don't you wait for me out in reception? I'll be right out," Ocean suggested, sensing both Darryl's boredom and a moment of opportunity. When Darryl left Aura's office, Ocean let his eyes fall gently on her face. She was truly beautiful, almost like Mona, but younger, softer, smarter. He had promised himself he'd stop making bad decisions with his dick, but she was too appealing to resist. Who knew? Maybe it wouldn't turn out to be a mistake. He didn't want to come on strong, so he asked casually, "Maybe you and I can go for lunch one day?"

Aura watched the way Ocean tilted his chin up as he asked the question, giving her the best possible angle from which to view his full lips, strong jaw and solid throat "I'd like that," she answered. She was glad he didn't ask her out to drinks or dinner. Lunch was innocent.

***

Aura and Ocean's lunch together started off with a bit of nervous tension which quickly lifted as they chatted about Jenson and the business of commercial advertising. Aura appreciated Ocean's good looks, but she had been with many attractive men. Kenny was tall, muscular and sexy too. What appealed most to Aura was Ocean's kind ways. He was quick to pull out her chair and get the door, and he didn't hint at sharing the tab or the tip. He spoke glowingly of his brother, finally admitting Darryl was not his biological brother. And, he didn't arrive with roses or lay on the pick-up lines to try to get her into bed in the least amount of time possible. He seemed natural and relaxed, which allowed Aura to feel likewise. When they finished a lazy two-hour lunch, they were quick to make plans to meet again.

***

Aura and Ocean were out on their third lunch date in two weeks, when Ocean finally suggested dinner. "Sure, under one condition," Aura began.

"Yeah, what?" Ocean asked with playful curiosity, slipping his hand around Aura's waist as he led her toward the door of the swank French restaurant.

"Let me pick up the tab for a change," Aura asserted.

Ocean raised a thick eyebrow and smiled, his brown eyes glinting. *Could this be love?* "No problem," he replied, brushing the soft ends of her hair lightly against the back of her navy dress as he opened the glass door to exit the restaurant.

Aura held his hands for a few moments longer than necessary to say goodbye. They had not yet kissed, and it was torture for her, so she turned her chin up to him and he quickly met her mouth with his own. His lips were as soft and sensuous as she had imagined.

***

When Aura prepared for her Friday night date with Ocean, she knew she'd have a hard time keeping her panties on all night. If he fucked anything like he kissed it would be *over* for her.

"Look at you, girl! You're absolutely sinful!" Dana laughed as Aura ran from her steaming opium bubble bath to her bedroom to slip into lingerie. Dana joked with her while she got dressed. "I'm gonna tell Kenny on you!"

"Shut up, Dana," Aura laughed. "Nothing's happened yet, so there's nothing to tell Kenny about." She slipped into her white satin bra and matching bikini panty.

"Damn girl, you look so good... I wanna fuckya!" Dana proclaimed with roaring laughter.

"Dana, you're a moron, you know that?" Aura said jokingly.

"Seriously, though. What did you tell Kenny?" Dana

asked.

"Nothing, just that I had plans to go out with some friends. Honestly, I think Kenny's getting kind of tired of me anyway. Things just haven't been clicking like they used to between us. It's like...he didn't seem to care that much anyway."

"Yeah, girl. He's probably thinking you freed him up to hang out with the boys tonight," Dana added.

Aura smiled, "You know, I didn't think of it that way. You're probably right." She slipped into the peach silk dress she bought for the occasion. "Do you think it's too much?" she asked Dana of the slim, short cocktail dress she wore.

"No, girl, it's perfect!" Dana beamed. "You could wear that to a work function, you know. It's not like it's *long* or anything I mean you're not taking him to McDonald's are you?" Dana laughed.

"No. Do you think it was stupid of me to offer to pay?" she asked as she began applying mascara and deep apricot lipstick.

"Nah, that's up to you. He's taken you out a few times for expensive lunches from what you've said. I think it's the least you could do if you really like him. Don't make him think you're cheap. Only cheap men like cheap women."

Aura frowned. "Shit, Dana, why do I feel nervous? I mean, we *have* been out before."

Dana laughed. "You're nervous because he's never been *here* before, and it's your first nighttime date together *and* you think you're gonna get laid tonight." Dana paused for a moment to consider her relationship with Ace. It felt good to be past this stage. She sighed. "Poor thing. It's almost like a first date. Better you than me."

"Yeah, dating sucks," Aura agreed.

Minutes passed before the apartment buzzer rang.

Aura's heart leapt when she saw Ocean at the door in a suit with a baker's dozen of red roses for her.

***

Dinner went well. They talked a lot about relationships, family, community responsibility and their shared Caribbean heritage. Aura was surprised to find out Ocean never attended college, but it didn't bother her. He was much more intelligent than many of the men she knew with all types of degrees. They joked about partying and dating, so when Ocean invited her back to his apartment for a nightcap, she was ready for whatever happened.

Ocean had asked her to carry one rose with her on their date, which he quickly confiscated when they entered his apartment. "Let me take this," he said as he adjusted the stereo, finding a Teddy Pendergrass CD. "Do you like him?" he asked.

"TP? *Please!*" Aura laughed. "I can't even *speak* to anybody who doesn't like TP!"

Ocean smiled and removed the band which had held his hair back. "Good," he replied.

Aura watched enraptured as his carefully contained locks were suddenly free to coast the shoulders of his jacket. Then, he removed his jacket.

"You're getting pretty comfortable," Aura noted.

Ocean laughed. "Oh, I'm sorry. Am I making you uncomfortable? It's just I'm home now; it's force of habit. I swear, this is it. The hair and the jacket; I'll keep my pants on." Ocean shifted nervously as he spoke.

"Ha, ha..." Aura responded playfully. She was glad to see he was losing some of his cool. She'd hate to be the only one.

"Ha, ha..." Ocean replied as he turned toward the refrigerator. A bottle of champagne was on ice. "How do you feel about champagne?" he asked.

"I love it," Aura replied with a grin. He had obviously done some careful planning for the evening. "Does this mean you knew I was gonna come back here?"

"Nooo..." Ocean began slowly, "It just means, if you didn't I was gonna get drunk on a bottle of champagne." He laughed, and she joined him as he handed her a crystal flute with the bubbly stuff.

She appreciated the fact that his place was well kept. Robert had been meticulous like that; Kenny was a slob. She hoped Ocean would be different from both of them.

Ocean joined her on the sofa. "To us?" he said with a questioning smile.

"To us!" Aura agreed as she clinked glasses with him. She wrapped her arm around his to take a few sips before setting the crystal flutes on the smoked glass coffee table.

It seemed that from that first sip of champagne the evening progressed breathlessly fast. First they just curled up on the soft new-feeling leather of Ocean's navy sofa listening to Teddy Pendergrass, then Marvin Gaye and Minnie Ripperton. Their conversation started with family and relationships again before growing political and value driven. They discussed work and social issues, while joking and occasionally stopping to kiss, until the kisses grew more frequent than the conversation, and Aura pressed her body against his hotly. *Was it too soon?*

"Hey you," Ocean said throatily as he rose softy from the couch. "Come here." He held her hand, gently guiding her into his bedroom.

When Aura looked inside, she was surprised to find red rose petals covering the cream bedspread. This was the kind of stuff that only happened in movies! "You really *are* a romantic, huh?" she asked as he lowered her gently to the bed, his mouth over her own.

Ocean laughed. "Honestly," he began, looking longingly into her eyes, "I have no idea." Then he laughed again, this time harder and more anxiously. "I swear, I've never done this before. Not that that's good, but you know what I mean. I don't have to throw petals on a bed to get laid!"

Aura looked at him stupidly. *What was he talking about?* She moved away from him on the bed.

"Shit, I'm sorry, Aura... Dammit, it's you, you know!" His tone was almost angry.

"What is it?" she asked softly.

"It's just that, I've never really tried this hard with a woman before. I mean, I've been with lots of women..." He threw his head back on the bed and stared directly at the ceiling fan above it. "Do you think the rose petals were stupid?"

Suddenly it was clear to her. She was wondering what his problem was. He had a minor ego bruise when she said he was romantic. She smiled and leaned over to kiss him, stroking his long mane of hair as she brushed her lips and tongue against his. "I *love* the rose petals," she murmured. With those words, she felt his response quickly change from uncertainty to gentle passion as he carefully freed her from her dress and removed his own clothes. He led her to the shower and they washed each other carefully before heading back to the bedroom. Ocean immediately nestled his head between her legs, relishing in the taste of her clean newness.

Aura was pleased by Ocean's desire to please her and his adeptness as he licked at her until she could no longer contain herself and erupted and smoldered like a volcano. He kissed her feet, calves and thighs as his locks brushed along her legs making the journey to her breasts and face. There was something different with him. She felt a different closeness than she had in a long time. Their bodies seemed to fit together like pieces in a jigsaw puzzle, as their minds had earlier in the evening.

The night was long with hot oily massages, long wet kisses and steamy showers. It was nearly dawn by the time they fell asleep, sweat-soaked in each other's arms.

***

The next morning, Aura rose before Ocean and reclined on the sofa with the newspaper she found outside his front door. She didn't think he'd mind, but was surprised when he seemed downright giddy about it. Here was a man she could get used too. The feeling scared the hell out of her.

Ocean Ryder
Spring 1992

Ocean was shocked as he watched the television coverage of the looting and burning in Los Angeles. He thought back to when he first came to the U.S., convinced that equality and opportunity were available for everyone. As he saw the sea of black faces stealing angrily, he couldn't help but wonder why no cameras were on white faces. Could it be possible that no whites stole during the riots? He found that rather difficult to believe. But he did know that careful editing was done with any type of filmmaking. So, when he watched TV news coverage of events, he concerned himself at least as much with what wasn't shown, as with what was.

"Hey, baby, let's look at something else," the woman beside him on his new sofa suggested. The sofa was supple and navy, and he was somewhat proud of it. Brandy was pretty and vivacious and he was happy with her. At 5'5", she was short for him, light-skinned and full-figured, not his usual type, but so funny and pleasant that they settled into an exclusive relationship over the past few months. She was a social worker at the organization that set him up with Darryl, so he had known her casually for years before they began dating. With her he felt secure and cared for. She came from a large, close-knit family in the Carolinas, and maybe some of her warmth was for that reason. He had actually become pretty good friends with her brother, Rick. So, they often hung out with Rick and his wife of two years.

"No, babe, don't change it. It's important that we see this. This bullshit. It's historic." Ocean's voice was filled with the annoyance and disgust that had overcome Black America after the King verdict. *Where do we go from here?*

Brandy shrugged her shoulders. What could *she* do? It was Friday night and here she was stuck with an angry boyfriend and her own feelings of disillusionment. She just wanted to avoid it…do something fun, but it didn't seem like fun would be part of their plans for the evening.

"Rick wanted us to come over for dinner. Do you want to go?" she asked. It was after 7:00pm, and if they were going, they really needed to get moving.

"Oh, I don't know. Maybe not tonight, babe," he said, resting his hand on her denim-covered thigh as he gazed hypnotically at the TV. He quickly turned and kissed her cheek. "I guess I'm not feeling all that sociable."

Brandy looked dejected.

"Don't mind me, though. If you want to go hang with your brother, go ahead. I'm probably not such good company tonight, anyway."

Brandy stood up. "Well, if you say so. I don't want to stay here and be miserable over this shit." She paused and looked sympathetically at Ocean. "I guess I'll just head out."

"Okay," Ocean mumbled.

And she left.

***

Not long after Brandy's departure, his friend Maleek called. "Ocean, man, what's up for the night? Is Brandy there?"

"Nah, man, she broke out. What's good?"

"Nothing's good tonight, man. You want company? I'm in the crib with one of my boys, we were thinking about passing through. You got beer?"

"Yeah, man, the fridge is stocked, you *know* that. I've been peeping this L.A. shit. It's just pissing me off. Come on by, man. Let's make it *boy's night!"* He roared, before mumbling off-handedly, "ehh...what the fuck?" Maleek modeled at the agency with him. He was a pretty decent brother, cool to hang out with. They had gotten into their share of "trouble" together before Ocean settled down with Brandy.

"Peace, man. I'll be over in a few."

***

"Thirty-five dead. Twelve hundred injured. Three thousand arrested. Two thousand buildings set ablaze," the newscaster announced.

Ocean stared at the screen through a haze of Heinekens. Beer bottles were strewn on the floor when the other men showed up, hours later.

"Hey, man." They exchanged greetings and took their places in Ocean's apartment, grabbing beers haphazardly. Maleek's friend's name was Craig. They drank beers for hours before deciding that three good-looking men shouldn't be cooped up in an apartment alone on a Friday night.

They roamed to a number of familiar clubs in Manhattan, flirting with women, but Ocean, at least, didn't touch any. The same could not be said of his companions.

It was 6:00am when he returned to his apartment. Three messages were on his answering machine from Brandy. The first concerned. The second annoyed. The third angry. She still didn't trust him, but what could he do?

***

Ocean called Brandy early Saturday afternoon. "Hey, baby, what's up with you?" he asked, a bit annoyed by the messages she left the previous night.

"Where did you go on Friday?" she asked; her anger was apparent.

"No place, some of the fells came by, and we hung out for awhile. No big deal, No reason to lose hair, hon," he said playfully. There was an extended silence on the other end.

"Ocean, I'm not losing any goddamn hair over this shit. I just don't understand why you told me you wanted to be alone and then you went out!" She was nearly screaming.

"I didn't tell you I wanted to be alone, Brandy. I said I didn't want to have dinner with Rick, and I was feeling antisocial. I said I probably wouldn't be very good company, and *you* left! I didn't tell you to leave. You're acting like I kicked you out or something. Ocean was annoyed that he was being pulled into an argument. He was hoping Brandy would want to go bike riding while it was still early.

"You're such a liar, Ocean," she fumed.

"Brandy, you know, I'm not lying. And, you know damned well, if you had been here with me I wouldn't have gone out with Maleek and them!"

"*Maleek?!* You were hanging out with *Maleek!* He's a fucking slut! What were you and Maleek doing together?"

Ocean could not believe he had to go through all this explanation to leave his house. He felt like he was talking to his mother. No, his mother *respected* him. He didn't do anything but go out for a few hours for drinks. What was the big deal? Besides, why did she have to curse *at* him like that? He hated to hear women curse in anger. It was weird, but he didn't mind it playfully, he just couldn't stand it when it was *abusively*. He lowered his voice before responding. "Look Brandy. Calm down and call me later. I can't deal with this right now." He hung up the phone and immediately felt guilty.

Maybe he'd take his bike out alone. The weather was nice and a ride would probably clear his head.

***

When Monday rolled around, Ocean and Brandy still had not spoken. He decided to give it a break for a few days. Maybe he'd even let her call first, although he doubted she would. In any event, he was preoccupied with the day he planned to spend with Darryl. He had promised to take him to a commercial shoot, and, since his agency was supplying models for a jeanswear company, he figured a tour of the studio would be good for him. At fourteen, Darryl had come a long way from when they first met. His grammar had improved, and he was not as impressed with street life as he once was. Ocean spoke regularly to Darryl's mother to keep abreast of his school and home situations. And, although she was very pretty and flirtatious with him, he steered clear of involving himself with her sexually, realizing the huge potential for problems.

When Ocean and Darryl arrived at the studio, they were greeted by some of the other models and actors. Darryl seemed awed by his surroundings—bright lights, beautiful people, cameras everywhere. Probably, he was most fascinated by the idea that money could be made easily here. But, as he met the set designer, the director, the makeup artists, and the models, he began to realize that no matter what occupation was held by any particular person, hard work was involved. Things were not as easy as they sometimes appeared. Even the models did their share of pavement pounding to land the gigs or the deals they had, and shoots could take all day under hot lights and heavy makeup.

After Darryl's tour, Ocean chatted briefly with one of the makeup artists on his way out. Then, for some reason, the clicking of heels on the floor caught his attention, and he turned to witness the thick black mane of a woman's hair swishing against the tapered shoulders of a lavender jumper. He watched as the woman walked away from him, glimpsing the side of her face as she turned. Then, her full face. She was truly stunning. Deep chocolate skin, just a few shades darker than his own, with a slim, curvy figure, pretty full lips, and beautiful, thick hair.

***

Ocean wasn't looking to meet any new women. He had grown accustomed to making love to Brandy. And, in a sense, sex with one woman relaxed him in a way that was different from all the juggling he had done in his past. Brandy was sexy and special. But even as he thought about Brandy and their commitment, he could not allow himself to ignore this woman. There was no crime in saying 'hello.' And, even if there was, he was *exclusive* with Brandy, not *in love* with her. Whatever that meant. Besides, he couldn't even see the woman up close. For all he knew she had no teeth, bad acne or spoke in tongues. It wasn't even like he was officially checking her out. Actually, by approaching her, he was really just looking to confirm her flaws. Now that made sense...after all, there had to be *something* wrong with her. Nobody was perfect.

So Ocean watched her for a few moments before making the move.

***

When Ocean introduced himself, the woman seemed a little taken aback. Her name was Aura. Quite an interesting name, he thought, but he didn't say so. She was pleasant, and surprisingly, prettier up close than from afar. At first she didn't seem to want to talk, but then she warmed up quite a bit. When she mentioned her position as media negotiator for an ad agency, Ocean asked if she'd be willing to give Darryl a tour one day. She accepted without knowing if Ocean would even be there. He wasn't sure why he found that impressive, but he did.

Aura managed to arrange for Darryl's tour pretty quickly, and Darryl seemed thrilled. Of course, Darryl was always ecstatic when he had an opportunity to miss a day of school. When the two of them arrived at WBG Advertising, Aura was wonderful. She wore some sort of grape-colored suit that showed off shapely legs and wide hips. As she walked them around, Ocean could barely understand what she was talking about. Her hair was not loose, but gathered into a ponytail with a black silk scarf. This woman was pretty, kind and classy, not to mention, outrageously sexy. Ocean had to smile to himself as she walked them around for most of the morning, finally returning to her office.

Ocean really appreciated Aura's effort. It was clear she had gone out of her way to be friendly to Darryl, despite his still-rough edges. And, she had given a detailed tour, explaining the various departments and introducing Ocean and Darryl to professionals in Creative, Trafficking, Media, Sales, Finance, Human Resources and the Production departments of her agency. She had clearly notified her supervisors and staff of her plans in advance, and everyone greeted them as if they had been expecting them. For the most part, it was a friendly sea of white faces, with a few minorities speckled throughout.

Before he arrived, he wasn't sure he wanted to date this woman; he did already have a girlfriend. But once he was in Aura's company, he knew he had no choice in the matter. This woman had it going on, and there was no getting around it. He decided to try to ease into things with a lunch date, and was happy, but not surprised, when she agreed.

***

Ocean felt a rising trepidation as he rode the subway to Aura's job. By the time he reached her office, his palms were moist with anxiety. He wiped them on his jeans as he waited for her to come out to the reception area. When he saw her, she looked gorgeous as usual in a forest green dress and black bolero jacket. Her hair was curlier today than he remembered. As it turned out, he was in a forest green turtle neck and black jeans, so, although he was casually dressed, he got a weird feeling that they were in some sort of synch. As the thought crossed his mind, he felt a sudden sickness wash over him. *This woman had him thinking about color coordination?* It could not be a good sign.

"Hey, it's good to see you again," he said, briefly holding her hand in greeting. "You look great," he stated simply, hoping she could not feel any remaining moistness in his palms. *Why were his palms sweating, anyway?*

"Thanks. You too," Aura said smiling. Her lips were covered with a burgundy gloss and she smelled faintly of musk perfume.

He ushered her through the doors to the building lobby and hailed a cab to a nearby restaurant. When they arrived, they were quickly seated by the maitre d', who was acquainted with Ocean from previous visits.

"This is a nice place," Aura commented.

"Thanks," Ocean responded. "I've been here a few times on business. Sometimes Reeva holds meetings down here."

"Reeva?" Aura asked.

"Oh, Reeva Johnson is the head of Esquire Models."

"What's she like?" Aura asked as the waiter poured her sparkling water.

"She's pretty nice. At first she comes off real hard, you know. But, as you get to know her... I mean, I've been with Esquire...what...four years now... As you get to know her, she's pretty cool... Real professional, but likable... She looks out for good deals for us...that kind of stuff." Ocean spoke through bites of buttered bread.

"So, you said you're Bahamian. How long have you been in this country?" Aura asked.

"Hmmm, let's see... I came here when I was sixteen, so it's..." He paused, realizing he was about to reveal his age.

"How long?" Aura prodded innocently.

"Oh, I guess about ten years," Ocean exaggerated slightly.

"Oh," Aura smiled. "And, you were sixteen when you came?" She didn't realize he was younger than she was. Maybe that was what was wrong with him. He was immature. "So, you're twenty-six, then. How much longer do you think you'll be modeling?"

"Fortunately, men seem to have a longer run in this business than women do. It's unfair, but it's pretty much fact," Ocean commented, not bothering to admit he just turned twenty-five.

"But the women make more money, don't they?"

"Yeah, that's pretty much the case too. I suppose it balances out." Ocean smiled. She seemed to know her stuff. By the time their food arrived, the conversation had gone from work to family.

"So how often do you talk to your mom?" Aura asked as she nibbled a piece of rigatoni.

"Usually, a couple of times a month. Not less than once a month. I should really plan a trip home. I haven't been there in a year." He looked into her eyes meaningfully as he began to talk about his home. "You'd absolutely love it. The sea and sky for days... It's truly beautiful. My mom would love you." He dropped his eyes with partial embarrassment. He couldn't believe he just said that.

"It sounds wonderful. I've only been to St. Lucia a few times since I came here. I keep telling my parents we should plan a family trip, but we sometimes have a hard time getting our schedules together." She smiled before adding, "I've been here since I was only two, so I don't really know any other home."

"I'd like to see where you come from," Ocean said noticing Aura's interesting features, the slightly almond eyes, high cheekbones, slender nose, and full mouth.

"Hmmm," she smiled, knowing he was admiring her. "So, is Darryl your only brother?" she asked.

"Oh, no, not at all. I have five brothers and one sister. Most are still in Abaco."

"Abaco?"

"Oh, yeah, that's the island I'm from." He smiled and continued. "Actually, Darryl's not my biological brother. When, I include him, though, I actually have six."

Aura raised her eyebrows. "You know, it's funny, I didn't think you two resembled each other enough. He looks more Spanish."

"Yeah, he's Puerto Rican and black. We met through Big Brothers, so I'm sort of his official big brother. Gosh, it's been three years already... It really doesn't seem that long, but I feel like he really is family now...it's weird."

"Gee, that's a nice thing to do. How did you get involved?" Aura wondered

"I saw an ad on the subway, and I just decided I wanted to try it out. Things were going pretty well for me, so I figured I should give something back... It's actually turned out to be a lot of fun most of the time. I mean it was tougher in the beginning, but now it's cool, and I see a lot of progress. I really feel more like he's my son or something."

"Yeah, it's a pretty big age difference. Do you have any kids?" Aura hated to ask, but it was one of the 'usual' questions.

"No, thankfully. I'm not ready for that just yet." He smiled. *Did this mean she had kids?* "How about you?" he asked.

"No, not yet." Aura's curls dangled around her face as she shook her head, 'no.'

Ocean and Aura began sharing jokes and the conversation lightened up considerably. As they got to know each other a little better, Ocean fell back into his feelings of comfort and control. When the meal was over, they lingered over cups of cappuccino, before he dropped her back at her office door.

He didn't try to kiss her goodbye, and she didn't seem to notice.

***

It wasn't until their third lunch date that they seemed to acknowledge the fact that they were sort of 'dating.'

Ocean flinched when Aura asked if he was in a

relationship. "Why? Are you?" was the best response he could come up with. She laughed. "Yeah, actually, I sort of am." She squinted as if in response to a potential blow. When she opened her eyes Ocean was gazing at her with what appeared to be some regard.

"So how long have you been seeing this person?" he asked, impressed with her honesty, but not quite ready to divulge his own situation.

"Not too long...about six months" she replied, examining Ocean's long eyelashes and thick brows before looking directly into his eyes.

"Is he important to you?"

"He's a nice guy, but I think he's beginning to lose interest."

Ocean smiled knowingly. "I find that hard to believe," he commented.

Aura smiled. "I guess I'm losing interest too..." She let her eyes drift over Ocean's mouth as she spoke. "Enough about me... So, what's *your* story? You're dating five women, right?" she said suggestively, playfully, and somewhat seriously. She imagined he was *not* a one-woman man.

Ocean smiled fully. She read him pretty well. "No, actually I'm seeing one woman for the past few months, but I have been known to date a few different women in my time."

"Oh, really?" Aura asked with curiosity, her brow rose.

"Yeah...what? Are you trying to convince me you've never dated more than one man at a time? You're beautiful. You've probably got men chasing you around like little puppy dogs." Ocean laughed and made little barking noises.

"Oh, stop!" Aura squealed.

"Oh, stop!" he mimicked her. "Come on now, girl! I know you've had your share of men chasing you around."

"Okay, so what?... You still didn't explain this woman to me. Is it serious?" she asked.

"Not as serious as you." He looked her dead in the eye when he said it, and Aura felt her heart leap.

"Stop it!" she giggled, her face flushed hotly.

Ocean looked at her seriously and grabbed her hand. "I *really* mean it." His tone was intense. "I don't run around saying this kind of stuff every day..." He paused, before adding, "You'll see." Ocean had been trying to take things slowly with Aura. Partly because of Brandy, and partly because he didn't want to screw things up. He knew dinner was long overdue, so he finally asked her out the following Friday. She was quick to accept, and he knew it would be hard to keep from touching her on an evening date.

When they exited the restaurant, he held her hands and quickly kissed her for the first time. Her lips felt as awesome as they looked, and she knew how to use them.

***

Ocean didn't give Brandy much attention in the weeks since their argument, but they did have sex a few times. He thought about Aura often from when they first met, but since their lunch Wednesday, she consumed his thoughts. It had been over two weeks since he slept with Brandy, and since then she had perfected the art of hanging up on his answering machine. The fact of the matter was he really didn't want to sleep with Brandy right at that moment. He didn't know if he'd want to later, but at the moment all he wanted was Aura. By Friday, he was as excited as a child on Christmas. If anything did happen, it had to be special.

He bought a new suit, thirteen boxed red roses and a couple of bottles of champagne. He cleaned his apartment and laundered his sheets. He even scrubbed the shower walls. Lucky for him, he had no appointments on Friday, so he was able to set aside the time for his frenetic house-cleaning and shopping.

At 6:00pm he finally relaxed. The place looked perfect. He caught a glimpse of himself in a mirror and stopped... *Was this really him?* He had always enjoyed a clean home, but it wasn't the cleaning that bothered him. He'd clean for any first date. Shit, he cleaned for himself...it wasn't that, it was how he was *feeling*. Geez, he felt like saying 'vulnerable.' He squirmed when the word popped into his head. It was as if there were a voice in the back of his head saying if he didn't clean, she wouldn't come...in more ways than one. Ocean smiled at the thought. Somehow the thought of sex always relaxed him, even in the case of Aura, where he really didn't want anything to go wrong. He knew he was a skilled lover, but every woman is different. He smiled as he wondered how she looked sweaty and naked... As his mind wandered, he felt a hard-on pushing against his sweats. Fuck, he thought. It had been two weeks, for god's sake; if he didn't get laid tonight he'd *have* to sleep with Brandy. He brushed his penis roughly, weighing his options... He considered jerking off, but decided against it. "Fuck," he mumbled aloud as he quickly stripped and jumped into a lukewarm shower. He sang a childhood song at the top of his lungs until the erection disappeared, then looked at his limp penis and said, "Okay, we made it through that time. Next time I don't know if I can be so strong... So, stay down until I call you!"

Thankfully, his penis did not reply.

***

When Ocean met Aura that evening, she was a sight

for sore eyes in a short pink dress. She shared a hip-looking apartment with a pleasant woman named Dana. Aura explained that they had been friends since childhood, and Dana was recently engaged to her brother. He was impressed by how loving Aura seemed. She talked about her parents and siblings as if they were all best friends. It was a closeness he envied.

Dinner went well. She had promised to pay, but he thought she'd let him if he asked, and was surprised when she didn't. He was tempted to fight for the check, but decided against it. It was nice to have a woman pick up the tab for a change. He didn't need her to financially, but he appreciated the gesture. It was also nice to go out with a woman who knew how to eat with a normal passion. Brandy probably over-indulged, and many of his previous girlfriends were nearly-anorexic models. So, when Aura ordered chocolate soufflé with warm raspberry sauce for dessert, he was sort of turned-on watching her eat it.

He was surprised to learn Aura had her own wild partying days to discuss. She was no angel. Actually, she reminded him of himself, and he found that comforting. He was happy when she agreed to come back to his apartment. He was even happier when they cuddled on his sofa with glasses of champagne. He had asked Aura to carry a rose on their date, leaving the remaining dozen arranged at her apartment. He took the single rose from her when she came in and tossed the individual petals on his bed cover. He thought it would be a nice surprise if they made it into the room later.

***

Their kissing had become a bit heated on the sofa, so Ocean guided Aura into his bedroom. She laughed when she saw the roses and called him "romantic." For a minute he felt like a real jerk, until he realized she meant it in a good way. From there things sailed along smoothly.

He kissed her and combed her hair. He had been dying to play with it from when he first met her, and was thrilled to finally have the opportunity to get close to her. He eased her out of her dress and was surprised by how toned and shapely she was. He knew she was slim, but you never know what you're in for the first time you see a woman naked. But Aura truly was beautiful, with clear smooth skin, small pert breasts and a full, round butt. He didn't want to rush her, so they took their time and showered together.

When they returned to the bedroom, he laid her down quickly and kissed her thighs and calves before venturing between her legs. She arched her back as he approached her with his mouth and hands. He wanted to please her more than he had wanted to please anyone in a long time.

Aura bit Ocean's earlobes gently, intermittently running her tongue along his neck and kissing his cheeks and mouth. He had just put his face next to hers again, after a long spell of oral sex, and, perhaps, she was expressing her gratitude. She traced her tongue along his nipples, trailing saliva down to his navel as she kissed his stomach and thighs.

He watched her as she took him in her mouth. She looked beautiful...but as he got more aroused, he became anxious to enter her, so he grabbed her hair at the back of her neck and drew her head up to his. He kissed her face and rolled her over onto her side. His hands travelled the course of her hips and thighs as he gently spread her legs and moved his hips toward her. He pulled a condom from the bed stand and handed it to her.

Aura placed the condom on him firmly, making sure to leave space in the tip for his ejaculation. She slid her body close to his, and wrapped her leg around his waist.

Ocean rocked his body into hers easily, enjoying this new terrain.

Aura's moans were slow and throaty, and she threw her head back against his pillow. She pushed her hands into his hair as he touched her from the inside.

Ocean pinched her nipples and kissed her eyelids as he rocked inside her. Finally, he moved his mouth to her lips and kissed her thoroughly. He felt so secure and wonderful inside of her, all thoughts of performing were gone. He felt relaxed. Her moans let him know everything was okay.

They looked into each other's eyes for awhile...until Aura got frenzied and turned her head away, her hips pumping wildly. Seeing her so excited, threw him over the edge and while he tried to hold back for a few moments, when he felt her begin to shudder, he couldn't contain his own excitement. They orgasmed together.

As Aura dozed off, Ocean squeezed a bottle of massage oil onto her back. He laughed when she jumped up. "Heeey, what are you doing?" she squealed with delight.

"Stay still... don't move," he said as he rubbed the oil into her skin.

"Uhhmm," she responded. "Am I under arrest or something?" she laughed.

"Yeah, you are. You've been bad," he said moving his hand between her thighs. "Now, I have to take you into custody."

Aura rolled onto her back, "Really?" she asked.

"Yeah," Ocean responded kissing her and moving his hand between her legs. He stroked her clitoris with his fingers. "What should I do with you?" he asked between kisses.

"Whatever you want," she responded throatily. She sighed with pleasure as he brought her to orgasm with his hands.

"You're beautiful, you know that?" he said after.

"Thank you." She kissed him on the forehead before running back into the shower. "Wanna come?" she asked playfully. "Exactly, what are you asking me?" Ocean replied, following her into the shower. They made love again as water crashed in the background.

When they returned to the bedroom, Ocean was surprised he had another hard-on. "Hey, baby, look what I got!" he stated joking, but proud. Holding back with Brandy must have paid off; he usually got only two hard-ons in a night.

"Uhmm. Let's see what we can do with this..." Aura touched his erection firmly with her hands. By the time the evening was over they were bundled in a sweaty heap on the bed, and it was past 5:00am.

***

When Ocean rose the next morning, he was disappointed that Aura was not by his side. He slipped into sweatpants and peered into the living room. He felt as though his heart skipped a beat when he saw her in nothing but a white satin bra and panty, fully engrossed in the *Times* crossword puzzle.

Sophia Boyd
Spring 1992

"So tell me more about your friend Sandy." Lynn Galliger leaned back in the soft brown leather of her office chair as she asked the question. It was a sunny afternoon in June, and the sun shone brightly through the wide venetian blinds. The faint background sounds of chirping birds and honking horns could not be silenced by window pane or curtain.

Sophia shifted restlessly on the green fabric chaise. "Well, Sandy's not why I've been coming here, but we *are* very close." It was just about a year since she entered therapy with the short, busty psychologist behind the desk. And, as the months passed, she touched on many subjects: her relationship with her mother, her sisters, and, of course, Ron, but she never disclosed the intimate details of her relationship with Sandy. *Was it any of it this woman's business?* She came primarily to resolve her feelings for Ron...feelings which had lent to many a sleepless night. She had no issue with her sexuality. She was beginning to wonder why she continued to show up and recline in the same green chaise once a week.

"Tell me about Sandy. She's your best friend, right?" She paused. "Most people talk a lot about their friendships...often to the point where they avoid why they really came. With you I find it strange that you seem to spend so much time with Sandy but seldom discuss your feelings for her."

"We're friends; that's all," Sophia explained defensively.

"Then why are you holding back?" Lynn countered.

Sophia examined the well-worn carpeting which covered the office floor. "What do you want me to say?" she asked, feigning innocence.

"I don't know, Sophia. What do *you* want to say?"

"I told you. She's my friend."

"I know what you told me. We don't have to discuss her, but you've been coming here for a year and you've never told me much about her. Has she helped you deal with your feelings for Ron at all? Do you talk to her about your dad? Your mom? Your sisters? Don't you ever ask for her opinion?" Lynn Galliger stood up and took a seat on the sofa across from Sophia. "When did you two meet?"

Sophia smiled, lifting her gaze to meet her therapist's eyes. "We met in college. Gosh, I've known Sandy for over ten years now." Her spirit lifted as she thought of her lover. It had been a long time since their college days at the Fashion Institute.

"And, how did you feel about Sandy when you met her?" Lynn continued.

"I thought she was pretty and fun. I had just gotten to New York, and I appreciated the attention she gave me." Sophia's eyes twinkled as she reminisced.

"Were you close right away?"

"We were, but it was weird when I found out..." Sophia stopped quickly when she realized what she was about to say. She looked at Lynn Galliger for guidance. *Did she really want to tell this woman about Sandy?*

"Found out what?"

Oh, what the hell? Just because Sandy was gay didn't mean she was. "Well," she began, "I found out she was gay." *There, she said it!*

Lynn Galliger frowned. She knew there was something going on with the mysterious Sandy. "So then, Sandy's gay?"

"Yeah." Sophia twisted the hanging piece of her head wrap as she stared at the carpet. So what if Sandy *was* gay?

"And in all the years of your friendship with Sandy, how have you been affected by her lovers?" Lynn paused. "I'm assuming your friend has sexual relationships with women."

Sophia looked at her therapist with annoyance. *What was the point of this?* Suddenly, she grew stony. "I don't want to talk about Sandy." She folded her arms in front of her in defiance. She paid for this woman's service. She didn't have to deal with any shit.

Lynn Galliger moved on to another subject.

***

When the phone rang, Sophia answered quickly, expecting it to be Sandy. The kids were with her Aunt Tyra for the weekend, and she and Sandy had made plans to go out with friends.

"SOPHIE?!" the voice on the other end boomed.

"Daddy?" she responded emotionally. She had been able to avoid her father's phone calls for years. Now, she could hear his voice on the other end, and it was all she could do to keep herself from crying. "Daddy?" she said again, almost asking, but knowing that it was her father.

"Oh, Sophie..." her father's voice cracked with emotion. "How *are* you?" he asked.

The tears came down her face alarmingly fast. She wiped them away quickly with a kitchen napkin. "I'm fine," she responded in the requisite way. Her mind quickly filled with memories of her father pushing her swing, picking her up from high school parties, attending her college graduation.

Suddenly she heard her father's tone change to desperation. "Sophie, *please* don't hang up," he begged.

"I won't hang up, daddy," she said in a high, shallow voice. The words crossed her lips before she could fully comprehend what she was saying. She had promised never to speak to this man again. This was the man who left her mother after thirty years of marriage to move to Florida. This was the man she hated.

"Oh, baby, I love you so much!"

Sophia could hear the pain and anguish in her father's voice, but she didn't know how to respond. She also couldn't stop the stream of silent tears which slid down her cheeks. *Where were they coming from?*

"I'm so sorry..." His words soothed her like warm oil.

"I'm sorry too..." Her words fell from her lips freely. *What was she sorry for?* For refusing to speak to her father for three years? For blaming him for her parent's separation? For denying him the chance to see his grandchildren? As she thought about her boys, she felt an unexpected wave of guilt. Who was she to keep them from knowing their grandfather? Sophia felt her composure begin to return. "So, how *are* you?" she asked.

"Not bad, Sophie...things are different now, but I'm good. The weather down here is beautiful year-round. You should come visit one day."

"Sure," Sophia responded distantly.

Mr. Boyd paused before adding, "Or I could come visit you in New York. You know I'd love to spend some time with you. I'd stay in a hotel...You don't have to worry about making room for me..." His voice became a near-whisper. "I just want to spend some time with you."

Sophia cleared her throat, as if in so doing she could distance herself from her own emotions. "Well, we'll see what happens... You know this thing with Mom is still tough for me to deal with. Let me think about it. I have your number. I'll call you." Sophia quickly hung up the phone before her father could protest.

She didn't have her father's number anymore, but she could get it from one of her sisters. That is, if she ever decided to call him.

***

It was 5:00pm and Sandy still hadn't called. Sophia was bored in the house without the kids, so she decided to go out to dinner alone. Sandy had promised to call before noon. It seemed this type of neglect was becoming more frequent in their relationship. In the beginning, this type of oversight never happened and Sandy's words were like clockwork. But now, any little thing could make her "forget" a date or a promise. Sophia didn't think it was that she didn't love her anymore, but after three years, their relationship had grown routine. At first, Sophia would think Sandy was in an accident or something when she didn't keep her promises, but now she accepted it as an inconsiderate habit on her part.

When Sophia arrived at Caribbean Corner, a pretty black woman named Mona seated her quickly. The heavy aroma of cooking food immediately made Sophia feel ravenous. As she examined her menu, she relaxed and took in her surroundings: the hard wood floors, African sculptures, framed photos of black leaders and celebrities. *Screw, Sandy!* She was glad she came out alone tonight. She didn't need Sandy or Sandy's gay friends to have a good time.

A young waiter came to take her drink order. She ordered a margarita and relaxed as she waited for her drink to arrive. It was nice to be out alone, without having to worry about her children. Sophia looked around at the various people in the dining area of the restaurant. There was a table with three young women who seemed like college buddies. A table with two men and two women... Maybe they were double-dating? A table with an older man and woman... Maybe it was their anniversary? They seemed very much in love. It took Sophia's thoughts to her earlier conversation with her father. They hadn't really discussed anything, but it felt like she opened a huge can of worms. Then, Sophia noticed a striking couple at one of the corner tables...a beautiful dark-skinned brother and his companion. Both looked like dreamy chocolate fudgesicles from some African fantasy. The woman was very dark with long black hair which curled at her shoulders over a tapered cream pants suit. The man had a chocolate complexion with dreadlocks that fell just beyond his shoulders and framed a stunning face. She wondered if either of them did any modeling. They gazed at each other as if there were no one else in room. Sophia smiled. They were obviously *new* lovers. That dreamy-eyed look wouldn't last for long.

Sophia was working on her third margarita when her food arrived: steamed red snapper, yams and greens. As she ate, she replayed her day in her mind: first the call from her father, then waiting hours for Sandy's call. This was definitely better. She noticed a young man at the bar who seemed to be watching her. Sophia smiled in spite of herself. He looked no older than twenty-five! At thirty-one, anyone younger than thirty was like a child to her. Although this particular baby looked quite appealing. He was tall, stocky and light-skinned, much like Ron had been. Sophia made a mental note to have a drink at the bar before she left.

***

"Hi, how are you?" the man at the bar asked as Sophia ordered her third margarita. She was feeling rather euphoric. "Oh, I'm just great. How are you?" she responded jovially, quickly stealing a bar stool as it became available.

The man stood next to where she sat. "My name's Brad. What's yours?" His eyes coursed over Sophia's voluptuous figure, barely hidden in stylish rayon overalls and long-sleeved black bodysuit. He could see the full curve of her breasts and thighs as she sat loosely at the bar.

"I'm Sophie," Sophia responded. This man was young, but quite attractive. He certainly seemed like a nice guy. They got into conversation, and Sophia talked about the fashion business. The man mentioned he was a stock broker, so they talked a little about Wall Street as he ordered her drinks. She felt relaxed and increasingly uninhibited, but not drunk at all.

"Hey, why don't we get out of here," he suggested as he quickly paid the drink bill.

"Where do you want to go?" she asked. It was getting late, and she knew she should probably head home. Then, she remembered she had no reason to head home. There wouldn't be anyone there anyway, and it would do Sandy good to wonder where *she* was for a change.

"There's a nice place over on Nineteenth Street... My friend works there. They have live music, if you want to go." Brad offered Sophia his arm.

"Sounds good to me," Sophia happily agreed. *Why not?*

***

Sophia laughed heartily with her companion as he led

her up the stairs to his apartment. "You know what, Brad?" Sophia began, carefully holding the railing of the staircase with one hand and Brad's shirted biceps with the other.

"What?" he responded with some annoyance. What could possibly be wrong? She was full of liquor that he bought. She was already *inside* his building. *She couldn't change her mind now, could she?*

Sophia pulled her arm away from his with some difficulty. "This is not a good idea... I've really had *waaay* too much to drink..." She slurred a bit.

"Oh, just come up for a little while..." Brad began, before pressing his lips against hers so that her back was flush against the painted yellow wall.

Sophia kissed him back, then turned her head to the side. She could feel the cold wall against her cheek as she spoke. "No, this is not a good idea..." She freed herself from his arms and stumbled down the steps and out of his apartment building.

Brad stared after her dumbfounded and considered following her, but decided against it. How could she do this to him? *Stupid bitch!*

***

When the phone rang the next morning, Sophia's headache pounded loudly in her head. "Oh, shit," she grumbled, grabbing the phone.

"Where the hell have you been?" an angry Sandy demanded.

"I'll tell you later," Sophia groaned. "What time is it?"

"It's nearly noon! You had me worried sick!" Sandy complained.

"Sorry, look, I'm tired. I'll give you a call back a little later." With that, she rolled over and went back to sleep.

***

"Hi, Sophie," Sandy stated carefully when Sophia picked up the phone.

"Ohhh, Sandy, I'm sorry I didn't call you sooner," Sophia said, apologizing quickly. It was Monday evening, and she had not returned Sandy's call on Sunday as promised.

"It's okay. I can understand if you're mad at me. You have every right to be," Sandy conceded.

"I am mad at you, but that's not why I didn't call. Honestly, I was just so busy. I had to get the kids from the Bronx last night, and things have just been hectic. You know how it can get..." Sophia paused before asking the inevitable. "So what happened to you on Saturday?"

Sandy swallowed before answering. "I got tied up with these fools." She sighed. "You know how Meg and Aretha can get sometimes. They got into a big fight so I was up at Barry's apartment watching the kids, and I didn't want to call you from there. Time just flew. I was just running around." Sandy referred to the lesbian couple they had planned to have dinner with that night. They were known for occasional physical altercations, and Barry, who was also gay, was Meg's best friend.

"So where did you sleep?" Sophia suddenly heard herself asking.

"I went home!" Sandy replied defensively.

Sophia smiled. *Whatever.* If she couldn't trust Sandy after three years, who could she trust? Clearly, not herself... She let her mind wander back to the staircase kiss in Brad's apartment building only two nights before.

"Sophie?" Sandy began. "I'm really sorry. I should have called. Can you forgive me?"

"Of course," Sophia answered.

"Let me make it up to you I'll come cook dinner for you and the kids Wednesday. Is that ok?" Her voice was pleading as if she were apologizing for more than she had admitted.

"Sure," Sophia replied simply.

***

"So how was your week?" Lynn Galliger asked the following Wednesday, as she peered across at the pretty light-skinned woman reclined in her green chaise.

"Pretty eventful, actually," Sophia admitted.

"Do tell," Lynn Galliger urged.

"I finally spoke to my father. He called and I happened to answer the phone. I also met a man..."

Lynn Galliger raised an eyebrow. She was certain Sophia was a closet homosexual, and suddenly inventing a man the first week after she pressed her about Sandy was a typical response. "Tell me about your father," Lynn Galliger urged, figuring it was easier to tackle the smaller problems first.

Sophia dropped her eyes slightly in response to the woman's question. "I don't really know how I feel about him anymore. At first, when I answered the phone, and it was him, I felt happy, overjoyed, really. I started crying uncontrollably like really sobbing." She looked at her therapist for a reaction. Lynn Galliger smiled and nodded her head as if she understood.

"But then after I stopped crying, I just felt the same, you know... Like I didn't really want to have anything to do with him." The therapist nodded her head.

"Now, I feel sort of guilty... Like I'm not being fair... At least not to my kids..."

"What about yourself?" Lynn Galliger urged. "Do you think you're being fair to yourself?"

"What do you mean?" Sophia asked.

"Don't you have the right to have a father too?"

Sophia paused, taking in the question. "I never thought of it that way... I mean, I do have a father, I'm just angry with him for what he did to our family..."

"From what you tell me, it's not what he did to your family, it's what he did to your mother... Do you feel you have to defend your mother from him?"

Sophia looked perplexed. "No... I mean, I don't think so."

"Look, Sophia, I'm glad you've finally spoken to your father. I think it's time for you to prepare to reexamine your relationship with him. Maybe you can start by talking to your mother."

"My mother won't speak to him anymore."

"Why don't you think your mother speaks to him?" Lynn Galliger asked.

Sophia's mind began to wander. *Why did she come here and listen to this woman talk once a week?* The problems with guilt feelings over Ron and the ensuing nightmares did seem to work themselves out after she entered therapy, but did she really need anything more? She could handle her relationship with her family. And, why didn't this woman want to hear about the man she met?! Shouldn't that be more important than the ongoing situation with her father?

"Sophia?" the woman said repeatedly. "Sophia?"

"Huh?" Sophia responded dazedly.

"I asked you a question," Lynn Galliger stated firmly.

Sophia sighed, pulling herself out of her day dreaming. "I'm not feeling so well, can I make up my time later?" she asked with disregard.

Lynn Galliger looked shocked. "That's not office policy, but we can certainly meet at another time."

"Thank you." Sophia quickly gathered her purse and

left the office.

***

When Sophia walked outside, she was pleased to have over a half-hour to herself before she got the kids from the babysitter. The weather was beautiful at eighty degrees with clear blue skies. She walked along the treelined blocks with a feeling of freedom. She had made up her mind; she wasn't going back to that woman! It wasn't that her therapy hadn't worked. It had, but she felt she reached the point where she should deal with her problems on her own. Granted, her little escapade the previous Saturday had not been particularly wise, but she didn't let it get out of hand. And, Sandy would certainly never need to know she kissed a man. She threw his number away as soon as she found it.

She slid her hands into the pockets of her linen blazer as she strolled along the sidewalks, occasionally stopping to peek in the window of a shop. Yeah, things were going well. She was back on track with work, her relationship with Sandy was stronger than ever, Timothy was doing well in kindergarten, and Marcus was happy with his preschool.

As far as the situation with her father went, she'd have to give that some time. She knew she couldn't keep the kids away from their grandfather for much longer. Maybe she *would* let him visit in a few months for the holidays.

***

Sandy cooked a wonderful dinner that night and the kids fell asleep early in front of the television. Things could not have been more perfectly planned. Sophia and Sandy had time to cuddle on the sofa after the kids were tucked in.

That night their lovemaking was particularly emotional, as if they sought to rectify the wrongs of the previous weekend. As usual, the kids had been sleeping for hours. What was unusual was Timothy's nocturnal journey to his mother's room, only to find his mother naked in the arms of her female friend.

"Oh, nooo..." Sophia began when she saw her son's shocked countenance at her bedroom door. She quickly grabbed her robe from beside the bed and followed Timothy, who had quickly run away. "Oh, honey..." she began as her five-year-old son padded back into his bedroom with embarrassment. She placed a hand on his shoulder, as her mind raced for what to say. She could think of nothing.

Timothy quickly jumped back under the covers of his bed with Marcus fast asleep beside him. His eyes rested directly on his mother's face in a curious fashion.

"Timothy?" Sophia said gently, responding to her son's peculiar expression.

"It's okay, Mom," her son said simply as he looked into her eyes with a precocious wisdom. Then, he turned onto his side, closed his eyes and drifted back to sleep.

***

The next evening, Sophia picked the children up from the sitter and busied herself with cooking dinner afterward. She hadn't discussed the previous evening with Timothy, and was still uncertain about what to say. She was, however, certain of one thing—she had to put her relationship with Sandy on hold. As much as she cared about Sandy, she could not handle a continuing relationship. She needed to find out what was important to her. *Would she have reacted the same way if Timothy walked in on her and Ron?* She wasn't sure, but she didn't think so. It was her own fault that she got so careless about locking the bedroom door. And, it was her own fault for not anticipating such an occurrence. She had some heavy thinking to do, and she needed to be alone to do it.

Aura Olivier
The Holidays 1992-1993

Aura looked at the light snow flurries which fell outside her office window. It was funny how things could change so quickly. With Christmas and the New Year on her mind, it was easy to get lost in thoughts of the previous December. She had just become involved with Kenny back then, and was hopeful things would turn out well. But, looking back, she knew from the beginning that it wouldn't work. She smiled as she recalled Dana last Christmas, as jovial as ever, but never even hinting things were getting serious between her and Ace. And, she remembered Angie and Pascal's quiet togetherness during Christmas dinner.

She put her hands on her hips and breathed deeply, watching the yellow cabs pass along the street below. This year would certainly be different. Angie and Pascal had gone their separate ways after five years together. Dana and Ace were making wedding plans for June.

And, she and Ocean were doing just fine. She knew it was more than that. She was in love with him, and it didn't feel scary anymore. It just felt good.

She sighed. *Yeah, love feels good.*

She tossed the plastic packaging from her lunch into the wastebasket under her desk. She had a busy month ahead of her at work with many large media buys underway. It had been weeks since she'd eaten out. Thankfully, it was Thursday, and the week was almost over. She had plans to go ice skating with Dana after work. It had been months since they'd been out alone together. Of course, neither of them minded. It just meant that they spent most of their free time in their foursome with Ace and Ocean. It was great, really. Ocean and Ace hit it off from their first encounter. And, besides, they lived together, so they saw each other often enough, although mostly as ships passing in the night, running in and out of the apartment...to and from work.

Aura was enjoying the holiday season, but she wished her sister, Angie, could find some happiness. She just hadn't been herself in the months since her split from Pascal. Aura had asked Angie to go skating with them, but she refused, saying she was too busy with work. She figured Angie probably didn't want to be around her and Dana when they were so happy in their relationships. Honestly, she couldn't really blame her. It must be hard for her to see Dana and Ace's relationship progressing so quickly when Pascal never even proposed to her.

***

As the clock approached 5:30pm, Aura closed her office door and changed from her red wool suit into a pair of loose-fitting jeans and a navy blue turtleneck sweater. On her way out, she deposited two games under the decorated tree in the reception area of her office. Her company sponsored a yearly drive to supply needy children with holiday toys, and she was happy to take part. She and Ocean had even spent Thanksgiving morning doling out food in a soup kitchen with Darryl. That was part of what she loved about him ̄ he was kind-hearted and responsible; he took his community seriously.

"Hey!" she called out, when she saw Dana at the rink.

Dana walked over to where she was in front of the

skate rental area. "What's uuup?" she asked in her usual cheerful way.

"Same ole, same ole," Aura said with a wide grin.

"Gosh, girl. You look good. That man must be taking *good* care of you!" Dana gushed melodramatically, as if she were a long-lost friend.

Aura blushed. "Oh, you *know* he is!" They ordered their skates as they spoke. "I haven't felt like this since I first started dating Tony...and I was so young then, it doesn't even count anymore. When I think about it, it was like I was a different person."

"Shit, Aura, that's over five years ago..." She paused as she laced her skates. "Wow, we've been friends a *long* time... And, we're getting *old!*" She stared at her friend with the shock of her realization.

"Yeah, I know," Aura admitted, lacing her own skates. "Before you know it we'll be turning thirty, all married up, with kids."

Dana giggled. "Do you know something you're not telling me?"

"Like what?" Aura replied.

"Like, who's getting *all married up?*"

Aura laughed. Dana could be so ridiculous sometimes. "I thought *you* were getting all married up!" she replied.

"Well, it sounded like I heard the word 'we' just now." Dana cupped a hand around her ear as if it would improve her sound reception. "Was I hearing correct? Now I know I'm not deaf, girl. Did I hear a 'we' or didn't I?"

Aura stood up on her skates. "Shut up, Dana, before I throw you down on that ice!" she joked.

"Do I hear a challenge? Girl, you know damned well I can skate rings around you... BACKWARDS!" She stood on her skates and slapped her knee with her laughter.

"Come on now. Who are you trying to fool? You better hold on to that bar. I know you're scared to let go!"

Aura joked, referring to the railing around the rink.

"Yeah, sure," Dana mumbled, letting the joking die down. "So, do you want to marry Ocean?" she asked on their way to the ice.

Aura simply skated off.

***

"That was fun, but I can't do that too often. All that cold is bad for me," Aura said as they boarded the subway to return to Brooklyn.

"Holy shit!" Dana exclaimed under her breath as she stepped onto the 'F' train.

"What?!" Aura mumbled before seeing who was on the train with them. She was shocked to see Tony looking back at her. As she walked into the middle of the car, he followed behind.

"Aura!" he said.

"Hi, Tony," Aura replied. She was surprised by her own lack of interest.

He and Dana nodded their hellos.

"I'm glad I bumped into you. I've been wanting to speak to you."

Was he for real? "Oh, really?" Aura responded "Why would you want to speak to me? I thought you and Robin were married and everything."

Tony dropped his eyes slightly. "We are."

"So what do you want?" she asked with annoyance.

"I can't tell you here. Believe me, it's important. Here," he reached into his coat pocket and pulled out a business card and pen. He carefully scribbled a number on the back of the card. "Call me at home when you have a moment. Really, it's important. Or, if you'd like I can call you."

"Nah, that's okay. I'll call you. This better be good."

Aura smiled nervously. What could he possibly want to talk to her about? Knowing Tony, he probably wanted some pussy. With that thought, she smiled at him again, but more casually. *He was such an asshole.*

"Trust me; it will be." With that, he walked to the other side of the car.

Dana waited until he was out of earshot before she spoke. "What was *that* about?"

Aura laughed. "I don't know, maybe he wants a second wife or something."

"Tony's a jerk, but he still does look *good!* Damn!" Dana laughed. "Shit, if I wasn't in love with your brother, I'd give him some my damn self!" she joked.

Aura cut her eyes at Dana playfully. "You are *truly* disgusting!" she stated, knowing she'd probably do the same.

***

Aura dialed Tony's number Saturday afternoon as Dana peered over her shoulder. Ocean and Ace had already left the apartment to pick up some groceries and run a few errands. They had all gone out partying the previous night at a club called The Potpourri.

"Hello?" a woman's voice answered.

Aura was not certain if it was Robin. "Hi, may I speak to Tony?" Aura asked. She could hear the phone being passed to someone else. Pretty rude. The person could have at least said, "hold on" or something.

"Aura?" Tony said, sounding somewhat sympathetic.

"Yes, Tony. You've got me. What was all that talk about on the subway? And who was that? Was that Robin?" She asked her questions with some annoyance. It probably was Robin—just plain ole rude!

"Yeah, it was...listen...I don't know how to tell you

this, so I'm just gonna tell you, okay?" Tony inhaled deeply.

"Whaaat?" Aura asked with rising dread. Her mind raced. What could Tony, of all people, have to say to her that would be of any interest to her after five years?

As Tony exhaled, he dropped the bomb. "I'm HIV positive."

Aura replayed her sexual encounters with Tony in her mind like a videocassette in fast rewind. She had worn condoms with him *sometimes.* Her heart began beating loudly in her chest, and her breathing took on a frenetic rhythm. Shit, *sometimes* couldn't save her now. Now, when she'd finally met the man she wanted to spend her life with...the man whose kids she thought she would one day carry.

Dana's mouth dropped open with shock. What could Tony have *said* to her?

Finally, Aura felt able to speak again. "Are you serious, Tony? Why didn't you call me sooner? How long have you known?" She couldn't believe she and Dana were lusting after Tony not even twenty-four hours earlier.

"I planned to call you Aura, but it's been a long time. I didn't really know how to reach you."

Aura's mind replayed her lovemaking with Ocean. He was downright meticulous about using condoms. Thank heavens for his good sense. She would never be able to forgive herself if she infected him with something as horrible as AIDS. AIDS... Shit! It was the first time since Tony said "HIV" that she allowed herself to think the deadly acronym. AIDS... Aura felt her tears stinging in her eyes. "Damn you, Tony. Haven't you done enough shit to me? How can this happen?" She choked back her tears.

Dana gave Aura a peculiar expression. She hoped the

conversation wasn't about what she thought it was about.

"Relax, Aura. I was just tested recently. I may have gotten it *after* we were together. But, I know I wasn't your first boyfriend either."

Aura tried to digest this new piece of information. She had thought he'd been with Robin since they broke up. Did this mean he wasn't faithful? She didn't have a hard time believing that at all...that eased her mind a bit. Maybe he got it *after* they were together. He was right, though, she wasn't a virgin when she started dating him either. *What a big fucking mess.*

She rummaged through drawers in her mind—with all the blood tests she had over the years for sickle-cell therapy, they must have tested her for AIDS at some point. She hoped. Her thoughts calmed her a bit. "What about Robin?" she asked, not entirely sure she cared.

"She's positive too," Tony admitted.

"Wow." Aura thought back to the all-night cram sessions they had together, the college parties they attended. She and Robin had been really close for awhile. "Is she sick?" she asked.

"Not too much. She's hanging in there." Tony's voice sounded pained.

Aura resisted her urge to ask more questions, detecting Tony's discomfort. "Well, thanks for letting me know. Take care of yourself." Aura hung up the phone.

"What was that all about?" Dana asked.

"Have you ever been tested for AIDS, Dana?"

"Girl, I get tested for every goddamn thing. AIDS, hepatitis, syphilis... You know I donate blood. They haven't sent me a card yet, so I figure I'm okay."

"Oh, yeah," Aura commented, realizing Dana's blood would be tested regularly from her blood donations.

"Is that what Tony said?!" Dana asked with nervous agitation. "He has AIDS?!"

"Well, he's HIV positive, so if he doesn't have it yet...he will..."

"Are you worried?" Dana asked.

"Shit, Dana. Of course, I'm worried. I just keep thinking I must have already been tested. I mean, it's five years ago... Shit, if I'm HIV positive, I have a lot of people to call..." She thought about all her boyfriends over the past few years. She had used condoms regularly, but had her share of occasional accidents. And, she knew condoms were no guarantee, anyway.

"What are you going to tell Ocean?" Dana asked.

"I'm not going to tell him anything. I'll just get tested. Maybe I don't have anything to tell him."

Dana frowned. "Are you sure that's the right thing to do?"

"What else can I do? I'm a nervous wreck as it is; I don't want to freak him out for no reason"

"Well, I guess it's your choice." Dana shrugged her shoulders and walked away.

***

When Ocean returned, Aura quickly took him aside. "I need to talk to you," she stated simply.

"Sure," he replied.

She walked him into her bedroom and closed the door.

"What's up, babe? You don't look so hot..." He paused when she didn't respond in any way. "Are you *okay?*" he asked, his voice filled with sudden concern. He wrapped an arm around Aura as he took a seat next to her on the queen-sized bed.

Aura breathed in deeply. "We've been together for what...seven months?"

"Oh, you've been *counting!*"Ocean said playfully. He kissed her forehead.

Aura remained serious as she searched for the right words. "I've sort of had a scare; a bit of a reality check." Aura searched for the right words. She couldn't tell him the truth, could she? "I just found out one of my old girlfriends is HIV positive."

"Oh, baby, that's horrible. Shit, that *is* a reality check, isn't it?" Ocean held her closer. "I've been tested Aura; I try to get it done once a year. I'm fine."

"I want us to get tested together." Aura paused before adding more firmly, "Soon."

"Sure, baby. Just let me know where you want me to be, and I'll be there." He held her chin in his hand and kissed her slowly. "Uhmmm. I'd love to slip out of latex with you." He winked.

"Ocean, we will *not* be slipping out of latex any time soon," Aura stated a bit harshly.

Ocean smiled, "Not even if I marry you?"

Aura blushed quickly, then laughed. "What makes you think I would ever marry *you?*" She punched his arm playfully, and buried her face in his chest.

"What makes you think I'd ever ask?" Ocean held her in his arms and chuckled lightly.

Aura felt a tear at the corner of her eye. *Suppose she lost everything?*

***

The blood was drawn the following Tuesday and while Ocean was convinced his results would be negative, Aura was crazed with trepidation for the next few days. She cried when she got her results. They were negative. She immediately called Dana.

"Dana Carlton speaking," the voice stated.

"Dana Dane! I'm back in business!" Aura nearly screamed with her office door shut.

Dana swallowed. "The results? You got them?!"

"Yup! I'm fine!"

Dana sucked her teeth slowly. "It's a good thing too, 'cause if you weren't fine I was gonna personally smack little Miss Robin in the head for you, and her sickly husband!"

"Damn, Dana, don't be mean!"

"Shit, Aura, if you're gonna get something like that, wouldn't you at least want it to come from someone you cared about...like Ocean or something. At least you could say it was halfway worthwhile."

"Dana, I could never say it was halfway worthwhile, even if the dick was solid gold and vibrating with a French tickler!"

"Aura, you are too much. Well, I guess we've all had a little wakeup call now. Fuck a Lycra spandex, now...all I need is a latex condom bodysuit. You know what I'm saying? Nowadays, this shit is just ferocious. You just never know..." Dana's voice trailed off.

"Has Ace ever been tested?" Aura asked.

"Are you kidding me? Aura, you know if he's sleeping with me for this long he's been tested. We've been together too long for that kind of nonsense. *And,* we're getting married. Come on, now!"

Aura felt like a totally irresponsible child when Dana made her comment. Dana always was pretty serious when it came to her nonoxynol-9 condoms, but she didn't realize she got tested regularly too. "Gee, I didn't know you were so serious, Dane!"

"Hey, I like living and I'd like to continue...you know? Anyway, girl, congratulations, but I've really got to run. I'm going by Ace after work, so I'll probably see you tomorrow."

"Okay. Bye, Dana Dane."

"Bye Aura."

Aura sighed with relief, and dialed Ocean's home number. He wasn't there but she left a message on his machine: "I miss you, boo. Call me when you get in."

***

When the phone rang, Aura was happy to hear Ocean's voice on the other end. "Hey, boo, what's up? Did you get your results yet?"

"Yesss..." Aura said playfully.

"Well..." Ocean said in kind.

"I'm fine!" she replied. "What about you?"

"I *told* you I knew I was fine," Ocean replied matter-of-factly.

"Well, you never know until you *know,* you know?" Aura laughed. It was good hearing his voice. They hadn't spoken all day. "So what's the plan for tonight?" she asked.

"Well it's Christmas time in The Big Apple. We can do whatever we want! Do you want to go see the tree?" he asked referring to the 80' tree at Rockefeller Center.

"Nah, I went skating there last week with Dana. Let's go to the World Financial Center," Aura said referring to a business and shopping complex on the river which had a huge public atrium. It was attached by a bridge to the famous World Trade Center, but was a big attraction in its own right in the summer and holiday seasons. "I think the Boys Choir of Harlem is performing tonight. Did you get the tickets for the Christmas Concert at Radio City Music Hall?"

"Yup," Ocean replied.

"Good. I got my Alvin Ailey tickets today," she said referring to the dance tickets she purchased. One of the things they had in common was a love of the arts. Whether it was a movie, museum exhibit, play, dance or concert, they loved to experience art together. And, they were lucky enough to live in a city where all of these things were at their fingertips, many for little or no cost.

"So, see you later then?" Ocean said, knowing her answer.

"Of course, babe." Aura grinned. "I love you." She said it without thinking. Shit... *What did she say?*

"I love you too." Ocean looked at the phone as if it had displayed his ace in the hole. *He gave his own hand away!* He swore he heard a Kenny Rogers song playing in the background of his thoughts, *"You've got to know when to hold them, know when to fold them, know when to walk away, know when to run..."*

"All right then," Aura replied recovering from his words. *She knew it!*

"Peace." Ocean placed the telephone receiver back in the cradle trying to maintain his cool. He *knew* he was in love, but why did he *say* it? He felt a lump in his throat and he grabbed a beer from his fridge and consoled himself. Fuck it... Love was okay. *Wasn't it?*

***

There was no snow, just bitter cold on Christmas morning. Aura was nestled in Ocean's arms and was surprised, for a moment, when she looked around the small room. She had forgotten where she was in the way waking travelers often do in hotel rooms. A pale peach comforter and blanket covered the two of them on the full-sized bed. She hadn't slept in her old bedroom since the previous Christmas and was surprised the room was kept the same as she had left it.

Her parents hadn't changed Ace's or Angie's rooms either. Sylvia and Donald Olivier knew they could make use of the space for storage, or straighten it up a bit for guests, but they wanted their children to have a comfortable place to stay when they came home. And, maybe they weren't too ready to face the fact that it was only the two of them living in the house now. After having kids for over twenty years, the reality was a bit unsettling.

"Merry Christmas," Aura mumbled into Ocean's ear.

"Mmmm, Merry Christmas baby," he mumbled in response, shifting lazily in the bed. He slid a hand around her waist, pressed his body against hers, and kissed her neck "What time is it?" he asked.

"It's still early."

"Good," Ocean whispered wearily. They had stayed up the previous evening drinking eggnog, singing Christmas carols and playing cards with Angie, Dana, Ace and Aura's parents. It was one of many times he had been in the company of her folks over the past few months. The first was Fourth of July weekend, when the Olivier's threw a big backyard barbecue. He enjoyed being around her family and particularly Mr. and Mrs. Olivier. Their relationship proved to him that love *could* last.

He slipped his hand inside the flannel pajama bottom she wore.

Aura smiled. Making love to Ocean was beautiful. They had both 'fucked' many times before, but when he touched her it was different. Now she knew what people meant when they talked about 'making love.' She had never really understood it before—not even with Tony...and certainly not with Robert, or Henry, or Mike, or Kenny or any of her other lovers. She was consumed by him, and with him. It was inexplicable, but Dana understood. A fleeting thought stretched across her mind: *Could Angie?*

She turned around and kissed him slowly, contemplating the state of her breath in the morning.

He kissed her back longingly as if morning breath never even crossed his mind. She reached inside his boxers. A full hard-on greeted her. She sipped from the glass of water beside her bed, then burrowed a path under the covers to the warmth beneath his shorts. And then, she kissed him there.

Ocean sighed and rushed his hand through her hair. He was in love. And when love and sex come together, everything is different. There was no comparison between her touch and that of any other woman. The reality of his feelings engulfed him, shocked him, *grew* him, because to love a woman *was* to be a man. He felt like Aura *made* him a man. Or, in a way he did. It didn't really matter because he was in her mouth right at that moment, and his thoughts were incoherent.

***

A 7' spruce stood center in the Olivier's living room, adorned with lights and garland and surrounded by gifts. The whole family was awake now, exchanging gifts, drinking hot apple cider and listening to Nat King Cole sing Christmas songs. Dana had spent the night.

Aura was a bit nervous when she saw the small velvet gift box that Ocean presented to her. *Was it a ring?*

Mrs. Olivier smiled thoroughly when she saw her daughter with her new boyfriend. It was obvious he loved her—the way he *looked* at her, the way he *talked* about her, the way he treated her family. A mother knows when a man is in for the long haul.

Mr. Olivier was pleased when he was in the company of Ocean and Aura, Dana and Ace. But when would Angie find *her* mate? The thought made him furrow his brows and frown.

Aura wondered what was on her father's mind.

Then she opened the box; it was a beautiful pair of emerald earrings. Aura thanked Ocean with a mixture of relief and disappointment. *Was she ready for a ring?*

***

"Dinner was delicious," Ocean complimented meaningfully. He hadn't had such a wonderful home-cooked meal in years, it seemed. His father's woman, Karen, couldn't cook a lick in comparison. Turkey, ham, candied yams, braised asparagus, fresh cranberry sauce, stuffing, pecan and sweet potato pies, ice cream. He was in culinary heaven.

"Yup, my moms can cook her *ass* off!" Angie agreed, taking a swallow of wine.

Dana frowned directly in the direction of Aura's sister. "Yeah, Mrs. O. Everything was truly delicious. Thank you so much for having me here. I know my parents hate me now." She lowered her eyes and smiled widely. "My mom must be going nuts." She brought her voice to a near-whisper, "But, she just can't cook quite as well as you can, you know?" She winked at Mrs. Olivier.

Sylvia Olivier laughed. She had seen Dana grow from a little tom-boy to her son's fiancée. What could possibly be funnier? And, Dana was a truly kind and likable person. She couldn't think of anyone she'd rather see Aaron with.

"Yeah, I guess your mom can't cook too well, huh?" Angie agreed, swallowing another gulp.

Dana cut her eyes at Angela. She could talk about her *own* mother, but she wasn't trying to open up the 'dis mommy' gates, you know? It was odd, but Angie had been different since she split with Pascal. She had become more obnoxious, rambunctious. Maybe she was just indulging her sorrows in too much goddamn wine, eggnog and cognac.

***

"Ahhh, home sweet home!" Aura said as she entered the apartment with Dana. They were returning home from a Kwanzaa event in the City. It was two days after Christmas, and neither of them had slept in their apartment for days.

"Yeah, I do miss my bed when I leave it for too long." Dana agreed. "Although, I hate sleeping alone now. I can't wait till I can live with Ace." She sighed.

"Well, you don't have too much longer now. I'm wondering if I should even renew the lease in February. If you're moving in with Ace, I can't see how I can handle this rent on my own, and Ocean's bed *is* mighty comfy!"

Dana smiled. "You're in love with him aren't you?"

Aura sighed like a heartsick school girl. "Yeah, I am."

"I *know* he's in love with you. All you have to do is look at him once. It's all over his face."

Aura grinned widely.

"You know, I love you Aura. I'm so happy for us. I mean we've had many a night when I thought we were both gonna have to go through our lives alone, you know. It's not that that's so bad... I mean, we were happy before we were in love."

"Yeah," Aura agreed.

Dana laughed. "But not being in love doesn't hold a candle to this shit!"

"Yeah!" Aura laughed. "It is a really good feeling... everything... Having you..." She looked meaningfully at Dana. "Shit, good friends are hard to find. And people change so goddamn much you never know how long a friendship will last. I mean, I remember when we played with my dollhouse together."

Dana laughed. "I remember when you lost your virginity to that guy with the giant gap between his teeth!"

"Yeah... God, I just knew he was *fine!*"

"That boy was the funniest looking thing I've ever seen. Thank God your taste got better!"

"Well you lost it to Mike Lonson, he was no charm!"

"He was Adonis compared to your little gap-toothed friend!" Dana laughed. "But seriously, we have been through a lot together. I remember when we compared pubic hairs!"

"Good Lord!" Aura squealed, embarrassed by the thought. "That was a *long* time ago!" She giggled for a moment before becoming more serious. "What do you think about Angie?"

"She needs to go out. She's bugging." Dana's frankness was always refreshing.

"Yeah, she seems to be hitting the bottle kind of heavy. Maybe I can get her to go out for dinner or something this week. We've hardly been talking at all lately."

"Yeah, well do something. She's starting to make me crazy. I wanted to smack her when she said something about my mom's cooking."

"You know she didn't mean anything."

"Aura, come on now! Everybody knows not to dis other people's moms!" Dana folded her arms across her chest.

"Yeah, true." Aura nodded her head in agreement. Dana had a point.

Suddenly Dana smiled and shifted around on the black bean bag. "You thought Ocean was gonna give you a ring, didn't you?!"

Aura laughed. "Girrrl... I was scared to open that thing!"

"I *know* you were!" Dana laughed.

Aura got more serious then. She frowned. "The thing of it is, I wasn't sure if I wanted it or not. So, when I opened it and it wasn't a ring, I wasn't sure if I was disappointed..." She kicked off her boots and pulled her feet up onto the sofa. "The thing is... I *know* Ocean. He *knows* I thought it might be a ring. He was teasing me." She gave Dana a perplexed glance. "I wonder why?"

***

Aura dialed Angie's work number the next morning. She had been spending most of her time and energy with Ocean, Dana and Ace, and after Angie's behavior at Christmas dinner (she was clearly drunk), she couldn't help but wonder if her sister was feeling abandoned. She and Angie had always been so close when they were younger. It wasn't until Angie got serious about Pascal that their relationship started to dry out. Pascal was quiet and serious, unlike Aura and Dana. Basically he bored everyone except Angie, who seemed to like having him around as some sort of security blanket. She had never really discussed Pascal's departure with Angie. All she knew was he had another woman. But, Angie was so different from the rest of her family members. When she hurt, she closed up like an attacked clam, and no one really knew what was going on inside of her.

Aura pushed her hair behind her ear, as she listened to the ringing on the telephone line. It was Angie's drinking that scared her most. Not because her sister was really drinking *that* much in excess, but because it was a drastic change of behavior for Angie, who barely drank at all under normal circumstances.

"Department of Social Services, Ms. Olivier speaking," Angie stated flatly. She sat at her desk in a brown wool suit, her hair trimmed to shoulder-length.

"Hey Angie, it's me!" Aura greeted.

"Aura?" Angie seemed surprised.

"Yeah, what's up?" Aura asked jovially.

"Damn, Aura you haven't called me at work in a long time."

"You haven't called me at work in a long time either," Aura replied playfully.

"Whenever I try to reach you, you're always busy with your new beau." Angie's tone was laden with sarcasm.

Aura immediately interpreted the harshness as a sign of her sister's pain. "Ohhh, listen, I'm sorry Angie. I know I haven't been all that available lately, and I know you've been having a rough time. Why don't we go see a movie or something this week?" She added gently, "I'll buy you dinner after…"

Angie cleared her throat; her voice was hoarse with anger. "Everything's so goddamn easy for you Aura; it makes me sick! The perfect goddamn job...the perfect best friend...the perfect little hunky boyfriend...even Ace can't leave you alone...you and stupid Dana!"

Aura was flabbergasted. *What had she done to deserve all that bullshit?*

Angie continued, her voice was thick with sarcasm, "No, Aura I don't want to go to a perfect little movie and dinner with you. Go play with your little friends and *my* brother. I'll talk to you some other time."

Aura heard the phone click. Her eyes were wide with shock. She didn't know if she should feel bad for Angie or for herself. She knew she hadn't been the world's most attentive sister for the past few months, but she did try. Besides, why couldn't Angie be happy for her? *Was that so hard?*

Aura felt the dull aching which had plagued her for the past twenty-four hours become more acute. She pulled painkillers from her desk drawer and took them with water before dialing her parents' travel agency.

"Olivier Travel," her mom answered.

"Mom, what's going on with Angie?" Aura asked, her voice shrill with her upset.

"Aura? Oh, I don't know honey. What happened?"

"I wanted to take her out this week, but she won't let me. She seems so angry. Did she say anything to you about Pascal?"

"Is she still harping about Pascal?" Mrs. Olivier asked.

Aura was surprised her mother didn't seem more in tune with Angie's situation. She spoke to her mother often, and just assumed Angie did too. "I don't know, Ma, I just figured that's what's been bothering her."

"I never liked that boy anyway," her mother admitted, sounding somewhat preoccupied.

Aura felt like her mom was totally missing the point. Of course, she wasn't entirely sure what the point was. Realizing she didn't want to get into the details of her conversations with Angie, Aura decided to let it go. "Never mind, Ma. I'll talk to you later."

"Okay, honey. Take it easy," Sylvia Olivier responded cheerily.

"Bye mom."

"Bye Aura." Aura placed the phone back in the cradle. She wanted to help Angie, but she did have work to do. *How do you help someone who doesn't want you to?*

***

"Oh… This is beautiful!" Aura said as she looked out onto the water from the deck of the cruise boat. She could see the Statue of Liberty in the distance.

It was cold, so Ocean kept his arms around her. "I wanted us to bring the New Year in special. It's our first

New Year together, you know."

Aura smiled. Sometimes she felt like she was in a dream when she was with him. It wasn't that she was giddy in love. They had passed that stage. This shit was for real. It was just that things had fallen into place so well that it seemed scripted from some beautiful fairy tale.

Then the countdown began. She heard the crowd aboard the boat yelling.

"Ten!" Aura got her noisemaker on the ready.

"Nine!" Ocean grabbed a handful of confetti.

"Eight!" Aura sipped her champagne.

"Seven!" Ocean put his hand in his pocket.

"Six!" Aura gave him a strange look

"Five!" Ocean smiled mysteriously.

"Four!" Aura laughed.

"Three!" Ocean suddenly felt a wave of anxiety.

"Two!" Aura licked her lips.

"One! HAPPY NEW YEAR!" Aura tooted her noisemaker. Ocean threw his confetti and placed a small velvet gift box in Aura's hand. Then, they kissed briefly.

"What is this?" she asked.

"Open it," he stated in the deep baritone she loved to hear.

It was pear-shaped diamond solitaire. She felt a tear forming in her eye.

Ocean got down on one knee. He felt a lump in his throat. "Will you marry me?" he asked.

"Oh, my god..." Aura began.

Ocean stared at her with a child's eyes. His heart was in her hands now.

"Of course! Yes! Oh my god!" A single tear slid down her cheek. Its warmth quickly turned cold in the midnight air.

He stood up, put the ring on her finger, and kissed her

thoroughly. She was going to let him keep her, and that was all he wanted. Aura was overcome with joy. Now she was not only in love, but she was contracted to spend the rest of her life making love to the man she was in love with. *What could be better?*

Ocean Ryder
The Holidays 1992-1993

Ocean parked his "new" 1989 BMW in an icy puddle outside the health club. He had purchased it six months earlier, finally giving in to his desire to own a car despite the inconveniences of driving in the city. He slid the red metal club over the steering wheel with the mindless ease of old habit as Maleek continued describing his weekend. Maleek was tall, muscular and caramel-colored. "Yeah, man, we were *all over...* The honeys were steaming that night, too! You should have been with us man."

Ocean laughed. He'd been out with Maleek many times. He knew exactly what it was like. And, he'd been out with scores of women *and* groups of women *and* groups of men... He'd done the party scene pretty thoroughly. He knew he wasn't missing a damn thing.

"Man, you laugh, but you didn't see what I saw. Shee-it, that girl got you going nuts, for now, but it'll end just like anything else. She must've put some kind of spell on you. Even Brandy never had you acting like that!" Maleek sounded dumbfounded and dejected. He shook his baby-capped head with disbelief.

Ocean laughed again. He wasn't sure why he offered to work out with Maleek. He seemed hell bent on ruining his relationship with Aura. "Damn, man, chill. Why's it got to be all that? A spell, man? Fuck that! I just like her, that's all." Ocean grabbed a towel and walked toward the men's locker room. *He wasn't under any goddamn spell.*

"Like? *Like?!*" Now Maleek had to laugh heartily, showing off his money-making grin.

"What?!" Ocean asked, suddenly defensive.

"Man, that girl got you whipped like my mom's eggnog!" He laughed again, removing his cap to reveal a bald head. He ran his hand over his scalp in his habitual way. "Whipped like Mr. Softee, like a chocolate shake, man!"

Ocean threw him a harsh glance, and the laughter died down.

Maleek smiled and quietly added, "Like Babyface, man."

***

Ocean met Aura at her job at 5:30pm. They were supposed to meet Dana and Ace at The Potpourri, a dinner/dance club in midtown Manhattan. Their relationship had become pretty serious over the past few months. He had quickly released himself from the confines of his relationship with Brandy, nearly immediately after his first evening with Aura. He remembered that first morning together well...eating pancakes, doing crosswords, making love on the living room floor. It was funny how things changed. He really didn't have any interest in any other women anymore. It wasn't even like when he was with Brandy and he just felt comfortable. With Aura he felt free, not confined like he had always imagined a serious relationship would feel. With Aura, he actually felt freer to be his true self than when he was alone. He certainly felt freer to be emotional, to feel. It wasn't like when he hung around with the guys tossing beers, watching sports or chasing women. With Aura, he could talk about the things that were important to him: family, art, career. It wasn't that he couldn't talk to other people about those things, but with Aura it just clicked. And, she was much cuter than any of the hairy guys he knew. Ocean smiled as thoughts of her leisurely washed over him. He was sitting in the reception area of Aura's office, a single rose in his hand. Maleek's comments crossed his mind. *Did buying her a rose for no particular reason mean that he really was whipped?*

As Ocean gave the rose a worried glance, Aura walked into the reception.

"Hi, baby!" she greeted. "For me?!" she asked sighting the rose.

Ocean stood and gave her a quick hug and kiss. "Of course," he replied, smiling. Seeing her response was more than worth the two bucks. *What was so wrong with falling in love?* Ocean flinched slightly at his own thought. He didn't know why love scared him so much. Okay, well maybe he did. Maybe it was because his whole life he heard other men talk about love as if it were some horrible disease you ran the risk of catching if you spent too much time with a woman you cared about. Or maybe it was because he heard of too many men doing crazy things for women...being disrespected...getting used...and maybe he just didn't want to take that risk...of being a fool...or being vulnerable...or out of control... He smiled at Aura so she wouldn't know what was running through his mind. He wondered, *was she scared to fall in love too?*

***

They danced all night. The lights in the club flashed dramatic colors as Aura swayed her hips rhythmically in a tight, black sequined dress. Ocean had never seen her quite like this before. It was driving him crazy. *She could really move.* He put a hand on her hip as he rocked his body next to hers. Dana and Ace danced nearby.

Aura called out, "Go Dana, get busy! That's right work it out, girl!" She laughed and smiled at Ocean. Her chanting could barely be heard through the thumping bass and wailing horns of the music.

Dana worked her stuff in a body-hugging red velvet dress. With a giggle she shouted, "Go Aura! Go Aura-Go!"

Ace made sure to keep his eyes on Dana as she moved to the beat. He noticed a few of the other brothers checking her out. While he was proud, he was also cautious with his woman. Besides, the bootie was bodacious, and he felt it was his job to guard it at all times. When they tired themselves out, the four headed back to Aura and Dana's apartment. Ocean drove through the lamp and neon-lighted streets with skillful ease. The dark pavement glistened with the dew of an earlier drizzle which struggled to freeze over, but didn't quite make it. Aura's hand rested gently on Ocean's thigh as he drove. Dana and Ace cuddled in the back seat. Ocean caught a glimpse of the two in his rearview mirror and had a feeling of being at peace with the world. *Was this what family felt like?*

When they got back to the apartment, they found their respective rooms quickly. They had tired themselves with the dancing, and Aura barely got into her pajamas, before falling asleep in her bed. Ocean locked the bedroom door and undressed. Then, he lay down beside her and wrapped an arm around her waist. She turned in her sleep and put her head on his chest. And it occurred to him that he always wanted to feel this way. Then, Ocean quickly fell asleep with Aura in his arms.

***

It was noon before he rose the next day; Aura was still nestled in his arms. He smiled. There was no getting around it... He really did love her. Even worse than that, he loved *being* in love with her. She slept late like he did. She partied like he did. He felt like she was the missing piece in a jigsaw puzzle, and now he was complete. Ocean smiled. He was making himself sick.

Aura opened her eyes and saw Ocean smiling at her. "Good morning, baby," she muttered softly, her voice thick with morning.

Ocean kissed her forehead. "Good morning, baby," he replied softly. He closed his eyes and drifted back to sleep for nearly another hour, before finally getting out of bed. Aura rose with him and headed to the bathroom.

Ace and Dana were in the living room watching television when Ocean walked in.

"Mornin', Ocean," Dana greeted.

"Hey, man, what's up?" Ace began. "You feel like going for a drive?"

Ocean laughed. "You mean, do I feel like driving your raggedy ass around Brooklyn?"

Ace laughed. "Yeah, man. That's exactly what I mean." His eyes were hopeful.

Ocean gulped down a glass of orange juice. "Sure, man. No prob. Just lemme take a shower first. Is that cool?"

"Yeah. Let me know when you're ready." Ace returned his gaze to the TV set.

***

When Ocean returned from running errands with Ace, he met up with Aura in a mood he wasn't sure he had seen before. She looked as if she had seen a ghost.

In a way, he supposed she had. She explained that she had just found out one of her old friends from college had AIDS and she wanted them to get tested. He knew they had nothing to worry about—he got tested regularly, but he agreed to it to ease her mind.

***

The first time Ocean told Aura he loved her it was entirely by accident. Actually, she pretty much tricked him into it by saying she loved him first. They were having a perfectly normal telephone conversation, planning their weekends for the month. Aura seemed thrilled her HIV test turned up negative, which Ocean found slightly disconcerting, but not too much so. In any case, things were moving along perfectly and Aura was about to hang up, but before doing so she said she loved him. Before he could think, he admitted he loved her too. Then, he hoped she didn't make a big deal of it. Thankfully, she didn't.

***

By the time Christmas week rolled around, Ocean was wearing his love more like an old sweater than a stiffly starched shirt. He had never really felt "in love" before, and initially it overwhelmed him with feelings of dread and fear. But he and Aura stayed up many nights working through their feelings for one another, and with each conversation he felt closer to her and more trusting. Whenever he spent time with her family, they made him feel right at home. Even his playboy father thought Aura was the best thing since sliced bread, encouraging him to "marry that girl before someone else does."

So he decided to take his father's advice.

She was everything he wanted in a woman, and he hated the nights he spent without her. She didn't try to control him. She didn't ask him for money. She didn't ask where he was all day, like he was cheating—she was confident in his love... She *knew* the deal. She was sexy, funny *and* smart. A little wild, but professional, beautiful and complicated, and everything about her kept him horny. And the sex...the sex was *sooo* different from all the times he screwed before her. He finally knew what it was to "make love." And with all this, she respected him. She didn't treat him like she had him wrapped around her finger, because she felt the same for him. And, he trusted her. He knew she didn't look at other men. Or, at least she didn't touch... Ocean smiled, everything felt good. Even when they argued, they played by the rules. She didn't curse at him in anger or call him names. They tried hard to discuss and compromise. She never laid a hand on him, and, of course, he would never lay a hand on her in anger. Ocean smiled at the irony... So many women were quick to scream abuse if a man tapped them, but would slap a man in the face or give him a good push without a second thought. The fact of the matter was, both men *and* women needed to control themselves to keep violence out of their relationships, especially if their parents had violent relationships. Ocean's thoughts trailed off.

"Sir, may I help you?" the gray-haired man behind the display counter seemed annoyed.

Ocean smiled. He had let his thoughts get the best of him He gave the salesman a strange look. "Did you say something?"

The gray-haired man cleared his throat. He wondered what this long-haired black man could want with diamonds, but he tried to hold his tongue; the man did look vaguely familiar. Maybe he was an actor, or something.

"Yes, I said, may I help you?"

Ocean flashed his money-making smile. "Yeah, I'm looking for two gifts for my girlfriend...one engagement ring, and something else that would fit into the same type of box...maybe a locket or earrings..."

The man raised his eyebrow. Finally someone who wanted more than a four hundred dollar ring. Could it be his lucky day?

***

When Ocean left the jewelry store, a wave of anxiety engulfed him. He knew he did the right thing, but the reality of his actions hit him like a sudden brick. He had just spent over three thousand dollars of his savings! The items in the inner pocket of his leather jacket weighed heavily on his mind. *Would she like them?* He felt a pang of nausea and leaned coolly against a bus stop shelter. His mind chased his worse fears for a few brief moments. Maybe this wasn't real… Maybe she wasn't real... Maybe he didn't deserve her... What could she see in him? Then, his reality returned as easily as it had left. He swallowed, feeling the crush of his anxieties quickly rise. He *knew* she would love them! He controlled his sudden urge to grin. He couldn't wait to see her reaction to the little ring box on Christmas morning. He relished in the thought of playing a joke on her.

***

When he got home he called his mother. "Mom, I'm gonna do it!" he stated quickly.

"Eddie?" his mother asked.

"Yeah, hi mom. I'm gonna do it... I'm gonna ask Aura to marry me!" His heart beat quickly in his chest.

"Oh, Eddie... I want to meet this girl... I'm so happy for you!" A tear formed in Mrs. Ryder's eye. Her son had found his happiness.

She gave Andrew Miller a quick glance. He rose and kissed her cheek.

***

Ocean wore a steady smile when he hung up the phone with his mother. It was obvious that she was thrilled. She encouraged them to honeymoon in Abaco, to which Ocean had no objection. He doubted Aura would mind. What next? He dialed his father's number without hesitation.

"Hello?" Karen asked.

"Oh, hi, Karen, it's Eddie. Is my dad around?"

"Sure, Eddie."

Ocean heard the rustling as the phone quickly changed hands. "Eddie?!" his father boomed. "It's good to hear from you, now that you're spending all your holidays elsewhere." His comment began with joy and ended with a degree of disappointment.

"Daaad!" Ocean nearly whined. He was calling to tell his father his news, and somehow Neville Ryder always managed to make him feel guilty. Couldn't he give the father pity stuff a rest?

"What, Eddie? I'm just saying... Karen and I invited you over for Thanksgiving and Christmas and you brushed off both invitations." Neville Ryder wondered if his nagging would one day gain him an invitation to the Olivier's home. According to Eddie, it was quite beautiful and Mrs. Olivier cooked better than Karen. Ideally, he wanted a solo invitation. Karen and the kids were driving him nuts!

Ocean grimaced. "Sorry, Dad. But, you make it sound

like I didn't come by at all. We came over on Thanksgiving; we just didn't eat with you. I don't know, we'll see about Christmas." Ocean frowned with a combination of guilt and annoyance. Then, he grinned widely when he remembered why he called. "Anyway, Dad, I just wanted to tell you something. I decided to take your advice..." He breathed deeply. "I've decided to ask Aura to marry me. I bought the ring today."

"Well, congratulations Eddie! I hope everything works out for you. That Aura is a fine woman, too." Neville Ryder paused briefly before asking, "So how much change did you kick out for the ring?"

Ocean smiled. He actually felt good about spending the money on *his woman.* "Over two G," he stated cockily.

Neville Ryder cleared his throat. "Two G? You mean two thousand dollars for a ring? Your mother's ring only cost me two hundred, and I thought *that* was too much!" Mr. Ryder's voice became harsh with anger. "You've got money like that to throw around and you expect me to repay loans to you? You should be taking care of your old man if you've got that kind of money to waste!" He mumbled under his breath, "Two thousand dollars..."

Ocean didn't bother to mention the five-hundred-dollar earrings he bought as a Christmas gift. It was clear his father couldn't share in his joy. He felt as if he had been punched repeatedly by his father's words, and his eyes burned with tears. *What was the point of feeling happiness if you had no one to share it with?*

Thankfully he heard a tone on the telephone line signaling another call was coming through. He abruptly ended the conversation with his father and answered the line.

"Hi, Ocean!" It was Mona's voice.

"Mona, long time no speak. How are you?"

"Not too bad...but, I really need to see you." Her tone suggested urgency.

A tear rolled into the laugh-line of Ocean's smile as a delayed response to his father's words. Neville Ryder was probably the only person who could upset him so easily. Ocean still sought his father's approval hungrily, and when he couldn't get it, it made for a painfully swollen belly. So, Ocean was happy to have the distraction of Mona's voice on the line. They usually touched base every month or so, but he hadn't *seen* her in over a year. "What's wrong?" Ocean asked quickly. His voice bore no hint of the lone tear on his cheek—He sounded sexy, casual, normal.

"Can I come over? I really need to talk in person."

Ocean didn't have much time to spend with Mona before meeting Aura later in the evening, but he felt needed so he agreed.

"Thanks," Mona replied simply. "I'll be there in twenty minutes."

***

"Oh, Ocean, I don't know what to do!" Mona hugged Ocean tightly before removing her long chinchilla fur coat. She wore tawny suede pants tucked into long brown heeled boots and a sheer ecru silk blouse. The lace from her white push-up bra was clearly visible, and the strand of pearls she wore rested gently upon her breasts.

Ocean eyed her from head to toe. Mona always did look fabulous. "What's the matter, babe?" he queried. "Can I get you a drink?"

"Yeah, a drink would be wonderful. Something strong. What do you have?" Mona made herself comfortable on Ocean's leather sofa. She crossed her legs and handled the stereo remote with ease, flipping through the preprogrammed stations, finally settling on jazz.

"This should do it," Ocean said, resting a stiff rum and coke before his guest. "Drink up."

"Thanks." Mona lifted the glass to her mouth and drank half of it in a sequence of long gulps. "Uhhh," she sighed. "Yeah, that's better."

"So tell me what's wrong..." Ocean began.

Mona frowned. "My marriage is *ruined!* Louie's seeing another woman. He says he's leaving me." Her voice was filled with the type of hurt and anger that one would expect to hear from a faithful spouse.

Ocean had actually valued his friendship with Mona over the years. *Was she really such a hypocrite?* He wasn't sure how to respond.

Mona continued, "I know what you're probably thinking, Ocean, but you're wrong. What went on between you and me was different... special..."

Ocean couldn't believe what he was hearing. Was the threesome with Dawn *special?*

"I mean, you know I care about you. I thought that the time we spent together enhanced my relationship with Louie... I never thought he'd leave me..."

Ocean frowned. What could he say? What she really meant, was 'oh shit, what am I going to do for a living now that my husband knows I'm about as faithful as a tomcat.' Ocean controlled his urge to smirk. Did she really just say she thought the sex they had enhanced her marriage? His mind wandered to Aura. Although she resembled Mona on the outside, they were like night and day on the inside. He and Aura shared the same ideals about marriage and family, ideals which Mona would probably never understand. Ocean knew Mona married Louie Robbins for financial security, and he doubted she ever loved him. It wasn't his place to judge, but it seemed a little ridiculous for her to be upset over her husband's impending departure, when she had behaved like a single woman for most of their marriage. He remembered the sound of his mother's voice saying, "You never miss your water till your well runs dry." Maybe, that was it... Maybe Mona didn't realize she wanted Louie until he said he was leaving.

"When did he say he was leaving?"

Mona swallowed the remainder of her drink quickly. "He didn't even speak to me. He just left me a stupid note on the refrigerator. They're vacationing in Cancun as we speak." She jingled the ice in her glass as a request for another cocktail.

Ocean had to laugh. "Oh, I know what that feels like," he said, nodding his head as he remembered Tasha's angry note five years ago. *Was it really five years?* He looked around the apartment with a curious interest: It was time for him to move into a house or a condo or something. Renting was worthless. He'd been throwing his money away for *five years!* He grabbed the glass from Mona's waiting hands and made her a second drink.

"I don't know what to do, Ocean. Louie and I have been together for a long time."

Ocean rested a hand gently on her shoulder. He was surprised at how bare her skin felt even with her blouse on, so he quickly removed his hand before remarking, "There's really nothing you can do, Mona. Just let it go; maybe it wasn't meant to be."

Mona glared at Ocean with outrage. "What are you saying? Are you saying you don't think I love him?"

Ocean was stunned. This woman was not the Mona he thought he knew. It wasn't that they were *that* close. They never discussed Louie. But, he did think she was *reasonable.* How could she screw around on Louie for years, and still manage to be upset when he ran off with some other woman? Mona had screwed women *and* men.

He doubted that he and Dawn were the only ones... It was clearly time for a change of plans... He just wanted her out of his apartment. He kissed her cheek. "Of course not, Mona. I'm sure you love Louie, maybe you two can patch things up. I don't know what I was thinking." He gave her his best apologetic look.

"You really think so?" Mona asked, suddenly fawn-like and charming again. The transformation was a bit startling.

Ocean smiled with his deception. "I don't see any reason why you can't."

Mona moved closer to him on the sofa. "I knew you'd understand, Eddie," she said as she rested her head on his shoulder. She slipped an arm around his waist.

Ocean felt his heartbeat quicken. Mona hadn't called him Eddie in years, and she knew he was in love with Aura. *What was she doing?*

Mona rubbed her cheek into Ocean's cotton sweater as her hand drifted across his thigh.

It had been a long time since Mona touched him intimately, and, for a moment he didn't want to stop her—it felt good. But he knew the difference between his dick and his heart, and an offhanded desire to screw Mona certainly wasn't worth jeopardizing his relationship with Aura. And besides, his mother always told him never to do anything he couldn't live with. He'd feel guilty every time he looked in Aura's eyes if he were to bed Mona now. "Look, Mona, I think you'd better go," he said rising.

Mona looked startled. "What's wrong, Ocean?" she asked.

"Listen, I can't help you patch things up with Louie, and I'm not gonna let you screw things up between me and Aura."

Mona looked perplexed. "But Aura would never

know," she pleaded suggestively.

"But I would know," Ocean stated simply, grabbing Mona's coat from the rack near the door.

She walked toward him with a carefully controlled bounce in her step, allowing her breasts to jiggle provocatively. "You know, Ocean, you just don't make any sense. You know I would never tell her." She smiled sensuously, "And despite what you say, I know you want to."

Ocean felt disgusted. Mona was very beautiful, and left to his dick alone, he would screw her; it was true. Thankfully, his dick didn't make decisions alone, because, at that moment, the rest of him was repulsed by her.

***

When he met Aura later that evening at the World Financial Center, he told her about Mona's visit.

"Are you serious?" she asked laughing. Ocean had told her about his relationship with Mona from early on...even about the threesome. She didn't like it, but she preferred knowing to not knowing. She felt secure in his love, and she just hoped that when she wasn't around he would do the right thing. She knew he was accustomed to being around beautiful women, so the opportunities would always be there. There was nothing she could do about it; it was the nature of his business. She just made sure he knew where she stood: if he screwed around he would lose her; it was as simple as that. Or, maybe she'd screw one of his friends and then he'd lose her.

Ocean touched her thigh as they sat on the marble steps of the huge public atrium. "It was unbelievable," he continued. "She came over crying about Louie leaving her when I know she's probably never been faithful to that poor man" His eyebrows furrowed. "People are funny," he stated simply. Then he threw Aura a playful but meaningful glare, "You better not even *think* about doing what she did."

She kissed his cheek "Baby, the day I sleep with another man is the day I call it quits on us." She looked seriously into his eyes. "I just wouldn't do it."

"I can't stand the thought of you with someone else."

Aura smiled. "Don't think about it; you have no reason to." Then she giggled, "Besides, *you're* the one with all these older women following you around telling you about their *husbands*... But you *know* I'll be gone before you can say 'where's Aura?' if I ever find out about you messing around with another woman."

"Ahem." Ocean pretended to clear his throat. "What's wrong with older women?" he asked playfully, tossing an arm around Aura's shoulders.

"Ha, ha." Aura smiled, "I'm only a couple of years older than you. Not like Miss Mona. How old is she now anyway. Forty?" Purple lights flooded the stage below, and an announcer introduced the Boys Choir of Harlem. Aura rested her head on Ocean's shoulder and watched the show.

***

"Are you crazy?!" Maleek asked, nearly falling off the treadmill.

Ocean laughed. "Nope." He pulled an ankle to his butt, stretching his quadriceps before beginning his run.

"But you don't know anything about her... It's only been six months... She might be crazy or something!"

"It's been almost eight months, and I know everything I need to know. She's perfect for me."

Maleek straddled the treadmill to pause for a moment.

His sweat dripped onto the moving belt of the machine as he spoke. "Well, at least have one of those two-year engagements or something."

"I don't want a two-year engagement. I want to many her."

"Well you can't marry her now. At least have a one year engagement." Maleek shook his head. "Shit, I can't believe you're actually doing this. You're gonna hate yourself later."

"Thanks a lot." Ocean laughed. "What should I do? Grow old looking at your hairy butt?"

"Grow *old?* Is that it, man? She makes you think you're old? You're only twenty-five Ocean!" Maleek was horrified.

"Nooo, she doesn't make me think I'm old. I know I'm not old."

"So then, *why?* " Maleek's voice was pained.

"Maybe you'll fall in love one day, and then you'll understand."

Maleek jumped back onto the moving belt to resume his run. "That's not love; that's insanity."

***

"Oh, thank you, baby," Ocean said, ripping the wrapping off the cologne Aura gave him. It was one of the expensive new designer fragrances she liked.

"That's not all!" she said excitedly. "Here." She handed him a bigger box.

Ocean unwrapped a kente-print silk robe and matching boxers. "Wow, Aura, this is beautiful!" he exclaimed, kissing her forehead.

"And finally..." she began, presenting a smaller box.

"Wow! You really went all out!" Ocean opened the smaller box. It was a single ruby stud earring.

"Thanks, sweetie, I love everything." He hugged her tightly. "This is for you," he said, paying careful attention to her facial expression. *Did she think it was a ring?*

"Thanks," Aura said. Ocean detected some trepidation. He couldn't tell if it was happy anticipation or nervous anxiety. She removed the gold curly ribbon and opened the velvet box slowly.

Ocean studied her face carefully. When she saw the earrings she was obviously surprised, but he wasn't sure if she was relieved or disappointed. He swallowed hard. He'd find out in a week.

"Thanks, Ocean!" Aura exclaimed. "Oh, these are beautiful!" She tilted the box toward her mother. "Mom, look!" She kissed Ocean quickly, before rising from the sofa and walking around to show off her gift.

"Emerald earrings! Oh, these are beautiful!" Sylvia Olivier gushed. "You found a man with good taste, Aura!"

Aura beamed. She showed her father. "Very nice, dear," he responded. He was a bit disappointed, though. He thought it was a ring box.

Dana, Ace, Aura, Ocean, Angie, Sylvia and Donald exchanged gifts for the next hour or so. Mr. Olivier made a pot of coffee while his wife heated apple cider for the family. Angie, Dana and Aura got to work mixing pancake batter while talking in the kitchen. Ace and Ocean sat on the living room sofa chatting.

"If you folks want something hot to drink, I suggest you come into the kitchen," Donald Olivier's voice boomed from the kitchen door.

"Dad, we can't all fit in the kitchen at one time," Ace complained.

"Then set the table for breakfast, Aaron. Let Ocean help you, I'll send Dana with the coffee." He paused. "Or do you want the cider?"

Ace and Ocean exchanged glances. "No, coffee's fine, Dad."

"Good."

Ace rifled through the china cabinet in the dining room for plates and silverware. The table was already covered with a solid red textured cloth. "It seems like I haven't seen you in a while, man," Ace stated.

"Yeah, you're probably right. The foursome hasn't been in full effect lately," Ocean agreed.

"You know, Aura thought you were giving her a ring," Ace commented in a near-whisper.

"What makes you say that?" Ocean replied.

"Didn't you see her face?!"

Ocean lowered his voice. "Do you think she wants a ring?"

Ace laughed. *"All* women want rings!"

Ocean laughed at Ace's response. "You know what I mean! Do you think she wants to get married? To me?" His tone hinted at his vulnerability.

Ace's tone and expression were suddenly serious. He walked closer to Ocean, nearly talking directly into his ear. "Yeah, man, I think she does."

***

Christmas dinner was delicious. Everyone seemed happy, except Angie who was clearly feeling left out. It seemed they had been eating and drinking all day, from their big breakfast to their even bigger dinner. She consoled herself with a few too many drinks and nearly drew Dana into an argument, but the spark did not become a fire and died out without ado.

Ocean wondered what Maleek would think of Angie as he chewed a piece of turkey. Maleek probably wasn't smart enough for Angie, but maybe he'd at least get her mind off that stupid Pascal guy. From what Aura said, Pascal was dating a twenty-year-old now, and made sure Angie knew about it. Ocean never liked Pascal; he was too insecure—a real asshole. And, it bothered him to see a woman as smart and pretty as Angie all alone. Granted, she was a bit heavy, but she still had a nice shape. She could still get play from guys.

"Why do you look so serious?" Aura asked.

Nothing, just thinking," Ocean replied distantly.

"I can smell the wood burning, baby. Don't burn down the house!" she laughed.

"Ha, ha," he stated sarcastically but playfully, resting a hand on her thigh. Aura had met Maleek only once, but maybe she'd have an opinion on it. He decided to ask her about it later.

***

He asked her in the car on the way to his father's house.

"Maleek? I don't know. I don't think they'd like each other, but make sure you ask Maleek if he's down first 'cause it would just make things worse if Angie says 'yes' and Maleek says 'no.'

"Hmm...I'm glad you said that... I wasn't even thinking about that." He turned his head as he backed into a parking space.

"Why don't you want to stay for awhile?" Aura wondered.

Ocean couldn't tell her that his father was a jerk, and he thought he might give away his engagement surprise. "We've been a bit on the outs lately. I just want to drop off a couple of gifts. We can spend time with them another day."

Aura gave him a curious look. "Let's take David out

one day soon. I like the little fella." She smiled when she thought of Ocean's four-year-old brother.

"That's a good idea. We can see a movie or something." He exited the car with a few gifts in hand. Suddenly, he felt really worried his father might blow everything if he saw Aura. "I have an idea. Why don't you just wait for me in the car?"

Aura frowned. "No, Ocean!"

Ocean grimaced. "I guess that would be sort of rude, huh?"

"Yes it *would!*" she replied haughtily. *What could he possibly be thinking?*

Ocean quickly kissed her cheek "Sorry, babe. You can come up with me, but I'm not going in there. If I go in, they'll never let me leave."

"Ocean, you *have* to go in. It's Christmas day!" She nearly whined.

How would he get out of this? He grabbed her tightly. "I know it's Christmas day, baby. That's why I want to spend some time alone with you. We spent all day with your family, now we have to spend all night with mine? Can't we see them later?" His voice was pleading.

Aura blushed. *He was so sweet!*

Whew! Ocean managed to drop the gifts off with his father without going inside.

***

By the time New Year's finally rolled around, Ocean was a nervous wreck. He had planned a nice evening on a dinner/party cruise boat, and Aura seemed to be having a good time. They danced and joked around while their ship circled Manhattan. She looked gorgeous as usual in a velvet cocktail dress, and he felt rather dashing, himself, in a tuxedo. She wore the earrings he bought for her proudly, and the hue of the emeralds complemented the plush forest green of her outfit. The night was cold, but clear, and they occasionally ventured onto the deck to catch a glimpse of the night view: The New York skyline, the statue of liberty and other passing boats.

As the hours passed his anxiety rose, but he had promised himself he'd wait until the countdown to propose. So, he waited nervously, hoping it would all be worth it in the end. He wanted to make it memorable for her, but when the cruise ship's emcee started to countdown the end of 1992, he felt weak in the knees. His heart pounded loudly in his chest and his face flushed hotly in the cold December air.

The next thing he knew he was on one knee and Aura was crying. But she said, 'yes,' and that was all he cared about. He held her and kissed her then like he had kissed no other woman. Aura was his passion.

Sophia Boyd
The Holidays 1992-1993

Timothy and Marcus trampled into the apartment with quiet exhaustion. Sophia had them out all day, shopping and seeing the sights. Now all three of them were tired. The boys removed their coats and plopped their tired bodies onto the sofa. Sophia reviewed the contents of her mailbox: a few bills, a catalog, *Essence* magazine... a couple of Christmas cards. She smiled; it was nice to have something besides bills to greet her. She surveyed the return addresses on the cards: one from Sandy and one from her mother. She swallowed. She hadn't spoken to Sandy since the incident with Timothy six months earlier. She hadn't even spoken to Timothy about it. He had never asked, so she didn't bother to bring it up. She wondered if he even remembered it at all, since he was half-asleep at the time.

She opened Sandy's card first, overcome by her own curiosity. She had changed her number three months earlier to avoid Sandy's calls, but she was still anxious for some communication. Sandy had designed the card herself with red, black and green oil paints against a black background. "Happy Kwanzaa," the outer flap read. Sophia smiled and opened the flap. The page inside was tan-colored with a message hand-written in black felt-tip, "Dear Sophie, I know that you feel we must go our separate ways now, but I want you to know that I will always love you, Timothy and Marcus. You and your children are an integral part of my life. You've always been my strength, and without you I can never be the same. I hope that one day you will find it in your heart to let me back into your life. All my love, Sandy." Sophia frowned and quietly ripped the card into tiny pieces as she sat at the gently scuffed wood table in her kitchen. She collected the pieces and returned them to the envelope. Then, she threw the entire package in the black rubber garbage pail.

Next, she opened the card from her mother. It had a snowy winter scene on the outside with a simple "Merry Christmas" inside. "Love, your mother," was all it said. Her sisters hadn't even signed it. Sophia put the card in the showcase area of the living room wall unit beside a collection of cards from her co-workers and business associates. "Thanks a lot Ma," she mumbled sarcastically. She knew her mother was upset that she wouldn't visit Jackson for Christmas, but she'd be even more upset if she knew why.

Sophia had invited her father to New York to celebrate Christmas and Kwanzaa with the kids, but she made him promise to keep it a secret from the rest of the family. She just wasn't ready to deal with their reactions. She hated going back to Mississippi. She hadn't been home for Christmas since her parents' divorce, opting to eat with her Aunt Tyra and Uncle Mac for the past three years. She allowed herself to reminisce her previous Christmases with Sandy, always eating alone with the kids at Aunt Tyra's before running home to Sandy's arms. *Oh well, times changed, so what?*

The kids seemed engrossed in the television, so she dragged the heavy shopping bags from her hall closet into her bedroom. She had what seemed like a ton of gifts to wrap for the kids and her family. Now, was as good a night as any to begin. It was two weeks to D-day, she thought with a sarcastic snicker. This Christmas was wearing on her like a pair of strappy stilettos—downright uncomfortably. She looked forward to seeing her father, but it also scared her. She hadn't seen him in years, and she wasn't sure what it would be like to eat with him alone. It would certainly be a first. And, she hadn't cooked a Christmas dinner since she and Ron spent Christmas together in 1988. She wasn't sure she remembered the fine art of preparing a turkey with stuffing.

She answered the phone on the first ring. It was Brad. He called her occasionally since they met at Caribbean Corner in June, and she did finally sleep with him once, but she had no interest in him.

"Merry Christmas, Sophie, you sure are hard to catch up with," he said.

"Oh, hi Brad," she offered casually. "Merry Christmas to you too." Her words were friendly but her voice was cold.

"I was just calling to see if you wanted to get together one of these days..." he began.

Sophia wished she had let the machine pick up. "Nah, I'm gonna be too busy," she stated with indifference.

"Oh."

"Yeah..." Sophia searched for more excuses. "As a matter of fact, I'm in the middle of something right now. Why don't you let me call you back?" she offered, knowing full well she had no intention of ever calling him. *Did she even know where his number was?*

"Oh, okay," Brad mumbled.

Sophia returned the cordless phone to its base

***

"Father, forgive me for I have sinned..." Sophia knelt

in the confessional with a feeling of bizarre comfort. She stopped going to church years ago, but over the past month she had a nagging feeling of needing to confess. It wasn't that she really thought God would only forgive her sins if she fessed up to the old white man behind the screen; it wasn't even that she felt she needed to have sins forgiven. But, she did have a feeling of loss. She felt alone, maybe more at this Christmas than ever before. She felt she had betrayed her mother reconciling with her father. She felt she had betrayed her family by living as a lesbian. She felt she had betrayed Sandy by not continuing to live as a lesbian. She felt she had betrayed her sons by denying them their grandfather. Overall, she just felt a deep guilt she couldn't seem to shake, and she hoped that by reaching back to childhood lessons in religion, she would find some reprieve. And, it was Christmas time after all, Christ's mass as she was taught. The fact of the matter was, whether she took it seriously or not, she was planning to celebrate the birth of Christ with her family. She wondered if Christ hated lesbians as much as Christians did.

***

Sophia held her father's hand as she walked down the aisle of the Kwanzaa Expo at the Jacob Javits Convention Center. Timothy and Marcus ran ahead, busying themselves with the crowd and the activity. She kept a watchful eye on them as they moved through the sea of black faces, calling them back when they seemed to be getting too far out of reach. She couldn't help but smile as she watched their matching blue jackets and little blue galoshes trudging through the wide halls.

Leon Boyd was a large man. At 6'1", 250 lbs., he was quite the big teddy bear, with a massive chest to carry his healthy belly. His grey eyes set deeply in his handsome face and dark brown hair waved behind a now-receding hairline. He wore a white turtleneck and blue sports jacket under the long wool of his grey tweed overcoat. And, at fifty-three, he was still quite attractive.

Sophia was clearly daddy's girl. She favored him with the shape of her face, her similar complexion, the angle of her nose and the fullness of her lips. No one could view the two together without guessing they were father and child, despite their clothing choices. Mr. Boyd was comfortably casual and conservative in his clothing, while Sophia sported her usual head-wrap. Today it was a lovely blue and purple African print. Her mildly relaxed hair peeked from one side in its usual manner. Her body was draped in a short purple swing coat of her own design, and her legs peaked from below in blue jeans and black ankle boots.

Her father flew into town the previous evening, and she was happy to bring him to the Expo. Black vendors from around the country sold their wares: children's books, clothing, art, jewelry, calendars...all with an Afrocentric perspective. It was a wonderful time to relish in their African-American culture. Sophia picked up books for the kids, skincare products and clothing. Her father bought art and literature. She was surprised at how easily they got along. It seemed the years apart had made her forget how good their relationship once was.

"Oh, Sophie, look!" her father exclaimed He had never been to such an event before, and he was excited by a mud-clothed teddy-bear. "Do you want it?" he asked.

"Oh, I love it, Daddy!" she admitted. She lost the abrasive timbre that had become habit since her split with Sandy; her tone was warm and child-like.

Leon Boyd moved into the crowd surrounding the plush toys, and quickly purchased the bear for his daughter. "For my little bear," he said in his most fatherly tone.

Sophia grabbed the bear and held it close to her. A father's love is like no other. *What could she have been thinking for all those years?*

***

"Grampy, read us a story!" Timothy gushed; his face glowed with satisfaction as he sat in his grandfather's lap. Marcus sat beside him, heady with his own anticipation of Santa's impending visit and his grandfather's dreamlike return.

"Sure, what would you like to hear?" Mr. Boyd asked, clearly thrilled with the request.

"Read 'Twas the night!" Timothy exclaimed.

"Why, I know that one by heart!" Leon Boyd replied happily, before reciting the famous poem. The boys were totally enthralled.

Sophia watched their interaction with joy. Her sons had found her father. It was a beautiful thing to see.

After the poem, Timothy brought books from his bedroom shelf, one by one. He seemed fascinated by the deepness of her father's voice, the largeness of his hands, and the roundness of his belly. She wondered, did they think that somehow her father was closer to Santa Claus than she?

***

Leon Boyd read to the boys for hours, and though they struggled with the Sandman, they both fell asleep before 9:00pm. Sophia helped her father tuck the young ones in.

"That was wonderful," Mr. Boyd admitted, taking a seat on the living room sofa.

"Thanks, Daddy. I'm sure the boys will appreciate tonight for a long time to come."

"It's my pleasure," he said sincerely. "And I must thank you, my dear. The Expo was wonderful. Tell me all about this Kwanzaa thing."

Sophia smiled. She had mentioned Kwanzaa once to her mother, and was greeted with such disdain, she never brought it up again. Her mother was raised as a Catholic, and all she wanted to hear about in December was Jesus Christ. But, Sophia had some problems with Christianity, and they could never agree on religion. After learning of the senseless slayings in the name of Christ during the holy wars... After recognizing the killings and bigotry that continue to this day because of organized religions... After realizing the relationship between the mind-control of religion and black slavery in the United States... The demonizing of African gods... The creation of white idols... The force-feeding of Christianity throughout the world through colonialism... After realizing all these things, she had a hard time understanding why so many blacks were practicing Christians. Even though she, herself, knelt before a priest just a few days earlier...for comfort...a salve...guidance... Yes, Sophia believed in God or *something,* and it wasn't the *teachings* of Christ she had a problem with, it was the *actions* of the people who smugly worshipped him as if it were a free pass to heaven. It was they who she found so misguided and unappealing. Were they so afraid to face their own dark shadows that they had to harass her with their subway preaching, abortion clinic bombing and fanatical screaming that they seemed to lose the very thing they searched for? Their own souls? Yes, she had tried to tell Beverly Brown Boyd that Kwanzaa was not a substitute for Jesus. And that Jesus was the most misquoted, misunderstood man in history. Of course, it all fell on deaf ears.

"Would you like some tea or something?" Sophia asked her father on her way to the kitchen. She wore a ribbed purple sweater over her blue jeans.

"Tea is fine, but some scotch would be better. What do you have back there for your old man?" her father asked, his tone teasing.

"No scotch, Daddy. I have a bottle of wine, if you want to share it."

"Wine sounds good... Now tell me about this Kwanzaa. Is this something you young kids came up with?"

Sophia smiled. "It's been around since 1966. I guess you could say it's something young kids came up with."

"So tell me Sophia, what does it mean?" Mr. Boyd stood in the threshold to the kitchen, as Sophia uncorked the wine bottle.

"Well, it was founded by a man named Maulana Kalenga after the 1965 Watts riots in L.A." She paused with contemplation. "It's based on a compilation of the African harvest celebrations, but it's not an *African* holiday." Sophia wondered if her words would seem contradictory. "I mean, it's not celebrated in Africa... It's a time to look at how we feel about the main principles of our lives as blacks in the U.S....as part of the diaspora...to reflect on what we've accomplished and to set goals for our personal growth in the New Year." She uncorked a bottle of Kendall-Jackson Chardonnay; her knuckles were still pink from being out in the cold all day.

"So there's no Santa Claus?" Mr. Boyd said teasingly.

"No, Daddy, there's no Santa Claus." She frowned. "Sometimes I wonder if Timmy and Marcus really need Santa Claus. I almost feel like I provide them with Santa by peer pressure alone. I like to see them dream, but I wonder if they really need to think they're entitled to gifts on the day of Christ's birth. Which, if you know anything about history, we know Jesus was NOT born on December twenty-fifth." She laughed then, heartily and dreamily. "But, you know, Daddy, it gives me so much pleasure to *play* Santa Claus; sometimes I think I do it more for myself than for them. The look on their faces is worth all the money in the world!" She leaned back as the tiny smiles of previous Christmases washed over her.

"So it's an African-American holiday. What else?" her father asked, genuine in his interest. He took a tiny sip of his wine as he watched his daughter speak. She was his charm. Marion and Denise were nice young women, but Sophia was a soldier. Her work, her children, and her strength were his salve. She made him proud.

Sophia spoke easily, with the professionalism she had come to learn through her years of work presentations. "Well, the celebration takes place on the seven days between Christmas and New Years Day. There are seven guiding principles for each of the seven days. In order, they are: unity, self-determination, collective work and responsibility, cooperative economics, purpose, creativity and faith. During the week-long celebration, you gather with family and friends and discuss what the principles mean to you. There are other aspects of the celebration that are more ritualistic, but I don't celebrate that way with the boys, at least not yet. Right now, I just concentrate on explaining the principles to them, and getting them to understand. Marc is still young, but Timothy is beginning to pick it up. I think I'll stop celebrating Christmas when Marcus is eight and Timothy's ten. By then, I suppose they will have both grown out of Santa Claus." Then, Sophia nearly jumped with her excitement as she remembered an important addition, "And, Kwanzaa encourages hand-made gifts and gifts that feed the *mind.*" She tapped her forefinger on her temple for emphasis, "not all this video game, toy gun crap." She led her father to the living room sofa as she finished her comment.

Mr. Boyd beamed with pride, taking a seat beside his oldest daughter. He only wished his wife and other daughters were interested in something so positive. He wondered what such a celebration might have meant to him, if such a thing existed when he was a young man. His daughters made him proud, despite the fact that he had no boys. Only Sophia gave him his little men, and he was more grateful to her for that than she would ever know. Sophia's boys were Boyd-Henderson's, and he hoped that one day soon he could convince her to drop the "Henderson." After all, their father had been dead for years.

Sophia was happy to disseminate information about Kwanzaa, but it was still her first full day with her father in years, and she had many questions. She turned a vulnerable countenance to him as she leaned back in the old couch, crossing her denim-covered legs, and fiddling with her purple-patterned head-wrap. "So Daddy, what really happened between you and mom?" The question seemed simple, but it took all of her composure and energy to ask it. She couldn't imagine what could be more difficult than the ending of a union which she had expected to last forever. *How do people divorce after thirty years? When do you stop loving?* She needed to *know.*

Leon Boyd grimaced. How could he respond? He knew he had never loved Sophia's mother, but what could he say? She was an adult, but how could he tell her such a horrible thing? Did the fact that his baby was thirty-two make her more able to deal with the pain of it all? Did the fact that she had given birth to two young boys make her more knowing? He didn't know. He reflected on his other daughters. They had never even asked about the separation, they had just accepted it like so much spilt milk—never angry with him or their mother. *What did that mean?*

Sophia was certain her father would not respond, so she turned her body on the tapestry antique sofa and grabbed the television remote. Surely, there was something on the tube to distract them both.

"Sophie," her father began, his voice deep with melancholy.

"What?" Sophia's tone was harsh.

"This is difficult to discuss."

"Whaaat?" Sophia repeated sardonically.

"Your mother and I were never in love, and she always knew it." *There, it was said.*

Sophia felt the flash of hot red anger burn in her belly and rise to her neck and face. The stream of tears came next; she felt dizzy. All the words she had heard over the years were now gaining meaning. Little things her Aunt Tyra said...her sisters...her mother...

Leon Boyd seemed shocked by his daughter's reaction. *Hadn't she always known in her heart?* "Sophie, you know your mother was pregnant with you before we married..." he began, as if this explained it all.

"Of course," Sophia replied, her voice cold but soft. She wiped her sliding tears with her fingertips. Her face was pink, and her eyes began to puff.

"Oh, baby, I never wanted to hurt you," her father said. "I mean, I just thought you *knew.*" He quickly put an arm around her. "Nobody *ever* told me that." Sophia leaned her head against her father's broad chest.

"But, Sophie, everyone knows this. I just thought you knew..."

Sophia sniffled like a wounded puppy. These final words meant it was all her fault. If she were never conceived, her parents would never have had to endure their horrible trial of a marriage. After all, that's all it was: a trial, a prison, a cage. Her parents never really had love or marriage. All they had were sleeping arrangements. Her mind drifted over the countless indiscretions her father had over the years. Women would call the house. Her mother would become enraged. The funny thing about it was if she had to choose, she *liked* her father more than her mother. He was a genuinely nice person trapped into marriage by his own moral ideologies. She couldn't really blame him: It was her own birth that was at fault. The thoughts raced through her mind like so much water rushing through a breaking dam. These were things she always knew in her heart, but never allowed her mind to translate to reality in her head. A second wave of guilt crushed her. She was toting around guilt over Ron, and Sandy, and even her relationship with her mother, but now...now she had to deal with the fact that her whole life...her whole family was a mistake caused by her conception.

"Daddy, I need to go to bed now," she stated quietly, simply. She left the mostly full wine glass on the small wooden coffee table, and stumbled drunkenly into her bedroom. It was not the spirit of the wine which left her drunk, but the intoxicating heaviness of her father's words...the reality that he force-fed her with one simple sentence: "Your mother and I were never in love, *and she always knew it,*" was a bit more than she was able to handle. She fell asleep in her clothing, passed out from the force of his words pounding so heavily on her mind.

***

Five days had passed with Mr. Boyd sleeping on a blue fabric futon in Sophia's living room, before Christmas day arrived. Sophia had recovered from her conversation with her father over those days. The initial shock of the story was worse than the reality of it. The fact of the matter was nothing had changed. Her father was still her father. She and her sons were still here. Her parents were still divorced. She still couldn't stand her younger sisters. When she accepted that reality, the rest managed to fall into place. Not easily, but gently.

As the boys unwrapped their gifts, dressed in superhero pajamas, Sophia boiled a pot of water for tea.

Her father rested casually on the sofa as he watched the boys in the dreamy euphoria of Christmas morning, which only lucky children experience. He was clad in a gray T-shirt and sweat pants. A question entered his mind, but he thought it better not to ask within earshot of the boys, so he rose and walked the paces to the kitchen. Sophia's apartment was certainly conveniently located in downtown Manhattan, but he wasn't used to living in such a small space. He walked close to his daughter before asking in nearly a whisper, "Do you keep in contact with their father's family?" At that precise moment he couldn't think of Ron's name.

"Ron was never close with his family. We were barely in touch...not in touch at all while we were married. I never hear from them." Her words were spoken with the quiet distress of long-recognized pain.

"Oh," her father said, wishing he could retract his question. He steeped his tea with slow deliberation, as he contemplated what this might mean to his grandchildren. "So, they've never known *any* grandparents?" he wondered aloud.

"They know ma..." Sophia started. "Well, sort of..." she admitted, finally. The kids had spent time with her mother probably less times than she could count on one hand.

"Oh." Her father spooned sugar into his cup with his head gently bowed.

"What is it, dad?" Sophie asked with some agitation. She could sense her father was biting his tongue.

"Just...well, how do you spend your time?" Then, he smiled with a sudden remembrance. "What ever happened to your good friend, Sandy?"

Sophia's eyes quickly darted away with a complex assortment of embarrassment and apology. "Sandy and I haven't spoken for awhile...we're sort of on the outs."

"Oh." Mr. Boyd felt sad at hearing the news, but he was certain a woman as smart and successful as Sophia had many friends, even though she hadn't introduced him to any over the past five days. "So who do you spend your time with?" he asked as he sipped his mint tea.

The question bothered Sophia, so she chose to ignore it by asking a question of her own. "What's your relationship like with Denni and Marri?" She hated to face the fact that besides her work and her children, she really had no friends. She blamed it on her late arrival to New York City—she wasn't born here—but in her soul she knew there was another reason; she just didn't know what it might be.

Mr. Boyd recognized his daughter's tactic to avoid his question, and he allowed her that luxury. After all, who was he to stroll into her life after three years to question her? Maybe it was best that she didn't respond. You're your sisters and I speak pretty often, but they don't really visit, and, of course, I can't visit them at your mother's house. They came down to Florida about a year ago, but that's it." Then he added, "But, they're nothing like you. You, my dear, are special. I'm so happy that we've finally been able to try and patch things up. I'm just so proud of you, honey." Her father gave her an earnest look of approval.

Sophia smiled. "Thanks, Daddy," was all she said.

***

Sophia spent most of Christmas day alternating between cooking and playing with the boys. Her father spoke to her as she checked on the turkey, wearing a bright green apron over a loose black velvet jumper.

"So how's the job coming along, Sophie?" Mr. Boyd was looking rather dapper in a grey tweed suit.

"Oh... The job is great, Dad. I've been working really hard." She basted the turkey as she spoke. "I just can't believe how many years I've spent there. It's going on twelve years now. I guess I'm getting a little restless, and the contract for my label's about to come up for renewal." She closed the oven, and turned around to face her father. "I don't know... I'm thinking about going to another design firm next year." She smiled, while adding, "Who knows?" with a shrug.

Her father gave her a serious look. "Why do you want to spend the rest of your life working for someone else?" he asked curiously.

"Huh?" Sophia busied herself with a side of ham which needed slicing.

"I said, why don't you start your own design firm, Sophie? You have twelve years of experience. You probably know the business inside out! And, you've got those folks making money off *your* designs! Why don't you keep your profit?"

Her father's questioning startled her. She had never even considered starting her own business. Where would she get the money? Who would she sell to? What if she failed? She smiled at her father; at least he had faith in her. "I don't think so, Dad..."

Leon Boyd smiled. "Don't say 'no' so fast, Sophie.

Research it. The day may come when you thank me for putting the idea in your head." He folded his arms across his chest with pride, nodding his head meaningfully.

Sophie smiled. "Okay, Dad."

"Can I help you with the ham?" he asked.

She sighed and handed him the carving knife. "Thanks."

"It looks like you and the boys will be eating turkey and ham all week then."

Sophia smiled. "It's a blessing...one less thing to think about for a week. At least I know what they'll be eating for lunch." She ran her fingers through her loose hair as she took a seat in the kitchen, quietly watching as her father carved the Christmas ham.

***

"Sophia!" Aubrey Clifford called across the wide airport corridor when she spotted her co-worker. Aubrey was only twenty-six and always smiling, as if the reality of life had not yet dawned upon her. She wore a long black coat over her jeans and boots, and covered her wavy auburn-dyed hair with a derby.

Sophia turned upon hearing her name and quickly recognized the woman. "Hey, Aubrey, what are you doing here?" Sophia asked. They were casual friends and co-workers, and she was happy to bump into her. Especially since her father gave her the acute feeling she was entirely friendless, and now here was Aubrey to prove him wrong. Pretty convenient.

"I just sent my parents back to Dallas... They were in town for *two weeks...* It was killing me! I'm lucky to still be alive!" She laughed at her own hyperbole, her lips curved into a bright orange smile around Pepsodent-white teeth. "What are *you* doing here?"

"Funny... Pretty much the same thing... My dad just caught his flight. I loved having him up, though. It was great." Sophia smiled with the memory. She would really miss having her father around. It had been a long time since she'd had another adult in the apartment with her... someone to talk to.

"Oh, that's nice," Aubrey agreed. "So where are you off to now?"

"I'm gonna grab a bite to eat. Do you wanna come?" Sophia asked, undoing the buttons of her purple swing coat. She held a wide-brimmed black hat in her hand, banded in the same purple wool as her coat. A long black scarf draped softly around her shoulders.

"Sounds good to me," Aubrey replied.

Sophia's relationship with Aubrey Clifford had not changed since Aubrey kissed her cheek a year and a half earlier. Sophia accepted her reaction to the kiss and the jeering man who called her a "dyke" as part of her paranoia over her own bisexuality/lesbianism. (She wasn't sure exactly how to describe her sexuality, and was even more annoyed that society made her feel forced to choose. She just couldn't believe everyone didn't have some degree of interest in both sexes.) In any event, she never commented on it, and Aubrey didn't do anything else she considered inappropriate, so it was a done deal... No big thing.

***

"Congratulations on the promotion, Aubrey," Sophia stated as a petite white woman seated them in an airport lounge. Neon signs dangled over the bar area announcing the various brands of beers and spirits which available. "I don't think I got the chance to say that earlier. You know, with Christmas and this and that, I've barely been in the office at all, but I did hear the news."

"Thanks, Sophia. That means a lot coming from you. What do you have planned for New Year's?" Aubrey removed her coat as she spoke to reveal a white angora V-necked sweater.

Sophie smiled nervously. It was a bit embarrassing not to have real plans for New Year's Eve when it was only a day away. But, Leon Boyd's woman, Elsa Tymner, threatened to find a new man if Leon missed spending both Christmas *and* New Year's with her. "Oh, I'll probably just go to my aunt's house with the kids... That's all."

"Oh, that's too bad. I have a great party coming up tomorrow night. If you didn't have plans, I would suggest you come." Aubrey flashed her a somewhat knowing grin and tapped her pumpkin-colored nails on the red and white checkered tablecloth. Then, she leaned into the table a bit, adding, "You know, why don't I just *give* you the information? Maybe you'll want to show up *after* midnight, when the kids are all settled."

"Sure," Sophia agreed politely. She did wish she had something more fun to do on New Year's than sit at home with the kids. (She made up the thing about her aunt's house so she wouldn't sound totally pathetic.) On the other hand, she really didn't think she wanted to hang out with Aubrey on New Year's Eve either. It wasn't that Aubrey wasn't a pleasant enough person, but they *did* work together, and she tried not to socialize too heavily with co-workers. She was friendly with most of her black co-workers, but there weren't a whole lot of those. As she looked at Aubrey's pleasant gaze, her father's suggestion returned to her like a replayed record. *Why did she want to spend the rest of her life working for someone else?*

"So, what else is going on with you, Sophia? How are the kids?" Aubrey asked, between nibbles of a Reuben sandwich.

Sophia seemed to snap out of her far-reaching thoughts. "Oh, the kids are fine," she replied simply. Then, she leaned in closer to Aubrey, "Have you ever thought about working for a black-owned company?"

Aubrey rolled her eyes with emotion. "Chile, pleeease! I'd be the first one running if I could find one! Wouldn't we all?" Aubrey's eyes returned quickly to her sandwich as if Sophia's question excited her and defeated her in the span of only moments.

Sophia nodded her head slowly. "Yeah, I guess we all would." Her statement was simple, but she made a mental note: if she *did* start a business, Aubrey would probably be willing to move with her. Then, another thought occurred to her. "What if you had to take a pay cut?" she asked.

Aubrey looked more pensive this time. "Well, I need to make money, I guess...but, if I thought I could do better there in the long run, it might be worthwhile. It would depend on the circumstances." She gave Sophia a questioning look.

"Oh, nothing," Sophia said, responding to the glance. "I've just been wondering why we don't have more black businesses."

"It's rough out there; that's why. Nobody has any money. Nobody knows where to get any money."

Sophia frowned. "Yeah, I guess, that's why." She thought about her father's words. *Research it.*

***

Sophia tiptoed down the red brick steps in front of her Aunt Tyra's home. It was half past midnight and the kids had finally fallen asleep. She slipped stealthily into the waiting cab in a body hugging chocolate-colored silk wrap-around dress with matching peau-de-soie pumps. Tiny onyx studs dropped delicately from her ear lobes and the gold choker around her neck. The driver kindly wished her a happy New Year, before taking her to the midtown address. Sophia responded graciously.

By the time she entered the hall, it was nearly 1:00am. A tuxedoed gentleman helped her remove the long camel-colored faux fur she wore. The hall was quite large, with shiny hardwood floors and high, exquisitely ornate ceiling molding. The dance floor was filled with seemingly happy people, laughing and shaking to the powerful music.

Sophia was pleasantly surprised. Aubrey had told her to dress up, but she had no idea the event would be this nice. She walked toward the bar area and ordered a margarita. She was impressed again. They had a well-stocked bar.

"Oh, Sophia!" Aubrey called out, walking toward the other woman. "You look wonderful!" she exclaimed. "Is this yours?" she asked referring to the design of the dress.

"Yes," Sophia replied. "I'm glad you like it."

"Like it?" she asked, nearly gasping. "Sophia, you make the most fabulous things! Maybe *you* should be our next big black businesswoman!" She laughed, making reference to their previous conversation.

Sophia blushed. "Well, thank you, Aubrey, I didn't know you felt that way about my stuff."

"Oh, absolutely!" Aubrey beamed. She leaned into the bar in her short, mango-colored slip of a cocktail dress and ordered a glass of white wine. Her neck and smooth caramel shoulders were free of the impediment of even spaghetti straps, graced only by a small strand of freshwater pearls.

Sophia found herself thinking Aubrey looked beautiful tonight. As the thought occurred to her, she was immediately worried. She did not want to get involved with a woman again, and she still had a sneaking suspicion Aubrey might be gay... "I'll have another margarita," she mumbled to the bartender.

"Sophia, are you okay?" Aubrey asked, giggling softly.

"I'm fine," Sophia replied. *Why didn't that woman ever stop laughing? Was there something funny?*

"You sure downed that margarita pretty fast. Does this mean you'll be hanging off the chandeliers later?" She laughed again; her breasts rose and fell quickly under her dress, leaving ripples in their wake.

"No," Sophia smiled politely. "I don't think I will be."

Then, a man walked up beside Aubrey. "Hi, Maleek!" she said, turning to face him "Maleek, this is one of my friends from work, Sophia. Sophia, this is my cousin Maleek."

Sophia was stunned. This man was gorgeous. For a moment, she thought she was wrong about Aubrey's sexuality—this had to be her boyfriend. He was tall, bald and caramel-colored with an awesome smile and striking features. He looked more in Aubrey's age range; she doubted he was over thirty.

"Hi, Sophia," Maleek greeted. "You look beautiful! It's a pleasure to meet you!"

Sophia couldn't control her own blushing. "Thank you." She added a bit nervously, "You're looking quite nice yourself."

"Thanks," Maleek responded. "How about a dance?"

Sophia's eyes asked Aubrey's permission.

Aubrey's eyes immediately gave it, so Sophia and Maleek headed toward the dance floor.

From that point it seemed the hours passed too quickly. Maleek was attentive and funny...not to mention model-gorgeous. Sophia hadn't felt this kind of restless longing for a man since the day she met Ron.

They laughed.

They danced.

They shared margaritas.

"Why don't we get out of here?" Maleek suggested at 3:00am.

Sophia threw her head back and laughed, her loose tresses bounced around her onyx-ornamented ears. The company of a man, the excitement and promise of this New Year, and the gentle comfort of her margaritas allowed her to laugh fully and womanly.

"Is that a yes?" Maleek asked hopefully. Sophia was a knockout, dressed to kill in a beautiful soft brown dress that clung to her curves like hot butter to a muffin. And, it was short, revealing shapely calves and solid thighs. She was healthy, the way he preferred his women. Yet she was different, much lighter than he would normally choose. He wanted her to fill the space in his bed *tonight.*

Sophia looked meaningfully into his eyes. She could see he was really interested in her, so she said her goodbyes and left with him. He kissed her in the cab, and by the time they reached his apartment they were both disheveled. He ran his hands through her hair as he unlocked his apartment door. When they entered he kissed her breasts and her neck, and guided her into the bedroom. Then he took her quickly and passionately.

Sophia sighed as she allowed Maleek to touch her. It had been so long since she allowed anyone to touch her body or her heart... She enjoyed the sensation of his bare lips against her breasts...and her mouth...and her neck...and his urgent intrusion into her body...holding her as if they were the only people in the world.

She wished she could have spent more time with him, but before she knew it, it was approaching 5:00am, and she'd be irresponsible if she didn't get back to her Aunt

Tyra's before daybreak.

"I've got to go," she whispered.

"I'll call you," Maleek mumbled, kissing her at the door.

"Definitely," she said, certain he would. She hopped into a cab with a smile on her face, feeling beautiful and wanted.

But, he never did call.

Aura & Ocean
Autumn 1993

"I do." Ocean smiled as he said the words, partially from his own joy, and also in a futile attempt to offset his own anxiety. In a church full of friends and family, after months of planning and thousands of dollars spent, it was clearer than ever—*this was definitely a big deal.* But as he curled his lips into a giddy grin, his disquiet was indiscernible to the crowd. In their eyes, Ocean was the charismatic half of a dream-like couple: the handsome, popular model, looking impeccable in a black tuxedo, accessorized with cream silk bow tie and cummerbund. *Aura* completed the fairy-tale union, stunning in an egg-shell brocade gown with a beaded train that rested leisurely on the altar. Her hair was swept high on her head, and a crown of lace and pearls accented her face. Her lips were frosted burgundy and Ocean waited with childlike anticipation for the moment he would be allowed to "kiss the bride."

When he kissed her then, he felt weak with excitement. Her small waist wriggled slightly under his hands as their lips paired. The "ohhs" and "ahhs" of the onlookers could be heard above the tender hush of expectant silence and the soft crackling of smoking altar candles.

Then, the well-wishers began to cheer as he and his bride walked the ornately tiled path out of the small church. Ace, Dana, Maleek and Angie followed close behind, completing the wedding party. Angie and Dana wore long violet gowns which hugged them to the hips; their lavender lace overlays hung bolero-style over the purple velvet, just covering their breasts. Angie had taken off a few pounds since she and Maleek began dating six months earlier, and the dress allowed her to show off her newly reclaimed figure.

Ace and Maleek wore tuxedos with lavender satin bow tie and cummerbund. The six formed a receiving line at the rear of the church, and soon the guests rose and shook their hands, kissed the bride and so on, in the usual fashion of weddings.

Ocean's mother, Dorothy, and her new husband, Andrew Miller, flew in from Abaco to attend. The two looked dolled-up in freshly starched cotton outfits under wool overcoats. They beamed, thoroughly ecstatic, as they kissed and hugged the bride and groom. The new Mrs. Miller hugged her so enthusiastically, Aura nearly dropped her bouquet.

Neville Ryder, Karen, and the three children: Nicholas-13, Ian-11, and David-5 were also in attendance. When they exchanged greetings with Ocean and Aura, they seemed a bit distant, and Ocean knew why. His father had been miserable ever since they discussed the price of Aura's engagement ring. He had even tried to get information on the price of their wedding bands, her dress, the reception, honeymoon, and whatever else he could think of. Ocean was disgusted by it. It was *his* money. His work at Esquire allowed him to clear $90,000 the past couple of years, and if he wanted to spend some of it on his bride, he didn't feel he had to answer to anyone, especially, his father, who he had been reluctantly subsidizing for years. It was true: Neville Ryder was his only biological father, but he wasn't much of a friend, and he was a questionable role model. Ocean would sooner take advice from Aura's father than his own.

Donald and Sylvia Olivier looked stunning in a tuxedo and peach sequined gown. They smiled excitedly as they hugged and kissed Ocean and Aura. Sylvia Olivier suddenly began crying.

"Oh, ma..." Aura smiled, as her mother rested her head on her shoulder.

"Two of my babies gone in only five months," Mrs. Olivier sighed reflectively, referring to Ace and Dana's marriage the previous June. "You two be good to each other," she said, glancing from her daughter's face to her son-in-law's.

"Of course we will," Ocean promised in his throaty baritone. His face was clean-shaven, and his hair was pulled back at the nape of his neck. His smile was unfading.

Then, Darryl Colon and his mother came for their hugs. Darryl was already fifteen and practically family. He shot up to 5'10" in what seemed like three months, had the beginnings of a beard and mustache now, and his voice had completed the change from pubescent to manly. Ocean kissed Mrs. Colon's cheek, then hugged Darryl by leaning into him and patting his back with both hands, the way men sometimes do. Then, the aunts and uncles from Aura's side of the family, co-workers and friends came to be greeted before heading off to the Caribbean restaurant where the reception would take place.

***

"I now present to you, the bride and groom—Aura and Ocean Ryder!" the announcer's voice boomed the good news as the two entered the restaurant dining area and took their seats at the head table beside Dana, Ace, Angie and Maleek. The room was mid-sized with mirrored walls painted with the works of Caribbean artists. The floor was a heavily shellacked wood, excellent for dancing, and the small circular tables were draped in specially ordered lavender cloths. A single white rose in a hand-sculpted wood bud vase adorned each place setting as guest souvenirs: The words "Aura and Ocean, October 15, 1993" were inscribed in the base. And, large Kenyan sculptures of kissing couples served as the centerpiece for each table. Their friends and family shouted excitedly as the couple was presented for the first time as husband and wife.

Aura and Ocean were thrilled to be surrounded by their best friends on such a momentous occasion. The nervousness that had been with them all day was quickly forgotten, as their friends and family consistently approached them throughout the cocktail period to extend blessings. When dinner was served the conversation was energetic. Dana, Ace, Angie and Maleek were clearly having a good time.

Aura was thrilled when the time came to toss her "throw away" bouquet. They all laughed when Angie managed to catch it.

Afterwards, Ocean removed the requisite garter and gave it a good send-off toward the group of single men who gathered to catch it. He watched excitedly as the garter travelled to the back of the room on a powerful toss, but his joy quickly subsided when he saw his father jump and successfully catch the item. *Did he have to publicize the fact they he and Karen never married?*

As best man, Ace had been emceeing the game. When he realized what transpired, he gave Ocean a sympathetic glance. "Okay, folks," he said with strained approval, "It looks like Neville Ryder caught the garter belt!" Ace faked enthusiasm, and wondered if he could avoid admitting this was Ocean's father. *How embarrassing!*

"All right, let's get Mr. Ryder and Angie together then..." his voice trailed off. This was pretty disgusting. He looked at Ocean for assistance. Ocean looked sick. Angie looked horrified. *Her sister's father-in-law was going to put a garter on her leg?!* Ace laughed, "Are you sure you qualify, Mr. Ryder? I thought you were a married man!" Ace was proud of himself, certain that they would be able to redo the toss.

"I'm not married!" Mr. Ryder declared defiantly, throwing Karen a harsh glance.

Ace swallowed. He supposed there was nothing he could do, so the music played while Neville Ryder slid a little lavender garter above Angela Olivier's knee.

***

It took the six of them awhile to recover from Mr. Ryder's behavior, but they refused to let it spoil the rest of the evening. Ocean was embarrassed, but there was nothing he could have done short of making a scene, so he apologized to Angie for his father and got on with the business of having a good time. The party was lively, as they both had hoped, and when it was time to leave, they weren't entirely sure they wanted to go. But after quick clothing changes and kisses goodbye, they boarded the limousine which would take them to the luxurious Plaza Hotel. Once they left, they were happy they had. Finally, they could get back to reality and spend some time alone together. The next morning they would catch a flight to Freeport, Bahamas where they would begin their honeymoon. From Freeport, they would cruise to Paradise Island, and finally, Abaco.

"Ohhh, I'm pooped out!" Aura exclaimed, throwing her body on the sofa in the posh suite. She wore a cream velvet jumper with an ornately beaded jacket of the same color.

"You're pooped?!" Ocean asked playfully. "At least *your* father didn't totally embarrass you and your entire lineage on *your* wedding day!" He sunk his body onto the sofa next to her.

"Oh, baby, don't worry about it. That's just the way your dad is. He thinks he's a stud." She laughed. "He is a good-looking man, you know."

"That doesn't mean he has to act like a dick," Ocean commented caustically.

Aura laughed. "Ocean, don't call your father a dick!"

"Uggh..." he groaned, slipping an arm behind her. "We're married now Aura..." he began, his voice suddenly throaty. Aura tilted her head back with excitement and anticipation. She knew he was about to kiss her.

"You know what that means, don't you?" he asked playfully.

"Whaaat?" she questioned.

"That means I can make love to you whenever..." And he kissed her. "Wherever..." And he kissed her again. "For as long as I want."

"Who told you that?" Aura asked, playing along.

"What do you mean who told me?" Ocean grabbed her hand and led her to the huge bathroom. "It's in all the husband manuals." He rested his eyes gently upon hers, then he allowed them to course over her face... her shoulders... her breasts... her waist... her thighs...

Aura laughed. "You should be locked up for looking at me the way you do!" she laughed. She leaned against the mirrored vanity as the stiletto heels on her cream snakeskin pumps sunk deeply into the plush beige carpet.

"You look at me the same way," Ocean replied, dead serious. He stood with his back to the wall on the opposite side of the deluxe washroom.

Aura felt the hot rush of her own rising desire. It was true. She loved him *and* she lusted for him.

"So what are you gonna do?" she asked, playing this game they both enjoyed.

"What do *you* want to do?" he asked toying with the buckle on his pants seductively.

Aura did not respond verbally, barely aware of the shallow puffs of air which left her parted lips in tiny gusts.

"Take off your clothes. I want to watch you undress." He did not ask—he demanded.

Aura smiled. "Ocean!" she exclaimed, with a fiery combination of puritanical embarrassment and heightened sexual excitement. The idea of being looked at, but not touched, was suddenly thrilling. Ocean had never made such a request before.

"Do it," he stated simply.

Aura's face burned hot as she removed the jacket slowly. She could see Ocean's erection rise under his clothing, but she resisted the urge to walk toward him. She removed the jumper slowly, first revealing the cream lace bra under the top, then the matching lace G-string under the bottom. She even wore lace garters and opalescent stockings for the occasion. When she finally looked up at Ocean in nothing but high heels and underwear, he was clearly weak with desire.

"All done," she said provocatively, tossing her clothing to the side.

"Finish," he stated simply. It took all the patience and self-control he possessed to keep from grabbing her and ripping those little lace things off, lowering her to the floor, and releasing this thing that was driving him crazy.

Aura felt her body grow weak. This *was* exciting. "You mean *everything?*" she asked, with a combination of real and pretended innocence.

"Yeah, everything...slowly..." Ocean accidentally bit his lip as he released that last word. *Yeah, slowly. This game was fun.*

Aura looked directly into Ocean's eyes as she unhooked the front of her bra, her small breasts sprung quickly when freed. She could hear his sigh. Then, she stepped out of her shoes, kicked a leg up onto the toilet and removed the stockings slowly... She unclasped the snap of her garter to release one stocking, rolling it slowly down the length of her long leg. When both stockings were removed, she slipped a burgundy frosted fingernail under the lacy silk front of her G-string panty and gently slid out of it.

Ocean looked at her naked before him until he could no longer take it, then he walked over to her and cradled her in his arms. "You are so beautiful...I can't believe you belong to me..." he said, burying his face in her neck.

"I...love...you..." She released the words like breaths between moans as she urgently kissed his lips and tore at his shirt buttons.

Ocean could feel the heat radiating off her body as she undressed him. He caressed her longingly, finally pulling the remains of his clothes off in a frenzy. He lowered her to the shaggy carpet quickly. His hands roamed her body lovingly; his fingers stroked her hair... neck... breasts... thighs... He massaged her buttocks with his hands, relishing in its roundness and fullness, enjoying the feel of her soft skin under his palms. Her body was hot, and that coupled with the sound of her voice and the joy of their day together made his passion more powerful than he had ever experienced. As he heard her repeat the words, "I love you," over and over, in the voice he had grown to adore, this new covenant warmed his heart: She was his wife, and the love they made now was sacred in a way it had never been before. He kissed her breasts then, tugging lightly at her nipples. "You're so beautiful, Aura. I don't know what I'd do without you..." He sighed. "I love you *so* much..."

Aura's eyes grew moist as she listened to Ocean's voice. He made a trail of kisses from her mouth, down her neck, breasts and stomach...finally reaching the warmth between her legs. She ran her hands through his hair, as he kissed her there with such passion and love she couldn't control her own response, and as she reached a riveting wave of orgasms she was unaware of the two lone tears which fell from her eyes.

Ocean moved his mouth away from her body and to her mouth in one quick shift of his weight, which forced his penis into her slippery warmth. He caught sight of her tears mingled in the dewy glow of her face—a testament to her love and her pleasure. Then, he closed his eyes, reveling in the intensity of his own delight. He could feel the gentle raking of her nails across his back, buttocks and thighs as she bit his neck and shoulders. Then, he felt the sweet relief of his own release as he came inside of her, arching his back tightly. He moaned loudly as waves of ecstasy overwhelmed him, then he dropped his head weakly, his lips brushing lightly against her neck "Aura..." he sighed.

Aura was surprised to see a tear had escaped Ocean's eye, but as she noticed his, she immediately became aware of her own lost tears. "Oh, baby..." she sighed, holding him in her arms. She loved him more than anything. Everything felt so new, like they had never made love before.

Aura loved the feeling of Ocean's sweat-soaked body next to hers. She didn't want to move...ever... So they held each other and fell asleep as husband and wife on the carpeted bathroom floor of their suite in The Plaza Hotel.

***

The beach in Freeport was long, stretching farther than they could see. The sand changed from soft white to deep beige as the turquoise waters crashed gently against it. It was Aura's first trip to the Caribbean in years, and she was thrilled to be there. Ocean looked delicious on the beach, shirtless with only drawstring running pants over his swimming trunks He sat on the beach lounger with a beer and a copy of Malcolm X's autobiography. Only a small white table with a large yellow beach umbrella separated Aura from him. She wore a white bikini as she relaxed to the sounds of Angela Bofill on her Walkman™. They were having a wonderful time: sunning and swimming in the day, then dining & dancing at night. As she turned onto her stomach she felt the return of throbbing pains along her back and thighs. She had hoped this wouldn't happen.

She reached into her bag for her medication with a wave of guilt. She opened the bottle without removing it from her bag, and popped two pills into her mouth before reclosing it.

"What's that?" Ocean asked. "You've been taking a lot of those lately," he remarked.

"Oh, just vitamins," she lied.

Ocean laughed. "Is that what makes you so energetic? Maybe I should be taking those too!" He reached his hand out to her, gesturing for the bottle.

Aura passed the bottle to him nervously. "It's for women only." She stated the lie she had planned over and over in her head for so many months. When they were dating, it wasn't very difficult to hide her pill consumption. She simply went to the bathroom when she needed a painkiller. Since they started living together seven months earlier, things became more difficult.

Suddenly her painkillers became poorly concealed "vitamins." It seemed she'd been lying for so long, she couldn't imagine how she could tell him the truth now. *How could she go on keeping this horrible secret from her husband?*

"What's the difference?" Ocean asked, noting the bottle of "made for women" vitamins that Aura handed him.

Aura swallowed, hoping he wouldn't open the bottle. "It has lots of iron and concentrated *ovaries!"* she squealed, pretending to be playful.

"That's disgusting, Aura!" Ocean peered at the label on the bottle until he saw a listing for ovary extract along with various vitamins and minerals. "Yuck!" He handed the bottle back to her with a chuckle.

Aura sighed a breath of relief.

Ocean shifted on the chaise to eye his wife more easily. "Why don't you join my gym when we get back to Brooklyn?" he asked. "I think we get a discount or something."

"Oh, I don't know..." Aura began. She would hate to have Ocean see the limited workout she was able to do; it would be embarrassing. She just didn't have the strength to work out the way a healthy person might.

Ocean smiled, unaware of Aura's displeasure, "Well, think about it," he stated simply.

Aura smiled. "Yeah, I will." Just as she spoke, a spasmodic aching attacked her shoulders. She decided to try to swim a few strokes. Maybe it would distract her from the pain.

***

The days and nights were long and tranquil over the two weeks of their honeymoon. They soared from island to island with the carefree abandon of doves in flight. Ocean was most excited when they made their final stop at Mr. and Mrs. Miller's house.

"Eddie!" his mother exclaimed, hugging him tightly. She stepped away from him on the wooden porch to eye him from head to toe. "You look beautiful...all tanned!" She kissed his cheek and held her son closely; a tear fell unexpectedly from her eye. "You make me so proud!" Eddie crushed the cotton dress his mother wore with his hug.

Aura looked on smiling "Hi, Mrs. Miller!" she finally greeted.

Dorothy Miller shifted her gaze from her son to her new daughter-in-law. "Oh, Aura!" she exclaimed. "You look so beautiful!" She hugged Aura and gave her a quick kiss before leading her into the home she shared with her husband, sister and four kids.

Aura immediately smelled the aroma of conch chowder which permeated the room. "Uhhmm..." she sighed.

"It's Eddie's favorite," Dorothy Miller responded with a wink.

Aura gave Ocean an admiring glance. "Your son has good taste," she conceded.

Ocean placed their bags on the living room floor and slipped an arm around his wife's waist. Only Andrew Miller and Aunt Mary were in the living room, and Ocean felt a bit disappointed. *Didn't the rest of the family want to meet Aura?* He allowed his mother to introduce Aura to Aunt Mary, and they all exchanged the requisite greetings before sitting to chat.

"So how was the big honeymoon?!" Aunt Mary asked excitedly.

Aura and Ocean smiled as they shifted their bodies on the fabric sofa, exchanging glances in a silent determination of who would answer. They both wore pale blue jeans and white cotton shirts; finally Ocean spoke. "It's been wonderful. We really got the chance to relax. Aura did some shopping." He glanced at her for elaboration.

Aura continued his thought. "Oh, yes! I found some wonderful carved sculptures and jewelry." She paused before continuing, "The beaches are beautiful...we've just been cruising for days it seems...I haven't felt this relaxed in years. When I get back to the office, they'll think I'm a new person!" Her sentences glided gently into each other, as if she were relaying a dream.

Aunt Mary frowned. "You're going to continue working?" she asked, clearly disapproving.

Aura threw Ocean a toned-down version of her *Is she for real?* glance, before responding. "Yes, I'm going to continue working. I enjoy my work, why wouldn't I continue?" Aura made a futile attempt to rid her voice of any sarcasm.

Aunt Mary frowned again. "So, who will watch the children?"

"What children?" Aura asked, seething.

Ocean smiled and sat silently. He loved Aura's independence, and even enjoyed when she got ticked off over this kind of thing. She was a woman to be reckoned with, as he was sure his Aunt Mary would soon recognize.

"Your children!" Aunt Mary stated patronizingly. *Was this poor child stupid?*

Then, Aura threw her head back and laughed heartily. "Oh, Aunt Mary, I'm so sorry. I was actually beginning to get upset. Sometimes, I just forget we have two totally different backgrounds." She paused hoping her words would prepare the woman for what she was about to say. "It's just that times have changed. I hold a prestigious position in a pretty high-powered field, and I make an excellent salary, as a matter of fact, I'm up for an increase." Her mind wandered for a moment as she thought about the decisions which would be made when she returned home. She was in line for promotion to Senior Media Negotiator, and, although she felt positive about it, it was not yet official. She collected her thoughts and continued speaking to a wide-eyed Aunt Mary. "I have no intention of giving up my career" she stated simply, folding her arms across her chest.

"My goodness" Aunt Mary sighed with disbelief. "You kids are so different nowadays!" She looked Eddie in his eyes. "This stuff doesn't bother you?" she asked, gesturing at Aura with her hand.

"Bother me?" Ocean asked incredulously. "I *love* it! Aunt Mary you would not believe the number of women out there who look at guys like me as a free meal ticket. Aura's not like that; I know she's with me 'cause she loves me." He rested a hand on Aura's thigh as he spoke.

"So when *do* you want to start a family?" Dorothy Miller finally asked. She had struggled to hold her tongue while Aunt Mary talked.

Ocean laughed. "I don't know." He looked at Aura for an answer. "Two years? Three years?" he asked playfully.

Aura laughed and rested her head on Ocean's shoulder. She wanted children badly, but she was scared to death of all the risks associated with going through a pregnancy with sickle-cell anemia. First, Ocean would have to be tested for the trait...a wave of guilt made her sick for just a moment.

"Are you okay?" Ocean asked, noticing Aura's cheek against his shoulder for a few beats longer than he thought normal. Aura jumped up. "Oh, yeah...I'm fine..." she lied. *Shit... What had she gotten herself into?*

***

Marvin, George, Shana and Michael were all home before dinner. They seemed thrilled to see their brother and meet his new wife, and each apologized individually for having to work that day. Ocean felt silly when he realized that the only reason he didn't see them sooner was because they were working! A few days of vacation, and he forgot all about real life responsibilities!

The six of them relaxed in the living room, drinking coconut rum and condensed milk over ice while they chatted. Ocean and Aura were busy describing the wedding and reception. Occasionally, Dorothy and Andrew Miller jumped into the conversation to describe Aura's dress or some other notable thing, but they stayed in the kitchen with Aunt Mary for the most part, leaving the "kids" to themselves.

"I can't believe how perfect you are!" Shana gushed to Aura. "And, you make him so happy!"

"Oh, stop, Shana!" Aura laughed. *If only she knew how imperfect she really was.*

"Why stop, Aura?" Ocean teased lovingly, "You *are* perfect for me!" he said, kissing her lightly.

Aura smiled. She really did love him more than anything in the world. Maybe that was why she was so deathly afraid of losing him.

***

Aura looked around the small patio of their hotel restaurant briefly, before spotting the only other young black couple there. Ocean noticed his brother quickly and tugged at Aura's hand as he led her to the small, peach-cloaked table.

"Hey so this is the new wife!" Barry said, smiling as

Eddie and Aura reached them. He stood up and hugged his younger brother. The last time they saw each other was only briefly two years earlier. Barry's memories of Eddie were mainly him at sixteen and preoccupied with trying to screw every little girl on the island. It was nice to see him with a wife who seemed to make him happy. Remembering that ten years passed like grains of sand through his fingers made him feel old.

"Wow, man!" Ocean exclaimed. "I barely recognized you! You should come visit me sometime." He stared at his older brother's goateed face for a few lingering moments, trying to press his image into his mind.

"Well," Barry began, giving Ocean a perplexed look "This is my wife, Hillary."

Ocean pulled himself out of his daze. "Oh, it's nice to meet you Hillary," he said holding her hand for a moment. The woman was beautiful with copper skin and wildly curly chestnut hair.

"This is my bride, Aura," he offered.

"Hi, Aura!" the woman greeted, giving Aura a peck on the cheek. "It's nice to meet you."

"Thank you," Aura replied. "I'm so glad I'm getting the chance to meet both of you!" She shook Barry's hand, and they all got comfortable in their seats. Turning her face toward Barry, Aura added, "Ocean says you two didn't get a chance to see much of each other last time he was on the island."

A waitress took their drink orders before he responded. "Yeah," Barry admitted. "I was going through a difficult time in my life," he stated somewhat apologetically.

Aura immediately felt embarrassed by her own apparent intrusion. "Oh, I'm sorry..." she said softly.

"Oh, no, that's okay. I used to drink pretty heavily, that's all." Barry's tone was pensive. "I don't know how I did it, but drinking became more important to me than anything else. I was becoming a different person..." His eyes wandered to the potted trees on the open veranda.

Hillary placed a comforting hand on his shoulder.

Ocean shifted in his seat restlessly. "Really, Barry, you don't have to explain anything. Aura didn't know..."

"No, that's okay. She *should* know," Barry replied authoritatively. He turned his face toward Aura. "I don't drink anymore, that's all. I like drinking root drinks like mauby or fresh ginger beer for the bitterness. I do miss that." He smiled. "Hillary and I have been married for almost a year now! I don't know what she sees in me."

"Oh, stop!" Hillary exclaimed. "You know exactly what I see in you!" she laughed as if she thought only Barry could hear her.

Then Barry actually *giggled* with her; that's when Aura knew for sure that everything was okay. He was acting like a lovesick schoolboy—worse than she and Ocean.

Dinner progressed smoothly; Hillary and Barry made for pleasurable company, and the weather was agreeable despite showers earlier in the morning. Aura was pleasantly surprised by Ocean's family. She had expected his brothers to behave more like his father, but they didn't seem caught up in womanizing. And, she enjoyed hearing their pure Bahamian accents, since Ocean's was barely distinguishable after ten years in the States.

So, the evening ended with promises to call, write and visit, and all four of them vowed to make the effort.

***

After three nights in Abaco, they packed to go home. Their honeymoon was as exciting and romantic as Aura had dreamed it would be: They scuba-dived, snorkeled, partied and sailed to their hearts content. Their evenings closed with long nights of lovemaking, and their days began with lazy mornings on the beach and decadent noon brunches. Aura just wished she knew how to handle the feelings of guilt that recurred whenever the pains from her sickle-cell got particularly bad. *How could she go on with this horrible lie?*

"Hey...are you okay?" Ocean asked, coming back into their hotel room from the patio. He was in the process of doing a final check for sandals, toiletries and any other belongings they might inadvertently leave in the hotel.

"Oh, I'm fine," Aura lied, tormented by her own dishonesty. She fussed with the suitcase on the bed.

Ocean walked up behind her and wrapped his arms around her waist. He rested his chin atop her head. "I hope things went the way you wanted." His tone was soft with the uncertainty of trying to console without reason. He knew Aura was keeping something from him. Something was troubling her. At least, he knew it in his gut, so he tried to comfort her naturally, lovingly. But his conscious mind had not yet fully realized this fact that on the fourteenth day of their marriage his wife already had a secret.

***

"Ocean?!" Aura called out as she entered the apartment they shared. They'd been living as husband and wife in Ocean's old bachelor pad for the past two weeks. "Ocean!" she called out again, walking through the rooms excitedly. He was nowhere to be found. She picked up the stereo remote and flipped through radio stations, finally settling on jazz, then she checked the answering machine; there were two messages.

"Hey, girl, what's up? Give me a call later." It was Dana.

"Hey, baby. I just wanted to let you know the shoot's running a little late tonight. I'm not sure when I'll get out of here. I'll see you soon. Love you." It was Ocean.

Aura smiled, then sighed. She wanted Ocean to be the first person she told about her promotion. *Oh well...* She picked up the cordless phone and dialed Dana.

"Hello?" Dana answered casually.

"I GOT IT!" Aura screamed excitedly.

"YOU GOT THE PROMOTION?!" Dana shouted back.

"Yeah! I'm so psyched! It's an even better deal than I expected!" Aura smiled with the satisfaction of sharing the news with her best friend. Next, she'd call Angie, then her parents.

"Girl, I don't know what I was thinking, *asking* if you got it... I *knew* you'd get it!"

"Thanks."

"So, where's Ocean?" Dana asked.

"Oh, he's working a little late tonight. He got a new gig with Sofeegear last week, so he's flying pretty high himself."

"I didn't know Ocean got a job with Sofeegear! Oh, her stuff is hot! What's he doing for her?" Dana sounded impressed.

"Her who?" Aura asked.

"Sophia Boyd!" Dana responded.

"Huh?"

"Haven't you heard of Sophia Boyd? She used to work with some uptown design firm, then she broke away with her own hot gear. Girl, she's a *mad* up-and-coming sista!" Dana laughed. "She's supposed to have an appetite for men, too."

"Oh, ha-ha," Aura stated only half-joking. "What's that supposed to mean? Do you know anyone who knows her?"

"Yeah, actually, I do. She went to F.I.T. with Leron and Troy," she said, referring to mutual friends from their high school.

"You still talk to Leron and Troy?" Aura asked with disbelief.

"I usually bump into Troy every now and then on the subway or something. I think he works near me." She paused, savoring this latest bit of gossip. "Anyway, Troy tells me Sophia used to hang out with some gay girl a lot back in college. I don't know if Sophia was gay or something too, but apparently nowadays she likes her men by the truckload. She was married and it didn't work out so now she's some kind of *man-eater*.

Aura couldn't help feeling a bit insecure. "I *know* Ocean's not going anywhere!" she lied. "I'd kill him if he did, anyway:" She folded her arms across her chest, realizing this lie of hers was wearing thin on her own sense of security.

"Oh, puhleeze, Aura! I now Ocean's true blue! But you know how miserable little insecure women get sometimes! Just make sure you're keeping those love juices flowing!" She laughed heartily then.

Aura laughed with her. "Uhmmm…the love juices are just *fine,* thank you." She smiled. Lovemaking with Ocean was better now than ever before. Her mind wandered to the previous night, and she felt a quick warmth below her navel.

Dana continued. "And you know…talk to him…make sure he tells you what's going on. All the loving in the world don't mean shit if you stop talking…"

Aura furrowed her brows. Dana's words rang true. She was going to have to tell Ocean about the sickle-cell. The fact of the matter was, it scared her to death. How do you tell someone you love that you have a horrible disease that could change both of your lives? And, even worse, how do you justify lying to someone you committed to spend the rest of your life with?

"Aura?" Dana asked after a long pause.

"Yeah," Aura mumbled.

"Shit, Aura, don't take me so seriously. You know Ocean loves you. You guys are newlyweds, for godssake." Her tone was filled with sudden concern. She knew she had a bad habit of exaggerating and running off her mouth sometimes, but she didn't think Aura would be so insecure. "Okay, so maybe she's not exactly a *man-eater*. You know how people are... She's probably just dating two guys or something... So what?" She tried to sound convincing. Troy apparently knew a girl named Aubrey who worked as Sophia's personal assistant, and according to Aubrey, she was a m-a-n-e-a-t-e-r!

"Oh, it's not that..." Aura mumbled. "Listen, Dana, I have to run. I'll give you a call a little later." She pressed the disconnect button on the cordless phone, before Dana could protest.

***

When Ocean came home it was nearly 10:00pm, and Aura was already in bed. She hadn't been feeling well for weeks, and she knew a crisis was coming on. By midnight, it seemed no amount of painkillers would sufficiently dull the pain.

"What's the matter?!" Ocean asked frantically as Aura rocked her body in the bed, crying.

"I don't know," she lied. "Would you drive me to emergency?" she asked.

Ocean's fear turned his face a chalky brown. "What's wrong?!!" Aura was clearly in agony, and he felt helpless. He couldn't imagine what might be wrong. Suppose it was something terrible?! Like a burst appendix...or a tubal pregnancy... His mind wandered. He and Aura had taken some chances with their birth control. *Could her pain be his fault?*

"Just drive me to emergency. I'm sure the doctors will help me." Aura's voice broke through the clutter of his thoughts. She stood up and slowly began putting shoes on. The cotton pajamas she wore to bed would have to suffice.

"Oh, my god, baby!" Ocean grabbed the keys, helped Aura out of the apartment building and into the car. Then, he ignored most traffic rules as he rushed her to the emergency room. When she got there, he was impressed by how she handled herself. He was busy ranting and raving, but Aura approached the doctors calmly, and before he knew it she was being taken to a treatment area.

"Go home, Ocean," she said, lying in her cot. Demerol™ entered her veins through the IV, and she was feeling increasingly relaxed.

"What are you talking about?! I'm gonna stay here all night if I have to!"

Aura's eyes were pleading. "Please, baby, just go home and get some sleep. It won't do either of us any good if you look like shit on your shoot tomorrow." She laughed to let him know she was feeling better. "I love you, Ocean, but I'm a big girl now. I'll be fine. We can talk later."

"Are you sure?" he asked.

"Yeah, besides, this stuff they're giving me is going to put me to sleep, anyway." Ocean didn't seem to want to leave, so she added, "The doctor says it's just a muscle spasm."

"Oh...okay, but only if you're sure you don't need me." Ocean held her hand as he spoke.

Aura smiled. "I'll always *need* you." She squeezed his hand, and he leaned over and kissed her forehead. "Just go to work tomorrow. It's a great account. Don't screw it up."

Aura drifted off to sleep, and Ocean finally went home.

***

Aura called Dana from her semi-private room the next day.

"Oh, shit, Aura! You had a crisis?!" Dana's mind wandered over their last conversation. She knew stress could bring on a crisis, and she hoped she didn't make a contribution with her comments about Sophia Boyd.

"Yeah, I need to talk to you though, Dana... It's pretty serious shit..."

"Whaaat?" Dana asked, concerned.

"I've been lying to Ocean about this..." Her voice cracked as she said the words.

Dana's mind raced. *What was she talking about?*

Aura's mouth was dry, and imminent tears poised on the rims of her eyes. "I don't know how I can tell him now...I just feel so guilty...I kept thinking he'd never have to know...But, I just haven't been feeling well..." She stopped to catch her breath and blow her nose. Her tears were flowing freely down her cheeks, so she wiped them with a tissue. "Suppose he can't forgive me? Suppose he doesn't want me anymore?"

"Aura, what are you talking about? Shhh... Calm down..." Dana was confused, but her voice *was* soothing.

Aura swallowed. "My *sickle-cell,* Dana. I never told Ocean about my sickle-cell." She kept her voice steady, but the reality of her words forced her tears to flow again. She shifted uncomfortably on the hospital bed.

Dana swallowed. *Could she be hearing right?* "What do you mean you never told him?" Dana asked, dumbfounded. She and Ace certainly wouldn't talk about Aura's sickle-cell, but it never occurred to either of them that Ocean didn't know. Dana's mind grappled with this new idea, trying to make sense of it. Angie probably wouldn't even discuss something like that with Maleek either, to create an opportunity for the news to get back to Ocean. Dana frowned. *Could this really be possible?*

"It never came up," Aura replied, suddenly defiant.

Dana's voice turned angry. "Aura, how could you *do* something like that?" She lowered her voice, realizing co-workers could hear her. "Aura, you have to tell him as soon as possible." Her voice was authoritative. "You can't marry someone and keep something like that from them... For god's sake Aura, suppose he wants to have children!"

A few more tears slid down Aura's cheek. "Dana, you're not being fair!" she screamed into the phone.

"No, Aura, it's *you* who haven't been fair..." Dana thought for a moment about her own wedding. "My god, Aura! I can't imagine Ace keeping something like that from me!"

Aura's supply of tears finally diminished, and her eyes dried up slightly swollen. "I thought you might have understood," she stated softly. "Never mind," she mumbled before returning the handset to the cradle. *If Dana was this angry, how would Ocean react?*

***

A solemn-looking Filipino doctor entered Aura's room, not long after her conversation with Dana. "Mrs. Ryder?" he asked.

"Ms. Olivier-Ryder," she quickly corrected him.

"Well, yes..." he began. "How are you feeling?"

"Oh, much better."

The doctor smiled." I have some news for you which we'll need to discuss. Last night when you came in we put a lot of drugs into you."

Aura smiled nervously. "Yes, I know. I was in a lot of pain."

"Of course. I understand that. On your chart, there was a notation that you were not pregnant."

"I'm not," Aura confirmed.

The doctor grimaced. "Well, Ms. Ryder, I have blood tests indicating a pregnancy. If we had known this yesterday, we might have considered different treatment options."

Aura's eyes widened and her mind raced. She knew she and Ocean were a little lazy with the condoms over the past few months, but she hadn't missed a period. "How pregnant am I?" she asked, horrified.

"You're probably not too far along if you haven't missed a period yet." He smiled at Aura. "Why don't you get some rest, tell your husband, and we can discuss it later. I'm ready to release you today if you're feeling fine. I can write you a prescription for a milder painkiller until you decide how you want to handle this pregnancy."

"Thank you, doctor," Aura said, smiling as he left her room. She immediately got a throbbing tension headache.

***

Ocean was shocked when he called the hospital and was told Aura had already checked out. He called the apartment and Aura answered. "What are you doing home?" he asked frantically.

"The doctor said I'm fine. He wrote me a prescription. How's work?"

"Everything's going really well... Are you sure you're okay?" Ocean's voice was laced with frustration.

"Yeah, I'm fine," Aura lied reassuringly. *There was no way she could keep this baby.*

***

When Ocean hung up the phone, he wondered why Aura was lying to him. He opened her "vitamin" bottle while she was in the hospital, and immediately realized some of the pills inside were not vitamins at all.

***

"Are you sure everything's okay?" Ocean asked when he saw Aura reclined on the living room sofa. He removed his jacket and hung it on his treasured Kenyan coat rack, before walking quickly toward his wife.

Aura smiled. She *was* feeling much better. "Everything's fine," she said, curling her feet under her on the leather sofa. Ocean frowned, then.

"What's wrong with you?" Aura asked innocently.

"When you were gone..." he began. He wasn't sure how to explain what seemed like snooping. *Didn't he trust her?*

Aura swallowed. *What could Ocean have done in the one night she was gone?*

Ocean cleared his throat. "It's just...I opened the vitamin bottle you have, and I noticed some pills are not vitamins. His voice was strained. He hoped she had a reasonable explanation...any explanation for carrying codeine in a vitamin bottle. He had taken one of the pills to a pharmacist to find out what it was. The whole thing made him feel horrible, like he was sneaking around behind her back. Of course, she'd have a good explanation.

Aura smiled nervously. "Oh, that!" she sighed. Her

mind raced for a good response, when she thought of one, she quickly relaxed. "Those are just painkillers for when I have my period. Sometimes I get really bad cramps."

Ocean exhaled. He knew she'd have a logical explanation. He smiled and kissed her forehead. "Sorry for being such a snoop," he apologized.

Aura smiled. "It's okay. After all, you're my hubby now. If anyone has the right to snoop, you do."

Ocean sat on the sofa beside her and hugged her tightly. "It's just...that hospitalization last night...it made me so nervous. I don't want to lose you."

"I'm not going anywhere," Aura replied, resting her head in her husband's arms as her guilt and shame created a dizzying wave of self-loathing. She wasn't sure if she was ashamed because of all the lies or if the disease itself embarrassed her. Sometimes she just felt defective, handicapped... She hugged Ocean tightly, controlling her urge to spill everything and beg for forgiveness. No, she couldn't tell him about the pregnancy; he'd never let her abort the baby, and the risk on her health and that of her child would be too high. No one understands sickle-cell, unless they live with it.

Sophia Boyd
Autumn 1993

"Thanks for everything," Sophia said suggestively as the man left her apartment. It was Saturday morning and Angel had given her a satisfying evening. She smiled when she closed the door. This was much easier. She had successfully mastered the skill of separating sex from love, and she was enjoying it. Sex was a human need, like water and air. Now love... Love was another story. She got love from her family: her father, her boys; she didn't need men for that. It was too complicated. The boys were with her Aunt Tyra every weekend for the past six months. It worked out well, allowing her the time she needed to get her business off the ground and satisfy her sexual appetite.

Sophia sighed as she thought about the months she spent celibate, partly for her own sake and partly for the boys'. Those days were over. Since Aunt Tyra and Uncle Mac become Born Again Christians, Aunt Tyra nagged her about the children's souls till she struck a deal: Aunt Tyra picked them up from school on Fridays and kept them until Monday. It gave the boys religion and it gave Sophia *time*.

She flipped through her Saturday mail with disregard: another letter from Sandy; she shoved it in the wastebasket without opening it; bills she set aside; a note from her father she opened promptly. It was a birthday card. It seemed he was the only one who remembered her birthday anymore. Sophia sighed with the realization.

She had a lot to do today. Despite the fact that it was a Saturday, the launching of her business filled her days—weekday and weekend. She smiled smugly to herself as she considered one of the new models. His name was Ocean, and he was absolutely beautiful. She heard through the office grapevine that he was newly married, but she sensed some discontent and decided she may as well make herself available to him. After all, a man like that wouldn't remain dissatisfied for long.

***

"So, Aubrey, what's the scoop?" Sophia asked excitedly, leaning across her modest desk.

"What do you mean?" Aubrey replied, straightening her jean jumper in the painted metal chair in Sophia's Downtown Brooklyn office.

"I saw you talking to him. Is he free?" Sophia questioned with serious interest.

Aubrey shook her head. "Sophie, I *told* you the man is married. Lay off, already!" Aubrey adjusted herself in her chair with indignation. Sophia was her boss, but the woman had been buck wild since she started her own business. She supposed she was fiending on power or something. After seeing her new M.O. with men, Aubrey was silently pleased that her cousin, Maleek, had not become involved with her. She did find it strange that Sophia never even asked about Maleek after hanging all over him at the party the previous January. She hadn't given it much thought at the time, though, being preoccupied herself with her new boyfriend, Ted, who she met that same evening.

Sophia gave Aubrey an annoyed glance as her concept of marriage quickly tossed about in her mind—it wasn't very meaningful. "I *know* he's married. I've *seen* his wife... They don't seem to be too happy..." Sophia licked her coral lips, "That means there's still room for me..." She crossed her black-spandexed legs, and laughed. *Yeah, there was definitely room.*

Aubrey frowned and lowered her voice. "Sophie, you've fucked just about every brother up in this place!"

Sophia snickered proudly.

Aubrey rolled her eyes in response. "Girl, you need to check yourself... I think you're losing it."

"Damn, Aubrey, you act like he's *your* man! Just tell me the deal!"

Aubrey gave Sophia a stupid glance. "I *told* you. He's *married...* They're *newlyweds* for shit's sake!"

Sophia interjected. "Well, he's not *acting* like a newlywed. He's acting like a man with something on his mind." She sighed. "And, that man is sooo fine, I just want to do the respectable thing and find out what that something is."

"Sophie, you're hopeless." Aubrey leaned back in the chair in frustration, sliding her hands into the pockets of her overalls.

"Whatever, just give me the scoop."

"There is no scoop Sophie. I think he's in love with her."

"Everybody's been in love once upon a time. It'll pass." Sophia shifted in her seat. "So, do you have any information for me, or what?"

"Well, I don't know much..." Aubrey paused in contemplation. "All I know is another woman's been looking for him on site."

Sophia's mind did circles. "Another woman besides his wife?" she asked in disbelief.

"Yeah."

Sophia nodded her head. It was so typical. Someone

would get to him before she could. "What does she look like?"

"She's kinda brown-skinned, but she always comes with a man. I think she's married or something too..."

"Oh..." Sophia considered what this new information might mean.

"Look, Sophie, I just think he's off limits. I think he's true to his wife..." She paused before imploring, "Leave him alone."

Sophia smiled. "Look, if he's really true to his wife, he doesn't have to worry about little ole me. She gestured across her breasts with her hands.

"Yeah, sure..." Aubrey rolled her eyes with disgust. She decided not to mention that Maleek and Ocean worked for the same modeling agency. Who knew what Sophia would want to do with that type of information?

***

Sophia curled up on her sofa after tucking the children into bed. Her mind ran lazily over her evening with Maleek nearly a year earlier. She'd been with many men since then, and her business was really getting off the ground, but, for some reason, he left her with a gap she had not yet filled.

She hated when she thought about that evening... Over and over again... She was no virgin before she met him, and she was no virgin now... Obviously he was just a pathetic asshole... Even Aubrey never mentioned him. *Then, why did that night still bother her so much?*

***

"Sophie, I read an article about you all the way down here in Florida!" Mr. Boyd exclaimed happily.

344

"Really, daddy?! That's wonderful! I suppose it's all good..." Sophia responded into her telephone receiver.

"What wouldn't be?" Mr. Boyd replied. "It seems everybody loves you in New York!"

"Well, yeah... I'm doing pretty well."

"Oh baby, you're doing absolutely fabulous! If word of your business is flying this fast, I know you're doing an excellent job!"

"Thank you, daddy. I'm glad you have so much faith in me... Everything's working out better than I had hoped."

"I told you it would. Never underestimate yourself, Sophie. You're so intelligent and talented. People dream of having a life like yours..."

Sophia sighed. *Yeah, right.* "Thanks, dad."

"What are you doing for your birthday?!" he continued enthusiastically.

Sophia frowned. Her birthdays usually passed quietly since her move to New York sixteen years earlier, except during her relationship with Sandy. She smiled with the thought. Sandy had always made a big deal out of it. Even Ron had never made a big fuss. "Ohhh, just working, I suppose," she began. "You wouldn't believe what my days are like now. I'm constantly busy..." she explained.

Mr. Boyd frowned. "Well, I'm sure you'll find something nice to do to celebrate. You know you can't work all the time." He paused before adding, "Success is a journey, make sure you enjoy the trip."

Sophia smiled. "Yeah, daddy, I know."

Mr. Boyd cleared his throat. "Well, I won't keep you. Take care of yourself and talk to you soon."

"Okay," Sophia agreed.

"I love you," Mr. Boyd stated simply.

"Love you too, daddy." She hung up the phone and stared at it for a few moments before returning to her work.

She was about to turn thirty-three, and she wasn't too thrilled about it. Thirty had been bad, and each new year seemed increasingly annoying. She wasn't sure if she would celebrate or hide out on November nineteenth.

***

Sophia wore a simple pair of charcoal cotton coveralls with a long-sleeved T-shirt peeking from underneath as she entered her downtown Brooklyn office at 10˙00am She exchanged greetings with Aubrey, Cyprus and Bobby as she made her way into her small, private office. When the demand for her garments surpassed her production ability, she had hired the two young men to handle bookkeeping and assist Aubrey. She had managed to negotiate a new deal to increase production, and now her focus was on making sure consumer demand increased at a predictable pace. She hoped to one day operate her own production facility, but for now she used an outside firm.

Sophia had spent the past few months working addictively and relishing this newfound desire which took her to a level of delight which was difficult to explain: Every time she entered this small simple office she felt alive...brand new...important...*loved?* The type of raw emotion she experienced when she kissed one of her sons on the cheek...made love to a new man...drew a new design...struck a new deal... Yes, it was difficult to explain. It was *passion.* And passion goes beyond mere words and images to a spiritual plane which can only be *felt.*

Sophia's passion *was* Sofeegear, and the Sofeegear look was catching on. Word of mouth and good public relations had definitely paid off. The concept had been so simple to her; it was fascinating that seemingly so many women and men were hungry for the Sofeegear look: bold primary colors in sportswear, and soft, natural Afrocentric rayons, silks and cottons in men and women's clothing. She filled a huge unrealized void; black people wanted fashionable garments at a reasonable price that catered to their complexion, heritage and cultural tastes.

Sophia leaned back in the metal chair of her office. She had not yet had the luxury of investing in leather or even pleather for that matter. She was quite uninterested in appearances. At this stage of the game, her primary concerns were increasing demand to match her stepped up production. That was where her print ad campaign came in. She was not prepared to buy ad space with major publications yet, but she was ready to produce a catalog with an 800 number which provided callers with distributing store location information. She and Aubrey had been working for weeks on determining their method of distribution, and she had tight deadlines to meet for the fashion shoots, layout and print production. She wanted to have at least one hot model in it, so she chose Ocean Ryder from Esquire for more reasons than one.

As she raised the receiver on her telephone to call a vendor, she was speechless when she saw Sandy enter her office despite Aubrey's protests.

"Happy Birthday," Sandy stated simply, seeming innocuous in a large olive green jumper, revealed sparingly by a long black wool coat.

"Sandy..." Sophia started, not knowing what to say.

"You never even called me..." Sandy began. She rushed her hands through her natural hairdo nervously.

Sophia swallowed. Sandy looked beautiful as always, and it was just like her to show up on her birthday, thoughtful as usual. She immediately felt guilty for not responding...not even reading her letters.

"Oh, Sandy..." Sophia finally uttered. She rose and

quickly closed the office door behind the other woman. Aubrey flashed a curious glance.

Sandy finally smiled; her dimples cut little grooves in her brown cheeks. "Well, can I have a seat?" she asked, handing Sophia a bunch of carnations and removing her coat. "It's not much, but I picked these up for you..." she offered.

Sophia looked at the pretty collection of pink and white flowers and sighed. It was very nice, indeed. "So what have you been up to?" Sophia asked, for lack of anything else to say. She thought her feelings for Sandy were dead. It was over a year since the incident with Timothy that ended their relationship, and she had spent her time trying to forget the security and happiness she and Sandy had once had together... Now, seeing Sandy, she could not forget the love she once felt for her. And, this...obviously if Sandy were going through all this trouble, this meant she really did love her deeply.

Sandy smiled. "You seem so shocked to see me Sophie... Didn't you get my letters?" Sandy asked baffled.

Sophia did not respond.

"You did read them, didn't you?" Sandy asked incredulously.

Sophia bit her lower lip and shifted nervously in her seat.

"Sophie?" Sandy quickly stood up and grabbed her coat. Her voice grew suddenly hoarse with hurt and anger. "You know, I can *almost* understand why you changed your number...and I can *almost* understand why you never called, *after over ten years of friendship and over a year as lovers..."* Her voice cracked as she uttered that last word. Her eyes quickly grew moist. "But, Sophia, I just can't understand why you wouldn't even open my letters?! *What's wrong with you?!!"* She nearly screamed her final question.

Sophia stood up quickly and reached to touch Sandy's cheek. She wondered how she might console her...

"Sophia, DO NOT TOUCH ME!!!" Sandy screamed, sensing Sophia's sexual interest. "If you read my letters at all, you would know I've been in love with someone else for months now!" She pushed her arms through the sleeves of her coat and stepped away from Sophia, before softening her voice and concluding, "Look, I'm sorry I came by. I thought you were expecting me." Then, Sandy walked out of Sophia's office and her life.

***

Sophia managed to concentrate on her work that morning, despite her ruefulness over Sandy's visit. She felt bad about the whole thing, but it was over with. There was nothing she could do. Sandy didn't even want her anyway.

She was fussing over figures on her computer when Aubrey walked into her office. "It's one-thirty, Sophia. Are you ready to break for lunch?"

"What time is it?!" Sophia responded, quite surprised. The hours had flown pass. She and Aubrey had made lunch plans to celebrate her birthday. "Oh! Give me one quick second. I just want to finish this up."

"Okay, I'm waiting in front," Aubrey replied, exiting Sophia's office.

When Sophia came out, she quickly threw her coat over her shoulders and walked down the building's steps with Aubrey. She left her young office assistant, Bobby, and her part-time accountant, Cyprus, in the office working. She and Aubrey walked a few blocks to a local Italian restaurant where they ordered wine and seafood.

"Ugh, what a morning!" Sophia exhaled finally over her glass of wine.

"Who was that woman, anyway?" Aubrey asked, recalling Sandy's visit.

"Oh...you don't want to know..." Sophia sighed.

"So did you make plans for tonight?" Aubrey asked.

"Nah, I'm just baking a cake with the kids."

"Sophie, you should do something! It's your birthday for goodness sake!"

Sophia lied. "When you get to be my age, birthdays are not what they used to be." Sophia frowned with the realization of another year past.

"Oh, gimme a break, Sophie. Look at your life! People would absolutely die for this! Your business is skyrocketing! Everyone's talking about you and your stuff. You should be absolutely thrilled! And all this at only thirty-three. You're a *baby!*" Aubrey grinned widely, thrilled to be first-hand to whom she was sure would be the next black super entrepreneur. Sophia's talent, willingness to work and knowledge of the business were extraordinary. Aubrey was convinced she was in the right place at the right time. All she had to do was stay loyal and maintain their friendship at all cost.

Sophia looked at Aubrey stupidly. *It was amazing how she could make a perfectly pathetic life seem wonderful.*

"That's it, Sophia, I'm inviting myself over tonight. I'll cook dinner." Aubrey contemplated her offer quickly. "Or, better yet, I'll charge dinner on the company expense account?" Her statement quickly became a soft-spoken question.

Sophia grimaced. She didn't want to see Aubrey tonight, she just wanted to be alone. Her mind wandered. Unless... unless... "I'll tell you what, Aubrey. Why don't you find out if Mr. Ryder is available for a dinner meeting tonight at my place?" Sophia's eyes shifted as she devised her plan. "If he is, then maybe you *and Ted* can come on over, and I *will* let you charge it on the company account." Sophia smiled, satisfied with her instructions.

Aubrey rolled her eyes. She'd like Sophia much better if she left married men alone.

***

"So, how are we making out?" Sophia called out to Aubrey from her office.

"Ocean says he'll be there...and Ted's available." Aubrey did not sound too thrilled. She worried about Sophia. And, from what she knew of Ocean, he seemed like a genuinely *nice* guy, she'd hate to see Sophia take advantage of him. Because no matter how other people felt, she thought men were the weaker sex, 'cause they couldn't seem to control that thing between their legs quite as well as women.

"That's great!" Sophia exclaimed walking to Aubrey's desk. "Make sure you get a few floral arrangements and plenty of food. Do you know what kind of food Ocean likes?"

Aubrey sighed. "I don't know... I mean, I know he's Bahamian. We can cater Caribbean food..." she suggested indifferently. "That's perfect!" Sophia was beaming. "You know, Aubrey, I think hiring you was the best decision I made since starting Sofeegear!" She rested a hand softly on Aubrey's shoulder.

"Yeah, yeah, yeah," Aubrey sighed playfully. "So what are you going to discuss with Mr. Ryder?" she asked with slight sarcasm. "Stop being such a prude, Aubrey. Really, it's no big deal." Sophia smiled knowingly.

Cyprus shifted uncomfortably at his desk in a white turtleneck and jeans. He was twenty-six, tall and brown with hair so short he was nearly a bald-head. He glanced quickly at Sophia as she spoke. He knew she was after Ocean, and he felt a bit embarrassed since he slept with her during the first week of his employ, only two months earlier. Sophia never bothered with him again after that, tossing him aside like a used toy. It wasn't that he cared that much. He was a good-looking guy—he could get other women. It was just that coming into the office and working for her every day while she conducted herself like a horny college kid was uncomfortable at best. But he enjoyed the work, and she treated him well as an employee, so he had no plans to leave.

Aubrey shook a finger at Sophia in an attempt to fill her with some guilt, but Sophia didn't seem to have any remorse for what she was planning to do.

"Here," Sophia said, handing Aubrey the key to her apartment. "Start getting things set up at my place. There'll be a nice bonus in this for all your extra efforts." She smiled with sincerity.

"Oh, you don't have to do that, Sophie, *it's your birthday!*" Aubrey gushed.

"Please, girl, just take care of business. What I'm trying to tell you is, you're still working." Sophia looked at the other woman seriously.

"Sooorrry," Aubrey whined melodramatically, taking the keys from her boss and heading out of the office.

***

When Sophia arrived home with the kids, the place looked wonderful. A white linen cloth draped a serving table of unknown origin, and arrangements of mixed color roses were dispersed throughout the living room. Food was kept heated by small burners, and the apartment smelled exquisitely of spiced meats, roses and burning candles. A frosted black cake sat boxed on the kitchen table, smelling faintly of rum and raisins.

"Oh, this is wonderful!" Sophia admitted as she walked through the apartment. It was nearly 6:00pm.

"What time did you tell them to come?" she asked.

"Ted will probably get here around six-thirty, and I told Ocean seven."

"Sounds good." Sophia watched as the boys ran into the back bedroom. "You look great!" she commented, noticing the attractive black pantsuit Aubrey now wore.

"Thanks! Listen, everything's taken care of out here. Do you want anything to drink?" Aubrey asked.

"Sure, why not? Pour me whatever you're having. I'm gonna try to get the boys ready."

"Sure." Aubrey went about pouring Sophia a glass of red wine, and watching while she cleaned the boys up and dressed them in starched shirts and slacks. By the time she finished it was nearing 6:45pm. The bell rang, and Ted showed up at the apartment door soon after. In about another half hour the bell rang again. Sophia wore a cream crushed rayon jumper that moved softly against her body. She had stopped cutting her hair for the past year, so it fell softly at her shoulders. Her lips were coated in a creamy chocolate and her eyes were lined lightly in brown. She inhaled quickly as she opened the door to her apartment and gasped when she saw a stunning Ocean, tall and black standing beside a beautiful tall black woman named Aura, his fucking wife!

Oh, great, Sophia thought. *Couldn't anything work out for her on her birthday?!*

Ocean and Aura exchanged greetings with Aubrey, Ted, Sophia and her two boys. Sophia felt like a complete idiot. She threw herself a party and ended up without even having a date. It was pathetic, and she knew it, but she wasn't stupid enough to let others know that she felt that way.

She immediately transformed herself into the gracious hostess: considerate and witty. She chatted about the business, flattered Aubrey, complimented Ocean, told

Aura how lucky she was and made her guests feel special and important.

The food Aubrey had arranged was spectacular, and they all enjoyed their meal. When the evening ended, she had successfully established a friendship with Ocean and given Aura a false sense of comfort. Things had not gone exactly as planned, but Sophia used her talent for turning adversity into opportunity. A lesser woman would have simply admitted defeat, but this worked out better than she could possibly have planned.

Aura, Ocean & Sophia
Spring 1994

"Aura, I have someone I'd like for you to meet," Betsy McPherson said cheerfully. As the director of the media department, she had been Aura's boss for the past five months.

Aura looked up from the contracts on her desk and saw the short middle-aged white woman with an attractive black man. She immediately smiled. In her industry the minority population was so small, it was always nice to see another black face. "Hi," she said, quickly rising from behind her office desk and extending her hand to the gentleman.

"Aura this is Marc Bryant, our new account executive for Jenson," Betsy explained. "Marc this is Aura Olivier-Ryder, our senior buyer for Jenson and a number of other accounts. Jenson is an excellent account. You two will have a lot of work to do together. "

"It's nice to meet you..." Aura said, allowing her voice to trail off. The man did not look familiar to her, although the name definitely rang a bell. He wasn't bad looking at all: tall, light-skinned, a bit stocky and bearded with a slightly receding hairline, but quite attractive in a camel-colored suit with a white shirt and brown striped tie.

"I'm very glad to meet you," Marc replied, stunned by Aura's good looks. She was tall, dark and slim with beautiful hair and a lovely little black suit that showed off her figure.

The three chatted briefly before Betsy ushered him off to the next office. It was Marc's first day on the job and he was busy meeting important co-workers.

When he left her office, Aura racked her brain trying to determine why the name seemed so familiar to her. She finally gave up, figuring he probably went to Syracuse U. She clenched the back of her pen between her teeth for a brief moment and made a mental note to ask him about it when she got the chance.

***

Prince Rogers Nelson wailed about Purple Rain while Ocean swept the bathroom floor. He couldn't wait until he and Aura could find a suitable condo to purchase, but until then, he was stuck sharing his old apartment with her. It didn't bother him much, but occasionally he did think about the array of women who'd been in and out of this place. *At least their bed was new.*

Ocean sang along with the record as he removed the small wastebasket out of its corner in the bathroom. He frowned when he noticed a small pink slip of paper jutting out of the groove between the bathroom sink and the wall. He pushed at it with the broom until it became dislodged. As he picked it up to discard it, he realized it was a cash receipt from a Women's Health Center for $259. His heart immediately sank. There was only one thing that cost $259 from a women's health clinic...an abortion. He looked at the date on the receipt: it was for January 1994—four months earlier. He tried to remember if anything strange happened in January, but nothing came to mind. If she was pregnant, why wouldn't she tell him? *Was the child for someone else?* Maybe he was just jumping to conclusions... Things had been wonderful between Aura and him lately. They went out a lot, hardly argued and made a lot of love... He smiled with the thought. Nah, it couldn't be an abortion. Aura would never do anything like that to him. Ocean felt a twinge of guilt for even thinking such a thing. He smiled as he remembered the feel of her lips on his erection that very morning... and continued to sing along with Prince. He would just ask her about it. *It was probably nothing...*

***

"Of course I wouldn't mind a lunch meeting, Marc," Aura responded to the question posed by the light-skinned brother before her.

"Thanks Aura. I really appreciate it," Marc replied as Aura's telephone rang. "I'll speak with you later, then," he said before quickly removing his head from Aura's office doorway, and walking the paces to his own office.

Aura waved lightly as he left. "Aura Olivier-Ryder," she stated simply as she answered her phone.

"Hey, honey," Ocean said.

"Hey, baby, what's up?" Aura replied.

Ocean stared at the receipt in his hand. "I was just wondering when you think you'll be home tonight?" he asked.

"Oh...I should be able to get out of here by six or so... Why, baby? What's up?"

"Nothing," Ocean lied. "I just miss you with all these late nights lately." Aura *had* been working past 8:00pm quite a bit lately. Ocean hadn't really even thought about it until he heard the words coming from his own mouth. *Did it mean anything?*

"Well you know I've been busy with these new buys... I've got a lot of new responsibilities since the promotion." She paused before adding, "I'm sorry, baby, but there's really nothing I can do about it." She breathed deeply staring at her appointment book. "I should be able to get out of here by about six. Do you want me to pick anything up on the way home?"

Ocean frowned staring at the pink slip of paper in his hand. "Nah, baby," he replied.

***

"Hi," Aura said wearily as she entered the apartment that night. She removed a long navy spring coat and positioned it on the coat rack, before falling onto the sofa beside Ocean. She rested her head on his shoulder and kicked off her shoes. It was 9:30pm. Ocean held her closely. She was obviously exhausted. When she called to say she couldn't get out of the office before eight or so, he was disappointed, but what could he do? Work was work.

By the time ten o'clock rolled around, Aura's breathing had grown steady and Ocean was not surprised to find she had fallen asleep in his arms. He watched her then, her face dewy, her eyeliner slightly smeared. She looked tired...very tired. He picked her up and carried her into the bedroom. Aura shifted her body in a haze of sleep, but when he laid her on the bed she did not awaken. Ocean kissed her mouth lightly as she lay sleeping. She looked sexy even now in black stockings and a short black skirt and jacket. He unbuttoned her jacket to reveal a burgundy lace bra, and wondered if he'd be able to undress her without making love to her.

He removed her skirt and stockings without waking her, but by then he had a hard-on that he wanted to use. He watched her sleep with adoration—he was sure the receipt meant nothing.

She protested softly without waking when he raised her body to remove her jacket. Ocean quickly hung her clothes in the bedroom closet. He looked at her longingly then...her dark chocolate legs and long waist sprawled against a mint green bedspread with only a burgundy bra and panty covering her. He reached inside his sweatpants and grabbed his hard-on, debating exactly what he might do with it. He didn't really want to awaken her, but he did want to make love to her.

He lowered the bed coverings and eased her under them as she groaned lightly. Then, he removed his shirt and pants and got into the bed beside her. He sighed as he pressed his body against hers, allowing his erection to rub against her thigh. She turned in her sleep pressing her back and buttocks against him. Ocean slid his hand around her waist and along her hip and thigh. Her skin was so smooth and soft... He moved her hair away from the nape of her neck and kissed behind her ears and along her neck and shoulders. She exhaled softly under his touch, but he was not sure she was awake. *Did it matter?* He unsnapped the front closure on her bra and massaged her breasts with his hands. He felt his heartbeat quicken as she moved a hand along his thigh...

Aura turned her face to his and kissed him. She *was* sleepy, but his touch always felt wonderful...and she would never deny him sex, partly because she loved having sex with him, and partly because she didn't want him to ever deny her.

Ocean was thrilled when he realized Aura had awakened. He kissed her boldly, passionately, leaving a trail of wet kisses from her mouth, down her chin and neck, finally reaching her breasts. He licked her nipples and massaged her breasts lightly as she moaned her approval. She was slippery with excitement when he touched the fuzzy warmth at the joining of her thighs.

"I love you..." he rumbled into her ear.

"I love you..." Aura sighed back as Ocean pulled at her burgundy lace panty. He reached into the nightstand for a condom, and quickly covered his penis before plunging it into her body.

Aura moaned and rocked her hips slowly as Ocean matched her movements. He held her hands and kissed her shoulders as the gentle rain of pleasure fell against both of them...making them sweat...and moan...and nibble...and squeeze...and bite...and sigh with ecstatic relief...and rippling waves of bliss...

***

Aura and Ocean both jumped when the alarm clock went off the next morning. "Ugh," Aura moaned as she slammed her hand on the snooze button and slid her head under the covers to hide from the daylight. Ocean wrapped an arm around her and threw the sheet over his head as well.

Ten minutes passed before they both jumped again. "Ugh," Aura moaned. "I hate mornings!" She stumbled into the shower and Ocean followed close behind. The crashing of the water seemed to awaken them both as they lathered and rinsed their skin.

Aura stepped out of the shower first. "I've been so busy lately... I'm sorry I couldn't get home earlier last night," she said as she hurriedly rubbed her breasts and stomach with vanilla-scented body oil.

"It's okay," Ocean replied, turning off the shower water and stepping onto the fuzzy bathroom mat with Aura. He glanced at the corner where he found the women's clinic receipt the day before. It would drive him crazy if he didn't ask her about it. "Aura, you've been to the Women's Health Center?" he asked without thinking.

Aura stopped on her way out of the bathroom. *What did Ocean know about the health center?* "What did you say?" she asked with controlled anxiety.

"Yesterday, when I was cleaning out the bathroom I found an old receipt from some women's health clinic..." Ocean hoped he didn't sound *too* accusatory. "It was for two-hundred and fifty bucks... I don't know; it just seemed weird... What costs two-hundred bucks from a clinic?" He tried but failed to control the annoyance in his voice.

Hearing Ocean's seeming accusation was all Aura needed to put herself on the defensive. She knew she had had an abortion, but it was too complicated to explain to Ocean at that moment. It wasn't that she didn't love and want to have his children; it was just that she wasn't ready.

She hadn't even told him about her sickle-cell. If he had the trait for the disease, they could pass it to their offspring, so he'd have to be tested for the trait *before* they decided to have children. And Aura knew her case of sickle-cell was much milder than many others. She was able to attend school and work. For the most part she led a normal life except for her bouts with lethargy and intense pain. Some sickle-cell patients were virtually invalids, flanked by constant aches to the point of horrible disability. She and Ocean would have to have a genuinely solid relationship (like her parents) before they endeavored to have children. After all, children were a *lifetime* responsibility. (It seemed she needed her parents more now than she did when she was five.) And Aura couldn't guarantee her health to go through a pregnancy let alone to live to *see* her children reach adulthood. *The fact of the matter was she loved her unborn children, and she wanted to plan for them.* She didn't want to take codeine and intravenous Demerol™ in her first trimester and risk the possibility of brain-damage to her child. *The world is harsh enough without setting your own children up for failure before they're born.*

Aura walked away from Ocean, allowing her annoyance to mask her pain and fear. She knew she had done the right thing. How dare he accuse her with the abortion receipt? Suppose she had just had a physical? She slipped into her bra and panty while Ocean looked on with a towel wrapped around his waist.

"Aura?! Why don't you answer me?!" he asked suddenly angry.

Aura looked at her husband from a seated position on the bed. "Ocean, I'm trying to get dressed for work! What's the matter with you?! You know I've been working hard and you have to come ask me some stupid shit *first thing in the morning?!*" She stood up and pulled on her pantyhose.

Ocean looked at Aura for awhile, trying to figure out if she was being genuine. She was obviously putting up a front. He inhaled. "Aura, why don't you just answer the damn question?" he asked trying to keep his voice even, while accepting the absurdity of his attempt. *She was pissing him off.*

Aura sighed in exasperation. "Ocean, I don't know what the receipt is for. It must have been a physical or something."

"How come you never told me about this *physical?"* Ocean asked. It was obvious Aura was lying to him.

"I don't know, Ocean. It's my pussy; I didn't think you were so concerned." She slipped into her shoes and began rifling through the closet for a suit.

Ocean allowed his mouth to curve into an unenthusiastic grin. He didn't want to fight with her. Whatever happened happened. Aura was right about one thing. Now was not the time to discuss it. Besides, she looked so damn good in her bra, panty, stockings and shoes. He walked over to her and grabbed her. "It's my pussy too, and I am concerned..." he whispered.

Aura turned away from the clothes in the closet. Her eyes were wet with tears.

"Oh, honey, I didn't mean to upset you like that," Ocean responded, unbalanced by her sudden display of emotion.

Aura hugged him as a tear made its course down her cheek. She hated having to lie to him. She hated arguing with him. But worst of all, she just hated when he was angry with her. "Ocean, it's not what you think. Please don't think such horrible things..." she begged, gripping his bare back with her hands as she rested her cheek against his chest.

"Oh, don't worry about it Aura. You know I love you," Ocean replied apologetically. He wished he hadn't made her cry, but he felt cheated by her tears. It was as if she played that unfair woman card...tears... How could he respond? Cry too?

"I know," Aura replied, holding him tightly. "Just remember I love you too..." With that, she released him, grabbed a suit and dressed quickly before heading to work.

***

After Aura left, Ocean had his coffee and bagel and left the house to run a few errands before meeting with Sophia Boyd over lunch to discuss their next shoot schedule. Since Sophia made her catalog a quarterly item. Ocean became identifiable with Sofeegear. He gave up the Jenson account to do Sofeegear exclusively. He knew he could make more money working on Jenson, a much larger company with a big ad budget, but his heart was with Sofeegear. He and Aura had decided that supporting the struggling black company was the right thing to do, even though Jenson was one of WBG Advertising's clients. Ocean's choice didn't affect Aura's position at all. Plus, Sophia's product served their community better: it was affordable, unlike Jenson's overpriced jeanswear collection.

"Hey, how's the wife and kids?" Sophia asked suggestively as Ocean kissed her cheek hello. She was seated underneath the outdoor canopy of a Brooklyn Heights restaurant.

"You know, you are absolutely funny," Ocean replied in his driest voice. He was being playful, but the reference to 'kids' brought back memories of his argument with Aura that morning.

Sophia laughed. It was a beautiful April day and Ocean looked amazing as usual. His hair fell lazily against his broad shoulders, and she felt proud to be in his company. She glimpsed the passersby on Montague Street as the waiter brought their water.

"So, how's business?" Ocean asked.

"Oh, it's going excellent. Everyone *loves* your shots!" Sophia gushed.

"Thanks."

"You know, it would improve your image if you weren't married," Sophia teased.

Ocean smiled. "Real funny, Sophie. If Aura heard you say that she'd pull off that head-wrap and smack you with it!" He chuckled heartily at the thought. Aura definitely would *not* appreciate Sophia's sense of humor.

Sophia rolled her eyes. "I'm only kidding!" she explained. "How *is* Aura anyway?" she asked, suddenly sounding genuinely concerned.

"Oh, she's fine. Everything's going really well..." Ocean's voice trailed off with distraction.

Sophia frowned. "That didn't sound too convincing."

Really...everything's just fine," Ocean replied, forcing a smile.

A red-haired waiter came and took their order. When he walked away, Sophia lowered her voice and continued. "You know, if you ever need to talk, I'm here for you, Ocean. I mean, I joke around, but you know I wouldn't do anything to hurt your relationship with your wife. I like it when you're happy, you know. It makes for better pictures..." Sophia smiled softly, hoping Ocean would confide in her.

Ocean sighed. "I'll keep it in mind, Sophie, but for now there's really nothing to talk about."

Sophia smiled. Ocean was such a nice guy, it was a shame he was having trouble in his marriage so soon. There was a time when she really did want to get Ocean into her bed, but now she wasn't so interested in that. He was still gorgeous, but she had worn herself out screwing around for a year. In retrospect, she blamed it on Maleek and Sandy. Maleek had really hurt her and Sandy had really confused her. At the time, casual sex had made her feel certain she was heterosexual while keeping her from getting emotionally involved with any one man. It worked for awhile, but eventually bored her. Now she was involved with a young man named Philip, one of her new sellers. She knew she shouldn't sleep with guys at her office, but she enjoyed the sense of control it gave her. Ohhh, who was she kidding? She'd love to have Ocean in her bed if he'd give her the opportunity. She'd recently moved to a huge co-op in Brooklyn, and she'd be happy to give Ocean a tour.

When the food arrived, the conversation quickly changed from small talk and flirting to business. They discussed a schedule of shoots and shows, store appearances and catalog signings. Ocean listened intently. Sophia was an attractive woman, but he found her much more exciting when she talked business than when she flirted shamelessly. When she discussed her business, her passion and intelligence became readily apparent. She was an extraordinary designer with an amazing willingness to work and a powerful vision. Sophia wanted to dress the black community...employ the black community...give back to the black community... Ocean found that much more appealing than the cream silk head wrap and short cream dress she wore. Although they weren't too bad either.

***

"Are you ready?" the voice on the end of the line asked.

"As ready as I'll ever be," Aura sighed.

"If today's not a good day, we can always reschedule," Marc offered, sensing her exhaustion.

Aura sighed. "Nah, I could use the break... Besides, I don't think things are going to get any better tomorrow."

"I'll meet you in reception in five minutes then?" he asked.

"How about ten?" she replied.

"Perfect." Marc Bryant hung up the telephone. When he met Aura in the reception area ten minutes later she looked perfectly relaxed.

"Do you know where you want to eat?" she asked her co-worker.

"I was thinking about the new Japanese place on Fifty-fifth," he offered. "Do you eat Japanese?"

"Mmmm... I *love* Japanese! I didn't even know there was a place on Fifty-fifth. It definitely sounds like a plan." Aura smiled. She needed a distraction from her work and her personal problems. It seemed Marc Bryant might fill such a role.

They walked the blocks to the restaurant in light conversation and some silence. The weather was beautiful, and it was easy to enjoy the walk without talking. The restaurant Marc chose had a lovely glass-enclosed veranda in its non-smoking area, so they opted to sit there. The spring sun streamed through a lattice of ivy beyond the glass wall and made glinting beams off the water glasses and tableware.

"This place is really nice," Marc commented. "I've never actually been here before."

"Yes, it's wonderful. Just the type of break I needed. I've been swamped. It's nice to take a breather." She inhaled deeply and took a sip of water.

Marc smiled. He was thrilled to be in Aura's company. She was pretty, friendly and clearly intelligent. Plus, she was the only other black person he'd met so far in a professional position at WBG. And, did he mention she was pretty?

"So how's your first week on the job shaping up?" she asked as the waitress poured her a cup of green tea.

"Oh, it's been hectic, but good." Marc looked into her eyes before adding, "You know, you're sort of the icing on the cake."

Aura shifted nervously. She knew a come-on when she heard one, but her last name was hyphenated for goodness sake! Didn't he know she was married? "Thank you," she replied politely before adding, "but you *do* know I'm married, right?"

Marc's facial expression immediately changed, and he leaned back in his chair. No, he had not known.

Aura read his expression easily. "Oh, I'm so sorry..." she began. "You didn't think this was..." She was at a loss for words.

Marc laughed. "No, I didn't think this was a *date,* but I didn't realize you were married."

"Oh, sorry," she replied sympathetically.

Marc laughed again. "You're too kind, Aura. It's not

your fault I didn't know you were married. It's really pretty stupid of me to assume you weren't, and I suppose I could have asked someone."

"Yeah, it's just...the hyphen...it makes me think people already know. And, besides, my band is a real giveaway!" As she remembered her ring, she gave Marc a stupid look. He *must* have known she was married. *How could he not notice her ring?*

Marc avoided her glance and ordered his meal "You know, one of my good friends had the last name Ryder, but I haven't spoken to him in years. I should really give him a call one of these days."

"Oh really? You know, I was wondering why your name seems so familiar to me," Aura admitted.

"What's your husband's name?" Marc asked, certain it wouldn't be Eddie.

"Ocean," Aura responded.

Marc thought how interesting the name 'Oshun' was. He wondered if it was African or something. "I don't know him," he stated simply.

"Well, I guess your name must just sound common or something," Aura reasoned.

"Oh, thanks a lot," Marc replied, faking hurt feelings.

Aura laughed. "You know what I mean!"

As their meals were served the conversation grew lighter and more interesting. She was enjoying her time in Marc's company. It even occurred to her that if she weren't in love with Ocean, she would probably date this stocky bearded man.

***

Ocean enjoyed a stroll alone on the Brooklyn Heights promenade after his lunch with Sophia. He had to stop by the agency before 5:00pm to meet briefly with Reeva

Johnson before meeting up with Maleek and Craig at a midtown bar. He hadn't been out drinking with 'the boys' in months. He invited Ace along, but he declined. Actually, it was funny to him how little time he and Aura had spent with Dana and Ace over the past few months. The holidays were pleasant, but it seemed things had cooled off a bit between Aura and Dana. He supposed it was a part of married life, although he wasn't sure it was a part he really appreciated. As he sat on one of the promenade benches looking out onto the water, he reminisced over the days the foursome had spent drinking, dancing, renting movies, going for dinner…whatever…it used to be *fun*. Nowadays it just seemed Aura was so busy with work, and when she wasn't, there was a certain distance between them that he really didn't understand.

Maybe what Maleek had said was true.

It did seem that things between Aura and him changed dramatically in these first months of their marriage. He loved her as much as ever, but he couldn't get around the feeling that something was missing.

He shrugged his shoulders in the light cotton jacket he wore and squinted his eyes toward the sun. Leaning his head back, he smiled. At twenty-six, he was a married man, and despite his doubts, he'd marry her all over again. He supposed this was typical of any new partnership. Sure, there'd be rough times ahead, but he knew Aura loved him, and whatever happened they would work through it. He wasn't just loving a woman anymore, they were a team…they were building a nation… He smiled thinking about the kids they would one day have.

A pretty light-skinned sister smiled at him as he sat on the bench. He smiled back. *Why not?*

She walked over to him.

He had not been expecting all that effort on her part, but it was the 90's. Women were becoming more and more forward.

"How are you?" she asked.

Ocean crossed his left hand over his right and looked down at his wedding ring seriously before responding. "Fine, thanks."

The woman took the hint and walked away.

Ocean sighed. He'd better get moving. Reeva would be pissed off if he didn't show up. It was 3:45pm when he boarded the uptown #5 train.

***

"Hey man *whaas'up?!*" Ocean roared, slapping palms with Maleek after spotting him at the bar. It was 5:54pm.

"What's up with you? I never see your married ass no more!" Maleek complained.

Ocean laughed. "Whatchu need me for, man? I thought all your women friends kept you occupied!" He ordered a rum and coke from the bartender and exchanged greetings with Craig and couple of guys he never met before.

Maleek's face grew serious. "Actually, they do man. I had to let your woman's sister loose too, man! She was sucking the blood out of me!" Maleek grabbed his own neck, as if choking himself to death.

Ocean threw Maleek a confused glance. "Who, Angie?"

"Who else? That woman's beautiful, but she's a fucking leech sometimes! I can't take a piss without consulting her first. I had to cut her loose. I'm just not ready for that shit, yet." Maleek paused as if he had given the situation between Angie and himself a lot of thought "I mean, I liked Angie and all, but it's like she has it in her head that we should get married just 'cause you married Aura... I don't know... Sometimes women act so damn stupid!"

Ocean thought about Angie for a few moments. She was so similar to Aura in appearance, but so different *inside...* It was amazing. He could understand where Maleek was coming from. Angie always acted like she was *looking* for a husband... That was the easiest way to scare a man away. Ocean was surprised she and Maleek dated for as long as they had. "So when did this happen?" Ocean asked, only partly interested. He didn't want to get this type of news before Aura. It was sort of womanish... gossipy.

"Ehhh... I broke it down to her last night. I told her I wanted to see other women." Maleek brushed a hand over his bald head. "That's usually the easiest way to do it. It would've been fucked up if I just came out and said I've been fucking *lots* of different women for a long time now, ya know?"

Ocean nodded. *Yeah, he knew.* "So what did she say?" he asked.

Maleek frowned. "It was kinda fucked up. First she asked what she was doing wrong, like that really mattered..." He paused as if he really did feel bad before adding, "Then she just told me to kiss her ass!" He laughed. "She grabbed her toothbrush and left!"

Ocean laughed. "Well, you ain't all that mothafucka! She'll be fine!" He gave Maleek a disparaging look before adding. "She probably forgot about your ass already!"

Maleek laughed. "Nah, mothafucka, I think she'll remember *my ass* if nothing else 'cause I was hitting that shit *correct!"*

"Well, I haven't heard a peep from Aura, so it couldn't have been *all that!"* Ocean slapped his knee with the thought. Maleek always acted like his shit didn't stink when it came to women, maybe Angie proved him wrong! "Maybe you just *thought* you were hitting it and she was only trying to stay awake!"

Maleek gave Ocean a stupid look. "Ha, ha, mothafucka," he replied drolly. "Anyway, I just thought you should know."

"Yeah, whatever." Ocean drained his glass and ordered another. The conversation left Maleek's discussion of Angie and moved on to work, basketball and other women. Craig and the other men gave their opinions on the basketball part.

After a couple of hours and a few drinks, Ocean decided it was time to head home. He missed his wife.

***

Ocean and Aura were both in a deep sleep when the phone rang at about 1:00am. Ocean was shocked to hear Mrs. Olivier's voice on the other end of the line at such an odd hour. She immediately asked for Aura, and Ocean groggily nudged his wife and handed her the phone.

"What?! OH MY GOD!" she screamed.

Ocean jumped in response to the tone of his wife's voice.

"Okay, ma, see you there," Aura replied, her tone deep with fear and frustration. *How could Angie have done what her mother said?!*

"What is it?" Ocean asked.

Aura roamed the darkened room in search of a pair of jeans. "Angie's in the hospital!" she wailed achingly. Now Ocean jumped out of bed too. "What's wrong with her?" he asked.

"Mom says she was picked up on the street!" Her voice was hysterical. "She has *alcohol poisoning!!!"*

"Oh, shit!" Ocean responded. He hadn't even

mentioned his conversation with Maleek to her, and he immediately felt guilty. As they drove to the hospital he relayed Maleek's story to a disgusted Aura.

Upon hearing the news from Ocean, Aura wasn't upset so much with Maleek. She really didn't care what he did. It was Angie. How could Angie let such a trifling man send her to the hospital? After all, it had to be the break-up with Maleek... Why else would Angie drink herself into a damn-near coma? She was disgusted, it was true, but she was disgusted with *Angie.* Life wasn't perfect. If anyone knew that, Aura did. We all have problems. But life is a gift...a one-shot deal. It comes with no guarantees and no apologies... *What the hell was Angie's problem?*

***

When Aura and Ocean arrived at the hospital they immediately saw Donald and Sylvia Olivier huddled over cups of coffee. The two exchanged hugs and kisses with the younger couple.

"Have you heard anything?" Aura asked her mother.

"Yes; she's recovering. They pumped her stomach..." Mrs. Olivier said, half-choking from her own distress. Angie was thirty-three years old. *When would she be happy?* Happiness wasn't something a mother could provide. Sylvia Olivier spontaneously began humming "God Bless the Child." What more could a mother want than a child who had her own? Aura had her own, and Ace had his own, but Angie just couldn't seem to get her own. She didn't *need* for her children to marry; she just needed for them to have their own.

Ace and Dana ran into the waiting area a few minutes later. "What's going on?" Ace asked, his voice hoarse with anguish.

"She's recovering," Ocean stated simply as Ace

hugged and kissed his parents. He felt guilty, in a way. He had, with Aura, introduced Angie to Maleek. But, Angie was a grown woman; he couldn't take responsibility for her lack of self-respect or self-esteem. The thought brushed across his mind quickly. What would he do if Aura told him she wanted to see other men? Anger enveloped his chest briefly, and he quickly sent his mind on other excursions. It was *not* an option.

Aura hugged Dana and her brother tightly when they arrived at the hospital. She knew she should have been thinking solely of Angie, but at that moment she was struck with her own sorrow over the loss of closeness they *all* once had: Dana, Ace *and* Angie. She missed the days when Ocean, Dana, Ace and she were inseparable... and Angie would occasionally join them with Pascal. As she assessed their present situation—Angie drinking too much, she and Dana barely speaking and the resultant loss of touch with Ace, she couldn't help but wonder what had gone wrong?

She loved Dana, but their friendship had cooled off considerably since she admitted she hadn't told Ocean about her sickle-cell. Maybe cooled off wasn't the proper term—it was pretty much frozen. They spoke about once a month as if checking to make sure the other one was still alive, but that was it. They hadn't *seen* each other in months. And, as for Angie, who knew? It seemed every time she tried to reach out to her, Angie attacked her, so she got in the habit of not bothering.

Aura really didn't know what *she* could do about Angie, but she felt certain she could fix things between Dana and herself. Seeing Dana face-to-face for the first time since the New Year made everything different. Dana was her best friend of twenty-five years. There was no getting around it. They had to work things out. They missed one another.

***

Aura didn't actually see Angie until she was home in her apartment the next day, embarrassed and alone. The doctors had only admitted her parents into the hospital room the previous night.

Aura brought her a dozen red roses for lack of a better idea.

"What's up?" Angie asked as she opened her apartment door.

"What's up with you?" Aura responded, somewhat annoyed. How dare Angie jeopardize her own health over some trivial man shit when Aura had to deal with a *real* sickness?

"Well, you know the deal, so what's up?" Angie replied bitterly. It was bad enough her drinking had landed her in the hospital, was she going to have to tolerate one of Aura's holier-than-thou speeches too?

Aura frowned. Her sister was four years older than her, and had always been a positive role model: she graduated high school with honors, attended college, got a good job and moved out on her own. Basically, she did the things her parents had taught her to do.

"Aura, if you're coming here to bitch, please save it for later." Angie pulled her knees into her chest on her living room sofa. She was clad in a T-shirt and sweatpants, with an Afghan draped across her legs.

Aura squinched her face with displeasure. She didn't want to upset her sister when she was vulnerable, but she couldn't control her own response. The fact of the matter was, Angie had been quite a bitch since Aura fell in love with Ocean. She supposed it was heightened by Dana's relationship with Ace. In a way, she couldn't blame her. It was pure luck that allowed both her brother and herself to marry only months apart. But what was she supposed to do? Apologize for being happy? Condone her sister's alcoholic behavior?!

"Look, Aura, I'm sure Ocean's waiting for you." Her words were stated as a dismissal. A sort of 'drop your sorry-ass flowers and leave' request.

Aura grew livid. *How dare her sister treat her that way?* She didn't have to be there dealing with Angie's bullshit excuse for an ailment!

Angie responded to Aura's facial expression. "Look, Aura, I really don't want to hear your shit. Thanks for the flowers." She turned her face toward the television. The six o'clock news was on.

Aura could not believe her ears! She had tried to spend time with Angie over the past year, but her sister always had an excuse. Why should she have to feel like she was holding their relationship together... And now she had to feel like she was holding Angie's *life* together. Aura inhaled deeply before releasing her feelings. She sat at the edge of the couch where Angie had turned herself into a human cocoon. "LOOK, ANGIE!" she began, emphatically. "I've had just about enough of this *bullshit!"*she screamed. "I don't know what's the hell's the matter with you. You should be happy for Ace and me, but you're not. You're just jealous. *It's disgusting!"* She inhaled deeply before continuing. "Angie, how could you *send* yourself to the hospital?" Aura's voice broke as she asked the question, not waiting for a response. "Don't you know *every day* I have to deal with my illness? I have to deal with this shame...this horrible thing? I have to deal with the reality of how people will react to me if they know that...in a way...I'm genetically damaged?!" Aura's eyes welled with tears. "What you're doing *kills* me!" Aura leaned her body closer to her knees for a moment before turning her head to look into her sister's eyes.

"How can you do this to yourself? Especially over a man like *Maleek?!*"

"Oh, Aura, shut up! You've never known heartache. Even the sickle-cell is not so bad for you. What do you know?!"

Aura swallowed the tears and which dripped down her throat before responding. "Angie, just because I don't whine like a baby every time something is bothering me, doesn't mean I don't feel. I do feel!" she wiped her cheek with the back of her hand. *"I DO FEEL!"*

"Oh, Aura, just shut up! You have this fucking perfect life... *I HATE IT!"* Angie sat apparently undisturbed while Aura fought her tears.

Aura felt the warm rush of tears down her cheeks. She'd been fighting *so* hard, *every day*...and to have it all summed up by her sister's simple judgment was more than she could easily tolerate. Most mornings she rose with some pain; most nights she went to bed with some pain. And, yes sometimes it got so bad she needed more than her painkillers could give; for god's sake she had not even told Ocean yet. Yes, she was lucky to have him, but she had so much more to deal with than Angie ever would. She had a horrible, disabling disease which she could never dislodge from her life. Instead of Angie feeling blessed, she somehow felt abandoned.

"Look, Aura, I feel bad for what you have to deal with, but the fact of the matter is you have a man who loves you, and I have nothing."

Aura knew this type of thing was coming, although a part of her just couldn't believe it entirely. "Is that what you think this is all about?!" she screamed.

Angie sat motionless on the sofa.

"Let me tell you something..." she began. "Until you find it in yourself to *love yourself,* you can never love a man." She sighed. "It feels so funny to try to tell my big sis this type of thing," Aura leaned back into her sister's sofa. "Angie, it's not about who they are, it's about who we are... who *you* are..."

Angie sighed with disinterest.

"Angie, if you go on with your life...thinking someone owes you something...you'll *never* win..."

Angie mumbled under her breath and peered at the clock on her VCR. *How long would she have to listen to this crap?*

"Honestly, what happened between me and Ocean was a fucking fluke—an astrological imperception or some shit... It's so hard for black men and women to find love in this world. When it happens it's such a beautiful thing, it defies reason. Never hold yourself up to that light for scrutiny. It's unfair."

Angie rolled her eyes. "So you're saying only *you* have the right to fall in love and get married? Gimme a break, Aura! Everybody does it. It's no big goddamn deal!"

Aura laughed. "Yeah, Angie, it *is* a big deal. Most people with any sense do not fall in love every day. It's rare and it's special and when it's right you'll know it, but nobody's gonna want to deal with a woman who's gonna fall off the deep end if things don't work out!"

"Oh, shut up, Angie, from what I hear, you didn't even tell Ocean about the sickle-cell, so what's up with all *your* love shit?!" Angie knew that last comment would shut Aura up. Ace had made her promise not to say anything to Aura about it, but who cared now?

Aura swallowed "Look, Angie, my relationship with Ocean has nothing to do with you nearly drinking yourself to death!" Aura stood up to leave. She slipped into her spring coat and kissed her sister on the cheek. "Listen, I'm sorry I yelled, but I didn't know what else to do. Maybe when you're feeling better we can catch a movie or something." Aura's look was genuinely concerned. She didn't want her relationship with her sister to get any worse, but she didn't know what to do. Angie was the only one who could take care of Angie—it was as simple as that. *Besides, what was the point of telling Ocean about the sickle-cell when she hadn't had a crisis for months?*

***

When Aura arrived home, she was still contemplating her 'discussion' with her sister. *Had she been too harsh?* She knew she had a bit of a chip on her shoulder because of her sickle-cell, and she wondered if she should have tried to control her emotions long enough to sympathize with her oldest sibling. She wasn't sure if tough love was what Angie needed right now—she must have felt horrible after the alcohol incident. But in reality it seemed to her that Angie was the one who had everything. She had her health. Angie could go to sleep at night knowing she could easily live to be a hundred, if she took care of herself. Aura didn't have that luxury. Sickle-cell anemia wore on her internal organs like a bad plague—it was coming between her and her husband, her and her self-esteem, and her hopes for the future, her and everything...

When she entered the apartment, Ocean was reading the *Village Voice* and listening to Earl Klugh while quietly sipping a Red Stripe beer.

"Hi, baby!" Aura greeted, thrilled to be away from her sister, and yet still haunted by the memory of her visit. She pulled scented red candles from a brown paper bag and set them on the kitchen table. "I was thinking of you," she admitted handing Ocean a Bloomingdale's bag.

Ocean smiled with the realization that Aura wanted to make-up. He opened the bag and removed a pair of silk pajamas. "I love it, but you know I don't sleep in this stuff," Ocean stated holding up the paisley-patterned sleepwear.

Aura laughed, throwing her body on the sofa beside him. "Well, you can wear it when it's really cold, or just to hang out alone. It *feels* really good." She winked at him and nuzzled her face in his neck.

Ocean stroked his wife's hair. *This shit beat the hell out of flapping with Maleek.*

"Anyway," she began, "I'm cooking you an amazing meal." She paused before adding, "I'm sorry about yesterday. I've been so tightly wound over work. Sometimes I think I'm a ticking time bomb. I was *way* too harsh with you."

Ocean sighed. *Her voice was music to his ears,* "You were right, Aura. It *is* your pussy!" He laughed. "I keep thinking it's mine, that's all!" He grabbed her waist through her navy suit, allowing his left hand to slide over her stockinged leg.

Aura looked deeply into his eyes. "It *is* yours," she said meaningfully before adding, "Sometimes I just forget. I'm still getting used to this marriage thing. The receipt was nothing; just an exam, but I hated the way you asked me about it." Aura was telling a partial truth. She could always admit the rest when the time came.

"So how's your sister?" Ocean finally asked.

Aura frowned. "Oh, I suppose she'll be okay. Honestly, I really don't know what to say to Angie anymore."

"Well, your father called a little while ago. You should probably call him back."

Aura sighed. "Yeah, I suppose so. I wish I had more to say to him. Angie and I pretty much just argued." She stood up from her position next to Ocean on the sofa and grabbed the telephone. The conversation with her father was brief as she relayed the gist of her confrontation with Angie. When she hung up the phone she left Ocean rifling through the various items in her grocery bag while she changed out of her work clothes. She planned to make cornished game hens with a sweet potato stuffing.

"Are you really making dinner?" Ocean asked with some amazement.

When Aura reentered the living room she laughed. "Stop acting like I never cook!"

"You never do!" Ocean countered playfully.

"Ocean, stop lying!" she rebounded. Granted, she didn't cook often because of her schedule, but she *did* cook on occasion. Aura busied herself with her ingredients, waving Ocean out of the kitchen area and handing him the candles to light. Although she left work early to see Angie, it was nice to spend the evening with her husband for a change.

When the phone rang, Ocean answered it. It was Sophia.

Aura frowned. She didn't like Sophia, and she was annoyed that Ocean didn't feel the same. She knew they had to work together on Sofeegear, and she was happy to see a sister get ahead, but she really wished it were a different sister.

When Ocean hung up the phone he mentioned a scheduled meeting for the next day.

"Watch out for that woman," Aura stated simply. She hadn't ever shared the information Dana gave her about Sophia's interest in men; she didn't want to sound jealous, but she wanted Ocean to know she was aware.

"I have no interest in Sophia," Ocean stated, enjoying Aura's obvious jealousy. He grabbed her from behind as she leaned over peeled sweet potatoes in jeans and a tank top.

"You'd better not," Aura replied easily. It was true she

didn't like Sophia, but she also didn't fear her.

Aura, Ocean & Sophia
Spring 1995

Sophia leaned back on the 'new' tapestry sofa which had recently replaced her 'old' antique. She had just dropped the boys with her Aunt Tyra, an arrangement which had outlasted both her aunt's desire to be 'born again' and her own desire to be 'free.' It wasn't that Aunt Tyra didn't go to church anymore, she still took the boys every other weekend when they visited, but at the ages of six and eight they had minds of their own now, and Aunt Tyra spent more time shuffling them from masses to church events than fixating on saving their souls.

Sophia sighed and stretched her arms; creating Sofeegear was probably the smartest move she'd made in her life—just as her father had suggested. She wondered what her dad was doing at that moment and toyed with the idea of calling him, but the fact was she really didn't have the time. Philip was due to arrive in a matter of moments, and, although she was not particularly enamored with him, they had been dating for over a year, long enough for her to become accustomed to his punctuality.

When the bell rang at moments past eight, she knew who it was and buzzed him in without question or response. Sophia would turn thirty-five in a matter of months and the presence of the attractive young man gave her a sense of her own vitality.

She pulled food from white cartons after letting him in.

There was nothing strange about a Chinese food dinner tonight.

"Hey, you look wonderful," Philip complimented upon entering the rustically decorated apartment. Sophia had a taste for all things old which he could not thoroughly appreciate, but she was still his boss—and his lover...so... So what?

"Thanks," Sophia responded modestly. She wore a lovely peach rayon wrap-around dress which seemed to have been cut explicitly for her curves...and it was. Her business was doing well, and she took no shame in requesting garments for herself. Her feet were pedicured and bare, the way she had come to enjoy them when she was home.

Philip removed his shoes immediately, out of habit and deference to Sophia's wishes. His feet were clean and free from cuticle overgrowth, mainly as a response to Sophia's suggestion. He was not unfamiliar with local nail salons, although he complained readily about the double pricing standard against men. Sophia was quick to remind him that men had every goddamn thing else so he should shut up and be thankful, and basically he did.

Philip's relationship with Sophia was one of both convenience and interest. She was quite beautiful, but at thirty-four and as his boss he felt she made too much of an issue of her position and her age at all possible moments. He was twenty-nine, and only five years younger, but Sophia left him feeling like a child. He had lived a life of quiet privilege and traditional upbringing, and Sophia's occasional references to dysfunctional family life, spousal abuse and rocky teen years drew feelings of confusion and even boredom from him at times. She seemed much older than her years, despite her curvaceous figure and adeptness in bed. Maybe that was part of the problem... She seemed *too* experienced in bed.

He enjoyed her willingness to slide her tongue over every part of his body, but he wished she did it out of true emotion, not habit. Not because he wanted her in a meaningful way; he enjoyed their somewhat casual relationship. (He occasionally had other sex partners.) He knew Sophia was not going to one day become his wife or anything. He just wanted a *feeling* from her. He wanted to believe there was no one else, however misguided such a belief might be.

"So, chow mein or lo mein?" Sophia asked, peering into the cartons on the beaten wood kitchen table which she had grown to adore, quite unlike Philip, who she had grown to *endure.*

"Both sound good," Philip responded.

Sophia wondered what she was doing with such an indecisive man. Chow mein and lo mein were worlds apart, but who cared? She couldn't have everything, *could she?*

Philip frowned as he watched Sophia empty the Chinese food cartons onto stoneware plates. She never cooked. And, the children were another obstacle. Sophia had two boys who he rarely saw. It wasn't that he wanted to; their absence on alternate weekends was a pleasant convenience. But what kind of mother did that make Sophia?

Sophia smiled in the fake way she had grown accustomed to when in Philip's intimate presence. She placed a steaming plate of lo mein, chicken chow mein and brown rice before her lover. *Who knew what he was thinking?*

***

"Aura Olivier-Ryder speaking," Aura responded to the telephone's ring, smoothing her royal blue skirt.

"Hey girl, what's up?" Dana asked.

"Hey, Dana!" Aura replied cheerily. "What's up on your end?"

Dana laughed. "Not much. I just figured I'd check you out, being Friday and all... How's work going?"

"Damn, Dana. There *killing* me here!" Aura laughed. "No really it's all good." Aura shuffled the papers on her desk. "What are you and Ace up to tonight?"

"Ace has a late court date, I was thinking about swinging by your crib..." she offered.

"Sounds cool," Aura admitted. She was pleased her relationship with both Dana and Ace was back on track after a year-long hiatus. Dana still didn't agree with her stance with Ocean on the sickle-cell, but they realized that a twenty-five year friendship and genuine love was not worth giving up over one issue which was sure to change eventually. They rarely discussed the situation with Ocean, although Aura was beginning to feel the need for her good friend's advice on the matter. She just hadn't been feeling herself lately. She'd been popping pills over the past week like a drug-addict, and she knew she was probably heading toward a sickle-cell crisis.

"Good, then. When do you think you'll be home?"

Aura sighed. "I'm feeling pretty crappy. I should be in early. Just swing by when you get off work," Aura offered.

Dana paused briefly. If Aura was going home early, she had to be feeling really bad. "What's Ocean doing tonight?" Dana asked.

"I don't know," Aura admitted pensively. "He's got a long shoot today. We didn't discuss the weekend. I guess we've both been wrapped up in work"

"Oh."

Aura laughed. "It's no big deal, Dana. Everything's fine," Aura said, responding to Dana's tone.

"Okay... So I'll see you later then?"

"Yup," Aura remarked.

They exchanged their goodbyes and hung up their respective phones.

***

When Ocean arrived at the apartment, Dana and Aura were watching a horror movie with a bucket of fried chicken and two beer bottles in front of them. Aura immediately paused the VCR when her husband came home. Dana twisted her mouth and shot Aura her 'oh no you didn't' look. The flick was just starting to get good!

"Hey, baby," Aura greeted, rising from the sofa to kiss her husband. "What's up?" she asked.

Dana rolled her eyes. She wanted to watch the movie.

Ocean kissed his wife and exchanged hellos with Dana as he removed his jacket. "Nothing much. What are you guys doing?" he asked, noticing the chicken and beers.

"Oh, just watching a horror flick," Aura replied. "Why, what's up?"

Ocean grabbed a beer from the refrigerator and took a seat on the couch. "Maleek paged me earlier. He wants to go down to Caribbean Corner tonight for drinks. Do you wanna come?"

"I don't know, I've been kinda worn out...and this movie just started fifteen minutes ago. When are you supposed to meet him?"

Ocean laughed, "When I get there!"

Aura smiled at her husband. He was so different with his friends than she was with Dana. "So when are you going to get there?" she asked, playfully.

"I don't know." He wrapped an arm around Aura on the sofa. "Maleek's not my goddamn woman. I'll see him when *I arrive!*"

Aura rolled her eyes. Sometimes Ocean was downright silly. "Whatever," she mumbled nestling her face into the warmth of his chest.

"So where's Ace?" Ocean asked Dana.

"He's got a late court date. Maybe we'll all come and meet you guys down at Caribbean Corner later on tonight."

"Is Ace coming here?" Ocean asked.

"Yeah. So, we'll probably just hop on the train and come and check on you guys. I wouldn't mind going there..." Dana's voice trailed off.

Aura looked to see if they had finished talking before restarting the movie.

Ocean seemed to take that as a cue to leave. He finished his beer, brushed his teeth, kissed his wife and left to meet Maleek in downtown Manhattan.

***

"Hey, what's up, man?" Ocean greeted, spotting Maleek's bald-head immediately at the bar.

"What's up?" Maleek replied, half-interested. He was occupied with a boxing match on the big screen TV above the bar.

Ocean hadn't been to Caribbean Corner since they added the television. He immediately realized he missed the old atmosphere. Was Louie trying to turn the place into a sports bar? He glanced around at the crowd. Making eye contact with Louie in the midst of a group of women; he gave a nod. Louie seemed to be enjoying his freedom since his divorce from Mona. Whenever Ocean saw him, he was surrounded by women. Louie was not a bad-looking man, but he supposed the young women were more attracted to his money than his middle-aged body. Louie had to be approaching sixty by now!

When a commercial came on, Maleek glanced over at Ocean. "Hey, man what's been going on with you?"

Ocean smiled. "Everything's cool." He was surprised to see Maleek's gaze remain on his face instead of scoping the room for women the way he normally did.

Ocean ordered a beer and watched the fight for about an hour, until it ended. It was nearing 10:00pm when he got a call from Aura saying she couldn't make it. He knew she didn't look so great when he saw her earlier...she seemed tired. Actually, he didn't mind if she stayed home. Sometimes he liked spending time away from her. He loved her company, but he also enjoyed himself when he was out alone.

"Yeah, Aura and them aren't coming out," he commented to Maleek who seemed occupied with popping peanuts into his month.

"Oh," Maleek mumbled distractedly.

"Whatever happened with you and Angie?" Ocean asked. Mentioning his wife's name made her sister suddenly pop into his mind.

"Nothing," Maleek said with a slight dose of annoyance.

"Daamn..." Ocean responded to Maleek's tone of voice.

Maleek looked at Ocean with astonishment "I'm sorry man. Am I acting stressed?" He leaned his head from one side to another, like a boxer stretching his neck muscles before a match. "I guess I *am* sort of wound up or something."

Ocean laughed. "I didn't know you were in *love* with Angie, man!" Ocean said, opting to torture his friend with sarcasm in his time of need.

Maleek laughed. "You know, Ocean, you're a real asshole!"

Ocean laughed. "Thank you."

"Seriously, though. I'm just going through some kind of shit, I guess. I haven't been feeling like myself." Maleek frowned as he thought about what it was that he was trying to express. The reality was, he didn't know *what* was bothering him. "As for Angie, we haven't spoken since we broke up. Maleek paused for a moment before giving Ocean an accusatory glance. "You *knew* that!" he admonished.

Ocean looked taken aback. "Damn, you really *are* weird tonight!"

"Nah, man, I don't know..." Maleek returned his attention to the large screen television while Ocean stared blankly at the back of his bald head. He didn't know what Maleek's problem was, but he didn't really want to stay to find out.

"Look, man, I'm gonna cut out..." Ocean began.

Maleek suddenly turned away from the television, his old self again...smiling. He slapped Ocean on the shoulder. "All right, peace, man we'll talk later."

Ocean exchanged the goodbye gesture and left the bar, shaking his head.

***

It was 6:00am when Aura realized her medication was not working. Excruciating pains racked her spine and legs. Ocean hadn't gotten home until early morning and he slept heavily in the bed beside her as she called her parents' house. She had no time to think as she waited for her father to arrive. She used her last bit of energy to quickly jot a note. *There was no sense in waking him.*

***

When Philip left the next morning, Sophia felt an odd

sense of relief. It was a feeling that was not entirely unfamiliar to her. Over the past couple of months, her interest in Philip was waning; there was no getting around it. She really didn't want to be manless so she tolerated her boredom without complaint.

Sophia scooped a Tanzanian roast into the coffee maker as she eyed the *Times*. This new apartment was huge and sunny, and she enjoyed the lazy mornings she spent alone. She considered calling her sons, but it was only 9:00am, still too early. She switched on the morning news and relaxed before busying herself with the many errands she had to take care of that day.

***

When Ocean rose that Saturday, he was surprised to find Aura was not in the apartment. A wildly scribbled note rested on the kitchen counter. It read: "Didn't want to wake you. Forgot I had a salon appointment. Aura." Ocean frowned. It was 10:00am, and Aura hated mornings as much as he did. It was unlike her to make any appointment so early on a Saturday. He brewed some coffee, grabbed the paper from outside his apartment door and settled on the sofa in his T-shirt and sweats. He liked to take his mornings slowly.

***

While Ocean calmly read his newspaper, Aura finally got some peaceful rest in a hospital bed with morphine in her veins and her parents at her bedside. Before she dropped off to sleep, she had begged them not to tell Ocean anything. She wanted to tell him herself.

***

By the time Aura woke from her drug-induced sleep it was after 8:00pm. She noticed a shopping bag with clothing at her bedside and a note from her mother. She smiled. Her mother thought of everything. It was just a pair of jeans and a sweatshirt, but she would need them when she checked out of the hospital. Aura's pain had subsided, it seemed. All she felt was the grogginess left by the drugs in her system.

"How are you feeling?" a doctor asked entering her room.

"Oh, much better," she replied.

The man smiled. "Good," he said reviewing her chart. "Just rest up. We should be able to let you out of here in the morning."

"Thanks," Aura replied. She watched as the man exited her room, before picking up the telephone. *What on earth would she tell Ocean?*

Ocean and Maleek were watching television when the phone rang. Ocean jumped and grabbed the receiver. He hadn't heard from Aura all day. He had called Dana and the Olivier's looking for her, but no one seemed to know where she was.

"Hello?" he asked.

"Hi, Ocean," Aura replied wearily.

"Aura, where are you?!" he asked anxiously.

Aura sighed, sounding defeated. "I'm so sorry I couldn't call you sooner. I can't explain it right now, but I won't be home tonight..." Her voice trailed off into silence.

Ocean muted the television. "What?!" He wasn't sure if he should be angry or concerned. He was a bit of both, but Aura's voice seemed so pained that his concern overrode his anger.

"Please, try not to be too mad at me..." she pleaded.

"I'll talk to you tomorrow."

"Aura, this is *not* okay..." he began, not knowing what else to say.

"I know it's not. I'll explain everything to you later, so you can understand." She sighed. "Listen, I really can't talk right now."

"Okay," Ocean replied. Then he heard the click as Aura hung up the phone.

***

When Aura checked out of the hospital the next day, her father drove her back to the Olivier's house. Her mother was in the living room with Ace and Dana when they arrived. "The jeans fit you well," Sylvia Olivier commented as Aura removed her jacket.

Aura walked over to her mother and kissed her hello. "Thanks, Mom." She gave Ace and Dana kisses as they exchanged hugs and greetings. Their moods were solemn.

"Have you called Ocean?" her mother asked as Aura took a seat on the sofa beside her.

The light sound of collective exhalations could be heard when Mrs. Olivier posed the question. They were all wondering the same thing. Surely, Aura knew she would have to tell him about her disease eventually. Why had she put it off for so long? Didn't she know she was only making matters worse?

"I called him last night." She sighed. "I still haven't told him yet, though."

Donald Olivier frowned. "Aura, I suggest you go home and tell him tonight."

"I will," Aura agreed. "I just need to relax for a while. When I get home, I'll tell him."

***

When Aura got home it was 8:00pm and Ocean was recovering from drinking a full bottle of coconut rum. He slept restlessly on the living room sofa, and Aura was careful not to disturb him. Clearly, it was not the right time to have a serious discussion.

***

Sophia tucked the boys into bed at 9:00pm. She had a big day ahead of her at work on Monday. They would be beginning the shoot for the winter catalog at 10:00am, and she had an 8:00am meeting with one of her vendors. Philip had cancelled their dinner plans for that evening. She wasn't entirely sure why she bothered with Philip. He was too young, bothered by her children and fearful of her success.

Sophia decided to try to get to bed early. She brewed a cup of herbal tea and began a novel she picked up earlier that afternoon. It was by a young black sister named Trish Ahjel.

***

When Aura left for work the next morning, Ocean was still on the sofa. It seemed he was in exactly the same position as he had been the night before. She left him a note on the refrigerator. "Sorry for everything. We'll talk tonight. Love you. Aura."

That was it, and she left.

***

Ocean didn't rise until after 9:00am. His mouth was dry in the wake of his overindulgence in liquor the previous night. He found a bottle of aspirin in the bathroom and orange juice in the fridge before noticing Aura's note. He quickly reclaimed his position on the sofa, note in hand. He swallowed the contents of the note along with the aspirins and juice. He had a ten o'clock shoot, and he felt like shit... *What was Aura trying to do to them?*

He thought he had been a good husband so far. He loved her. He tried to be fair. *How could she just disappear for days at a time?* Suddenly, he felt his anger rise. Didn't she know how many women would love to have him? He smiled. Even, Sophia was dying for a taste of the Ryder jewels. He smiled again. Then, he held his head in his hands. *Who was he kidding?*

The fact of the matter was, it didn't matter who wanted him, it was who *he* wanted. And Aura was all he wanted. That was why he married her.

***

"Ocean, why don't you join me for lunch?" Sophia asked delicately. Ocean had not been himself all morning, and although the shoot was going well, she wished he could be more cheerful.

Ocean sighed. It definitely sounded like a good breather. His weekend with Aura was weighing heavily on his mind. He hated to admit it to himself, but he hurt inside. The hurt was deep and he didn't know what to do with it. Plus, he had a hangover.

"What do you have in mind?" he asked.

"Why don't we go to the Parker Meridian?"

"Sure," he replied without the benefit of a thought.

Sophia smiled. *Why wouldn't she?*

***

Aura was haunted with thoughts of Ocean all morning at work. She thought she'd be able to wait until the evening to speak to him, but when the clock approached 1:00pm she wondered if maybe a lunch date could patch things up until the night. She sighed, running her hands over the canary yellow linen skirt she wore. She was thinking too much. It was giving her a headache.

"Hey, Aura, what's going on?" Marc Bryant asked, peeking into her office.

"Oh, hi, Marc!" Aura replied feigning happiness. It was important not to let her personal life interfere with her work.

"Have you eaten yet?" he asked. He eyed Aura in her yellow suit and white blouse. She looked beautiful, as usual. He had been working with her for about a year now; he had dreams about her, and he wondered if she ever cheated on this mysterious spouse he had never met.

"No, but I think I'll make some..." she began, "with my husband."

Marc frowned as Aura picked up the telephone, but he remained in earshot.

"Oh..." he heard her say. "They went to the Parker Meridian?" Marc continued to listen to Aura's telephone conversation. "Oh..." she said as he listened intently. "Okay." He heard the click of the phone being hung up.

"Where are you going?" he asked standing in the hallway outside of Aura's office as she grabbed her purse and rushed to the elevators.

"I'm meeting my husband for lunch," Aura replied with some hesitation. *She was sick of Sophia.* A business lunch was one thing, but Ocean had never mentioned a lunch meeting with Sophia for Monday. He should have been busy with the shoot. They shouldn't even have the time to lunch at a *hotel* of all places! Marc knew her tone hinted at problems in her marital life. Maybe there really *was* an opportunity here. Without thinking, he left WBG's building and took a stroll to the Parker Meridian. *He had nothing to lose.*

***

"So what's the matter with *you* today?" Sophia asked an apathetic Ocean.

He played with the ravioli in his plate. "What?" he replied.

"Ocean!" Sophia said, raising her voice only slightly.

"WHAT?" Ocean replied, raising his voice to her level.

"You're not yourself today." She paused, before adding, "Don't fuck up my shoot!"

Ocean leaned back in the restaurant's chair. "Look, Sophie. I thought this lunch was supposed to relax me." He looked at her painfully before gulping his martini. "I've had a rough weekend. What do you want from me? I thought the shoot was going well."

Sophia sighed, fussing with the burgundy wrap on her head. Ocean was even more tempting when he was upset. Vulnerability was always a turn-on. "Have another martini," she suggested. "You look like shit."

Ocean had to laugh at her comment. He was a model, and he looked like shit. Ha, ha...

"Listen, finish your food. I have a room upstairs for the buyer's reception tonight." She smiled contritely. "Why don't we go relax for awhile after?"

Ocean eyed Sophia carefully. *Whatever.*

"I've never seen you like this before..." Sophia began. For a moment her mind was flooded with thoughts of camera people, lights, and the reality of the shoot. *Did they have time to relax in a hotel suite?*

"Remember when you said I could talk to you?" Ocean began, brimming with the newness of his martinis.

"Yes?" Sophia replied expectantly.

"Well, I might need to talk..." He felt the words cross his lips, but as he gulped his third martini he wasn't so sure what the significance was. If Aura loved him... If Aura loved him... If Aura loved him she would have come home on Saturday night.

***

"Relax," Sophia encouraged a worn-out Ocean.

"Everything's bad now," Ocean mumbled. What difference did it make if he talked to Sophia? His own wife wouldn't have anything to do with him. She was gone all weekend. All weekend.

"Ocean," Sophia started, eyeing the way his hair fell against the pale blue of his denim shirt. "You know I'm always here for you."

"Sophie, you're a great woman," Ocean began through the haze of martinis. "I don't know what's happening between me and Aura..." he finally admitted.

"Don't worry," Sophia said as she brought her body closer to his.

"I won't," Ocean said simply. Then he felt the urgent need of a kiss pressed against his mouth. Sophia's lips felt good.

"Don't worry," she said again, rushing her hands through his hair.

Ocean began kissing her, contemplating the softness of her skin and what she might look like naked.

"It's okay," Sophia continued, enjoying the feel of Ocean's body finally resting against hers.

Ocean groaned. "You're beautiful, Sophie," he admitted, "but I can't do this. I have to find out what's going on with Aura."

Sophia frowned as the hard black body pulled away from her. She hated men who were in love. At least, she hated men who were in love with other women. Then she felt a twang of guilt. The man *was* married.

Ocean tucked his shirt back into his pants, and they boarded the elevator to the lobby.

***

When Aura reached the hotel it was nearing 2:00pm and the restaurant's maitre d' was certain Ocean and Sophia had finished their meal. She sighed. Oh well...When she turned to leave she was surprised to see Marc Bryant. It was good seeing him. For a moment, he made her forget why she was there. They chatted in the hotel lobby and Aura was able to forget her problems. Then, she saw Ocean exiting an elevator with Sophia's arm wrapped around his waist.

"I'm so sorry..." Marc began, recognizing Aura's anguish. *This* was her husband? A man who spent his afternoons exiting hotels with other women?

Aura watched as Ocean and Sophia left together. She wasn't sure why she didn't call his name. She should have, but she was too choked up to speak. *Did this mean he and Sophia had been screwing around all along?*

She swallowed quickly and pretended everything was all right. After all, Marc was a co-worker. And, work was work. She had to maintain control.

Marc watched intently as the man and woman left the hotel. The woman seemed hot, but it was the man that caught his attention. For some reason, he seemed familiar. "What was your husband's name again?" Marc asked with some distraction after Ocean left the lobby.

"Ocean," Aura replied. *What was the point?*

"What kind of name is that?" Marc responded.

"It's really a stage name. He was born Edward," she stated matter-of-factly.

Marc was frozen for a moment. *Edward?* Could this be the same Eddie he had known years back? Yes, the walk; that was definitely who it was.

Aura gave Marc a perplexed look

"I know him," Marc stated.

Aura was surprised for a moment, then she sighed. *That* was why Marc's name had seemed familiar. He had been on the guest list for their wedding!

***

When Ocean arrived home that evening, Aura was huddled on the sofa in her pajamas, a carton of ice cream in hand. He did not speak when he saw her.

Aura felt the heaviness of his silence deep within her. How would she begin to tell him? To tell him that she'd being lying for as long as they'd been together? To tell him she had a secret which would change both of their lives forever? To tell him she had had an abortion? To tell him she saw him leaving a hotel elevator with another woman? Thoughts flooded her mind more swiftly than she could take and before she knew what she was saying she heard herself talking. "I'm sick... There I said it... I'm sick... Sick, sick, sick... There I've said it..."

Ocean turned to look at the woman he married. *What the hell was she talking about?* SICK?! Sick, was something they could work through. He thought she was *sleeping* with someone else!

Aura's face turned ruddy and tears began to stream down her cheeks.

Ocean watched in painful fascination. She wasn't making any sense.

"I didn't want to have to tell you, Ocean...about the painkillers I take...when I've been hospitalized...I always hid it..." She looked at her husband in agony. "I just didn't want to lose you..." she said, hysterical with her own tears.

Ocean resisted the urge to touch her...to console her. He was angry and he wanted her to know that. He wanted to figure out what the hell she was talking about... He was in pain and he wanted her to feel pain too. He didn't want to relieve her in any way. At that moment he wanted her to feel miserable.

Aura accepted the fact that Ocean would not try to make things any easier for her. How could she blame him? She had pretty much thrown him into the arms of another woman. She examined the hard wood floors of their living room as she spoke, too ashamed to look Ocean in the eyes. "Sickle-cell anemia runs in my family..." she began. "That's the reason I had to be hospitalized after we got married..." Aura paused to look briefly at Ocean's stunned countenance. "That's the reason I had to abort our baby... I found out when I was in the hospital..." Aura looked up quickly when she heard the rustling of clothes. She watched as Ocean slammed the apartment door behind him.

***

"What's the matter with you?!" Maleek nearly screamed to a disheveled Ocean.

"Nothing, man." He realized how ridiculous his response was as he placed a shopping-bag full of Heinekens on Maleek's kitchen counter. "Fuck, man," he sighed, correcting himself, "Everything." He pulled at the tie in his hair with his hands letting his hair spring loose. It seemed that damned thing was giving him a headache, or increasing the pain of the headache he already had. Ocean fumbled through Maleek's kitchen drawer until he located the bottle-opener and opened a brew. He put the rest of the beers into the refrigerator and threw himself onto Maleek's sofa.

"This had better be good," Maleek began, immediately realizing he didn't need to finish his statement. Ocean looked like he'd been through a war. "You know I cancelled a date for you," Maleek admitted lightly.

"Yeah, man, I know. Don't you ever want anything more out of life than a fucking date, Maleek? Is your life really just about pussy?"

Maleek looked at him stunned. He hated when Ocean criticized his lifestyle like his own shit didn't stink. Ocean had had his share of living for pussy too! "Fuck you!" was all Maleek could come up with in response, but that response satisfied him so he took a seat on the love seat across from the sofa where a seemingly pained Ocean sat with a Heineken bottle at his lips.

"Look, man, just don't fuck with me tonight. I need to talk to someone, and you're the best I could come up with." He laughed suddenly then, realizing his own ludicrous actions. "I actually stopped by my dumbass father's house tonight." He sighed. "Lucky for me, he wasn't home." He stared at the corner of the living room where the ceiling met the walls. "God only knows what kind of shit advice that dumb fuck might have given me." He groaned aloud, frightening his friend with its intensity.

Maleek gave him a seriously concerned look. He'd never seen Ocean like this before. This confirmed it finally. It was about a woman...a stupid fucking piece of ass placed on this earth to control men's goddamn lives. What woman was worth going through all this shit for? He resisted the urge to grin when he recognized the answer. *None.* Maleek sat up in his chair haughtily with this realization. Whatever Aura did had to be terrible. Finally, Ocean would be a free man again. They could shoot the shit like back in the day.

Ocean looked at Maleek with anguish. Where should he begin? Should he even begin to tell this supposed friend about him and his woman? Fuck... he sighed. Why not? The fact of the matter was, Maleek *was* his best friend.

"She lied to me..." Ocean began, struggling against the burning of his tears. Maleek suddenly wished he could leave. He'd never seen one of his male friends cry, and if that was what Ocean was about to do, he didn't know how he would handle it.

Ocean leaned his head up towards the ceiling, controlling his need to let go. He walked to the bathroom without saying another word and stared at himself in the mirror. *Was this what it was all about? Being a man? Who gave a fuck if he shed some tears over his own goddamn woman? His wife?! !* He looked at the tears that fell the course of his cheeks, and in a strange way he felt a sweet relief. The image of tears on his face brought back memories of childhood. He heard the scornful voices telling him men don't cry, denying his right to feel, to be human. "Fuck'em" he grumbled at his own expression, suddenly getting the urge to scare the hell out of Maleek by leaving the john with un-wiped tears. Fuck'em... He reentered Maleek's living room with a tear-strewn face and a smile.

Maleek gave him a horrified look. *What the fuck kind of shit was this?!!*

When Ocean saw Maleek's look, he laughed for a moment and looked away, but each time he looked at Maleek again, the brother looked like he had seen a fucking ghost or something! Actually, each time he looked at Maleek after a few hearty laughs, he laughed harder.

Maleek stared at Ocean like he had lost his mind. *Was this what a nervous breakdown looked like? SHOULD HE BE CALLING 911?!!*

When Ocean finally calmed down, Maleek asked ever-so-gently, "Yo, man, are you okay?"

Ocean sat quietly on the sofa at that point. "Yeah, man, I'm okay; it's just that you're such a dumb mothafucka. Like you've never seen a man cry before."

Maleek didn't see the humor. "The only man I ever saw cry was dying from an asthma attack," Maleek stated flatly. *What the fuck was this shit?* He could've been out with Beatrice. He didn't have time for Ocean to lose his goddamn mind...in *his apartment of all places.*

"Damn, Maleek, you're shit is more fucked up than mine, I never realized your heart was so goddamn cold. I mean, you're acting like you've never experienced *a feeling* in your life..." Ocean's voice trailed off as he listened to himself speak. *He sounded like Aura.*

"Damn, man, you even sound like a woman now!" Maleek suddenly roared. The word 'woman' was bitterly derogatory.

Ocean stood up quickly, suddenly pissed off. *Who the fuck did Maleek think he was talking to?* "Maleek, you better not come to me with no dumb shit, now, 'cause you know I'm upset." He paused before barking, "DON'T FUCK WITH ME, I'VE GOT ENOUGH SHIT ON MY MIND ALREADY!" His words were a warning that Maleek immediately understood. Actually, Maleek was happy that Ocean was still a man. That crying shit threw him off for a minute.

"Peace, man. Word up, I'm sorry..." Maleek began in a quick attempt to console his friend. "Just chill, man. I should've never said that shit."

Ocean lay out on the sofa and stared blankly at the

television. "Fuck it, man. Put in a movie or something. Just forget about it."

"You know, Sophia and I had a thing once..." Maleek admitted, in attempt to start conversation and relieve Ocean of thoughts about his own problems.

Ocean shifted his head quickly in response to Maleek's words. "Get out, man! You and Sophia... my Sophia?" he asked stunned. "Yeah, man, a while back... I *did* her and everything."

"That's funny, man. She knows you work for Esquire. How come you two don't keep in touch?"

Maleek sighed. In retrospect he wished he had. "I don't know, Ocean. I sort of wanted to but I fucked up. She's beautiful, smart, cool... a bit on the edge, but I kind of liked it."

"Damn, Maleek, you should rescue her from that asshole she dates." Ocean suddenly remembered his own life, and rested his head wearily on Maleek's sofa. *Who was he to give advice?*

Maleek finally ventured to ask the question. "So what's up with you and Aura?"

Ocean sighed. He felt better since Maleek admitted his own little secret. "She's..." he considered his words. No, he couldn't tell Maleek about the abortion. That was *too* personal. "She says she has a disease...sickle-cell anemia... She was scared to tell me, that's all."

"Ohh..." Maleek kept his silence.

"I mean, how do you marry someone and not tell them you have a chronic ailment?" He paused before asking, "Do you know anything about sickle-cell?"

Maleek frowned. "Nah, man, not much... I mean I have a cousin who's kid has it but we're not all that close."

Ocean sighed. "Fuck it, man. Put a movie on. I just don't want to see her tonight."

Maleek did as Ocean asked.

***

"What's the matter with you?" Sophia asked Ocean during the shoot the next day.

"Nothing," Ocean stated simply.

"Do you want to go for lunch?"

Ocean smiled. "No, but I know a guy named Maleek who would love to do lunch with you."

Sophia felt her heart skip a beat. Was he talking about the same Maleek she'd been brooding over for what now felt like forever?

"Here," he said, handing Sophia Maleek's business card. "Call him. It can't hurt. Maybe he's grown up a little."

Ocean enjoyed this temporary sense of power. He hadn't even told Maleek he would do this. What the hell? He'd tell him later.

***

When Ocean came home Tuesday night, Aura was lying in the living room. She looked as if she had not moved since he saw her the previous evening. Doritos and potato chip bags were strewn on the floor. "How was your day?" he asked.

She looked at him with swollen eyes. "I didn't go to work," she mumbled.

"Do you want to talk?"

"Yes."

"Why don't you take a shower or something," Ocean suggested, still unwilling to give her his forgiveness. He didn't even know the whole story yet. He had to be sure...

Aura stood to leave the living room. Before entering the bathroom, she peeked her head into the archway between the living room and the hall. "Please don't leave," she whispered.

Ocean swallowed. He refused to let himself get emotional. He *needed* to know what happened. "I won't," he stated sternly, searching the fridge for orange juice, not turning to see his wife's face.

***

When Aura returned to the living room, her wet hair was twisted into a braid and she wore jeans and a black tank top. She approached Ocean on the sofa, but he quickly moved away. She, instead, took a seat on the large navy leather recliner. "I'll try to explain everything..." she said.

Ocean did not look at her, at first, he just listened.

"I was always so scared to tell you," she began. "I've been fighting this thing my whole life, and I suppose part of the fight was denial..." She waited, giving her words time to wash across Ocean's psyche.

Finally, he looked at his beautiful wife...pained, aching, and partially wet... But, he did not speak.

"Have you ever heard of sickle-cell?" she asked.

"Not really."

Aura leaned her head back. It was always so difficult explaining her disease. And she had never even explained it to any man before, except her first boyfriend who ran from her as if she were a leper. She cringed with the memory. "It's a hereditary blood disease. It's pretty much exclusive to blacks and people of Mediterranean descent. It gets its name from what it does to my blood cells. They're not all round like healthy cells; some of them are shaped like a sickle or a crescent-moon. It makes it difficult for blood to travel through my body. Sometimes they clot..." She put a hand to her wet hair for comfort.

"The pain is more than I can describe with words... It can get very bad."

Ocean turned to look at Aura. Was this it? Was this what she was going through? She was scared to tell him she was in intense pain?! He leaned back into the sofa. He didn't want to hear anymore, but at the same time he did. He loved her like he had loved no other person in his life...not even his mother, and certainly not his father. Was it him? Was it him that made his own wife doubt his love so much? Did years of drinking, fucking and drugging turn him into someone whom even the own love of his life couldn't completely love? Thoughts flooded his mind, but he dared not speak. What could he possibly say? That he hated her for lying? That she had no excuse? And what about their baby? *Their baby?!*

Aura waited until Ocean seemed ready to hear more. "The pain can be a daily thing," she continued. "I have to take a lot of painkillers." Aura turned her face away from her husband as she admitted another lie. "The vitamin bottle..."

Ocean felt his chest tighten.

"The pills were not for cramps." A tear fell from her eyes right when she thought she had none left. It seemed she had spent all of the previous night and day crying. "It's all the same." Her body shook as the words left her lips.

Ocean could no longer stand the sight of Aura in such agony. He wasn't sure what he had to give to her, but he walked over to where she sat sobbing on their recliner, and he held her in his arms. As she rocked gently with the agony of tears, he had to ask... He couldn't let it go... He had to know... "Aura, why would you abort our baby?!" he finally wept along with her. His arms wound tightly around her waist. The feel of their tears mixing on their pressed cheeks, felt *good* in a way neither of them had ever experienced.

Aura turned her lips to his cheek and kissed him gently. "When I found out about the pregnancy..." She paused realizing she had to face up to another lie. She inhaled deeply. "When I went into the hospital for muscle spasms, it was the same thing."

Ocean rested his head in her lap now. *Was this too much for him to bear? Would her lies ever end?*

Aura stroked her husband's hair, "That was when I found out about the pregnancy..." Her tears sprung anew with the realization of what she had done. "If I had known about the pregnancy, maybe I could have endured the pain..." She swallowed realizing she was still lying. "Ocean, it's just too much for me... I could *not* have endured the pain... even if..."

Ocean squeezed her knees tightly as he listened to her story.

"It was... I don't know... They gave me heavy intravenous painkillers that night... It could have caused damage to the fetus... I couldn't have the baby, and I was still too scared to explain..." Aura shook in the chair. "Ocean, I'm still too scared to explain... Maybe I'm just weak or something, but if it weren't for this weekend, I don't know if I ever would have told you. I kept thinking the time would come when it would feel right. But, it still doesn't feel right. I still wish you didn't have to *know*... Know that I'm not the woman you wanted me to be... What or who you thought I was..."

Ocean turned his head to his wife in sudden disbelief "Aura, I *want* to *know* you... I *want* to *love* you..." He kneeled on the floor beside the armchair. "Loving you has given me more than anything else in this fucking world!" he nearly screamed. "Who I've been with other people doesn't mean *shit* compared to who I *am* with you!"

Aura relaxed slightly, her breathing slowed to a more

normal pace. Had she told him everything? She ran through the lies in her mind... the vitamins... the hospital... the abortion... the sickle-cell... There was nothing else... *And he was still there...* She wrapped her arms around him and held him tightly.

Ocean lifted his chin from her lap to her face and he kissed her gently. "There's no one else?" he asked, confirming his relief.

Aura looked at him with shock. What was he talking about? "Of course not," she moaned tugging at his neck as his hands ran across her thigh.

Ocean pulled at her hair upon hearing her response to his question. "I love you," he rumbled as tears made the trip from his eyes to his chin. "I didn't marry you to give up on you..." Ocean swallowed before continuing. "Aura, this shit is for both of us, for our children, for the world... I wanted you to be my wife because I wanted a wife one time...one time only."

"Do you really still love me?" Aura asked, choking on her tears as Ocean kissed her.

"I couldn't stop if I wanted to..." He picked her up and carried her into the bedroom where they made love in a bittersweet way... A way neither of them had *ever* experienced before.

Like newborn babies they wailed...and moaned...and screamed and sighed...and released, relished and accepted their vulnerability...their newness in each other's arms... *So* this *was love... It hurt while feeling more beautiful than anything they had ever felt before...*

Aura, Ocean & Sophia Autumn 1995

Aura looked out the large bay windows of the bedroom as the sun glinted soft streams of light across the wood floor. She groaned lightly with the start of this new day and shifted under the thick blue blanket and black comforter which covered her lean body. She could not believe it was October already. Tomorrow would make two years since she and Ocean married. She wriggled her hips under the blue bed sheets, annoyed by their cold.

Ocean groaned and threw an arm around Aura's waist, pulling her body close to him.

She sighed. His side of the bed always seemed so much warmer.

"Happy Anniversary," he muttered coarsely, only barely awake.

Aura smiled as she mingled her thighs with his under the bed covers. "Happy Anniversary," she replied.

Ocean leaned up on one elbow and looked at his wife. Here they were. They had made it. In a sunny new duplex condominium, with many bad memories behind him, she was with him, and he was with her... Still...

Aura sighed as she glanced the digital clock on the dresser. It was 9:00am on Saturday, and, although they both enjoyed sleeping in on the weekend, they had big plans for the evening and much work to do. Aura slipped out of bed, despite Ocean's protests. "Where are you going?" he mumbled.

"I'm gonna make some coffee..." she teased, realizing he was his usual horny self. "We've got a lot to do today."

"Ugh..." was Ocean's only response as Aura left him and his hard-on alone in the room. He pulled a pillow over his head in quiet rebellion. Mornings *still* sucked.

***

"Have some," Aura offered as Ocean exited the bathroom, still looking like the weight of a new day wrecked havoc in his life.

"Thanks," Ocean said, accepting the coffee cup presented to him. He looked at her closely before admitting, "You know, there was a time when I wasn't sure we would make it this far." Then, he kissed her forehead.

Aura looked at the black and white tiled floor of their large kitchen. *Yes, she knew.*

"Oh, I didn't mean it like that," Ocean began, easily reading his wife's response. "You know; it's just...We've both been through a lot."

Aura looked at him sincerely. "I suppose that's true..." Her body contorted into a low-lying crescent moon, as if under a sneak attack.

"So, how are *you* feeling?" he asked, still unaccustomed to the reality of Aura's world—her life. Days of pain he wished he could rob from her and give to someone who deserved them... Or keep for himself.

Aura sighed. *She was fine.*

Ocean gulped his coffee. "Well, I'm gonna start trying to get things together. I'll check on the DJ. Maybe I can pick up Dana and Ace later."

Aura smiled. "Yeah..." She raised her eyes to her husband's. "Angie's really come around," she said, out of nowhere.

"Yeah," Ocean admitted. There had been a phase when neither he nor Aura could tolerate Angie's presence, but it seemed that since her hospitalization things slowly worked themselves out. According to Aura, she had come into contact with a good shrink. Ocean didn't know much about psychiatrists, but if it worked, he was pleased.

Aura's body slinked into sudden sadness. She really had no reason to be unhappy; it just seemed bad memories haunted her.

Ocean grabbed Aura in her white terry robe. "Stop it, woman" he jousted playfully.

Aura broke out of her spell. "I'm sorry," she apologized, not entirely sure for what she sought forgiveness. She shrugged her shoulders. "It's just that after all we've been through, with us, and Angie, and that thing with Sophia..." She gave Ocean a semi-harsh glance. She *did* believe him when he said he never slept with her. "It just seems that things are *too* good now... Like the calm before the storm or something...like it will all blow away...or I'll wake up and find out I'm dreaming..." She sighed. "There's so much suffering in the world. Who are we to know better?"

Ocean looked into Aura's deep brown eyes. "You know something. Aura, this is why I love you." He smiled. "Okay, maybe it's only part of the reason." He grabbed her then, and held her close.

Aura exhaled leaning her head against his chest.

"You're, always thinking.... You think about other people and it's beautiful. He kissed her forehead. "It's cute...but nobody ever said that in order to be righteous you have to be miserable."

"I know."

"Aura, god knows, we all have our own cross to bear."

"I know."

"Look, I'm gonna go out and try to do the million things you want me to before the party tonight. Cocktails start at four, right?"

"Yikes!" Aura exclaimed with the realization. It was already past 11:00am. She couldn't imagine why she decided to start the party so early... Then, she remembered, she and Ocean wanted to get the guests out and have time to themselves at a reasonable hour.

"So, I should be back in a few," Ocean said, quickly kissing Aura's lips.

"I'll see you later!" she called out as he grabbed his coat and slammed the apartment door.

***

When Ocean came home after 2:00pm, Aura was busy fixing curry goat, escovich fish and lasagna. The aromas filled the first floor of their Park Slope duplex, filling Ocean with a deep feeling of love... *Wasn't it love when a woman cooked like crazy?*

"Hey, baby," he said, grabbing her hips as she leaned over the stove.

"Hey," she responded lightly. She was exhausted from a busy day of cooking.

He looked around at their new place. They'd only been living there for the past two months, and it was immaculate. The living room was huge and uncarpeted with a new calfskin sofa, loveseat and recliner on the outskirts of what they hoped to temporarily be a large dance floor for the evening. White venetian blinds leaned against the bay windows behind soft white curtains. Two rubber plants stood in huge wicker pots on the side of the windows and the glass entertainment center took up nearly an entire wall. The place looked beautiful, and Ocean knew he would not enjoy it as much if it had not been decorated by his wife's hand.

"So what's on the menu?" he asked.

Aura nearly giggled. "Ocean, *you* know!" she squealed. They had discussed their menu for what seemed like days at a time. She still found it silly that he got so excited when she cooked—okay, not just cooked—*threw down!*

"Tell me again," Ocean sighed, rubbing his slight stomach.

"Curry goat, lasagna, salad, rice and peas, conch stew, escovich fish, cake, champagne..." She smiled then. "Oh, and my favorite dessert..."

Ocean raised an eyebrow. *What was she talking about? Sex, maybe?* He looked at her in her small tank top and realized he was more than willing to oblige.

Aura laughed. "No, not that!"

Ocean slid his hand along her breasts.

"Will you *stop?*"Aura squealed. She was lying without remorse—she loved Ocean's touch whenever... But she *did* have food to prepare.

"So then what *are* you talking about?" he asked.

"I'm making chocolate soufflé," she admitted, suddenly uncertain. She allowed her eyes to slip to the black and white patterned floor."

Ocean stepped away from her. "Wow... Isn't that French or some shit? Isn't that like... what chefs make or something?" he asked facetiously.

"Oh, Ocean, *shut up!*"Aura responded, playfully.

Ocean laughed. It was funny how women could get insecure over cooking. He decided to give her a break. "Anyway," he said, pulling items from a bag. "I got the shrimp platter and the crab claws."

"Thanks, honey," she replied.

Ocean looked at his watch. "Is everything under control out here? Where's Dana?"

"She called to say she wouldn't be able to come early. It's okay, though. Everything's fine." Aura paused. It was nearing 3:00pm. "Ocean, go take a shower!"

Ocean smiled with a degree of sinister. "Okay," he replied.

***

"I'm back," Ocean boomed as Aura finally found a moment to recline on the sofa, waiting for use of the bathroom.

"Well, it took you forever..." she started, slowly turning, until she saw her husband's head... Her mouth dropped with awe...

Ocean had shaved his head clean, bald!

"OCEAN! "Aura screamed.

Ocean laughed heartily.

*"What did you do?!"*she yelled, still overcome by the shock of her normally hairy husband turned suddenly hairless. Her eyes coursed his face in waves... He looked so...so...different...

Ocean smiled, running a hand along the smoothness of his scalp. "I owed you one," he said. "I had a secret of my own."

Aura ran up to him and touched where *all that hair* had once been. "How could you make a decision like this..." she began running her hand along his scalp, suddenly feeling this new wonder of a husband... a man she suddenly didn't know...

Ocean kissed the warm mist of sweat on her neck. She had been working hard. He peered at his watch briefly... It was 3:30pm, and he knew black people never showed up for a party on time...

Aura's eyes were still wide with the realization: *Ocean had cut off all his hair!*

"Hey, it's almost party time," Ocean began. "Let's do something."

Aura sighed while her mind screamed: *Ocean had cut off all his hair and didn't even consult her!*

Ocean read the look on his wife's face. "You deserve it," he explained.

Aura looked like a frightened doe.

"You never told me about the sickle-cell," he said ushering her up the five steps to their bedroom area "I had to plan a pay-back."

Ocean sprawled her body across the king-sized bed as Aura glared at him as if she had never seen him before in her life. In a way it was true, she had never seen him like this. Ocean had relieved himself of his sense of helplessness. Aura's secrets could be forgiven now. He had branded his own school of tender retaliation.

As Aura slipped out of her jeans and Ocean slipped into her, they both accepted it... This retaliation felt *good*.

***

Aura showered and dressed quickly after her bout of 'quickie sex' with the man who for a moment seemed to be a new lover, but thankfully...and lovingly was her own husband.

When Ocean entered the kitchen, Aura was putting the soufflé into the oven.

"Isn't that a lot work? Why didn't you just buy one?" he asked.

Aura smiled. *Why didn't she?* "Because sometimes you've got to do things for yourself to make them worthwhile." She closed the oven door and sighed. "You know," she began. "I was always scared to make one. It's silly, I guess. I just thought I didn't know enough about cooking or whatever."

Ocean looked at her with honest regard.

Aura sighed. "You know... Sometimes you just have to do it for yourself. No one else's chocolate soufflé could possibly taste as good as my own, even if it's bad," she admitted.

Ocean looked at his watch; it was nearing 4:30pm.

Aura continued her thought. "It was like I never had the courage to make one before...it's a complicated dish. The ingredients must be handled carefully or the whole thing can explode or fall in the oven."

Ocean shot Aura a horrified look. *Was she serious?* This was taking dessert to the final frontier... He grinned, as he recognized the silliness of his own thoughts.

She laughed. "I guess...sometimes you have to do for yourself even if it means trying something new and risking failure, even if it's a big failure." She paused as she thought about her words. This soufflé shit surely seemed to hit home, "They say successful people are the ones who fail the most, you know? Because they're the ones who try the most."

Ocean realized again why he found his wife so fascinating. *She was courageous and vulnerable, and somewhat nutty!*

Aura brushed a hand over Ocean's bald head, before continuing what now seemed like a serious metaphor. "Sometimes you need to take a chance, to have *courage* that things will come together *perfectly*." Aura stopped then, hoping her husband could read between the lines.

Ocean sighed. His 'old' hair was tucked in a pillow case in the bathroom, and she had not even asked about it.

***

"So you finally made it!" Ocean said to Ace and Dana as they entered his home.

"Wow...the hair looks great, Ocean!" Dana exclaimed. "Or should I say the head!" she said laughing. "Aura must've freaked out!"

Ocean palmed his baldie as memories of Aura's tongue on his scalp just a little while earlier ran across his mind. "She got over it," he said.

"Where is Aura anyway?" Dana asked. She walked away without waiting for an answer, and immediately found her girlfriend in the kitchen. "Girrrl... Everything in here looks good!" she exclaimed, hugging her friend.

"Thanks," Aura replied.

"I have news!" she squealed delightedly.

"What?!" Aura asked, knowing Dana's news could be anything. She turned toward Ocean and Ace in the living room as if they might have some inside knowledge.

Dana laughed as Aura uncorked a wine bottle,

"No, thank you," Dana said, pushing her wine glass away,

"What?!" Aura asked, knowing full well what that might mean.

"Baby, tell Aura the deal!" Dana said calling out to her husband in the living room.

Ace and Ocean entered the kitchen in response to Dana's call.

Ocean looked at Dana and Aura, stunned.

"Oh..." Ace began, grinning at his wife and grabbing her waist. "It looks like they'll be a new Olivier in the clan."

Aura grabbed Ocean quickly. "Are you serious?!" she asked.

Dana jumped up and down in a navy cotton jumper. "Yes! Yes! Yes!"

Aura screamed as she hugged her girlfriend. "I'm so happy for you! How pregnant are you?!"

Dana sighed as she rubbed her belly. "My midwife

says I'm just around two months."

"Oh...Dana, I'm so happy for you!" Aura replied. She grabbed her brother then, she felt *too* happy...something had to give. "Congratulations, stud!" she squealed resting her head against his shoulder.

"So, when are you and Ocean gonna give Kayla a cousin?" Ace asked.

"How do you know it's a girl?" Aura flashed Ocean an inquisitive look. *Who knew?*

"We don't know, Aura, we just have it in our heads. We'll be able to find out soon enough. For some reason, your brother wants a girl as much as I do! But, of course, we'd be happy with any healthy baby." Dana felt a pinch of guilt when she said "healthy." *Would Aura be able to have a healthy baby one day too?*

"Kayla, huh? Were gonna name our baby Hope," Ocean said as he ogled his wife in her short sequined dress. "I don't care if it's a boy or a girl. Hope." He paused contemplating his words. "That's the name..."

"Ocean, Aura will *not* let you name your son, Hope! You're so crazy!" Dana giggled outwardly, but deep down she knew exactly what he meant.

As six o'clock approached, guests started streaming in at a steady pace: Donald and Sylvia Olivier, Maleek and Sophia, Darryl and his mother, Angie, Marc Bryant, Reeva Johnson, Ted and Aubrey, Craig... Neville Ryder had not been invited. He was busy living with a new twenty-eight-year-old girlfriend. He left Karen pregnant, six months earlier. So, thanks to his dad, he had a 'mom' who could be his girlfriend and siblings who could be his children.

"You look good," Aura said, complimenting the always well-dressed Sophia. She had been dating Maleek for a few months now, and it seemed all was well between them. Even Angie didn't seem bothered by this new relationship. It was true what Ocean had said. Angie had come a long way... She was finally happy despite her singleness. It even seemed she relished in it with a bunch of new hobbies she'd taken up.

Other friends came to join the party throughout the night.

And Aura served her soufflé to an expectant crowd.

***

Sophia rose early, as usual. By 9:00am she broke the urge to run away from herself. She grabbed the telephone and dialed an all-to-easy-to-remember number.

"Hello?" Sandy asked.

"I'm sorry about everything..." Sophia began, peering at a still-sleeping Maleek in her bed. She was falling in love again "How are you?" she asked her friend, finally able to make amends.

Sandy smiled. "I'm just fine."

"Cocoa Riser"

(noun) A fan of Chocolate Soufflé who acknowledges she is sexy, funny, smart and so much more, and also wants to improve the global condition by working in community to reach common goals for our men, our children, our neighborhoods and ourselves.

"Cocoa Riser" Discussion Questions

1. Could you relate to Eddie's desire to have a family history different than his reality? What do you think about his realization that if his history were different, he would have a different life, not necessarily a better one?

2. What did you think of Ocean's strategy to take Darryl to a movie only if he would go to a museum?

3. "Too many damn people in one place, piled on top of each other like so much cattle, with guns and drugs sprinkled on top and poverty fencing them in." Have you experienced the urban projects? Do you agree with Ocean's assessment? Do you know anyone who escaped the projects? How did they do it?

4. Did you think Sophia made the right choice in ending her relationship with Ron when she did? Do you think she ever should have married him? Could you relate to her feelings of guilt?

5. What did you think of Aura's dad's "everybody hates everybody" speech? Do you believe "we all hate because our hate is part of our fear, and we fear what we don't know?" How do you think this relates to current issues like gay marriage and terrorism?

6. What did you think of Donald Olivier's pep talk on the way home from the hospital? Was he effective in teaching his daughter gratitude? Do you believe as he does that we would be more grateful if we focused on the news instead of "soap operas?" Do you believe that "obstacles and change are the only things we can really count on?"

7. How did Ocean's visit home affect him? Don't we all need "food" from home? How do we define "food" and "home?"

8. When Sandy tells Sophia "I just don't want you to wait until the burden's too much for you to bear." When is the appropriate time to get mental health assistance?

9. What did you think of Sophia's rant about religion? Was she being a hypocrite, since she had just visited a priest for confession?

10. What did you think of Sophia's struggle with her sexuality? How would you label her? Do you believe her sexuality needs a label?

11. Could you relate to Angie's character when she seemed to be the only one not in a 'perfect' relationship? It seemed therapy and developing hobbies helped her find herself. Do you have hobbies that help you keep your sanity?

12. What did you think of Aura's Chocolate Soufflé analogy, comparing it to fear of the unknown, developing courage to face potential failure and her own fear of being honest and vulnerable with her husband?

Visit "Chocolate Soufflé Book" on Facebook or use the link below for ideas on how to get your book club, family, group of friends or organization more involved.

Let's Rise Up!

https://www.facebook.com/Chocolatesoufflebook/

Printed in Great Britain
by Amazon